Kate Callahan had seen Rich Spencer hundreds of times over the last two years. But never before had she seen him as anything more than the man with a camera on his shoulder. The competition.

But today, she finally saw him. Really saw him.

Light brown hair that looked as though he'd just stepped out of a windstorm. He had a toned physique, under his cream sweater and loose-fitting jeans. And his eyes....

Kate swallowed hard.

His eyes were the color of the Caribbean Ocean sparkling in the bright sun. She shook her head, trying to rid her mind of the sudden urge to skinny-dip in the salty water.

The tropical waters focused on Kate's face for only a moment before roaming slowly over her body as though she stood before him without a stitch on. His lips pulled at the corners, forming a sexy, knowing smile.

www.morgankearns.com

ISBN: 1-4392-5563-6
EAN13: 978-1439255636

Visit www.MorganKearns.com to order additional copies.

Thank you!

As I began this adventure, there were many people who rooted for the story, and me. To them, I say thank you! All the fans of this story, this is for you! It was truly a labor of love; complete with tears.

A huge thanks to Kim, Katie, and Debbie!

To my children, thank you for letting mommy write.

And last, but not least, thank you to my beloved husband. Without your encouragement and understanding, none of this would be possible. I love you!

To Rich, Kate, and Jesse:
Thank you for sharing your story with me,
for giving me the honor of telling your tale.
I hope I did it justice!

Fade
to
Black

(Deadlines & Diamonds)

Morgan Kearns

Part One

A New Beginning

One

Was it possible to be completely content and nervous as hell all at the same time?

Kate rubbed at her stomach with little hope of calming the butterflies that were waging war on her digestive system. She inhaled a deep breath and let the soothing scent of her lover fill her lungs. Lifting her head from his chest to check the clock, she wondered if ten more minutes would really put her that far behind.

Leaning up on an elbow, she moved a dark lock of hair from Jesse's tanned forehead to admire his masculine features. Her finger traced the strong contour of his jaw before coming to rest on his plump lip. She could stay like this forever, but really needed to act responsibly.

"Jesse." She wiggled back and forth, trying to shake him awake. His soft snores continued. "Jesse, honey, it's time to get up." Her fingertips tickled their way up his sides and he shifted under her touch.

"Hmm?" came the groggy reply.

Tipping her head, she pressed her lips to his square chin. "I'm getting in the shower, but you need to get up. You have to get to the shop. You said last night that you had a full schedule today—and you have to finish that fancy Ferrari before noon." His arms tightened around her, pulling her closer to him, and Kate could feel his hard contours pressing against her through her pajamas.

"Can't we just call in sick?" he asked in a hoarse, morning whisper. His normal bass voice was made even deeper by the lack of use. Teeth grazed the sensitive skin just above her collar bone and an involuntary gasp made her reaction obvious.

There were few things Kate loved more than snuggling with the man who held her heart, but.... *Be responsible*, she reminded herself. "Jesse." She slapped playfully at him. "I can't call in sick on my first day."

"Damn." He sighed before kissing her in an attempt to change her mind. "Are you *sure*?"

Kate laughed lightly. "Yes, I'm sure." She placed her hand on his tan, sculpted chest and pushed him back until he lay flat on the mattress. Then, tucking her knees under her, she inched her way up his body, leaving a trail of kisses.

Now it was his turn to gasp.

Finally at his lips, she whispered, "I'd love to spend all day in your very capable hands..."

"But...," he anticipated her next word.

"*But*, I have to get ready for work." She started to crawl out of bed. "And so do you."

His arms wrapped around her like a steel trap. "I love you, KC."

"I love you, too." Their lips met and his tongue swept along her bottom lip, a slow, deliberate effort to frustrate her self-control. "Jesse," she warned as she fought the smile that tugged hard on the corners of her mouth.

"Oh, fine," he groaned. "One more kiss. That's the price to unlock my arms." He tightened his hold and rocked her back and forth.

Through the soft cotton of her pajama top, Kate was very aware of the warm skin of his chest. His fingers lightly moved over her back, and the simple strokes calmed her better than Calgon ever could. "I don't know, that's a pretty stiff fine," she teased before gladly paying it.

He released his hold and cleared his throat. "So, did you know that I'm an environmentalist?" Jesse's question came from nowhere, said in all seriousness.

"Since when?" Kate asked over her shoulder as she crossed the bedroom toward the bathroom.

"Oh, come on, Kate, conserving water is important in the desert. How 'bout we shower together?" He climbed out of bed and started toward her.

Kate laughed, shaking her head. "Jesse Vasquez, if you get in the shower with me, I'll get very little *showering* done."

A dark eyebrow raised, a mischievous grin lifted his lip while his brown eyes twinkled. "Exactly."

"Don't you come near this door," she warned, her finger accentuating the demand.

He looked down at his toned body, and Kate couldn't help but take in every sculpted inch. "Come on, KC, I'm in desperate need of..."

She shook her head again, amused yet determined. "Jesse, I can't. I'll make it up to you tonight," she said through the crack in the door, "I promise."

The truth was that Kate now needed a cold shower after Jesse's attempts at seduction— *Damn! That boy has talent!* –but she forced the knob toward the scalding temperature she loved. She leaned under the spray and quickly soaped, sudded, and rinsed her body and hair. Without the distraction of Jesse's persuasions, Kate was left with the how's and why's of where she was going today.

KHB.

Her first day on the new job. She stepped out onto the bathmat and wrapped a towel around her as a lump formed in her throat that she tried to stomp down with

incessant swallowing and a glass of water. Not that
either worked.

After towel drying her hair, Kate bent her head over
to blow some body into the auburn locks. The air was
warm against her scalp and goose bumps covered her
skin. She flipped her head up and the curls fluttered to
rest just above her shoulders. A few strategic pulls of the
straightening iron and it was sleek with only a slight
curl at the ends.

In the mirror, her green eyes twinkled, widened as
the mascara wand extended brown lashes into black
ones. She blinked to make sure all the lashes were
covered. She smiled, loving the new brand of mascara.
With lips puckered, neutral lip gloss added a subtle
shine, and a few swipes of blush along her cheekbones
were the finishing touch. Kate slipped an ivory cami over
her head, slid the matching lace thong into place, and
walked back into the bedroom.

Jesse, who was back on the bed, fell against the
pillows in a dramatic display. "Oh, come on, Kate, are
you *trying* to cause me pain?" he asked, practically
panting.

She smiled at his awareness and winked as she
added salt to his already bleeding wound. "You know,
I'm not wearing a bra."

Jesse jumped out of the bed, flew across the room,
and jerked her into a bone-crushing hug. His lips
roamed over her exposed skin with an almost frantic
intensity. "Please," he whined, "I'm good to go. There'll
be no need for foreplay." His persistence was a huge ego
booster, but Kate knew that if she let this go on, she
would definitely be late—and that wouldn't look good on
her first day.

She gave him a quick chaste kiss and pulled out of
his embrace. "Later, Jesse. I have to get ready for work."

He followed her into the closet and pulled out a

turtleneck sweater and a pair of his XXL blue sweatpants. "Here, this is the perfect outfit for your first day. Sophisticated and—"

"Ridiculously frumpy—not to mention that it covers everything?" she scoffed.

"Yes." He nodded, looked guilty, and then stuffed the clothes back into place on the shelf. "I don't want those perverted newshounds drooling over my woman."

"*Your* woman, huh?" She hated when he got jealous and possessive.

He paused and Kate wasn't sure if another fight was on the tip of his tongue. "I love you and I couldn't bear losing you."

Jesse was a confident guy, normally. It was his insecurities when it came to her innocent relationships with other men that made the hair on the back of Kate's neck stand on end. She brushed the irritation aside, not wanting to add pissed to her emotional buffet, and stepped into his arms. Her fingers ran over his muscles lying just beneath the skin. "You don't have any reason to be jealous."

"I know it's stupid," he said as he kissed her hair. "You haven't even stepped foot inside the building, and I'm already antsy as hell."

Kate wrapped her arms around Jesse's waist and kissed his bare chest. "You have nothing to worry about. You already have me. I'm not going anywhere." It was as though she'd said those same words a thousand times over the years and she wondered if he would ever believe her.

"It's not *you* I'm worried about." He raked his fingers through his hair. "Damn, I wish I had a ring on that finger of yours." He lifted her left hand and pressed the ring finger to his lips. "Someday. Soon."

She melted into his embrace, enjoying this side of him much more. "I don't need a ring to know that I'm yours, Jesse. I love *you.*"

"I know." He tilted her chin up, his brown eyes full
of concern. "I just can't help but feel like this new job of
yours is going to change our lives forever."

"You worry too much." Kate kissed his chest again
and slapped at his bare butt, a loud smack resonated
around them. "Why don't you get some clothes on?"

× × ×

"Shut that damn thing off!" Shea Spencer shrieked at
her husband. Driving her elbow into his back to brace
herself, she slammed her fist into the snooze button of
his alarm clock. "It's 6:30 in the frickin' morning. Why
are you getting up so damned early?" Her French-tipped
fingers rubbed at her permanently made-up eyes, then
flipped long blonde extensions over her shoulder before
huffing back against the pillows.

"Just go back to sleep," Rich responded, using his
elbows to lift his body off the mattress. Nasty, red
scratches that he felt before were now visible, streaking
from pecs to abs.

"It's her, isn't it? How can you be going to your lover
after what we did last night?" Her accusatory tone made
his blood boil.

His hands clenched into fists, frustration
overwhelming him. "What we did last night? What we
did last night?" He could already feel the sting of the
deep grooves running all the way down his torso, which
added fuel to the inferno festering in his gut. "*That* was
nothing more than getting off, and you know it."

"Go to hell, Rich."

"I'll meet you there," he retorted with a snarl.

Her response was to snort then she yanked the
covers up over her head as if to hide from the world.

What he'd tried to convince himself was a great

marriage, filled with love, was nothing more than an ongoing war with the occasional screw. Rich wanted a happily ever after, always had. He'd thought what they had was true love. Then, one day, Shea came home, having quit her job, and turned into someone he didn't even recognize—or want to.

Rich glared at the childish lump of a woman, whose beauty was truly only skin deep, before climbing out of bed. He was just grateful that she'd shut her mouth and wasn't pressing him anymore about his alleged infidelity. Being unfaithful was something that wasn't an option to Rich. He believed in marrying forever, remaining with the one you'd promised to love. Every day that went by, though, his resolve weakened. Damn the vows that made it impossible to stray from the evil woman who had replaced his wife.

Spending the night in Shea's bed last night was a mistake. He'd only intended to wait until she was asleep before he made his retreat, but his body betrayed him and sleep overtook him. Celibacy was going to have to be his new way of life. He couldn't trust himself to flee her bed. He was just grateful that last night her insane side had been mostly dormant.

In the shower, the water did exactly what Rich expected—it stung like a bitch. Shampoo bubbles moved along the trail of water and burned when they reached the deep, raw marks. Shea had dug her nails into his skin and torn through the flesh, trying to mark him. Rich wasn't stupid, he knew that she was leaving evidence for the lover he didn't have.

He stepped out onto the fluffy white bathmat and used a towel to wipe off the water. He gingerly patted his chest with the towel before wrapping it around his hips and stepping in front of the mirror. Hair the color of caramel stuck out in every wild direction and Rich ran a brush through the unmanageable strands. After brushing his teeth, applying some deodorant—and Neosporin—he opened the door.

"Who is she, you sonofabitch?" Shea screamed as his cell phone flew across the bedroom at him.

He ducked to the side and it slammed against the wall. The back popped off and the battery slid under the dresser. "What the hell is your problem?"

"*She* is my problem."

"She who, Shea? There is nobody else." Not that Rich hadn't wondered what it would be like to live with a wife that actually loved him. "Look, I'm going to work." He reached into the dresser, pulled out a pair of jeans, grabbed a shirt from the closet and retreated to the guest bathroom to get dressed.

Two steps short of the safety of the hall, he remembered the phone and turned to retrieve the pieces. It was a good thing he'd invested in the military model after the last time Shea had chucked the little electronic device into a wall. Doing so had saved him from having to pay the ridiculous deductible more than once.

Rich flipped on the light in the bathroom and carefully flicked the lock into place before sifting through his clothes. "Damn," he muttered. "Commando in jeans isn't comfortable."

✕ ✕ ✕

Well, this is it, Kate thought as she stood outside the five-story building that housed KHB-Salt Lake and would be her new home away from home. Her hands ran down the front of her steel gray slacks, smoothing away any fresh wrinkles. With the matching jacket pulled tight around her, she grabbed her heavy coat and threw her laptop bag over her shoulder.

Nervous energy bubbled in her every cell. She'd heard that this was one of the best stations in Utah, but now that she was here, she couldn't help but second guess her decision to leave the comfortable for the frightening unknown. A frigid autumn breeze kicked up and blew a lock of hair into Kate's face. She tucked it behind her ear, wishing like hell she'd taken the time to actually speak with the people she'd be meeting, for all intents and purposes, for the first time today.

She walked through the foyer, one foot in front of the other, until she stood in front of the reception desk.

"May I help you?" the receptionist asked, her reading glasses perched on the end of her nose.

"Yes, Kate Callahan to see Dale Morris," Kate said with a smile.

"Of course. Just take a seat and I'll let him know you're here." She motioned toward the open room Kate had just walked through.

"Thank you." Kate was much too nervous to actually sit. So instead, she resorted to perusing the lobby. The warm burgundy and gold hues were welcoming, and the low sounds coming from the television, of course tuned to Channel 17, eased some of her tension. Faces of their main anchor people smiled back from pictures that adorned the walls.

"Kate."

She turned. "Dale." She extended her hand toward the man that was the same age as her father, but with more honey blond hair than distinguished gray.

He took Kate's hand in his strong grip and shook it gently. "We're so glad to have you as part of the News17 family."

"Thank you. I'm glad to be here." And she was.

The news business wasn't new to Kate. She was good at it, and could eat, breathe, and sleep breaking news. Unfortunately, the glass ceiling was alive and well in some newsrooms, and she prayed that this one was just as she had heard—shattered. Ambition ate at her.

She wanted the anchor chair. To be the face on all the billboards. Maybe even end up in New York.

"Come with me and I'll introduce you around." He motioned to the receptionist. "This is Lydia. Lydia, this is Kate Callahan, our newest reporter."

Her gray curls bounced with her nods as the phone began to ring. "Nice to meet you, Kate," she said before turning to answer the incoming call, "Thank you for calling News17, your extended family, how may I direct your call?"

Kate followed Dale through another set of glass double doors where he called, "Jordan."

Smack dab in the middle of the newsroom was the assignment desk—the hub of every news organization. Three men looked up and Kate couldn't begin to guess begin to guess which one was named Jordan. The red-haired man, who sat behind the desk, waved as he talked away on the phone. The other two stood with their arms resting on the top of the chest high assignment desk. They were waiting for their next task— or shooting the bull.

She recognized both of them, had worked alongside them in the field for two years while she was their competition. Kate hadn't cared then to even learn their names, and this moment was the first time she'd taken the time to notice more than just the cameras they carried around.

One of them looked like a body builder, his sleeve straining against the muscle of his bicep, with blond hair, cut short in the back with longer curly locks on top. He smiled and his dimples nearly swallowed his cheeks.

The second man had light brown hair that looked as though he'd just stepped out of a windstorm. He had a toned physique, under his cream sweater and loose-fitting jeans—much more Kate's type than was his muscled friend. And his eyes.... Kate swallowed hard. His eyes were the color of the Caribbean Ocean sparkling in the bright sun. She shook her head, trying to rid her mind of the sudden urge to go skinny-dipping in the salty water.

The tropical waters focused on Kate's face for only a moment before roaming slowly over her body as though she stood before the group without a stitch on. His lips pulled at the corners, forming a sexy, knowing smile.

Jesse was right about the bra, she thought wryly. Embarrassed, she brought her arms up and crossed them in front of her chest, successfully covering any hint of what he was doing to her.

"Rich," Dale said, and *Rich's* eyes moved to their boss's face, allowing her to finally breathe again, "Nate, I'd like to introduce our new reporter, Kate Callahan."

"Welcome to the family," Nate said, holding his hand out.

The redhead hung up the phone. "Yeah, *boss.*"

Dale groaned. "Please don't call me that, Jordan."

"Sorry," Jordan laughed unapologetically, and then turned to Kate. "Who do we have here?"

"This is Kate Callahan, our new reporter," Rich informed him, turning to smile at her.

"These SOB's ever get out of hand, you just let me know." Jordan slapped Rich in the back of the head.

"Thanks." Kate raised an eyebrow at Rich. "I'll remember that." There was something about the tingling in the pit of her stomach that came from his simple eye contact that made her nervous to be around this Rich guy.

"Who are you going to send her out with today?" Dale asked.

"Um..." Jordan looked between Rich and Nate. "I guess..."

"I don't have an assignment yet," Rich offered, a

little too eager for Kate's comfort.

Kate glanced down at her left ring finger and cursed the fact that Jesse hadn't put a token of his love on it—yet. Jesse had been right about the attention she'd get from her new co-workers. But it wasn't the way Rich looked at her that had red flags waving in her head; it was her traitorous body's reaction to him.

"Sounds like she'll be with Rich, *boss*," Jordan said.

Dale ignored the use of his title, patted her shoulder. "You're in good hands, Kate. Rich's one of the best."

Kate's eyes drifted to the man standing next to her. He smiled, and the tingles returned to her stomach. *That's what I'm afraid of.* "Thanks, Dale."

"News meeting in fifteen minutes. Jordan will show you to your desk." He looked at Jordan, who nodded. "She'll be next to Clayton Tate." Nate and Rich groaned while Jordan laughed. "Stop it, you guys," Dale warned through a chuckle of his own as he walked away.

Clayton Tate was one of their main reporters and Kate had seen him on TV. He was a decent reporter, although, his snow white, blonde hair and pasty complexion weren't exactly Kate's taste. She adored tall, dark, and handsome.

Her thoughts flashed to Jesse, standing in all his glory this morning, bathed in golden sunlight as it cascaded through the window. Kate's breath caught in her lungs at the sight in her mind's eye.

Another round of snickers brought Kate out of her thoughts, and she hoped they hadn't noticed that she'd zoned out on them. "What's so funny?" she asked.

"Clayton isn't his real name," Nate said through his laughter.

"Really?" She shouldn't have been surprised. It was common practice in the industry to change or embellish your name to make it more marketable or reputable.

"Yeah, his real name is Greg Jeffers."

"But he thinks Clayton Tate is a better *'anchor name'*," Rich explained, using his fingers to make air quotations.

"Kate, don't call him anything but Greg. It pisses him off," Nate insisted.

"I'm not really into pissing people off," she said in a miniscule voice that annoyed the hell out of her.

"What's the matter, Kate? You afraid of rockin' the boat?" Nate tipped his head to the side, his gaze a question mark.

Kate gulped as she realized that she'd more or less defended the guy everyone thought was an idiot. "No, I—"

"Nate, don't," Rich said as he reached out and slammed his fist into Nate's shoulder.

"What?" Nate asked, his brow furrowed as his face questioned Rich's knight-in-shining-armor act.

Rich ignored Nate and smiled at Kate, which didn't do much to ease the nervousness in her gut. "We wouldn't want to make her do anything she's uncomfortable with, would we?"

"Nope," Jordan said as the scanner started buzzing with a car fire downtown. "Can you guys take this somewhere else? I've got to get crews moving. Nate, get ready to roll. I'll text you the address."

Rich waved his hand toward the center of the newsroom. "Your desk is this way."

Kate followed him and Nate matched her pace. "Hey, I'm really sorry."

"It's okay. The new girl gets a truck load of crap until she proves herself, I get that." Kate didn't turn to acknowledge him further.

"No." He shook his head. "We have one rule around this place; we tease because we love. If we don't like you, we ignore you or we make it painfully obvious you're a pain in our ass. It's easier for everybody that way. I think that we're gonna like you just fine."

"Yeah," Rich looked over his shoulder and winked, "we like you already."

Kate felt that there was an undertone of something more in his statement, and should have been mortified by his flirtations, but instead her heart pounded wildly in her chest as those sapphires twinkled at her.

"I'm off to the barbecue. Have a great first day, Kate," Nate said before heading to the photographer's lounge to grab his equipment.

The photog's belongings were kept in a room that had cabinets on the bottom and windows on the top. It kind of resembled a giant fishbowl, with no privacy to the people within its walls.

"Here we are," Rich said, "your desk." The faux burgundy walls would barely come up to her head while she was sitting down, but it was still hers alone. "Ladies room, coffee machine, and microwave are over there. Editing is through that opening." He pointed to the back wall, to a doorway that was large enough to drive a truck through.

"News meeting in the conference room in five," Dale's voice boomed over the loud speaker.

"Come on. Let's get you a notebook and a pen." Rich then led her to the supply closet and helped her retrieve a white reporter's notebook and a couple of blue pens before he weaved through the cubicles to the conference room.

Through the bank of glass that made up the front of the conference room, Kate could see her new colleagues waiting for the meeting to start. She took a deep breath, trying to calm her nerves, and turned to glance at Rich, who once again smiled at her.

Damn, that smile!

He winked. "Now, get in there and get us a great

story." He gently shoved her in the back, which she was grateful for since her feet seemed to have been stuck to the floor.

"Ah, Kate," Dale said, "let me introduce you to everybody."

One-by-one he named each person seated around the long, rectangular table. Kate took an empty seat next to Olivia, a tiny woman in her late twenties. Her hair was the color of ink, flipping out at the ends where it rested just above her shoulders.

After Kate received her assignment—turning an old woman with nine cats into a piece that resembled hard news—she half listened to the rest of the meeting while tracing the grains in the mahogany table with her finger.

"Okay, people, let's cover the black," Dale said, clapping his hands together once.

The room erupted in chatter and the shuffling of papers. Kate stood and turned to see Rich sitting on her desk, talking on his cell phone. His brows were furrowed, his eyes narrowed. It appeared that his teeth were clenched, but it was obvious that his fists were. Kate's curiosity was piqued and she wondered who could bring so much negative emotion out of that man.

"Hi, I'm Olivia," a voice said from next to her. "I hope you'll like it here."

Lost in her thoughts, and not really paying attention to Olivia, who barely came to her shoulder, Kate muttered, "That's interesting."

"What's interesting?" Long lashes fluttered while Olivia's brow formed a V.

Kate couldn't exactly voice that she was intrigued by the guy deep in conversation at her desk, so she resorted to the last bit of talk she knew they'd both heard. "Let's cover the black."

Olivia laughed, a friendly, high-pitched sound. "Oh, that's just Dale's way of saying that without us, there would be nothing for people to watch…except black," she added with a shrug.

"I figured that's what it meant. I'd just never heard it used as a pep talk." It was hard to concentrate on the conversation unfolding in front of her as she continued to watch Rich's fiery exchange.

"You'll learn that Dale is a great boss. He's a hardass when he has to be, but he's usually quite easygoing," Olivia explained.

"So you're a producer, huh?" Kate asked as they began the short journey across the newsroom to her cubicle.

"Yes, 5:00 and 6:00," she answered from right on Kate's heels. "So who are you going out with?"

"Jesse."

"No." Olivia laughed. "Which photographer is assigned to you today?"

"Oh." Heat rose in Kate's cheeks. "Rich."

Olivia nodded, satisfied, pleased. "Listen to him. He's very good at what he does. He won't lead you astray."

"Thanks, Olivia."

"Anytime." They reached Kate's desk, and Rich was just closing his phone. He forced a smile that didn't relieve any of the frustration in his intoxicating blue eyes. "Be good to her, Rich," Olivia warned.

"Of course," he said to her before turning his attention to Kate, "Well, what's our story?"

"Hundred-year-old woman with nine cats," Kate groaned, already feeling defeated.

"When we're done, it'll be so good, they'll want to lead with it."

Kate wished she could be as confident as her photographer. She raised an eyebrow. "Not even you're that good, Rich."

"Good luck, Kate," Olivia said as she started to walk

away, then she stopped and smiled over her shoulder. "I can't wait to hear about Jesse," she said before walking off toward her desk.

Olivia's mention of Kate's best friend and lover, hung in the air like a dud grenade. The mood was awkward as she searched her brain for something to say, just letting the seconds tick by in silence.

Rich saved her when he cleared his throat. "We need to swing by HR and get your press pass and key card, and then we're off to make nine cats, breaking news."

His humor broke the tension, and Kate couldn't help but laugh as she grabbed her bag, ready for any adventure that the day held.

Two

The only sounds in the vehicle were the clicking of the keys on Kate's laptop and the soft thump of the music coming from the radio. After picking a few soundbites, the story would be good to go. It wasn't going to be as bad as she'd originally thought, thanks to Mrs. Watts and her interesting family. Kate saved her work and closed the computer.

Rich cleared his throat, concentrating a little too hard on the road as he spoke, "So, who's Jesse?"

"My boyfriend," she answered without any hesitation.

He paused for a long moment then asked with *lots* of hesitation, "How long have you been going out?"

"We've been dating off and on since high school." Her shoulders lifted in a shrug. She hadn't expected to be discussing Jesse on her first day, with another guy. Especially with a guy who did funny things to her body, made her feel things she shouldn't.

"Off and on?" he asked as one corner of his mouth lifted into a smirk. His cell phone rang, and he groaned when he looked at the caller id. "Hey, Shea." His full lips flattened out into a line as his eyes closed for a long second then he said, "Just heading back to the station." The voice on the other end was high-pitched and didn't sound happy. "Um hum." He paused while the woman continued to shriek. "I know. I'm sorry...Okay, we'll talk about it when I get home...No..." He closed his eyes, rubbing at them with the hand that wasn't steering, and sighed, "Kate."

Sitting next to a man that was getting his butt handed to him on a platter made Kate beyond uncomfortable. She shifted toward the window and concentrated on the passing scenery.

"Who's Kate?" came the piercing question through the phone, clear as day.

Kate cringed, and out of the corner of her eye she watched Rich pull the phone away from his ear in an attempt to avoid permanent hearing loss. "I can't do this right now, Shea."

"No because you're doing *her* right now," she screamed before the line went dead.

There was a loud snap as Rich closed his phone. "Dammit."

The silence that followed was excruciating. Whoever this Shea person was, there was little doubt she was a tad nuts. Who speaks that way to someone they love? Kate had never screamed at Jesse that way—no matter how angry she'd been at him. And to insinuate that she and Rich...

"I'm sorry you had to hear that," Rich's voice was quiet.

Kate was embarrassed enough for the two of them. And she couldn't bring herself to look at him, even though he was doing his best to avoid her gaze. "It's not your fault," she told him, meaning every word.

Neither of them said any more until they pulled into the parking lot, then Rich cleared his voice and whispered, "Shea's my ... wife."

"Wow, sounds like she really loves you." There was a heavy dose of sarcasm to the phrase and as soon as the words left her mouth, Kate regretted putting a voice to her thoughts. They were callused and just flat out mean. "I'm sorry."

"No, you're right." He cut the ignition and the topic of conversation in one fluid motion. "Go show 'em what you've got, Barbara Walters." He gently put his knuckles into her shoulder, bumping her lightly. "Make me proud."

Rich had proved to be everything she'd been told. He was a great photographer, capturing the essence of the little old woman and her intriguing story. Because he was so talented, it made the job of writing to the video an easy one. The pictures by themselves could have told the tale without her.

"You ready?" Rich asked from outside the editing bay door. "It's time to get you ready for the live shot."

Kate glanced at him before asking her editor, Ivy, "Are you okay if I leave?"

Ivy looked up. "Yeah, I'm just going to drop in the last two shots and then you're all set."

"Thanks." Kate plucked her bag from the floor by the door.

"You bet," Ivy responded, sending the tape zipping into rewind.

"Let's go," Rich hurried Kate toward the lobby. "I've got us set up in a great spot."

The difference in their height quickly became apparent as Kate found that she had to almost run in order to keep up with Rich's long strides. Kate's phone beeped, signaling a text message and Kate pulled it out of her jacket pocket.

Kate, I'm watching. Knock 'em dead. Jesse

A smile crept onto her face and she punched in her response as Rich glanced over his shoulder, trying to hide a scowl.

Be home soon ... hope you're ready. Kate

"Jesse?" Rich asked in a tone that sounded bitter.

"Yeah," she couldn't help that it came out as a sigh. The phone beeped again.

I'm STILL ready.

She laughed and slid the phone back into her pocket, put the IFB into her ear, and rehearsed the intro that would soon be on live television. She paced along the wall in the foyer, the heels of her shoes making soft clicking noises as she moved.

"Two minutes, Kate," Rich cued.

She took her place in front of the camera and the butterflies began to assault her stomach. Closing her eyes, she thought of Jesse. It was his support that got her over the fear of being in front of people.

"The camera is me," he'd said in the very beginning

of her short career. "You aren't talking to anyone but me. And there's nothing you can say that will stop me from loving you."

"In five, four, three..."

In her ear Kate heard the voice of Leslie Williams, the main anchor, "And we'd like to welcome Kate Callahan to the News17 family."

Kate smiled and nodded, seeing only her reflection in the lens of the camera. "Thanks, Leslie. I'm happy to be here."

"Kate's here with a story about a grandma, nine cats, and a huge heart. Kate?"

"Emma Watts is a woman who is not only nearing the century mark, but also has a heart as big as they come."

The audio from her package flowed through her earpiece, and Rich gave her a thumbs-up. The producers gave cues for the next few minutes while Kate waited for her turn to speak again.

Rich pointed his finger at her and smiled. "Go."

Kate delivered the tag, "If you'd like to donate to help Emma with her crusade to help injured felines, you can get the information on our website."

"Thanks, Kate," Leslie's voice echoed in her ear.

Kate flashed the smile she was getting paid for and gave another nod.

"Clear," Rich said.

And with that, her first day was painlessly over. "Thanks for everything, Rich. I appreciate all your help today."

"It was my pleasure. You're going to do really well here." He wrapped one of the camera's cords around his arm and tossed it next to the wall.

"Thanks." She turned, embarrassed by his praise.

"Oh, Kate, you have to stay for the post mortem," he said, another cord formed a bundle, then added it to the pile.

"The what?"

He chuckled, pulling the camera from the tripod with a click. "It's what Dale calls the meeting after the show."

Her cell phone beeped with a text message, but before her hand could even reach into her pocket, her heart stopped, shocked by Dale's angry bellow, *"Kate Callahan and Rich Spencer ... in my office ... NOW!"*

Rich's eyes widened and Kate's stomach hit the floor. The two of them walked to Dale's office without exchanging a word. Through the plate glass window that overlooked the newsroom, Dale's expression was furious.

"Have a seat," he said through gritted teeth. "Would you like to tell me exactly what you were thinking with that piece?"

"Um," she stammered, "I was trying..."

"Trying isn't good enough for my newsroom, Miss Callahan," Dale growled, his eyes moved from Kate to Rich and back again.

Miss Callahan? Crap! Her stomach rolled. So much for her aspirations of sitting behind the anchor desk.

"I only accept the best." His expression softened and a smile tugged at his lips. "And you two are a pretty good team." When he finished his words an explosion of applause and laughter came from the doorway behind her. "Jordan, I want Kate and Rich together as much as you can swing it."

"Yes, *boss,*" Jordan said with a smirk.

Dale groaned. "If you weren't family, I'd have to fire you just for irritating me."

"But I am family, Uncle Dale," Jordan laughed. "I mean, *boss.*"

"Get out of my sight, *nephew,*" Dale ordered with a shake of his head.

"Tell Elaine hi for me," Jordan called over his shoulder.

Dale ignored Jordan's reference to who Kate could only assume was Mrs. Morris, and looked at Rich. "Would you excuse us?"

"Sure." He stood and tossed her a reassuring smile before he walked out, closing the door behind him.

"Are you okay working with Rich?" Dale asked, his fingertips pressed together.

"Um ... yeah, I have no issues with him. He's a talented photog and seems like an okay guy." *Not to mention good-looking.* As the thought crept into her thoughts, Kate was grateful she'd been able to avoid blushing.

"He's the best we've got." Dale took a sip of his Coke and looked over her shoulder, out the window of his office—probably right at Rich. "I liked what I saw today, Kate. You took a fluff piece, not even a very good one, and turned it into something truly newsworthy. Impressive."

"Thank you, sir." Her body began to heat with embarrassment that praise always seemed to cause, a trickle of sweat ran down between her breasts.

"Dale." He corrected, chuckling as he shook his head. "Don't let that bonehead nephew of mine contaminate you. I prefer a casual newsroom."

"Thank you, Dale," she said with a smile.

"I'm only 'sir' if you've screwed up," he added with a wink. "You'll learn that I don't give out unwarranted praise. By the same token, if I think your work was crap, I don't pull punches there either." He smiled. "With you and Rich as a team, I don't anticipate the crap discussion taking place very often."

"Let's hope for never," she said with a strangled laugh. Her heart pounded hard in her chest as she sat in front of the man that controlled her future.

"Are you okay working Thanksgiving?" His sudden shift in subjects caught Kate off guard. "Do you have any big plans or are you free to work?" He leaned back in his chair and waited.

Her thoughts flew to Jesse and her promise to make him an intimate dinner, just the two of them, with all the trimmings. Although the thought terrified her—cooking was not her thing—she'd promised, and... "Well, I kind of..." she sighed. "I'm sure I can move my plans around so that I can work at least half a day. Would that be alright?"

He nodded, leaned forward, and wrote her name on the giant desk calendar on his desk. "The holidays are hard to schedule around here."

"I'm sure." She could only imagine how hard his job had to be, juggling the schedules of all the people working in his newsroom.

"Talk to whomever you need to and let me know which cast works best for you. I have the perfect story for you."

"Will do. Thanks, Dale."

"Thank *you*, Kate."

She brought her feet under her and stood. She didn't look back as she exited Dale's office and pulled her phone out of her pocket.

KC, U did gr8! Only U could pull of something like that! Can't w8 2 finish what we started this morning. Jesse

"Hey, Kate," Olivia called from across the newsroom. Jordan stood so close they could have easily been wearing the same jacket. "There's a bunch of us going out for drinks, wanna come?"

"No, thanks." She would have enjoyed hanging out with her new friends, but she'd promised Jesse that she'd hurry home. She hefted her bag from the desk to her shoulder. "I really have to get home."

"To Jesse?" Olivia asked with a knowing giggle.

Heat, and subsequent color, flooded up Kate's neck and into her cheeks. "Yes, to Jesse. I ... um ... promised that I help him finish something."

"Suit yourself," Olivia said, tossing a love struck gaze to the man at her side.

Jordan wrapped his arm around her waist and pulled her even closer. "Goodnight, Kate. We'll see you tomorrow."

Kate waved and headed toward the back door. Rich and Nate were deep in conversation as she passed the photographer's lounge, and they didn't even acknowledge the wave she gave them. Nate's voice was low and harsh, "Haven't you had enough, man? A nuclear waste dump is less toxic than that woman."

Rich leaned toward Nate, but Kate was too far away to hear his hushed reply. Pushing through the glass doors, she pulled the keys out and opened her phone, dialing the numbers that would give her the sexy, deep voice of comfort.

"Hey, babe, how was your first day?"

"Good. I'm tired," she sighed.

He chuckled. "Not too tired, I hope. We have a date."

She smiled, imagining the twinkle in his dark eyes. "I'm never too tired for you, Jesse. Do you want me to pick up some dinner?"

"Nope, just hurry home. I've missed you."

"I'll be home in about a half hour."

"See you then."

×××

Rich's situation was a difficult one. He and Shea had been together for a long time, but it was getting to the point where a future was something he no longer wanted with her. She had turned from the loving person, who could melt his heart, to someone he didn't even *want* to recognize.

Being an only child, Nate was the closest thing Rich had to a sibling. The two had been friends since sophomore year at UNLV. Nate was the only person Rich trusted with the sensitive matters of his heart. Although every time Rich spoke to his best friend, he knew he ran the risk of ridicule. And lately, Nate had been a little more honest than was necessary.

"Haven't you had enough, man?" Nate asked. "A nuclear waste dump is less toxic than that woman."

Rich leaned in close and lowered his voice to a snarl. "Don't you think I know that?"

Nate shook his head. "I can't keep giving you advice you refuse to take, my friend. What do you want me to say?"

"I don't know," Rich groaned, dropping his head into his hands. "She crossed the line today, insinuating that Kate and I..." His fingers ran through his hair in an attempt to dislodge some of the frustration his body was feeling. "The worst part is Kate heard her say it."

"What do you care if Kate heard it or not?" He stopped and dipped his head to meet Rich's lowered gaze. "Rich, what aren't you telling me?"

"Nothing. There's nothing going on between us. We've only known each other for—" Rich glanced over at the clock. "Fourteen hours."

Nate followed his gaze to the clock and started to gather his things. "Look, I've got to get home to Roxy. She wants me to pick out a wedding cake tonight."

Rich debated giving Nate a bit of crap over the girly task, but decided to just let it die on the tip of his tongue. "Go home ... and keep in mind that I like raspberry."

"I'll remember that." Nate laughed and slapped him on the back. "I wish you happiness, Rich. I just don't know what to tell you to make it happen."

"Yeah," he sighed, "I wish it were only that easy."

"Hey boys," Olivia's voice called from the assignment desk. "You wanna get a drink with Jordan and me?

"Nope, I'm going home. Good night," Nate said before turning to disappear out the back doors.

"Rich, you in?" Jordan asked.

"I should probably get home." But then thoughts of what he was going home to flashed in his mind, and he quickly changed plans. "Yeah, I'm not up for alcohol tonight, but I'll go hang."

"Cool, we'll meet you at Fuzzy's in fifteen." Jordan took Olivia by the hand and the three of them walked into the night.

"I just have to get some gas. I'll see you in a few," Rich answered.

One of the perks of being a news photographer was getting to save his personal vehicle the mileage, not to mention what it saved in the financial department by someone else footing the bill for most of his gas.

With his tank full, Rich headed in the direction of Fuzzy's. His phone buzzed, and without even looking, he knew who the text message would be from.

Where the hell are you?

He sighed, feeling like a trapped animal, waiting for his master to show up again with a stick.

With Olivia and Jordan. Be home soon.

Within seconds, the phone made its presence known again.

If you loved me, you'd come home instead of PLAYING with your friends!

Her constant, unsubstantiated suspicions, that he was having an affair, were getting old. Rich had never given her any reason to doubt him. His pathetic heart had been hers from nearly the first moment they'd met.

He couldn't help but wonder what had gone wrong; which fork in the road had brought them to this miserable junction. The only time she spoke to him these days was to yell or criticize. They hadn't made love in months, it was just angry sex that left his body marred by scratch marks, and his heart aching.

Jordan was standing on the steps and smiled as Rich walked up. "You thirsty?"

"Parched," Rich answered. "Where's Olivia?"

"She went inside to get us a table." Jordan stuffed his hands in his pockets. "You okay?"

"Yeah," he grunted.

They walked in to find Olivia sitting at a table in the corner. "Hi, Rich," she said before placing a passionate kiss on Jordan's mouth.

"Um ... *hello?*" Rich pointed out, uncomfortable by their uninhibited public-display-of-affection.

"Sorry. I just can't help it," she giggled and kissed him again quickly.

The truth was Rich wasn't embarrassed. He craved the kind of love his friends shared. He wanted, desperately needed, to love the way Jordan loved Olivia, and every cell in his body ached for the touch of a woman who adored him.

"What can I get for you?" Fergie, the waitress, asked, a pen pressed to the notebook held between her long fingers.

"Corona for me," Jordan said.

"Um, I'm thinking something fruity." Olivia continued to look at the menu. "I think I'll have a strawberry daiquiri."

"And for you?" She looked pointedly at Rich.

"Just bring me a Dr. Pepper, thanks." He handed her the menu he hadn't even cracked open.

"Anything to eat?"

Rich shook his head, but Olivia answered, "Yeah, bring us an appetizer sampler platter."

Fergie smiled and took the menus. "I'll have it right up."

"Thanks," Olivia said as Fergie walked away. "So, Rich, what do you think of Kate? Dale was impressed by the piece she put together."

Wow. What did he think of Kate? She was beautiful, smart, quick-witted.... "She's really good, asked all the right questions without leading the interview too much. I think she's pretty easygoing. Not too annoying or demanding."

"Speaking of which ... how is the psycho bitch these days?" Jordan asked.

Rich groaned. "Shea's fine. Thanks for asking."

"Stop the act," Jordan said. "She's making you completely miserable. You can't hide it from us. How long have we known you?"

"Five years." Rich stared at Fuzzy, a giant of man with Fergie's name tattooed on his upper bicep, who was making a drink behind the bar. He didn't want to look at the friends who knew him too well.

Olivia reached out to cover Rich's hand where it rested on the table. "Rich, in that time, you've gone from a fun-loving, happy guy to a miserable excuse for a human being."

Rich's phone buzzed and Jordan rolled his eyes.

Are you going to bother coming home?

"Rich," Olivia whispered. "Are you okay?"

"Yeah, it's just the same old crap."

"Here you go," Fergie said over the sound of plates and cups being placed on the table.

Rich waited until she walked away before he reached for his shot of caffeine. "I'm a bucket full of fun, aren't I?" he said with a bitter laugh.

"Rich, what can we do?" Jordan asked.

"Buy me a backbone or Shea a new personality."

They both laughed, and then Olivia said, "Do they sell those?"

Rich chuckled, only for their benefit, and the phone buzzed. "Dammit. I should probably go before she sends the police to look for me." After tossing a five on the table, he grabbed his jacket. "I'll see you guys tomorrow."

"Bye," they said in unison.

Speed was something that made the blood course through his veins. He lived for it. Loved to race go-carts, and always beating Nate was an added incentive. But, anytime he was heading home, his speed was easy to control. The longer it took, the better.

His phone buzzed three times during the short twenty minute drive.

Much too soon for his liking, Rich pulled into the driveway and sighed. He ran his hand over his face, scrubbing his stubbled chin. Every light in the house was on, and there was little doubt that it was going to be a long night. Slipping the key into the lock, he turned the key and opened the door. "Shea, I'm..."

A vase came hurdling across the room and shattered on the wall next to the door, sending pieces of crystal flying in every direction.

"How's *Kate*?"

Three

Kate's tired feet dragged the rest of her body up the last flight of stairs to the door that was home. Slipping the keys into the lock, she opened the door. There was a soft, romantic glow inside. "Jesse?"

"In here, babe."

She walked around the corner to see Jesse standing next to the table, dressed in black slacks and a white shirt with the sleeves rolled up. The first few buttons still open to reveal a portion of his sculpted chest. Long tapered candles flickered in the darkness next to two place settings.

Her hand flew to her mouth. "I can't believe you did this."

He shrugged and walked over to meet her. "Technically, I didn't make dinner, Sophia did. She's a good friend." He ran his hands over her shoulders and slipped her arms out of the jacket. His lips met the skin just below her ear, which caused goose bumps to break out on her warm skin. "I missed you today."

"Hmm," she moaned, leaning into his body. Her head fell back. "I missed you, too."

"You hungry?"

"Um hum." Kate's knees threatened to give out, so she grabbed onto his strong upper arms and pulled herself closer to him.

"What's wrong?" He chuckled, knowing exactly what kind of affect his breath on her ear had, and where it would lead if the love bites continued.

"Nothing," she lied. "Let's eat. I would hate for all Sophia's hard work to be for nothing."

He pulled out her chair and slid it in once she was

comfortably seated. "You really did great today. It was kind of a sucky story."

"Hey!"

"But you turned crap into something really good." He sat to her right and lifted the lid on the casserole dish that was in front of them. "Viola!"

"Spaghetti, Jesse? Sophia helped you make spaghetti?" Kate laughed, thinking of his best friend's wife making such a simplistic dish. "Certainly you could have—" Her words were cut off by his finger on her lips.

"Please just shut up and eat. This isn't all I have planned for tonight." He raised a sexy eyebrow and winked. "And the next part's even better than Sophia's cooking."

"Well, when you put—"

"Huh, uh, uh," he reprimanded, "what did I just say?"

Kate leaned over and kissed his cheek. "Why don't we just skip dinner?"

"'Cause it would hurt Sophia's feelings." He lifted her hand and kissed it. "At least taste it, so it won't be a lie when you tell her it was fabulous." He dipped his fork into the pan, twisted it and held it out for her to eat.

She purposefully ran her tongue sensuously over her upper lip. His breath caught and he closed his eyes, inhaling a staggered breath. His fork clanked as it hit the plate. His chair slid back across the hardwood. He took her by the hands and pulled her into his arms. She gasped into his mouth as his kisses began to overtake her control.

He scooped her into his arms and headed for the bedroom, stopping only to blow out the candles in the main room. "I don't want to be interrupted tonight, especially not by the fire alarm."

He laid her softly on the bed and crawled over her as she slid backward to accommodate both of their bodies. Strong, warm hands slid under her camisole and up her sides until they reached their destination and she gasped in approval.

"I wasn't sure I liked the idea of you not wearing a bra today. But now—" He let out a hoarse laugh. "—I'm so totally okay with it."

She chuckled softly against his lips and reached for the starched cotton that obscured the contours of his chisled chest. Her fingers tugged at the fabric that was firmly in his pants and moved her hands up the soft skin of his back, grasping at his bare shoulders in order to pull his body closer to hers.

A trail of hot, moist kisses moved their way from her lips to her neck and down to her collar bone which caused her breathing to become unsteady and her heart to race. His fingers gently shifted the strap of her camisole, replacing its existence with his lips.

One by one, her fingers unbuttoned the cotton barrier between her and the chest of the man she loved. With his skin exposed, she moved her hands across his muscles which jumped at her touch. She continued her exploration, over his shoulders and down his arms.

She gasped as Jesse raised her cami up to kiss the flat surface just above her low-riding slacks. Then his fingers moved to the zipper and slid it down to reveal the ivory lace beneath. His breath left his lungs in a whoosh. "I can never get enough of you, KC." The weight of his body vanished then he stepped away from the bed.

"Jesse ... where ... are you ... going?"

He lifted her into his arms and carried her into the bathroom where more candles burned, giving off a romantic glow. He sat her down next to the large bathtub and turned on the water, filling the tub with bubbles and the air with the scent of vanilla.

His eyes twinkled in the candlelight and a smile spread across his full lips. "Now, let me help you." He found the hem of her camisole and lifted it up and over her head. Her hair tumbled onto her shoulders. He slid her pants down over her hips and reached for her panties.

"Huh uh." She pushed his hands away. "You first." Her fingers seductively roamed down his chest until they reached the waistband of his pants. She tugged at the button and made quick work of the zipper. They both gasped. "Commando, Jesse?"

One corner of his lip lifted as did one brow. "Like I

said, I have big plans for tonight."

She pushed the pants down his hips and they fell to the floor, leaving a whole lotta naked skin temptingly close to her. Her eyes swept him appreciatively from head to toe. Rough hands grabbed her then reached for the satin and lace of her panties. "Now can I finish?" His voice was rough with desire.

"Please," she breathed.

His large hands grabbed her by the waist, his thumbs slipping between the thin piece of satin and her skin. In one fluid motion, the fabric was gone. Again she was in his arms, his lips on hers. He placed her carefully into the warm water and stepped in next to her. He dipped down into the bubbles and pulled her so that they were facing each other, her legs straddling his.

He kissed her lightly. "You really did a great job today, KC."

"Thanks," she sighed as her body reacted to his touch. "I'm going to really like it there."

"Good. I'd hate for you to be miserable like at the last station." He kissed her shoulder. "Meet any interesting people?"

"The News Director, Dale, is great. He has a sense of humor, which always helps. A producer named Olivia, cute little thing, and I'm pretty sure she's married to the Assignment Editor, Jordan."

"What about your photographer? He seemed to have done a good job for you." His body stiffened and his voice was tight.

She stiffened too, lifting her eyes to glare at him. "I'm not doing this with you, Jesse. Not again."

"What?" He acted as though he was seriously offended by her reaction. "Well, let me ask you this...Is he good looking?"

Kate stood, furious, and sent water spewing over the sides of the tub. "I am done. This night is done. Good night, Jesse."

His fingers grabbed for her, but she jerked away from his touch, stuffed her still wet arms into the sleeves of her robe and stomped out of the bathroom. She glanced at the bed for only a second before deciding that sleeping next to Jesse was not going to happen tonight. His constant suspicions made her livid.

Did it matter that Rich was good looking, that he was smokin' hot? No, it didn't. What mattered was that Jesse felt the need to ask. She wasn't sure if she'd made her point, or just caused him to be suspicious of something that didn't exist.

✕ ✕ ✕

Kate was already awake when the alarm went off. She'd been at KHB for a full week now, and couldn't seem to get Rich off her mind. Luckily Jesse hadn't pushed the issue and didn't seem suspicious. He'd been loving, voracious.

She rolled over to hit the snooze button, realizing that last night's events were going to haunt her all day, in more ways than one. Three hours of sleep was not enough, no matter what wonderful, earth shattering, activity kept you up. Her whole body felt the effects of Jesse's body possessing her; the good kind of ache that left your mind reliving the past.

After gathering her clothes, she headed into the bathroom, turned on the water and stepped under the hot water that would help her muscles relax enough to get her through the next twelve hours.

When the water finally ran cold, she turned it off and grabbed at a towel. She stood in front of the foggy mirror and combed through her hair. Her reflection began to show itself as the blow dryer evened out the humidity in the room.

"What the..." She tipped her head to the side. "Dammit!" Her fingers moved over the marks that marred her normally white skin. She threw the door open, letting light flood the room where Jesse still slept. "Jesse Vasquez, you are so dead!"

He rolled over and squinted at her. "Why?"

"How am I supposed to go on air with these—" She inclined her head to reveal her neck. "—*hickeys* on my neck?"

"I thought you liked when I sucked on your neck." A

huge arm flopped over his face to block the light. "You didn't seem to object last night."

She closed her eyes, fighting off the images of their fabulous lovemaking session last night, took a deep breath to calm herself, and glared at him. "Jesse, you have to be more careful."

He laughed unapologetically. "I promise that next time I'll put them in a place where no one will see." He stood, letting the sheet caress his body until it lay motionless on the bed. "Come on," he said, walking toward the closet, "I'll help you find something to wear."

× × ×

Three hours of sleep was not enough. Rich's whole body hurt, especially his neck. He leaned his head against the wall in the photog lounge and closed his eyes. Last night, Shea had screamed, yelled, and destroyed everything she could get her hands on before finally retreating to the bedroom.

"Good morning," Nate said from over his shoulder.

Rich continued to rub at his neck. "Morning."

Nate studied him for a second then asked, "What's wrong?"

His fingers ran over a knot and caused an involuntary wince. "I must have slept funny on my neck."

Nate sucked in a breath and blew it out between his teeth, making a soft whistling sound. "Dude, that's what you get for sleeping on a couch in the den. You should at least invest in a futon."

Rich narrowed his eyes at him. "Thanks for the sympathy, man."

Nate shook his head. "Come on, are you really *that* scared she'll kill you in your sleep?"

Rich sighed, again remembering how unbalanced she was last night. "I sleep behind a locked door, don't I?"

His best friend burst into laughter. "Oh, I almost forgot about the time she shaved your genitals."

"I'm just grateful that's all she did to them." He'd

not told Nate about his serious lapse in judgment the other night, and he had no intention of sharing that little bit of information. There was no need to give Nate more ammunition.

"So what happened last night?" Nate buried his head in his locker.

"She threw a glass of wine on me at dinner last night." Rich plopped down in a chair. "Then chucked it into the wall."

"What? Why?" Nate whipped around to look at him, his mouth hung open.

"I'm not sure. She yelled until 4:00 this morning about all the ways I've ruined her life. Then she started in on all the affairs she insists that I've had."

"But you haven't—"

"No! Not even an emotional one."

Nate shook his head. "Are you sure she hasn't—"

"Rich Spencer to the assignment desk." Jordan's voice said from overhead.

"Well, I guess that's the end of this conversation," Nate noted.

Rich nodded. "I'd better go see what he wants." And seconds later, he stood in front of Jordan. "What's up, man?"

"I'm going to have you go out with Kate again today. Is that okay?"

Being Kate's photographer wouldn't make Shea happy, but then again, nothing did. There was something about the girl—with auburn locks that looked so soft he had to fight the urge to stroke them, and jade eyes that seemed to peer into his very soul—that made Rich want to get to know everything about her. A dangerous, slippery slope, he knew. "Yeah, sure."

"Good morning," a soft voice called from the entrance of the newsroom. He turned around to see Kate walking toward her desk. She waved and his heart jumped.

It was ridiculous to have any sort of feelings for this woman who had just entered his life a week ago. But there she was, doing nothing except looking absolutely beautiful in a black turtleneck that was tight enough to reveal her shapely figure. She smiled and her eyes twinkled, causing his heart to melt.

You're married, his thoughts reminded him as his heart continued to pound in his chest, and his mouth went dry.

"Morning meeting in five." Dale's daily message came over the PA.

He couldn't tear his eyes away as Kate fumbled through her things. "Good morning, Rich. How was your night?" Olivia asked from next to him, her arms full of papers.

"You don't want to know," he grumbled as his feet took on a mind of their own and followed her toward Kate.

"Hi, Kate," Olivia said. Kate looked up and smiled first at Olivia, then at Rich which caused his heart to jump into his throat while his stomach did flips. "How was your night?" Olivia asked her. Color rose in Kate's cheeks. "That good, huh?" Kate's only response was a nervous, uncomfortable giggle while she anxiously fiddled with the fabric around her neck. Olivia tipped her head and scrutinized Kate's appearance for a moment before she started to laugh. "Kate? Does the turtleneck have anything to do with what happened last night?"

Kate gasped and the pink in her cheeks turned to beet red. "Jesse got a little overly rambunctious, that's all."

A twinge of pain stabbed at Rich's heart. It took a few seconds for his brain to register the emotion as jealousy.

"Olivia. Kate. We're waiting on you," Dale called from across the room.

Kate grabbed her things and hurried toward the conference room. Her auburn curls rested on her shoulders. Her turtleneck was tucked into the slim waistband of her black slacks. She had a tiny waist and a perfect...

"Rich, do you have any extra batteries?" Nate yelled. "I need to get out of here, and Tommy isn't here with the keys."

Rich tore his eyes away from their focus, and turned to see Nate's reproachful stare. "I think I might have some in my lock-up. Let me check for you." He knelt down, fumbled with the keys, found what Nate needed, and handed them off.

"Thanks, man." Nate dropped the AA's into his microphone. "Can I ask you something?"

"Sure." The words left his mouth, and he instantly wanted to take them back. Nate knew him too well.

"What are you doing?" The question and Nate's face were full of disapproval.

"What do you mean?" he asked with faked innocence.

"I see how you look at her, Rich."

"I don't know what you're talking about," he lied.

"Okay." Nate shook his head. "I guess we'll go with that for now." He picked up his gear and threw it over his shoulder. "Have a good day, Rich."

"Yeah, you too," he said into his locker, avoiding Nate's eyes.

Love at first sight had always seemed like a fallacy, but maybe there was something to it after all. Rich had only known Kate Callahan for a short time, but there was little doubt that he was developing feelings for this new reporter. And, for the first time in his life, he considered making Shea's paranoia a reality. The consideration caused his heart to hammer in his chest, blood raced through his veins. His breath caught in his throat when a small, warm hand rested on his shoulder.

"Rich." Her voice was like that of an angel.

My angel. Oh, how he wanted that to be true.

Looking over his shoulder, he was struck speechless. Almond-shaped eyes, gold flecks set off the intensity of the jade, with long fringed lashes blinked. He opened his mouth, but couldn't convince his vocal cords to work.

"Are you ready?" she asked softly.

He stared at her for another moment, finding his voice. "Um ... yeah." He shook his head back and forth in an attempt to not look like a total moron. "Where we headed?"

"We're breaking news today," she announced.

"Breaking news?" He was honestly surprised.

"Yeah, Clayton, Greg ... whatever," she laughed and it was a glorious sound, "was *not* happy about it either. Before the meeting he was hitting on me, and then..."

"He hit on you?" Rich was surprised by the anger in his voice. So was she, it seemed, as she tipped her head and examined his expression while her delicate fingers rubbed at her turtleneck sweater. *Be cool. You have no right to fall for this girl.*

"Yes," she said quietly. "But then after Dale assigned me to breaking news, he was ... well, you could say he was pissed."

"I'm sorry about that."

"Don't apologize. He's the jerk." She shrugged.

"He's just used to getting that gig. What story did he get?"

She laughed and bent down so that their faces were only inches apart. The smell of her minty breath was almost his undoing. He closed his eyes, fighting her effect on him. "The baby elephant at the zoo."

His eyes shot wide in shock as a smile spread across his face. "Dale gave him ... fluff?" The thought of "Go-Get-'Em Greg Jeffers" reporting on baby elephants nearly caused a case of hysterics.

She straightened and laughed with him. "Yeah, he's so ticked that I don't think I have to worry about him hitting on me anymore."

"That's good," he sighed, staring into her eyes.

She stared back, scrutinizing whatever she saw on his face. "Yes. Yes, it is." Her hand moved up and rubbed at the spot on her neck. "Jesse was worried the guys would hit on me. He can be the jealous type."

Jesse, the BOYFRIEND, you idiot! The mention of the man in her life was like a slap.

"It makes him crazy when guys pay attention to me." She sounded detached, worried.

"Kate and Rich, move out," Jordan's voice rang out overhead. *"Breaking News."*

Rich jerked at the sound of their names, lost his balance, and fell over on top of her. Kate sucked in a breath, her eyes wide, penetrating his. Their noses touched slightly before he was able to pull away from her. Her whole body went stiff under him, and it seemed that she'd stopped breathing.

Kiss her, his thoughts echoed the feelings of his entire body. Instead, he leaned up onto his knees and stood, offering her a hand. "Sorry about that."

"You sure do apologize a lot, Rich." She reached up, took his hand and he pulled her to her feet. It took every ounce of self control he had not to wrap her in an embrace. "Especially when it's not your fault." She smiled. "We'll need to cure you of that."

"Sorry." He cringed as the word left his mouth.

She laughed. "See? You did it again."

He threw his gear over his shoulder. "Do you have everything?"

"Yep. Let's go."

The gentleman that his mother had raised wanted to open her door, and he had to remind himself that she was a co-worker. Nothing more. It was surprising how much that revelation hurt.

His phone buzzed with their assignment.

Amber Alert ... 4-yr-old girl ... 59th South and 15th East

Rich couldn't help but groan. His stomach suddenly felt sick. "Looks like we have a missing little girl."

"Oh, no." Her body shifted so she was looking out the passenger window. "Reporting on hurt kids makes me hate this job," she whispered.

"Yeah, me too. Let's hope there's a happy ending," he agreed.

"I love happy endings."

His thoughts easily moved to having Kate as his own—his perfect happy ending. "Yeah, me too."

The ride to the scene was a quiet one. Rich's thoughts plagued by the beauty in the passenger seat. Hers were probably on the task at hand—finding the missing little girl. As they pulled up to the scene, the police were setting up their command center. Kate didn't even wait for him before she headed into the throng of people.

Rich shouldn't have been surprised. This was how Kate Callahan rolled. He'd watched her since she burst onto the scene two years ago. Thought she was beautiful then, but she was all business. Never took the time to get chummy with anyone but her sources. So, of course, she beelined it for the sheriff.

"What can you tell me?" she asked, gripping her pen for his response.

"Press conference in ten minutes, Kate."

"Oh, come on, Reggie." She was right on his heels as he started walking away. "I'm sure there's something you can give me now," she pressed.

He stopped, turned with a dramatic roll of his eyes, then smiled. "Kate." He tsked his tongue, then whispered, "The mother thinks that the father took little Mary out of her bedroom sometime early this morning. He was just released from prison two weeks ago."

Kate gasped, but didn't react further as she jotted down some notes. "Did she have a restraining order against him?"

"Yes," he verified.

"Damn," she muttered and made more notes.

"Well, I've got to get the PIO ready for the press conference." He pulled a flyer off his clipboard and handed it to her. "You didn't get this from me." He winked and headed in the direction of the Public Information Officer.

"Thanks, Reggie." Kate turned on her heel and smacked right into Rich's chest. "Oh, sorry."

Rich chuckled and stole the chance to run his fingers through her silky, soft hair. "Now who's apologizing?"

She slapped at his chest, her face turned from playful to serious in a flash. "Is the live truck here?" He nodded and motioned over her shoulder to where the microwave signal was being sent to the mountain. "Good." She pulled her phone out of her pocket, pressed some buttons and put it to her ear. "Dale, yes. Press Conference is in five, but I'd like to cut in now. Okay." She closed the phone and looked at Rich. "Let's get a move on, Spencer, we go live in two."

"Damn, girl, you certainly get things done." He raced to catch up with her as she ran over to where the cables were set up to send their signal back to the station.

Leslie's voice tossed to her, "Kate Callahan is live at the scene with more on this developing story. Kate."

"Thanks, Leslie. We're here near 59th South and 15th East where an Amber Alert has been issued for four-year-old Mary White. If you have seen this little girl—" She held up the flyer, and Rich focused the camera on the sweet, smiling face on the page. "— *please* call 800-555-1402. A news conference is scheduled to begin any minute and we'll bring that to you live."

"You're clear. Go get ready for the conference," Dale's voice said in his ear.

Kate had heard him too and was already heading over to the crowd by the makeshift podium. Rich added a microphone to the pile and stepped back, setting up the tripod just behind Kate's shoulder. Through the chaos of the upcoming press conference, Rich was surprised to see Nate setting up his camera with "Go-Get-'Em-Greg" clambering for a spot up front.

Rich stepped over and whispered to Nate, "What the hell is *he* doing here?"

"*Greg* insisted that this little girl needed him." Nate looked through the lens and chuckled.

"No, that baby elephant at the zoo *needs* him," Rich growled.

Nate laughed as Greg walked up.

"Rich," Greg said dismissively.

"What the hell are you doing here?" Rich growled, daggers flew from his eyes.

"Covering breaking news," he scoffed with an exaggerated eye roll. "I knew you were dense, Richie, but this is slow, even for you."

Rich's fists clenched as did all the muscles in his jaw. "Kate is breaking news today."

Clayton tossed his head back in a mocking laugh. "Why don't you let your little *girlfriend* fight her own battles?"

His accusation was an even harder blow than he

meant it to be, and Rich was grateful when an interruption rescued him from having to comment. "Ladies and gentleman, we're going to be starting in just a second. You know the drill. We'll make a statement then we'll have a few minutes for questions."

Dale's voice entered their ears again, "Would someone like to explain to me why I have two crews on this, *Clayton*?"

The arrogant ass lifted the microphone to his mouth and whispered, "I just thought—"

"You just thought that you would totally disregard what Jordan had assigned you, and decided to do your own damn thing?" Dale growled.

"Well, when you put it that way. Yes, I guess that's exactly what I did," Clayton stammered.

"Stay through the press conference then get your butt back to the zoo," Dale said in a tone that was so calm it sent chills down Rich's spine.

"Yes, sir," Clayton said defeated, then turned to Kate, "Head to head, huh, honey?" He looked her up and down in a way that made Rich's blood boil. "There's more to reporting than a pretty face and big boobs."

Rich took a step toward him, only to have Nate's hand grab onto his bicep. Nate's voice was low, right next to Rich's ear. "Easy, Casanova, punching him out would be rewarding, until Dale canned your ass." Rich filled his lungs with a deep breath, and he tried to coax his clamped fists to relax enough to run the damned camera. "Dude, what is going on with you?" Nate hissed in a hushed whispered.

"I don't know," Rich answered honestly.

"Well, you'd better figure it out because the protective caveman crap is going to get you into trouble—in more ways than one," Nate warned.

The press conference started, and Kate did great. She asked all the right questions, making Greg look like the rookie. With the final question asked and answered, the crowed dissipated.

"Come on," Kate whispered as she tugged lightly on Rich's jacket sleeve. "Let's interview some of the neighbors."

For the next twenty minutes they went door to door, asking neighbors what they'd seen. It was weird that nobody had seen or heard anything. It was as if this little princess had disappeared into thin air. Kate looked defeated, her shoulders drooped, as they headed back toward the microwave truck.

Suddenly her head jerked to the left. "Shh!" She turned around and stared at Rich with wide eyes. "Do you hear that?"

He nodded, then lifted the camera onto his shoulder and hit record with his thumb. "Go ahead. I'm rolling."

The two of them cautiously walked up between two houses to a small shed. "Be careful," Rich whispered, suddenly wondering how smart of an idea this was. There was no telling what—or who—might be in there. The front doors were slightly ajar, and there was a whimpering coming from inside.

"Mary?" Kate said softly as she pushed the doors farther apart.

Oh, please let it be Mary, Rich thought, for more than one reason. A kidnapper with a gun would have been really bad.

But Kate was fearless. "Mary, are you in here? It's okay. I'm a friend."

A weak cry came from behind a water barrel in the corner. There between the plastic jug and the wall of the shed was the most glorious sight, Mary White with smudges of dirt on her tiny, tear-stained cheeks.

Rich stood back and focused the camera on the events playing out in front of the lens. Relief rushed through his veins. The little girl was safe—and so was the woman who was more special to him than she should be.

Kate crouched down in front of the little girl. "Mary, I'm Kate. Everything's going to be just fine." Mary whimpered. Kate reached out to the child huddling against the wall. "I promise that nobody will hurt you."

"Daddy. The police," she said.

"Your daddy isn't here, and the police are looking for *you*," Kate assured her. "They think you're lost, honey."

Tiny fingers added more dirt to the cherubic face as she brushed away her tears, then uttered a large sniff as the crying stopped. "I'm not lost," a small voice whispered as her tiny hand reached up and grabbed onto Kate's outstretched hand, holding tightly and rushing into Kate's arms.

"Come on, honey, let's get you back to your mommy." Kate scooped the little girl into her arms. Pink bunny slippers flopped wildly as Kate took off on a run. "I've got her! Reggie! We've found her. We found Mary!"

Keeping the camera firmly on his shoulder, Rich was careful to keep enough distance between them to get the Emmy award-winning video.

"Oh, Mary!" screamed the girl's mother as she ran toward Kate.

"Mommy!" Mary yelled, reaching out to her mother.

"Oh, thank you. Thank you," her mother said through her sobs.

"Where did you find her?" Reggie asked as he took Kate by the arm and led her away from the crowd.

"Go," she hissed at Rich, "get me the good stuff."

The crowd headed toward the awaiting ambulance where the EMT's gave Mary the A-okay, and everyone breathed a collective sigh of relief. There couldn't have been a better outcome to this story.

Rich began loading his gear into the back of the news vehicle and called in to let Dale know what had gone down.

"She *found* the little girl?" he asked in disbelief. Never in the five years he'd been at KHB had Rich heard Dale 'giddy', but here they were.

"Yeah. It was awesome," he gushed.

"Please tell me you got it on tape."

Always the News Director, Rich thought with an audible laugh. "I'm offended you have such little faith in me, Dale." He paused, taking a year off Dale's life before saying, "Of course I got it all on tape. That's what you're paying me for. After you see it, could we discuss a raise?"

Dale laughed, but didn't respond further on the subject of a pay increase. "I'd like to have you two live at

5:00 and 6:00. Do you think you can get an interview with the mother?"

"If anyone can, it's Kate." She was full of surprises and Rich loved surprises.

"I don't doubt that now. Where is she?"

"She's with Chief Brown. He's probably debriefing her."

"Have her call in when she can. Great job today, Rich."

"Okay, sure thi-...." A scream from behind him sent a shot of adrenaline racing through him. *Kate.* He turned to see an enormous guy with his arms around her, holding her back against his chest. Her feet moved as she tried to flee, but his grip seemingly tightened.

"Let me go!" she shrieked.

Instinct kicked in, and Rich began running to save his beautiful damsel in distress. For the second time today, he was willing to deck somebody for this girl.

The arrogant attacker smiled, . amongst the swarming scene of law enforcement, as he returned her feet to the ground. "Easy, KC."

Casey? Rich stopped dead in his tracks and watched in horror as Kate turned to the guy with short, jet black hair and naturally tanned skin.

Her body careened itself into his arms as a round of feminine laughter filled the air. "Jesse, what are you doing here?"

A two-by-four to the head would have hurt less than the realization that struck him. As Jesse swung her around, Kate's arms were wrapped tightly around his neck. She kissed him. With no other option, Rich turned and sulked back slowly toward the Explorer with the giant 17 on the side, wishing like hell he couldn't overhear the conversation between Kate and her boyfriend.

"We watched you all day, and when you did your final report, I told Josh I was taking my lunch break. You hungry?"

Rich found his breath held painfully in his lungs while he waited for her to answer. "Oh, Jesse," she sighed. "I'd love to...."

"But..." He sounded so disappointed, and Rich didn't even try to fight his smile.

"But, I really have to finish up this story, and I still have to check in with Dale."

Rich chanced a glance over his shoulder just in time to see Jesse's face fall. It was pathetic that he should feel any kind of gratification that she was choosing to stay working with him, rather than have something to eat with the competition. But then she leaned up on her tiptoes to kiss his chin, and the sense of triumph died in his churning stomach. He turned back to the open doors of the news vehicle, busying himself with ... something. He was concentrating too hard on the conversation happening behind him only to have her next words plunge into his heart like a dagger. "I'll make it up to you tonight." There was a long pause and then she giggled.

Rich turned to see Jesse's lips pressed just below Kate's ear and couldn't stop the growl that gurgled in his gut. Their relationship was surely going to destroy him, one painful piece at a time.

Four

The next week flew by doing follow-up stories with Mary. Kate was the only one she'd speak with, and consequently, Clayton and the other stations were jealous as hell of her exclusive with the little girl who'd had the whole state looking for her.

"Morning meeting in five."

It was nice to have the five minute warning. The ability to eliminate the watching of the clock to work on other important matters was a huge help. She opened yet another email, and began to type a response when a voice spoke her name. Her eyes flicked from her computer screen to Dale's smiling face. "Yeah?"

"I hope it's okay with you, but I'm going to give you a fun story today." He rested an arm atop her cubicle wall.

"Fun?" A knot developed in the pit of her stomach.

His eyes twinkled as he smiled. "I'm just thinking that you could use a break from hard news for a day or two."

"Oh," she said as the damned burning started in her eyes. *Stupid emotions.* This job was important, she wanted the anchor desk too badly, to screw up and get demoted. She bit on the inside of her cheek.

He must have seen the tears and stepped around the wall to drop down in front of her. "Kate, this is in no way a punishment. This last week with Mary has been hard. I've seen it wearing on you." His voice was soft, reassuring.

She wanted to deny his statement, but couldn't. He was right. Being with Mary, and seeing the fear in her innocent eyes when she talked about her father, *was* taking its toll.

"I want you to enjoy some of the fun stuff for the next few days, and then we'll get you back on the hard stuff on Monday. Deal?" He offered a wink and another smile before he stood.

"Whatever you want, Dale." Kate was glad her voice didn't sound as defeated as she felt.

"Kate, I can assure you, you're doing a fantastic job. This has *nothing* to do with your ability. I'd just rather not have you crispy-crittered when I need you to be on your A-game. You understand?"

"Sure," she lied.

In her time since college, she'd been in three newsrooms and never once did a News Director care whether or not she was feeling frazzled. Either Dale was *really* caring or she'd royally screwed up. She was betting on the latter.

He smiled. "Let's go. I'd hate to be late for my own meeting."

Kate walked into the conference room and took a seat next to Olivia. Kate like Olivia a lot. They'd become fast friends and sitting side-by-side was comfortable, easy, the norm. Everyone was talking about their plans for Thanksgiving tomorrow. Of course, they all included family and turkey. Since Kate now had to work, the intimate feast with Jesse was being substituted with dinner at Sophia and Josh's early in the afternoon so that she could work the ten.

"Okay, everybody," Dale called everyone to attention and got right to business. "Clayton, I'd like you to take breaking news today."

Kate could have sworn she heard a 'yes' come from Clayton's general direction. His eyes met hers, and he smiled as though he'd accomplished something really phenomenal. He was gloating. She almost expected for him to stick his tongue out.

"Kate—" She looked up to meet Dale's gaze. He pointed at her with his pen. "—I'd like you to cover turkey bowling with the governor." Clayton snickered, but she didn't take her eyes from Dale's face as she nodded. The last few assignments were made, and then

Dale concluded with, "Let's cover the black."

Kate jumped up and hurried out the door, her eyes scanning the ocean of desks for Rich so that they could get over to the state capital by 10:30.

"So Katie," a voice called from behind her, "how does it feel to be demoted to covering 'turkey bowling'?"

She whipped around to glare at Clayton. "You know, *Greg*, turkey bowling with the governor is a tradition. I'm happy to cover the traditions that the viewers have come to adore."

"You just keep telling yourself that." He smirked as his eyes roamed hungrily over her body.

"Kate, you ready?" Rich asked with a hardness to his voice that made Kate wonder how much of the exchange he'd heard.

"Yeah, let's get out of here. We're bowling with the governor today." She gave Clayton another death stare and then turned, slamming right into Rich's chest. "Oh," she gasped. "Sorry, I didn't realize you were so close."

Clayton made a snide comment that she didn't catch. Rich chose to ignore it with a roll of his eyes and a sarcastic snort. He followed Kate to her desk where she grabbed her bag. He remained silent until they were in the car and, after he started the vehicle, he said softly, "Kate, why are we bowling today?"

Tears began to burn her eyes again, and she fought to control her emotions. "Dale doesn't want..." She paused, trying to relieve some of the shaking in her voice.

"Kate, he doesn't want...what?" Rich's voice was so worried it nearly pushed her into the sobs she'd been fighting.

She cleared her throat. "He said he doesn't want me to get burned out."

Rich chuckled. "Oh, is that all?"

"Is that all?" she squeaked as the first tear rolled down her cheek. Out of the corner of her eye, Kate watched as his right hand made a motion toward her, only to pull back quickly and grab onto the steering wheel so hard his knuckles turned white.

"Kate, he does that, especially with emotionally

draining stories. You're very good, and it would be detrimental, in the long run, if you got burnt out. Take the reprieve, and let's go bowling." He reached out and wrapped his hand around hers. "Honest, Kate. You'll be back to kicking Clayton's butt in no time."

"Thanks, Rich." She did feel better, and the innocent contact did things to her that she couldn't bring herself to admit.

"Anytime." He squeezed her hand and smiled as his phone rang. His eyes left hers and looked down at the caller id which abruptly changed his mood. He let out a sigh before answering, "Hello?"

Kate had come to realize that Rich was in a loveless marriage. His wife was completely nuts. Her voice never changed from its high pitched shriek from that first day. She was belligerent, belittling, and made constant references to her suspicions of there being something between Rich and Kate, which was ridiculous because Kate loved Jesse.

His phone closed with a snap, and he let out a long, frustrated exhale. They both pretended as though the last few minutes hadn't occurred. Neither of them knew what to say, so they resorted to silence.

Finally the state capital came into view, and Rich spoke, "Have you covered this before?"

"Yeah, when I was at Six."

"So you know what to expect?" He was trying to act as though he wasn't rattled, but she could sense his frustration.

"Yep, no biggie. This story practically writes itself."

And Kate was right. Two hours and four crazy wife phone calls later, she and Rich were headed back to the station. His phone rang *again* and he closed his eyes, let out an exasperated breath and answered, "What? I'm trying to work."

Then the screaming began, "How dare you not answer the phone when your *wife* calls? What if there was an emergency and I really needed you?"

"Do you?" he said through clenched teeth, the muscles of his jaw working ferociously.

"Huh?" Shea was confused but still irritated.

"Is it an emergency?" His voice was too calm. "Do you really need me?"

"No, but—"

"Shea, I am trying to work here."

"Are you with *Kate*?" The way Shea snarled caused the hair on the back of Kate's neck to stand on end.

Rich ran his fingers through his hair. "I told you that Dale has me working with her. You *know* that I'm with her."

"Is she pretty?"

Rich turned to look at Kate, his eyes pleading. "I guess if you like that type," he said, adding a nonchalant shrug.

It was interesting to Kate that his indifference stung, but it did, and not just a little bee sting either. It was more like the one you'd get from a scorpion the size of a Scion. And the last thing Kate wanted to do was reflect on the whys of that dangerous question.

"Is she your type, Rich? Do I have a reason to worry?" The interrogation continued.

"Shea, I'm not having this fight with you again."

"That's not an—" Her voice was cut off as Rich closed his phone.

The ginormous purple elephant was again seated uncomfortably in between them, and words started coming out of Kate's mouth before she could censor them. "Feel free to tell me to mind my own business."

His jaw was still grinding his molars into nubs as he said, "Okay."

Well, don't stop now, Kate! She took a deep breath, and added another elephant to the herd. "Have you always been so miserable?"

The hard lines of his face turned even harder. His eyes narrowed, teal flashed to navy, and his tight lips formed a frown. "Excuse me?"

"I've heard the way she speaks to you, Rich." Kate twisted in the seat to face him. "Nobody deserves to be treated that way, least of all you."

Rich sniffed, coughed, and ran the back of his hand across his eyes, then gripped the steering wheel hard.

Kate wondered if this topic had nearly driven him to

tears and she felt horrible, his agonizing silence added to her guilt. "I've noticed you don't wear a ring," she whispered. "If I had a sexy husband, I wouldn't ever let him take it off." She laughed awkwardly as she realized she'd just called him sexy.

He glanced at her sideways with an evil smirk on his lips, but didn't comment further on the fact that he'd picked up on her slip of the tongue.

"Is that your choice or hers?" Kate continued.

Rich turned and his eyes met hers. Behind the beautiful, oceanic blue was a sadness she'd never seen before. Her heart broke for the man sitting next to her. "Would you like to hear the story, Kate?"

It wasn't until he broke off their stare to concentrate on the road that she was able to breathe, and attempted to choke down the lump that had worked its way into her throat. She whispered, "Only if you want to tell me?"

He smiled, but sadness still remained in his eyes. "How about we go get some lunch, and I'll tell you all the sordid details."

Guilt boiled in her veins. "I'm sorry, I..."

"It's okay."

Kate was beyond curious. But... "I don't want you to tell me anything you don't want to. I didn't mean to pry."

The smirk was back as he said, "It will be nice to finally get it all off my chest. I've not even told Nate the story. He thinks I just stopped wearing the damn piece of platinum because I'd had enough."

"Have you had enough?" It appeared that the you-can't-ask-*that* sensor in Kate's brain had been turned off.

He pulled the vehicle into a parking space outside a sandwich shop and turned off the engine. His body shifted toward her and he took her hand in his. Heat spread from the point of contact.

The contact should have made Kate uncomfortable, even angry. Instead her heart was pounding in her chest, and her breathing had all but stopped. Her brain was screaming at her to pull away. She didn't though, she just stared into his face anticipating the answer she hoped was coming.

✕ ✕ ✕

Kate's question echoed in Rich's head. *"Have you had enough?"* That was the same thing he'd been asking himself for the last twelve months. The first year of their marriage had been loving, full of laughter and enjoyment. But just before Shea quit her job at Raskey's Law Firm, everything changed. She became cold, distant, mean spirited, and paranoid.

Again Kate's sweet voice returned to his thoughts, *"Have you had enough?"*

His body acted on its own and shifted toward Kate, taking her small hand into his. The contact made his heart skip a beat, and as he looked into her eyes, he felt more passion for her than he'd ever felt for anyone in his life. He leaned in toward her and held his breath while his eyes drifted closed in anticipation.

"Rich," she breathed, "you were going to tell me why you don't wear a ring." Her big, innocent eyes blinked.

"Right, my ring." He forced his back against the door and rubbed at his finger. "Shea came home from work one day and said that she couldn't work at Raskey's anymore. She insisted that things were just too hard. She'd always loved that job, and her quitting seemed to have come out of nowhere, but she was adamant that—"

"Did she have an affair?" Kate cringed as the question flew from her mouth.

"No, why would you...?" He stopped mid-sentence as Kate's question sunk in. *Had Shea had an affair?* That would explain the distance, the anger, the paranoia— well, everything. "I don't *think* so."

"Sorry, I won't interrupt anymore." She acted as though she were locking her lips and tossed the invisible key over her shoulder.

"It's okay." Rich began to contemplate the possibility as he continued the story. "She refused to even go back for two weeks, she was just done. We argued. We fought, but she never would give me an answer. She simply left a great paying job with full benefits to go work at the

Gap in the mall for nearly minimum wage."

"Weird." Kate shrugged.

"Yeah, it was. Then a new reporter started, I came home from work and she asked if I had met her. Of course I had, and Shea went ballistic. She started yelling crazy things about me cheating on her. Which, I promise you, Kate, I never have. *Never.* No matter how bad things were between us."

Kate nodded and blinked slowly, letting out a controlled breath. Her reaction made him wonder if she was actually relieved he'd remained faithful.

"Anyway, the next morning while I was in the shower, Shea came into the bedroom and took my ring off the dresser. She cut it with some type of clippers and then beat the pieces with a hammer. When I got out, there was nearly nothing left of it."

Kate gasped. "Oh, my."

"So that's the reason I don't wear a ring." He held up his hand to show off his naked fingers.

"Did she ever say why she did that?" Kate's head shook back and forth in disbelief.

"She said that the pieces signified what I'd done to her heart."

"Goodness."

Talking to Kate was so easy—so natural—and in the next few minutes, Rich had managed to spill the horrifying details of the last year of his life. "Then the night of Jordan's bachelor party, I came home completely plastered and woke up to find that she'd shaved my ... my boys."

Her eyes widened and a strangled giggle burst out of her. "I'm sorry. It's not funny, but it..."

Rich chuckled. "It sounds like something that would happen in a frat house, huh?"

"Well, yeah." Her face turned serious for a moment as her eyes stared at him. "I'm seriously worried about your safety, Rich."

There was a long pause while his eyes drank in the sincerity of her face. He cleared his throat and continued, "That night I started sleeping in the den with the door locked. I stopped at Home Depot and bought a deadbolt that only I have the key to." There was no need to tell her that he'd slipped up a few weeks ago.

"That's good," she sighed. "Was that all she did?" She rested her hand on her knee and leaned toward him.

He laughed. "You have no idea what that woman has put me through. Once, she stuck condoms to my car." It surprised him that the laughter continued—and that it was alright. It felt so natural to confide in the angel sitting next to him. "It wasn't just wrapped ones either. She'd unwrapped every single one and stuck them all over my car."

She raised a hand up to cover her mouth, *trying* to stifle a giggle. "Oh, Rich, I'm so sorry. No wonder you're miserable."

"I'm not *completely* miserable," he corrected. "I do have some really great things in my life."

"I am so glad to hear that." She looked truly relieved. "Do you want to talk about those? It's probably a happier list."

"Well..." *You.* "I love my job." *You.* "I have some really good friends." *You.* "I'm close to my mom and dad." *You.*

Her eyes dropped to her lap and watched as her fingers played with a loose string. Painful silence stretched on for only a few seconds, which felt like lifetimes, before she reached for the door. He opened his and walked around to meet her. He wanted to take her hand and escort her into the sub shop where they would have lunch. Instead, he jammed his hands into his pockets and purposely kept his distance.

As he held the door to the restaurant open, she turned to him, "Thank you for telling me all of that."

"Thank you for letting me unload all my baggage onto your shoulders."

"If you ever need me, I'm here." She wrapped her tiny hand around his forearm, sending a delicious warmth surging from the point of contact, and squeezed. "I want you to know you can count on me."

Having her hand on his skin made his body react in ways it never had. He looked down into her eyes which were so clear he swore that he could see directly into her soul, and fought the urge to kiss her.

"What can I get you?" came the voice from the kid behind the counter.

"Um." Kate looked at the menu above the head of the college student waiting to take their order.

Rich ordered his usual turkey on wheat, and waited at the register while Kate told them what she wanted on her sandwich. "I'm paying for both orders," he told the girl with the blond ponytail. "And give me two large drinks." He swiped his card as Kate came up to his side and started to pull out her wallet. "I got it."

"How gentlemanly of you," she laughed. "Thank you."

"You're welcome."

They found a table and he took the cups. "What would you like?"

"Coke, please."

He hurried to fill the cups, cursing the slow machine, and returned to the table. "Here you go."

"Thanks." She took the cup from him and their fingers brushed just enough to make his heart to skip a beat. "Be careful, Rich, people will think we're on a date."

"Would that be so bad?" he asked hopefully.

The question hung in the air for nearly an eternity. Her big green eyes just stared into his. "Um," she paused for an uncomfortable second, "well, yes, it would—"

If that don't take the wind out of a guys' sails.

"—since you're married and I'm...going to be."

Rich shook his head, slumped into the chair across from her, and ignored the fact that he'd just humiliated himself in front of an angel. "Thank you for letting me talk about my disaster of a marriage."

"Anytime." She smiled. "You can tell me anything."

That I love you? There was no way he could ignore the feelings that were consuming every cell of his body. He reached over and curled his fingers around her hand. "Thank you, Kate. It's nice to know that you're willing to listen to me whine about the last miserable year of my life."

"Which reminds me of my original question—" Her eyes twinkled the most beautiful shade of jade. "—have you had enough?"

"I don't know," he told her honestly as he pulled his hand back. The movement was surprisingly painful. "I've never been a quitter, and I vowed to.... Better or worse, you know?"

"Can it get any worse?"

"Probably not."

"Do you still love her?"

Another question he'd asked himself a thousand times a day for the last year. "A piece of me will always love the woman that I married, but it's a tiny piece." He paused and played with the wadded up straw wrapper, trying to decipher his thoughts, his feelings. He must have been silent for a little longer than she would have liked because she cleared her throat and changed the subject.

"Are you doing the family thing tomorrow?"

Tomorrow. He groaned. "Yeah, it's the year for her family. It's nice because they're local, so we don't have to travel."

"But...?" she said, sensing that there was a big 'but' coming.

"Her family isn't exactly supportive of our marriage, and some of them are a bit unstable."

She raised an eyebrow and the corner of her mouth. "Like Shea?"

"No, not like..." He was surprised by his defensive response. She took a bite of her sandwich and chewed slowly, her eyes avoiding his. "Yes, just like Shea," he finally whispered.

Kate finished chewing and took a long, slow sip of her drink. "Sorry to imply—"

"No, it's okay." He shook his head. "I've just been defending her for so long that it's become a habit."

"Rich, how can you defend the fact that she mangled your wedding band, or that she sticks condoms to your car, or shaves your..." Color started to rise in her cheeks. "Your *boys*. There's no excuse for that. I'd *never* do anything like that to Jesse. *Ever.*"

Hearing *his* name on her lips and seeing the adoration in her eyes caused real, physical pain as though someone had reached in and was using brass knuckles to massage his heart. Rich cursed his memory as it chose that moment to recall Jesse swinging her around in circles the day of the Amber Alert.

A loud slurping noise brought him out of his agonizing thoughts. Kate smiled, her pale skin turned an exquisite shade of pink under the dusting of freckles on her cheeks. "Excuse me. I guess I need to get some more." She held up her cup, shook the ice still in it, and slid the chair backward.

"I can get it for you." He started to stand.

She shook her head. "No, you need to finish up. I have to get this story edited."

They finished lunch, the newscast, and finally the shift without saying much to each other. Sitting alone in the photographer's lounge, Rich's mind replayed everything that had happened today. She'd been so quiet, probably worried she'd offended him, or said more than she should. The truth was, she'd given him a lot to think about.

His marriage *was* awful. He *was* miserable. But the most important thing he'd learned today was that he couldn't live without Kate Callahan in his life. After only a few weeks Rich loved her, and had no right to. She was happy and in love with someone else. He was certainly at a crossroads in his life. Was he ready to give up on Shea? Was their future dead?

Kate's laughter rang through the newsroom, and he looked up to see her sitting on the corner of Olivia's desk, the two of them laughing at something on the computer screen.

There was another path he could take.

But would it be any less painful than the one he was already on? There was no guarantee that the woman he loved would love him back. Chances were better than not, she would probably stay devoted to the man already in her life.

"Goodbye, everybody," Kate's voice called.

With a nervous heart, he quickly stood up, ran his fingers through his hair and, as she turned to smile at him, his decision was made. The two of them walked into the parking lot together. It hurt that he wasn't going to see her tomorrow. He missed her already. His arms ached to pull her into a hug, to show her exactly how much she meant to him.

"Well, goodnight, Rich." She flashed him a smile. "Good luck tomorrow with your house full of crazies. I'll be thinking about you."

"I'll be thinking of you too ... while you're working." *While you're eating. While you're sleeping.* Then thoughts of who she was sleeping *with* crowded into his brain. Utterly painful.

She began to walk away from him, toward her car, and he hurried to close the distance. "Oh, Kate."

"Yeah." She turned and her hair fanned out before settling around her face.

"You aren't pretty," he blurted. Her brows narrowed in confusion as her face fell. He shook his head, his lips lifting at the corners. "I think you're absolutely beautiful." He winked at her. "Definitely my type."

✕ ✕ ✕

Rich happened to be leaving the same time Kate was, and they said their goodbyes as they walked through the parking lot to where their cars were parked. The fact that he was going to be spending tomorrow with a house full of nuts bothered her a great deal. And the more she thought about it, the more uncomfortable she became.

"You aren't pretty," he said.

All the air left Kate's lungs, and she could feel the tears stinging her eyes. She wasn't so naïve as to think that she was a super model or anything, but his words hurt more than just her pride. The thought of Rich Spencer not thinking she was at least pretty caused more pain than she thought possible.

Burning instantly started in her eyes. She took a step back and was about to turn away before the tears fell, embarrassing her further, when he took a step toward her as his eyes continued to bore into hers. She wanted to look away, to look anywhere except the intoxicating face staring back at her.

"I think you're absolutely beautiful." He winked. "Definitely my type," he whispered, before turning on his heel and walking away.

Her first instinct was to run after him, to get clarification. *His type?* She didn't want to be his type. She was Jesse's type.

Her ringing phone interrupted her thoughts. "Hello?" She snapped at the poor person on the other end of the line.

"KC? Is everything okay?" Jesse asked, worried.

His voice was all Kate needed to calm herself. She turned to face her car and smiled. "No, everything's fine. You can't imagine how much I needed to hear your voice right now. I love you, Jesse."

"Wow, what brought this on? Not that I'm complaining."

"It's just..." She looked over her shoulder to see Rich drive away. "It's been an emotional day."

"I'm sorry."

She climbed into the car and turned the key. "I'm on my way. Will you be there when I get home?"

The sound of metal and air guns could be heard in the background. "No. That's why I was calling. I have to work late since we're off tomorrow and Friday. I'm so sorry."

"It's okay." She sounded disappointed to her own ears. "How long are you going to be?"

"Probably three hours or so. Will you wait up?"

"Of course. I really need to be with you tonight." If for no other reason than to solidify her feelings for him and convince herself she didn't feel anything for Rich.

"I love you, KC. I'll see you in a bit."

The line disconnected, and she was again alone with her thoughts. The CD player was going to be her only salvation. She turned it on and enjoyed the hard notes and beats of her newest CD, which made her thoughts muddy in her head.

The dark apartment wasn't at all what Kate needed

to lighten her mood. She needed Jesse to wrap her in a hug and make the rest of the world disappear. She flipped on the lights and headed straight for the bathroom. A nice warm bubble bath would have to be what she used to get her mind off of the comment made by Rich.

She slid into the tub, submerging herself into the hot water and fluffy bubbles. *Definitely my type,* her mind chanted. His *type*? *His* type? What was *that* supposed to mean? He was married for crying out loud. And she was in love with Jesse. There was no way she would ever feel anything for Rich.

Rich.

His name echoed in her mind as did his words. Kate replayed everything about their conversations since the time she began working with him. His jealousy at the thought of Clayton hitting on her, and the events of today were enough to make her believe he had feelings for her—more than the professional, platonic friendship they were supposed to have.

I have to know, she told herself as she climbed out of the bathtub, sending water splashing over the sides and onto the fluffy white rug.

Kate didn't even take the time to dry off. Instead she wrapped her robe around herself and headed for the phone. She dialed the familiar number and waited for a voice to answer.

"Hello?"

"Hi Monica, it's Kate." Her heart hammered in her throat.

"Oh hi, Kate, what's up?"

"I um—" *What the hell are you doing?* "—I need to get a hold of Rich, can I get his number?" *You're playing with fire!*

"Sure thing. One sec."

Hang up, NOW!

The phone clanked against the desk, and then Monica was back and rattled off the number.

"Thanks."

"No problem. See you tomorrow."

"Yeah, tomorrow." Kate stared down at the numbers

that seemed to glare back from the paper in accusation. If she dialed them, nothing good could come from it. Kate had no business calling another woman's husband to ask him to clarify exactly what he meant by her being his type, no matter how horrible the marriage was. Nor did it matter how psycho Shea was. Rich was still married to her.

And Kate's heart belonged to Jesse.

She walked into the kitchen and pulled out a Coke, took out a cup and filled it with ice before dumping in the bubbling brown liquid. While the bubbles subsided, she paced in front of the notepad by the phone. This was a decision that couldn't even be discussed with anyone. Olivia was too close to the situation, besides she'd known Rich for far longer. Her only other friend, Sophia was... Well, she'd tell Josh and Josh would tell ... Jesse.

What are you doing?

Staring into the face in the mirror in the entry way, Kate spoke to the only confidante she had, "Who cares if the gorgeous guy with the intoxicating baby blues has feelings for you? It doesn't matter. What you have with Jesse is wonderful." Over her shoulder, from the opposing wall, was a picture of Jesse with her in his arms, kissing her.

The memory flooded her thoughts and she smiled.

It was just before they moved from Arizona. She'd just received the call saying that she had her first job after college. Jesse threw a party and convinced all their friends to come to wish her good luck—and goodbye. As people started to leave, he took her hands. "KC, I can't bear for you to leave me."

"I know, but we'll call every day and I'll come home as much as I can, and you can come..."

He leaned down and rested his forehead against hers as he traced circles on her back. "I don't want to be away from you for one minute, let alone weeks or months at a time."

Tears burned her eyes as she leaned up on her tiptoes to kiss him. The anticipation of being away from him ate away at her heart. "I know how you feel, Jesse, but what do you expect me to do?" The first tear made a trail down her cheek.

He chuckled as his thumb stretched out to brush away her tear. "I expect you to let me come with you."

Kate's brows furrowed in confusion, and she took a step back so she could see him better. "What? Jesse, what are you saying?" Her brain was working overtime trying to comprehend what he was telling her.

"I'm saying that I bought into a garage, and I'm moving out there with you."

The next thing Kate knew she was throwing herself into Jesse's arms, while wrapping him in a chokehold, kissing his cheeks and lips. "Are you serious?"

"If it's okay with you."

"Okay ... with me?" There was no way to contain the excitement, and relief. Tears streamed down her cheeks with increased force as she pressed her lips to his.

A flash interrupted their moment.

She studied the picture, running her finger over the people who looked so happy. They were happy. They *are* happy.

Her thoughts returned to Rich and the horrendous conversations she'd overheard, and the sad stories he'd told her as verification of Shea's lack of mental stability. Kate picked up the pad and stared at the numbers. *Curiosity killed the cat,* she told herself. With a flip of her thumb, the phone opened and she pressed the first three numbers, only to close the phone again.

Rich's words floated through her mind again, *"I think you're absolutely beautiful. Definitely my type."*

What the hell is that supposed to mean?

She curled up on the couch, with the pad, her phone, and her Coke. Her co-workers would be doing the 10:00 cast, so she flipped it on to see what was happening. The voice speaking was far too familiar, "And with photographer, Rich Spencer, I'm Kate Callahan reporting for News17, your extended family." They'd re-run her package from earlier.

"I think you're absolutely beautiful. Definitely my type."

After sucking in a deep breath, holding it, and exhaling slowly, Kate worked up the courage to dial the numbers ... and she did.

Her heart seemed to pound harder with each ring of the phone. She held her breath until a voice answered, "Hi Kate, I've missed you." The sound of his deep, comforting voice was all it took to erase any doubts or curiosity she had.

"Are you coming home soon?" she whispered.

"Yeah, I'm actually just locking up. KC, honey, are you okay?" Jesse always knew her too well.

"I'm just really tired." It wasn't a complete lie.

"Go ahead and climb into bed, I'll be home in about fifteen minutes."

"Hurry."

He chuckled, and she could hear the engine of his car starting in the background. "I'll be home soon."

The phone closed with a snap, and she laid it on the table, plugging it in. She picked up the pad and stared at the numbers, then pulled the top page off and shoved it into her purse. She took one more look at the girl in the mirror and waved a finger. "You are not allowed to call that number unless it's business related."

Her whole body felt exhausted. Kate stripped off her robe and laid it across the bottom of the bed. The blankets were cold against her skin, and she couldn't wait for Jesse to come home so she could curl up next to his warm body.

As soon as her head hit the pillow, her eyes drifted closed.

Five

"Kate." Her whole body began to move gently back and forth. "KC, sweetheart, it's time to get up."

"Hmm?" she groaned, snuggling into the warm body next to her.

A chuckle rumbled below the skin next to her ear. "I'd love to hold you all day, but..." She ran her fingers up his side and he laughed, brushing her hand away. "Do you really want to play that way?" he asked, kissing her neck. "It seems to me that you're pretty ticklish, right here." His tongue brushed along the hollow space below her collarbone and she squealed.

"Okay, okay. I don't want to start something that you're going to win."

He wrapped his arms around her and his hand reached around her back, pulling her closer to him. "Come on, we have to be at Josh and Sophia's in an hour."

Kate slid her hands down his back and under the waistband of his boxers, holding a firm cheek in each hand. "I'll just starve," she said as she squeezed. "Please."

"You're killing me, KC." He closed his eyes and let out a deep, frustrated sigh. "I promised Sophia we'd be there by 11:00."

"We'll be quick," she promised, leaning up to kiss his jaw.

"Not this morning." He ran his nose up her neck then ran his tongue along her earlobe. He rolled her over so that she was on her back and he was on top of her, balancing his weight on his arms. His lips lowered to hers, but just before they touched, he chuckled, "Get up,

KC." He kissed her softly and climbed out of bed, stripping of his boxers as he headed toward the bathroom.

The shower turned on, and Kate lay back against the pillows, frustrated in more ways than one. Kate was also frustrated with herself. She had no right to worry about Rich the way she did. The fact that he was spending the day with his wife shouldn't bother her. Nor should she be relieved that he spent every night *alone* behind a locked door. Certainly he was getting pleasure somewhere. He'd promised her that he'd never cheated on the crazy woman lucky enough to be his wife.

"KC?" The sound of Jesse's voice jerked her out of her thoughts.

Kate's eyes met his, and he smiled as he rubbed the towel over his short black hair. "Yeah?"

"Are you going to get up?"

Kate smirked as her mind crawled momentarily through the gutter. She raised a suggestive eyebrow while seductively letting her eyes roam down his body to the towel that hung low on his hips. "Shouldn't I be asking *you* that?"

The deep rumble of his laughter filled the air. He shook his head and reached down to pull the towel away.

Her breath caught in her throat at the sight of him standing completely naked in front of her. The male anatomy wasn't something Kate considered beautiful, until she'd seen the forever tanned skin that covered the muscular body of Jesse Vasquez.

"Nope." He replaced the towel and walked back into the bathroom. "Now, get up."

Two can play at that game, she thought as she ran fingers through her hair on the way to the bathroom.

Jesse was standing in front of his sink, brushing his teeth. Kate stood in front of the mirror and ran her hands over her breasts, moaning lightly, "Jesse."

He dropped his toothbrush in the sink and stared at her reflection with eyes wide while his mouth hung open.

"Oh, Jesse, I need you."

His head shook back and forth in a desperate attempt to remain in control. He rinsed his mouth out, never taking his eyes off the erotic motions of her hands. "Huh uh, Kate—" He turned to look at her. "—this isn't going to work." He walked over to turn the shower on. His hands stopped her before she got to the one place that would be his undoing. "This is *not* working." The towel twitched, revealing his lie.

"It's not, huh?" She raised an eyebrow and whipped the white cloth away. "It looks to me like it is totally working." She ran her hand down his abdomen and brushed him ever so lightly with the tips of her fingers.

He sucked in a breath of air. The sound of victory.

"Why, Jesse Vasquez, where is your self control now?"

His mouth crushed hers as he left a trail of kisses from her mouth to the tender space just below her ear. "You are evil, Kate," he whispered before brushing her hand away so he could lift her into his arms.

She wrapped her legs around his waist as he carried her to the shower.

He set her on her feet and kissed her passionately. As the shower door opened, he kissed her one more time. "You are very persuasive, babe, and if I let you, you're going to make us late."

"But—" she stammered in surprise.

He kissed her lightly on the tip of her nose. "If we're late to Josh and Sophia's, then you'll be late to work."

"It's okay."

He chuckled, kissing her on the forehead before easing her under the stream of hot water. "If you're late for work, you'll never forgive me. Now, hurry." He quickly strode away, leaving her alone to finish getting ready.

✕✕✕

After being forced to endure a cold shower, Kate's teeth were still chattering as the dress slid its way into place on her body. She should have been angry for his refusal, but turnabout was fair play. Heaven knew, she'd shot him down more times than she could count over the years.

"You ready?" Jesse asked from the bedroom.

"Yeah," she called back, "just about." After walking through a spray of perfume, she headed out to meet him.

He was dressed in a pair of dark blue jeans and a long-sleeved navy dress shirt. His back was to her as he searched through the drawer for a pair of socks. "I was thinking we should take two cars." He stopped mid-sentence as he turned and their eyes met. "You look beautiful."

She rubbed her hands down the front of her cream dress. The simple tailored A-line design came down to the knee and had a matching jacket.

"When did you get that dress? I'm thinking it's not at all appropriate to wear to the office." He flashed a suggestive smile and arched a sexy eyebrow. "I'll bet it'd look amazing on the floor."

Kate rolled her eyes and answered his first question, "I got it for the new job, and just haven't had a chance to wear it yet."

"It's definitely a keeper." He turned back to the task of finding his elusive socks.

After grabbing the matching heels out of the closet, Kate headed for the living room. "Hurry, Jesse, we're going to be late," she teased, laughing as he launched a rolled pair of gym socks at the doorway, purposely missing.

Laptop, purse, keys, her mind ticked off the list of things she'd need to take for work later. She lifted the bag to her shoulder, and the thin piece of paper in her purse carried the weight of a bag of wet cement.

"Ready?" Jesse whispered from right behind her as he placed a kiss just below her ear.

"Um hum," she whimpered as her knees reacted to his hot breath.

He chuckled, "Have you got everything?"

"Yeah." She grabbed her things and Jesse ushered her out the door.

Standing outside her car, Jesse kissed her sweetly on the lips, lingering just a moment longer than necessary. "Okay, sweetheart, I'll follow you. Do you remember the way?"

"Yeah, I'll see you in a few."

Kate sunk down into the seat of her well-maintained Volkswagen Jetta. Her lower body slid under the steering wheel, Jesse leaned in for one more quick kiss before he returned to his full height. "Drive safe."

"Promise."

He nodded and closed the door. In the rear-view mirror, Kate watched Jesse walk over and get into his car. His smiling face looked over to meet her gaze, he nodded and she put the car in reverse, pulled out of the space and headed in the direction of their Thanksgiving dinner.

× × ×

"Come on," the screeching continued from the other side of the bathroom door, as did the incessant pounding. "Would you hurry up? You know how my family feels about tardiness."

Rich turned toward the door and put his hand on the handle. He filled his lungs with a long, deliberate breath before opening the barrier between them. As soon as her furious face came into view, he rolled his eyes. "Tardiness, Shea? Really, how old are we?" A smile spread across his face as he slipped passed her.

The sound of a snort followed by the loud, obnoxious clanking of her shoes pursued him toward the den, his sanctuary. "Rich."

"Hmm?" Rich grunted, refusing to even slow his pace.

The clanking stopped and he heard her stomp her foot. "Rich," she whined.

He turned around and met her gaze. "Oh, come on, Shea," he mocked, using a Mr. Belvedere accent as he pressed his fingertips together. "We would hate to be tardy, wouldn't we? Your family hates that so."

Fury flashed in her eyes. "How dare you?" she hissed.

"I don't know, maybe I've finally found my spine."

"Rich, what changed between us?" The mood in the room changed from acid to syrup so fast he almost laughed.

Memories of all the hell she'd put him through rushed at him, giving him the courage he needed to finally call the shots. *Yes,* he concluded, *I have finally had enough.* "Honey, I didn't change. You did. And, for the record, I'd like to know what caused it."

She started to wring her hands together. "Nothing ... *caused* it."

"Well, you're sure as hell not the same woman I vowed to love forever." He took a deep breath and launched the next question into the air, come what may. "Did you have an affair?"

She looked like a deer in the headlights, just waiting to be plowed over by a semi. Her voice dropped low and she finally blinked. "Rich, you're a wonderful husband, and I guess I'm just—"

"Forget it," he snapped, and turned his back on her, jammed his wallet into the back pocket of his jeans and grabbed his phone and keys. "I'll meet you there."

"Wait. What will they say if we..."

"Honestly, Shea, at this point, I don't care what *they* say."

His feet were headed out the front door before he even realized what he'd said—or done. *Damn, it's going to hit the fan.* There was no way she was going to let his speaking to her that way just simply slide without any kind of retaliation.

He pushed the keys into the ignition, and with a flick of his wrist, the engine began to purr. What a comforting sound. The new feelings that were coursing through his veins were that of strength, power. It had been so long since he'd taken any kind of control in his marriage.

The feeling was liberating.

If nothing else, Kate had given him a new outlook on his, until now, pathetic existence. He'd become only a shell of himself—been drowning, his lungs burning fiercely. Kate was that first breath of fresh air after emerging from the depths of despair.

Since confronting Shea about an affair, Rich was sure that the possibility was real. Her lack of denial or excuses was enough to verify that she most likely had.

How could I have been so stupid? Nate had suggested it in the very beginning. Why had Kate's insinuation held more value?

Kate.

It was 4:00. Kate would be heading into the station to get ready for the 10:00 newscast. He groaned. His heart missed her more than he had a right to, more than he *wanted* to. His entire body ached to simply see her.

A red light stopped him, and the proverbial crossroad became very real. If he turned right, it would lead him to the station—to Kate. Turning left would take him to dinner—to Shea. That was the choice, wasn't it? Kate or Shea.

The light turned green and the choice was made. His heart pounded as each new intersection took him closer to his destination. Anxiety built in the pit of his stomach as he turned the engine off and opened the door, heading in the direction of the building. His hand shook with nervous energy as it ran through his hair and he composed enough courage to actually open the door and walk inside. His eyes quickly surveyed the room.

"Rich!"

His head jerked in the direction of his name. "Hi, Olivia."

She giggled as she shook her head, the black strands tickling her tiny shoulders. "I kinda figured I'd see you at some point today."

"Oh, yeah?" he asked, trying to sound nonchalant.

"She's not here," she said with a grin.

"Who?" His eyes still scanned the room in hopes that Kate would appear out of thin air.

"Rich, Kate's already out on a story and won't be back for hours."

"Oh ... no ... I forgot..."

Another burst of giggles started. "Yeah, yeah, you can say whatever you want, but you and I both know why you showed up here today."

He didn't even bother lying to her. His silence told her everything she needed to know.

"So, how'd you get away? Aren't you supposed to be at Shea's family's?"

"Yeah, they only live a few miles from here, and I..."

"And you thought you'd just drop by to *check* on things."

"Something like that," he mumbled. "Well, I guess I'd better get over to dinner."

"Do you want me to leave *anybody* a message?"

"No ... just pretend I was never here." He didn't want to appear any more pitiful than he already felt. Kate didn't need to know he'd stopped in to see her on his day off, when he was supposed to be with his wife. *Dammit!* "Bye, Olivia."

"Goodbye, Rich, have a nice dinner."

He waved over his shoulder and was out the door, in his car and driving out of the parking lot before his mind had even processed what he was even trying to accomplish. This situation was getting volatile.

He had a wife he didn't want and wanted a girl he couldn't have.

Dammit! Irony sucks!

The car came slowly to a stop outside Shea's sister's house. The red BMW revealed that Shea was already here. He wondered what excuse she'd used for his unfortunate *tardiness.* She appeared on the front porch and hurried out to meet him, an unfamiliar smile on her face. "Hi, baby," she called. "Is everything okay at work?"

Adrenaline bit him in the ass and he searched her face for any kind of animosity, but she just smiled. *Oh, right, her cover story.* "Fine."

She reached out to take his hand, but he stuffed it into his pocket. If she wanted to put on a charade for her family that was fine, but Rich refused to make it any easier for her to fool them into thinking everything was wonderful between them.

Shea's sisters also appeared in the doorway; ShyAnne with her high-maintenance platinum hair and Sharlice was the more subdued of the three. Both of them still carried an animosity for Rich that he never understood.

"So Rich," ShyAnne said in a tone that dripped sugar—and venom, "How are *things* at the office?"

"ShyAnne!" Shea hissed.

"What?" ShyAnne kept up the pretense, twisting a lock of her hair around her finger in faked innocence. "I'm only interested in what he's *doing* at work."

"ShyAnne." Ray wrapped his arm around the waist of his wife, leaned close to her ear, and whispered, "That's enough." He extended his hand. "How are you, Dick?"

"Rich."

Ray ignored the correction and kept right on talking, "Life treating you good?"

"Alright. You?"

He kissed ShyAnne on the cheek. "I can't complain."

She looked up at him with adoring eyes before they turned to ice as they focused again on Rich. "I'm going to help in the kitchen," she snorted before clomping away.

Ray reminded Rich of Squiggy on Laverne and Shirley, complete with the squeaky voice and slicked back hair. The disgusting little man watched until his wife was no longer visible then returned his attention to Rich. "ShyAnne says that things aren't good between you and Shea."

"Oh, yeah?" Acting dumb was the safest way to respond to that. Commenting in any way was like stepping into a minefield naked, without even the protection of a cup.

"Yeah." He leaned in closer and Rich could smell cheap alcohol on his breath. "Shea told her that you've moved into the den, and added a deadbolt."

"Has she now?" Rich kept his voice flat, emotionless.

A bark of laughter burst from Ray. "We've all been there, Dick."

"Rich."

Ray waved his hand dismissively. "Yeah, yeah, Rich. I understand more than anybody how *passionate* the girls can be. But those that fight hard, can *love* even harder." He raised his eyebrows suggestively and shot an elbow into Rich's side. "You catch my drift, there,

Dick?"

"Rich."

"I mean, I understand the need for sleeping behind a locked door every now and then, but to completely move out of your own—"

"Excuse me." Rich cut him off, and weaved his way in toward the television and no more questions. *Man rule 712: No talking during sporting events, except to tell the ref he's a dumbass.*

Ryan, Sharlice's husband, sat quietly, as always, in the chair in the furthest corner of the room. He was polar opposite of Ray, still sporting the physique of his college football days. "Rich," he said, patting the arm of the couch next to him. "Utah State is up by three."

Rich sighed in relief at the much needed normalcy of that statement. "Wow, close game."

"It's been a real nail biter," Ryan noted, his eyes on the TV.

"Dinner's ready," Sharlice called from the dining room.

"Well, I guess we'll just have to TiVo it." Ryan laughed. "What did we ever do before the ability to record stuff?"

"We missed a lot of nail biters," Rich said with a chuckle and followed the other man into the snake pit.

Shea gave Rich a weary smile and patted the seat next to her, which he took out of nothing more than obligation. There was no need to bring any more tension to this party. After a quick blessing on the food, the feast began. Everyone picked out their favorites and passed the bowls and platters on to the next person.

Rich's phone buzzed, signaling a text message and his heart jumped with anticipation. *Is she thinking of me too?*

Shea's scrutinizing eyes searched his face as she forced a smile. "Do you need to get that, *honey?*"

"I probably should just in case there's some sort of emergency at work."

ShyAnne snorted and rolled her eyes. "Yeah, like…"

"ShyAnne," Ray interrupted the snide comment that was sure to finish that statement.

Rich walked back into the living room and opened his phone.

You okay, man? Nate

It shouldn't have surprised him how deflated he was to see that it wasn't from Kate. But it hurt. He wanted her to be the one checking on him. He swallowed his wounded ego, and typed back.

Yeah. Thanks.

He closed the phone, and turned to walk back into the dining room, but stopped to enter another message.

Kate, Just wanted you to know I'm okay. Rich

His fingers itched to type that he missed her. He loved her. He wanted her. But he left the message as-is, hit send, and headed back to take his place next to Shea.

ShyAnne leaned over to Sharlice, whispered something, and they both erupted in hysterical cackling that grated on him. The fact that his name had been clearly mixed into the hissing didn't help his bad mood.

Rich's best attempts to ignore them were futile as he tried to enjoy the delicious food that was on his plate. Instead, their stares and continued giggling were wearing on his already fried nerves. "Excuse me."

"Is everything okay?" Shea placed her hand on his forearm.

He yanked his arm away from her as though her hand was on fire. "Yeah, I just need to go to the bathroom. I'll be right back."

The face staring back from the mirror looked absolutely exhausted. He'd only been here an hour, and already he felt like he'd been through the wringer. He ran some cold water and splashed it onto his face, then dried it on a towel.

Curiosity was killing him. Would Kate answer his message?

He reached into his pocket and... The phone wasn't there. *Shit!*

Panic sunk in as he rounded the corner to the dining room just in time to see Shea setting the little black thing down on the table. Her face was tight and her eyes were calm. Too calm.

✕✕✕

Kate didn't realize just how much she enjoyed working with Rich until she was stuck with Tommy. He was married to Leslie, the main anchor, and their constant text messaging and lovey-dovey phone conversations were enough to make the strongest stomach hurl.

"Yes, sweetheart, we're just heading back now, and then I'll be home and in your arms before you even know it. I love you, too. Goodbye, baby. Kiss kiss."

Dude! Grow a pair! Kiss kiss? Kate stared out the window and tried desperately not to gag. The beep of her phone saved her sanity. She didn't even check the caller id. Any excuse to ignore the guy next to her was a good one.

She smiled at the text from Rich, glad that he was surviving a house full of crazies and carving knives. For the moment, at least. Tapping the phone against her lip, she debated on whether or not a response was wise.

After going back and forth for a few minutes, she decided that surely he wouldn't have sent it if he didn't want some sort of response.

Rich, Glad you're okay. Things aren't the same without you. Kate

She didn't even put her phone away, grateful for the distraction from having to carry on a conversation with the ever dull, Tommy Williams. Honestly, they should offer hazard pay for going out with him. After practically doing his job for him, pointing out the shots that were needed, she was now stuck in a confined space with him.

Kate's heart jumped at the single beep, and she cursed the excitement she felt.

Of course, I'm okay, bitch! I'm with my WIFE!

"Damn!" That message had not come from Rich, but how did Shea get his phone?

"Is everything okay?"

Her heart pounded so hard in her chest, for a moment, she wondered if that was what Tommy was asking about. She managed a nod, and concentrated on her now erratic breathing.

"Damn, Kate, are you going to hyperventilate or something?"

"No ... I'm ... fine," she gasped.

"The hell you are." He eased the truck over to the side of the road, threw it into park and ran around to open her door. "Get out."

"Really ... I'm ... fine."

"Shut up and get out." He took her by the arm and tugged. "You need to walk around for a minute then you'll be fine."

She took his advice and walked around on the shoulder of the highway, gasping for the wind Shea's message had expelled from her lungs. Leaning over with her hands on her knees, Kate took deep breaths, only to have another wave of panic strike.

Rich.

What was Shea doing to him right now?

There was no way Kate could call him. That would only make things worse. *Damn.* Why did she have to care about this guy so much? She shouldn't. Didn't want to, but couldn't help it.

"Come on, Kate, let's get back to the station. I have a dinner to get to."

Her body slumped back into the passenger seat, and she leaned a cheek against the cool glass, closing her eyes. What had she done to poor Rich?

Tommy pulled up to the front of the building and stopped the vehicle. "My shift's over. I got dinner waiting for me. Hope you're feeling better, Kate." He handed her the video footage they'd just gotten and barely waited for her to close the door before speeding off.

At least he didn't use his boot to get me out of the car.

The newsroom was even more deserted than it had been earlier. Olivia was still sitting at her desk, which was a surprise. Jordan was at the desk next to her, an even bigger surprise.

"Oh, good. I'm so glad you're finally back." Olivia waved her over.

"What's up?"

"Robin left sick, so I'm covering the ten." Her fingers flew over the keyboard, adding letters, words to the script she was working on.

"I'm sorry."

She ignored the condolences, and kept talking, "There's a tire fire on the west side—"

"Oh, do you want me to—"

"No, Clayton's already on it." She stabbed a piece of turkey and put it into her mouth. "Hmm, thanks, Jordan."

"Hey, if my baby can't come to Thanksgiving—" He waved his hand over her plate, smiling. "—I bring Thanksgiving to my baby."

She giggled and finished chewing. "Clayton, fire. So that leaves me without an anchor." She just left the statement hanging in the air, waiting for a reaction.

Kate looked between Olivia and Jordan for another moment before realization hit. "You mean ... me?"

A grin spread across Olivia's face as she nodded. "Yes, you. I already called Dale and he okayed it. So you're on, girl."

"Wow, that's awesome."

Then Olivia frowned.

"What?"

"Can you still turn your other story?"

"Oh, yeah, sure. I'll go slam it out myself, and have it ready to go in an hour." Kate blew on her nails and rubbed them on her collar. "No problem." She secured her bag back up on her shoulder and turned, before stopping. "Hey, Jordan?"

He looked up. "Yeah?"

"Would you mind calling to check on Rich?" She'd tried to make her voice sound indifferent, but failed miserably.

His brows narrowed with the questions he wanted to ask, but didn't. "You bet." He gave a wink and picked up his phone.

Relieved, Kate headed into editing, her own phone at her ear. She desperately wanted to check in on Rich, but called Jesse instead—to share her good news.

"Hello?"

"Hey, guess who's going to anchor the ten?"

"Are you kidding? That's awesome, KC! Good for you."

"Thanks. I've got a lot to do. I just wanted to let you know."

"Okay. I'll see ya on TV."

"Bye." Kate walked into the audio booth, recorded the track for the package and returned to the editing bay, closing the door, sealing herself in silence. The pictures zipped through the monitor as a hiss from the glass behind her alerted her to someone entering.

Jordan stuck his head through the crack between the door and the wall. "He didn't answer," Jordan said. "I just thought you'd want to know."

"Thanks," she sighed.

"Is everything okay?" His brows furrowed, his eyes asking a thousand other questions.

"Yeah. Sure. I mean, I don't know."

"What happened, Kate?" He stepped inside and closed the door. "Is Rich okay?"

How much did Jordan know about Rich's situation? Kate didn't know, and it certainly wasn't her place to divulge any information.

"I'm just worried about him, that's all."

"Did something happen with Shea?" He raised an eyebrow. "She's crazy, you know."

Kate glanced over her shoulder at him. Her goal was to sound like it was no big deal. And she failed. "Yeah, she sent me a text message, and I'm worried."

"She *what*?" He gaped at her.

"Never mind." She turned her attention back to the task in front of her and ignored the eyes she could feel still staring at her. "I'm sure he's fine, Jordan." The door opened and started to close again. "Jordan?"

"If I hear from him, I'll let you know."

"Thanks." The drama of what might be, needed to take a back seat because she had to concentrate on what was happening right here, right now. Kate had a deadline breathing down her neck that wasn't going to give.

✕ ✕ ✕

The whole room was quiet, except for the scratching of the chair on the wood floor as Rich slid it out so that he could sit down. Everyone was purposely looking at anything other than the woman sitting next to him.

Something had happened while he'd been in the bathroom, and he didn't have to be a betting man to wager every last dime he had on what it was. Kate had texted back.

With every ounce of dignity and self control he had, he covered the phone with his palm and slid it into his pocket. He stabbed a piece of turkey with his fork and popped it into his mouth. The once delectable, moist meat was now the consistency and flavor of cardboard.

The soft chinking of forks against the fine china continued around him, but the group refrained from any kind of verbal communication.

Rich took a large swig of wine and continued chewing. A thousand emotions were running through him, but ultimately, he felt like an ass. Shea had accused him numerous times of being a cheating bastard, even though he'd been completely innocent. Technically, he still was—physically.

Emotionally, though, he had very much strayed from the promise to remain faithful to Shea. He'd imagined making love to Kate. Craved it. Enjoyed erotic dreams he ached to become reality. Hoped that one day…

"Rich," Shea's voice brought him out of his thoughts as she spoke right next to his ear, "your whore called."

His blood began to boil and his fists clenched, as did his jaw. Instead of shrugging off her insult, like he should have… "Don't ever call Kate that. She is *not* a whore," he snarled, scooted the chair away from the table, and stood.

She stood to meet him, her glare colder than the ice floating in the water pitcher. "So you're not denying there's something between you?"

Sharlice leaned forward, resting her chin in her hand.

"Shea, I am not having this conversation in front of an audience?"

Her hands were clenched into fists as she stood there seething. "Why not, Rich?"

"Yeah, why not, Rich?" ShyAnne's whiney voice chimed in. "We're *family.*"

"You're not *my* family," he spat, striding toward the door.

And with that, the Mikasa flew. A plate full of food soared past him like a Frisbee and smashed against the wall.

He turned to meet Shea's murderous gaze. "There is nothing between Kate and me. She is nothing more than a friend. In fact, she has a boyfriend that she is absolutely crazy about." His voice was strong, defiant, for which he was grateful.

Every last one of his words was true, but hearing them out loud caused his heart to become very heavy in his chest. He wanted to be able to tell Shea that he had feelings for Kate. That she cared for him too. But, that wasn't right either. As long as he was married to Shea, there was even less of a chance of a future with Kate. That needed to be rectified.

Shea and the rest of her family were motionless as Rich dared any of them to contradict what he'd just said. His overwhelming instinct to defend and protect Kate was raging, and he would do so even if it came as a detriment to him.

After an awkward silence, he took his jacket off the back of a chair by the door and stepped out into the sanity of the real world.

"Rich, wait," Shea called from behind him. "Honey, wait."

He whirled around and glared at her. "Honey? Are you kidding me?" She reached out toward him and he jerked away from her grasp. "Hell, no! We are so not doing this right now. You've already produced enough of a drama in the house."

"I love you," she whispered.

"I'm sure you *think* you love me. But, Shea, the way you treat me can in no way be construed as love.

Disdain? Hatred? Yeah, that's how I'd perceive it."

She started to cry, dropping her head into her hands. "I'm sorry," she sobbed. "We can work through this." She walked over and leaned against his chest, and being the pathetic fool he was, his arms eased up around her.

"Shea, honesty is important in a marriage."

She sniffed, and he hoped there wasn't a trail of mucus left on his shirt. "I know."

"Have you always been honest with me?"

She launched herself out of his arms and put her hands on her hips. "So that's how it's going to be, huh? You're feeling guilty, so you're going to throw it back on me."

"Whatever, Shea." He opened the door to the car.

"Rich, no." Hysterics returned. "We can go to therapy."

"*We* don't need therapy.... *You* need therapy."

The look of hatred in her eyes was one that Rich had never seen before. He wondered if he had finally pushed her too far. She stood in the middle of the road, hands on her hips, glaring down the street after him as he drove away.

Going home was going to be hell tonight. There was little doubt of that.

He thought of Kate and was afraid he'd put her directly in the crosshairs. His only hope was the Christmas party next week. If Shea saw with her own eyes how happy Kate was with Jesse, how much she loved him...

Damn. That would protect Kate from Shea, but what would it do to him? It was a pain he did not look forward to.

His phone was still in his pocket and was a nuisance as it pressed funny into his hip. He reached in and pulled it out. It was off. Shea had turned it off. If there was a heaven, that's all she did.

After flipping it open and turning it on, Rich pressed some numbers and held it to his ear.

"Rich, you okay?" Nate truly sounded concerned.

He laughed bitterly. "Do you have time to talk?"

"Sure, we're just hanging out at Roxy's parents'. Come on over."

"I don't want to impose." But he didn't want to be alone either.

"Rich, come over. It might be helpful for you to talk to Roxy's mom anyway."

Claudia Reynolds was one of the biggest names when it came to divorce lawyers. She was the best. 'A real shark' was how she was regularly described. If anyone could give Rich sound advice on how to handle things with Shea, it would be her.

"Okay, see you in a bit."

An hour later, Rich was seated comfortably in the Reynolds' living room. The conversation had gone from wedding plans to the game that Utah State finally lost, to bank business, then to Robby Jr.'s recent success at the U.

When there was a heartbeat and a half of silence, Nate winked and opened his mouth. "So, Claudia, Rich has a real piece of work he needs to get rid of."

"Nate," Rich hissed then turned to Mrs. Reynolds, embarrassed. "I'm sorry. Please ignore him."

Nate laughed. "You should hear some of the things she's done to him. I'm sure some of them are near criminal." He then began to rattle off the events of Rich's life that were humiliating in private; but being aired to a group of near strangers, they were utterly mortifying.

Rich prayed that if life was fair and good, that the floor would open up and swallow him whole, chair and all. Then, with any luck, the chair would squish him like a bug.

To his surprise though, there was no laughter—well, except from the guy he once regarded as his best friend. Rich would soon be interviewing new applicants for that title. His eyes shifted around the room, meeting each of the people staring back at him. There were many emotions in them; humor, sympathy, pity, compassion, and understanding.

Mrs. Reynolds smiled. "I've pretty much heard it all, Rich."

He nodded, feeling validated for the first time since

all of this started.

"So what are his options?" Nate asked.

She turned her head slightly in Nate's direction, but kept eye contact with Rich. "That depends on what Rich wants to do. Have you had enough?"

There was that question again.

His mind mulled the question over and over while the silence in the room dragged on. There was no pressure for him to answer. After several minutes he looked up at her. "Yes, I have."

The older blonde woman was as beautiful as her daughter, Roxy, and her eyes were kind as she smiled at him. "Rich, divorce is never an easy decision, but sometimes it is for the best. No one can decide for you, and you have to be a hundred percent sure that it's what you want because if she contests it at all, it probably won't be pretty."

His lips pulled into a tight smile the rest of his body didn't feel. "If I try to divorce Shea, she *will* contest it, and she *will* make it difficult."

"You have other options," she continued, listing possibilities that included counseling, legal separation, or keeping things status quo. "Do you feel that she's a threat to you?"

Nate's bark of laughter interrupted the silence that hung in the air due to Rich's lack of response. "He sleeps behind a door that has a dead bolt."

Mrs. Reynolds didn't acknowledge Nate's outburst, and Roxy chided him in a whisper, "Nate, this isn't about you, or your opinions. Please keep them to yourself."

"Sorry." He dipped his head, looking more like a scolded child than a strong, confident man. He smiled an additional, silent apology to Rich.

Rich tipped his head slightly, acknowledging Nate, but said nothing for a long time. The ticking of the large clock on the wall—and Nate's incessant fidgeting—being the only sound to break the silence. "I guess I have a lot to think about," Rich said. "Thanks for talking to me, Mrs. Reynolds."

"Claudia, please." She stood, walked over to a date

book sitting on a table near the fireplace and pulled out a card, holding it out to him. "If you decide you need to talk some more, don't hesitate to call me."

"Thanks." He looked down at the card that could save him.

Claudia rubbed her hands together then asked, "Now, who's ready for dessert?"

Nate jumped to his feet and was heading in the direction of the kitchen before she'd even finished the question. Rich slumped back into the overstuffed chair and leaned his head against the soft leather, closing his eyes.

Someone cleared his throat, and Rich opened his eyes to see Mr. Reynolds standing in front of him. "I know you're in a hard place, Rich. I can honestly say that I don't envy you at all."

He had no idea how little he would truly envy him. The Reynolds only knew about the horrible events in his marriage. They didn't have any idea of the depth of his feelings for a girl who was very much emotionally involved with another man.

Mr. Reynolds looked over his shoulder to make sure that the two of them were, in fact, alone. "Rich, there is no excuse for the way she has treated you; belittling you, emasculating you." He placed a hand on his shoulder. "You don't have to live that way. If..." he paused, then clarified, "*when* you're ready, let Claudia help you."

"I will," he said, knowing that it was only a matter of time before that phone call would happen.

He smiled and winked. "I'll make sure she gives you a good deal too."

Rich laughed at his attempt to lighten the mood, but it was truly more of a courtesy to the man who had opened his home on a holiday made for family than because he found real humor. "Thanks, Mr. Reynolds."

"Rob. Please call me Rob."

"Thank you, Rob. Honestly, I didn't come here for free legal advice."

Rob Reynolds tossed another look toward the kitchen. "We know. If you had, you wouldn't have gotten it. But any friend of Nate's is a friend of ours. Now let's go get some dessert before Nate eats it all."

Six

Kate walked up to the desk where Olivia feverishly typed on her computer, unaware of anything going on in the room behind her. "Okay, Olivia, your story is ready. A minute thirty-six."

She turned around and smiled. "Thanks, Kate." Her black hair was in an uncharacteristic disarray due to the number of times she'd run her fingers through it.

Jordan looked up from his computer. "What would you like me to do next?"

"*You're* writing?" Kate asked, sounding more incredulous than she'd actually meant.

He looked at her, letting irritation crackle between them. "I did go to college, Kate."

She shook her head, her hands flailing in an attempt to apologize. "No, no, I didn't mean..."

Olivia saved Kate from her stammering. "Just pick anything in national and pound it out for me. Thanks, babe." She smiled lovingly at Jordan.

"Sure thing, hon." He winked at her, stood and grabbed his notebook without so much as glaring at Kate. Not only had she offended him, it seemed that he was really pissed.

Olivia watched until he walked back into editing. She sighed and put her hand on her chest. "Damn, I love that man."

Kate laughed. "I hadn't noticed."

"Honestly, I don't know what I'd do without him today."

Kate's eyes roamed the deserted newsroom again. "Yeah, where are all the PA's?"

"Robin was supposed to produce and she's sick—*allegedly*." The fact that Olivia sounded so doubtful of the validity of Robin's illness made Kate laugh. "I was going to *assist* while *she* produced tonight so I'd have some extra time off for Christmas. Chris is the only other PA." Olivia looked over her shoulder, leaned in and whispered, "Jordan can write three stories for every one of hers, and he's out of practice."

"Do you want me to write something?"

She glanced up at the clock. 9:30. "Um, no, I'd rather you proof what you're going to read on air. If you don't like it, change it. You're the one who's got to say it on air."

Olivia and Kate were the only ones in the newsroom, which was unheard of on a weeknight. "Is Monica around or is Jordan pulling double-duty too?"

"No, she's here somewhere. Technically, he's still off. He must really love me, huh?" She asked the question with a cheesy smile on her face, already knowing the obvious answer. The man adored her.

"I would dare say that Jordan has some sort of feelings for you, Olivia," Kate said over her shoulder as she walked to her desk and logged on to the rundown. She began going over the scripts that she would be reading in less than thirty minutes.

Less than thirty minutes.

An onslaught of butterflies began their assault on her stomach. Why a girl with public speaking issues would decide to be a reporter, Kate would never understand. But here she was.

Her phone beeped with a text message.

You'll do great. Talk to me. Love you! J

A sigh escaped her lungs. Of course, he would know that she was nervous.

Thanks... Love you, too!

A few of the stories were in need of reworking to make them sound intelligible, and Kate made the changes quickly. As she was just closing the rundown, Olivia and Jordan walked over to her desk, holding hands.

"You ready?" Olivia asked, practically giddy for

Kate's chance to prove herself.

Jordan offered a smile of encouragement—and forgiveness. "Don't worry about earlier. It won't the last time you stick your foot in your mouth...just don't do it on the air."

Kate stood, laughed lightly, and grabbed her jacket off the back of the chair, pulling it on to her shoulders as the trio walked toward the studio. "Let's go cover the black."

The familiar music began and Kate smiled into the camera. "Good Evening, I am Kate Callahan filling in for Leslie Williams. Tonight we start with breaking news. A tire fire is lighting up the night sky this Thanksgiving. Clayton Tate is live at the scene and has been following the story all evening. Clayton, what can you tell us?"

The master of all things arrogant began his description of the scene and interviewed a fire spokesman who had been dragged away from his holiday as well. Kate fumbled with her scripts to make sure they were all in the right order. Teleprompters were great unless they took a dump and left you needing the hard copies.

Jordan appeared off to the side of the set. He offered a two-thumbs-up and smiled. "You're doing great."

"Thanks." She felt a little awkward getting praise, but was grateful it wasn't the other kind of response.

When Clayton was finished, Kate thanked him and began relating the rest of the day's news; the economy, the latest in the Middle East, and numbers from the Salvation Army on how many people they'd fed today. She waited while the weather guy delivered the forecast and the sports guy regurgitated the scores from the college and professional football games that had been played in the last twenty-four hours.

"We end the night with the lucky bird that was pardoned by the President." A fluffy white turkey was flitting around in front of a bunch of stuffy politicians, flashes signaling that still cameras were also documenting the event. "He'll live to see another year. Thanks for letting us be part of your family this Thanksgiving and always. Good night."

"Fade to Black. Roll Commercial," the voice of the director said in her ear. "Good job, everyone."

"We're clear," came a voice from behind the studio camera.

Kate was just gathering her scripts when Olivia and Jordan walked around the corner, holding hands, looking somber.

"Dale called."

Kate's stomach fell through the floor. The news director calling during a newscast was never a good thing. Praise simply didn't come that way. "Oh, yeah?"

"He'd like you to call him."

Crap! The butterflies were back as she walked away from them toward her desk. Her hand had just picked up the phone receiver, and had entered the first few numbers to call Dale when a commotion over her shoulder stopped her. She replaced the phone and stood, bracing herself.

Clayton entered the newsroom through the back door like a hurricane ready to strike land. "That's crap and you know it," he was telling someone on his cell phone. "I don't care. We should have traded." He paused, listening to the person on the other end of the line as he closed the distance. "Whatever. I guess it's in the past, huh?" He didn't even say goodbye to whomever he was talking to as he closed the phone and slammed it down onto his desk. "How dare you?" he hissed at Kate.

"What'd *I* do?" she asked, her defenses up.

Clayton was seething as he raged in the newsroom. His fists were clenched at his sides, and he literally spat as he spoke. "You stole *my* job!"

"I didn't steal anything," she answered in a voice so calm that he actually huffed at her. She rolled her eyes. "You were out on a story, and I just happened to be here when Olivia needed an anchor."

His normally pasty skin was an unnatural shade of red, and Kate expected steam to spout out of his ears— or the top of his head to blow off like in a cartoon. "Like you would have ever set foot behind that anchor desk if not for your best buddy, Olivia."

Kate heard Jordan's approach before he actually

spoke, "Clayton, you don't know what the hell you're talking about. You need to back off." He stepped in between the irate guy and the girls. His hands made fists then relaxed at his sides.

"Yeah, that's right, Jordan, jump to her defense." Anger poured off of Clayton in waves.

Jordan opened his mouth to speak, but Olivia placed her small hand in the center of his chest and stepped forward to address the accusations herself. "Listen, Clayton, you're the one who ran out of here like a bat out of hell when the call came in on that fire. You're the one who left *me* in a lurch. If you want to be pissed, that's fine, but look in the mirror. You have no one to blame but your egotistical, chauvinistic self."

"Screw you," he yelled, grabbed his phone, and turned on his heel. He looked like an angry, spoiled child as he stomped his way out the door.

"I guess I'd better call Dale," Kate whispered, her blood hammering in her veins.

Olivia giggled. "It's not bad, Kate. I was just messing with you. He was really happy with how things went. He probably wants to just pass along the 'atta-girl' himself."

"Please don't do that," Kate muttered as she picked up the phone, punched in the numbers, and waited for Dale to answer.

"Oh, Kate," Jordan whispered, "Rich called back, he's okay."

Relief washed over her, easing a ton of the anxiety that had only moments before plagued her. There was no chance to respond to this newest information because Dale answered, "Hello?"

"Hi, Dale. It's Kate. Olivia said you wanted..."

"Kate, great job. I really liked what I saw tonight. You're a natural. And I'm glad you're ours. Enjoy the rest of your night, and thank you very much for stepping in on such short notice." There was a smile in his voice.

She hung up from Dale, relieved and excited. It was nice to hear his praise even if she was too tired to enjoy it. Her whole body was exhausted. Between the stress of Shea's text message, worrying about Rich, and then having Clayton come completely unglued for something that wasn't even her fault; she was tired—emotionally more than physically.

Jordan had said that he'd talked to Rich, and that he was okay, but that did little to ease Kate's worry. She needed to see him with her own eyes, safe and sound, in one too-handsome-for-his-own-good piece. With a sigh, she pulled on her coat and slung her bag over her shoulder before heading toward the door. It opened, a cold blast of air hitting her in the face, and then her heart stopped at the sight of the man standing in front of her. Kate couldn't remember the last time she'd been so happy to see someone.

The world seemed to pause around them in that moment, as they just stood there, looking at each other, neither of them even blinking. The corner of his mouth finally lifted on one side, forming the smirk that always seemed to make her heart skip a beat. "Hi," he said shyly.

✕✕✕

As if his voice broke whatever spell she was under, she shook her head, a huge smile spread across her face. The bag on her shoulder fell to the floor with a thud, and she began to run toward him, closing the distance in a matter of seconds. "Rich," she said, launching herself into his arms. Her breath was heavy against his skin as her lips pressed against his cheek for an intoxicating few seconds. "I was so worried about you."

His arms tightened around her, cherishing the feeling of her soft, warm body against his. He lowered her to the floor and rested his chin on her head. She fit perfectly. This, he decided, was the greatest sensation in the world. He chuckled. "I like this reception."

She wiggled against his chest, and he held her for just another moment before letting her slip from his grasp. She took his hands in hers and held them out as if she were examining him for injuries. "Are you sure you're okay?" Her voice was breathless as she began her panicked interrogation. "Shea must have gotten my text message because—"

"I'm sorry."

She shook her head defiantly, refusing to let him take the blame that was his alone, and dropped his hands. "No, I'm the one who shouldn't have even sent you a message. It's my fault. You're married, Rich. You were with your wife. I crossed the line."

He ached to touch her again, but forced his hands safely back into the security of his pockets in an attempt to make them behave. "Did you get a response?" She nodded. "What did it say?"

She laughed bitterly as her cheeks turned pink. "Let's just say I knew right away it wasn't from you ... even though it had your name at the bottom. It certainly reminded me of my place—as your *friend*."

"May I see it?" She held out her phone and he opened it to read the newest text message from his number. All the air flew from his lungs in an agonized whoosh. The thought of sweet Kate getting this was... "I am so sorry she sent that to you. She had no right."

Kate studied his face for a long moment. "It's okay, really. I have to admit that it did surprise me though. How on earth did she get your phone?"

His fingers raked through his hair then he shook his head. "It fell out of my pocket when I sat down at the table. I'd gone to the bathroom when your message came in. Shea was just setting the phone back on the table when I got back."

"She must have been really pissed," she said with a smile.

A humorless laugh erupted from his gut. "You have no idea. She threw her plate at me when I left."

She laughed. "Food and all?"

"Yeah." He smiled at her. "I'm sorry, Kate. I shouldn't have brought you into this. It's just that I..." His heart was screaming at his brain to tell her the truth, to tell her how much he cared for her, but his head had stopped his tongue, and there was no restarting the declaration now. Not yet. "I knew you were worried and wanted to let you know I was okay. That's all," he lied.

"Are you going to be okay going home tonight? I

wouldn't want something to happen to you." A playful smile graced her lips and she winked. "While you're asleep."

"You can bet I'll make sure the door's locked."

She placed her hand flat against his chest. "You do that. I'd sure miss you if you weren't around. Working with Tommy today was torture." She laughed, and took a step away from him, her eyes twinkling. "If I had to hear his sticky sweet conversations with Leslie one more minute, I might have gotten physically ill."

"That bad, huh?" The conversation was so natural, so comfortable, Rich never wanted it to end.

"Yeah, that bad." She shook her head and rolled her eyes. "You're not allowed to be off anymore."

"Are you saying that you missed me today?" he teased, wanting desperately to hear her say that she had.

"Of course I missed you, Rich." She sighed and glanced down at her watch. "I really need to get going though. Jesse'll be waiting for me."

Rich's heart went from jumping out of his chest to being body slammed in a matter of seconds. She was going home—to Jesse, the man who held her heart. He hoped that the inward grimace hadn't made its way to his face, completely betraying him.

She brushed her fingers against his hand. "Goodnight, Rich. I'll see you tomorrow." Her hand retreated and curled around the straps of her bag, hoisting it back to her shoulder. "Be careful tonight. I know it would piss her off, but if you need me, you can call me. I'm here for you, Rich."

Those thoughtful, caring words began to sink in, and warmth filled his veins. The fact that she cared, even a little, meant the world to him. Gave him hope for the first time in ... well, years.

"You could come home with me. We'll pull out the hide-a-bed."

"Yeah, I'm sure Jesse would love that," Rich scoffed.

She bit down on her lip and looked at the floor. "Oh, he's more of a lover than a fighter...and I really need to get home to him," she lied through a fake smile.

Despite his belief her words weren't completely truthful, a huge lump leapt into Rich's throat, making it hard for him to swallow, let alone speak—or even breathe. "Oh, okay," he croaked. "You shouldn't keep him waiting then." The words were bitter against his tongue. "Goodnight, Kate."

His feet wouldn't move and his lungs refused to breathe as he watched Kate walk out the doors. She was going home—to Jesse. And her reference to him being 'a lover not a fighter' left little doubt what they would do once she got there. The thought of another man caressing her, tasting her, loving her, sent bile rushing up the back of this throat and his knees nearly gave out.

The ringing of his cell phone rescued him from himself, catapulting him from the white hot memory of Kate to the frigid blizzard that was Shea. With a quick push of a button, Rich sent the call to voicemail, not wanting anything to do with her right now. What he needed was a drink—a strong one.

"Hey, Jordan." Rich walked up to where the guy was perched on the corner of Olivia's desk.

"I'm glad you're alive, my man," Jordan said with a cocked brow.

"Yeah, thanks," Rich responded sarcastically. The muscles in his shoulders were tense, and he wondered at what point they'd snap. He shrugged, hoping to release some of the pressure. When it didn't, he rolled his head loosely on his neck.

"Wanna talk about it?" Jordan asked.

"Not really. You aren't up for a drink, are you?"

Jordan glanced down at Olivia, who nodded. "Um, sure, but I doubt anyplace will be open. We can go to my place."

"Oh ... right." Rich didn't want to make a nuisance of himself, but the thought of going home was not one he wanted to consider. "No, I think I'll..."

Olivia smiled. "It's okay, Rich. I was going to go right to bed anyway. You two can have some guy time."

"Are you sure?"

She smiled. "Absolutely, mi casa es su casa." She gathered her things and took Jordan's hand. "So, we'll see you there in a little while."

"If you're sure." Rich was skeptical.

"Don't be ridiculous," Jordan scoffed. "You can even sleep on the couch if you'd like."

"No, that's okay. Not going home tonight wouldn't make things any better. Shea's already suspicious as hell, even though there's nothing..."

"Is it really nothing?" Olivia asked quietly. Rich's horrified eyes met hers and she smiled. She'd meant no accusation in her question, just a simple perception. "I see the way you look at her, Rich. Not even Shea held your attention like Kate does. Have you fallen in love with her?"

Yes. "No. Of course not. I'm married."

"To a psycho bitch," Jordan reminded him. "Kate would be so much better for you."

"Kate loves Jesse." And with those three words, Rich successfully cut off any further discussion of the woman, who only a few short minutes ago had been wrapped in his embrace.

The three friends gathered their things, and Olivia handed off the reins to the incoming producer. "Good night," she called over her shoulder as they hurried out the door and into the frigid night. They stood outside their cars for only a moment before Rich deactivated the alarm on the car, a chirp filled the silence.

"We'll see you at home," Olivia said as she disappeared into Jordan's blue Mustang. Jordan tossed a wave over the roof of the car then also disappeared, the engine roaring to life.

Rich followed the familiar round taillights, but fifteen minutes into the drive, he decided that avoiding home was not going to do anything but add to Shea's aggravation, and consequently, his own.

Three rings later, Jordan picked up, "Yeah, man."

"Hey, I'm just gonna go home. There's no sense delaying the inevitable."

"You sure?" he sounded even more skeptical than Rich felt.

"Yeah, I'll see you tomorrow."

Jordan chuckled. "I sure hope so."

"If not, call the police." It was meant as a joke, but there was a strong sense of warning in his tone that both men knew existed. He closed the phone and tossed it into the passenger seat. At the next light he flipped a U-turn, and headed in the direction of the brewing storm that was waiting to unleash its fury.

The house was completely dark, eerily so. Rich wondered with a sense of panic what Shea had planned for him when the lights turned on. The garage door went up and her car wasn't there.

Hesitantly he opened the door to the house and called, "Shea." Only silence answered. She'd called, but surely, she wouldn't stay away. A strange combination of relief and dread were warring in his gut as he opened the phone and dialed voicemail.

"Rich, I can't stand to look at you right now. I thought it was best if I stayed with Sharlice tonight." She paused. "I love you, and I'm sure that we can work through your infidelity. I just need some time to process what you've done. I'll call you tomorrow when I've had a chance to calm down."

A round of honest-to-goodness, come-from-your-toes laughter burst out of him. The audacity of that woman. *My infidelity?* "Oh, good hell." A tear slid down his cheek as the hilarity of the situation continued to feed his amusement. She thought she'd caught him in some form of fornication.

And for a split second, he wished she had.

Even though he hadn't seen Kate's text message, he doubted that she'd offered to meet him at a hotel in twenty minutes, or given any other sort of invitation that would give Shea *proof* of an affair. There wasn't an affair—at least on Kate's end. For Rich though, he would have gladly accepted any offer Kate proposed.

No, I wouldn't.

He couldn't do that to Kate. She deserved better than simply being the other woman—the mistress. She deserved to be the one and only. And right now, she was Jesse's.

Lying on the cool leather of the couch in the den, with the door securely locked, he flipped on the television. It was a silly thing to record the newscasts, but he always did. It made him a better photographer to see his work—his mistakes—playing out on the illuminated box. Tonight, he would enjoy watching Kate's anchoring debut. He sighed and concentrated on the big green eyes, long lashes, and full lips speaking from the TV. He didn't want to give into sleep, but lost the battle.

Seven

Kate snuggled into the warm body next to her, and enjoyed the comforting sound of light snoring. Last night had been everything Jesse promised it would be. Her finger gently traced the muscles of his defined chest, causing him to shy away from her touch. "You shouldn't scratch me, KC. That's not very nice."

She laughed lightly, and continued to run her fingertips over his sensitive, ticklish sides. "I would hardly call this scratching. Did you sleep well?"

"Alright."

"Just alright?" she asked, surprised because she'd slept great.

He nodded, and tucked her under his arm. "I've got something that we need to talk about." There was a seriousness in his tone that sent her adrenaline into overdrive, and her mind raced with the possibilities.

"Whatever it is, Jesse, you can tell me." She sounded anxious, but it was nothing compared to the anxiety she felt.

He twisted a lock of her hair around his finger, and kissed the top of her head, then sat up to get a better look at her face. His eyes focused on the curl wrapped in his hand. "Dad's not doing very good."

Kate shifted to look at him. His eyes were worried. "Is it that bad?"

"They're thinking it's terminal." He bit on his lip as his voice cracked. He coughed to cover the emotion. His eyes filled with tears that he wouldn't let fall.

"Oh, Jesse, I'm so sorry. What do we need to do?"

"I'd like to get down there as soon as I can."

"Absolutely, what are you thinking?"

"We have a little time, and I know you can't go with me." He tightened his hold on her. "So, I'll stay for the party next week, then go home for a couple weeks and hopefully be back by Christmas."

Her heart ached at the thought of being without him for even a day, but *weeks*? She swallowed her own desires and the lump that formed in her throat then blinked back the tears that burned in her eyes. There was no need to make this harder for Jesse. Besides selfishness wouldn't do Tony a damn bit of good.

"I'll miss you," she said quietly, not braving any kind of volume.

He lifted her chin with his finger and pressed his lips to hers. "I will miss you every second."

The tears that had only been threatening before knocked on her clamped eyelids. "Um, I'd better get ready for work." She pulled out of his embrace and jumped out of the bed, and hurried into the bathroom. She stepped into the shower and let the tears disappear in the spray of water.

She cried for Tony. She cried for Jesse. And pathetically enough, she cried for herself. Her selfish side wanted to beg him to stay, but she couldn't do that to him, because he would. He would stay by her side while his father lay on his deathbed.

Showered and dressed, though emotionally drained, she put on a smile she didn't feel and walked out into the bedroom. Jesse was still in the bed, leaning against the headboard with his arm behind his head. "You okay?"

"Um hum," she lied as tears betrayed her.

"Come here," he said, reaching a muscled arm out to her. She raced across the room and curled up in his arms. "It'll be okay. He'll be okay." He chuckled. "And I'll only be gone a couple of weeks."

"I know. I'm just being a stupid, emotional girl." She sniffed and rubbed at her nose.

"It's not stupid for you to miss me." His strong hand engulfed both of hers and he squeezed gently, supportively.

"I don't want to make this harder for you."

His gentle palms came up and rested on the sides of her face, wiping at her tears with this thumbs. "It would be harder to leave if you weren't emotional. I'll be back soon." He kissed her softly. "Besides I don't leave for a week. No more tears, sweetheart, you'll ruin your makeup. Instead of thinking about the time we'll be apart, think of the great reunion sex we'll have. In the meantime, we'll have lots of farewell sex."

She laughed, and playfully slapped at his chest. "It's all about the sex with you, isn't it?"

"I'm a guy, KC." His hand reached around and squeezed her rear. "Now, get yourself to work. Hurry home so we can start saying goodbye." She shook her head. He always had a way of making her smile, lightening her mood when she needed it most. His lips brushed ever so lightly against hers. "Have a great day, honey."

× × ×

The newsroom resembled a beehive as Kate strolled through the bustle of people toward her desk, a drastic contrast from yesterday, but nothing out of the norm.

"Well, look who it is, Little Miss Story Stealer," Clayton snarled.

Kate offered him a dramatic eye roll, and said, "Are you kidding? How old are you, twelve?" She sat down with her back to him. She glanced around the newsroom. Rich and Nate seemed to be deep in conversation in the photog's lounge. Rich's eyes met hers for only a moment, his face expressionless. She waved, but dropped her hand awkwardly when he was already looking back at Nate.

"He's no Jordan, but he certainly falls into the eye-candy category," Olivia said.

"Huh?" Kate asked, tearing her eyes from the two men behind the glass.

Olivia shook her head and rolled her eyes dramatically. "Oh never mind, it's time for the morning meeting." Her arm threaded through Kate's as she stood. "Come on."

An hour and a Tate Tantrum later, Kate was headed to find Rich. He was sitting on a chair in the photographer's lounge; eyes closed, legs spread, forming a yummy V, with his head leaned against the wall behind him. He looked so peaceful, so handsome. His lips were turned up in that glorious smirk of his and Kate wondered what he was thinking about.

Her cell phone rang, and he startled, sat up quickly and nearly sent himself into the floor. "How long have you been standing there?"

Just long enough to notice how hot you are. "Just got here." She opened her phone, grateful for the chance to compose herself, and pressed it to her ear, but didn't take her eyes off him. "Hello?"

"Kate." Anna Callahan conveyed a week's worth of anxiety into that one word. She had a way of worrying about things that didn't need the waste of energy, and Kate was sure that this call was about the very subject she wanted to avoid.

"Hi, Mom. I'm just on my way to a story. Is everything okay?" Rich stood and started to get his things ready. He bent over and her eyes stole a quick glimpse of his perfect rear end. The way it looked in those tight blue jeans made her want... *Stop it!* She shook her head and tried to look at something else— anything else.

"Yes, everything's fine. I just haven't heard from you in a while. I'm guessing you know about Tony."

"Yeah, Jesse got the call yesterday." She walked over and sat down in the chair Rich had vacated, and debated on how high on the rudeness scale it would be to just hang up on her mother.

"Is he coming out?"

"He'll be leaving a week from Sunday." The burning sensation began in her eyes at even the thought of him being gone. She blinked frantically, trying to keep the tears at bay and ducked her head to keep her face hidden from the other person in the room. Now was not the time for Jesse to be leaving. Her heart was in turmoil.

Anna sighed. "That will be good."

There was a long pause, and Kate asked, "Mom?"

"He's bad, Kate. Are you sure you can't come too? Jesse'll probably need you."

"I wish I could, but I can't get away right now." She paused then said, "Look, Mom, I've got to go. I'll have to call you later." She closed her phone without waiting for a response, and turned around to meet Rich's curious gaze.

There was little doubt from the look on his face that he wanted to ask about what he'd overheard, but instead he flashed a warm smile and offered a hand. "You ready?"

She nodded, took his hand, squeezing it in hers. "I'm glad you're alive." She disconnected the contact and slid her hand into her pocket, trying to wipe away the heat that his touch had caused.

"Me, too." He chuckled and strode toward the door with the camera hanging off his shoulder. "Where we headed?"

"Downtown, there's an immigration protest." They got into the vehicle and Rich started driving. "So, how bad did Shea freak out last night?"

"She didn't," he said with a casual shrug. "She left a message saying that she could forgive me of *my* infidelity, but needed some time to herself." He rolled his eyes, and chanced a quick glance at her.

She was sure that her mouth fell open, and hoped that she wasn't completely gaping at him. "Infidelity?" she squeaked.

He cleared his throat and concentrated a little too hard on the road. "Yeah, you."

"*Me?* She thinks that you and I ... that we..." she stammered.

His eyes stared through the windshield as his hands tightened into fists on the steering wheel. "Um hum."

"Why would she...? Do you have...?" Kate wanted to come right out and ask if he'd given his wife a reason to suspect there was something going on between them. It frightened her that a part of her hoped he had. "Rich?"

He eased the vehicle to a stop at a light and faced her. "Kate, I think you are the most amazing woman I've ever met."

Kate cursed her body's involuntary reaction to his words; her heart pounded in her chest, her lungs struggled for breath. Hearing him say things like that to her wasn't good, but wanting to hear them was even worse.

He smiled. "I know that you're in a relationship and that I'm married." He cringed. "I would never ask you to do anything you're not comfortable with. You deserve better than that."

Kate's mind was swimming with what it was trying to comprehend. Rich wasn't making sense. Or was he? *Does he have feelings for me?* Is that what he was trying to tell her?

"Kate, Shea is crazy. She's jealous...and any conclusions she's come to have been all on her own."

"So, what are you saying, Rich? Do you have feelings for me?" Pathetically enough, she wasn't sure how she wanted him to answer that question.

The light turned green, and her question hung in the uncomfortable silence. He steered the car into a nearby parking lot and slipped it into park. He shifted in the seat so that they were facing each other. "Kate, my life is really confusing. I'm not going to pretend it's not. There aren't a lot of things I'm sure of right now, but I do know that I wouldn't want to go a day without seeing your smiling face, hearing your voice, stealing a touch of your skin." He paused, his blue eyes sparkled brightly. "You're my reason for waking up in the morning."

"Wow," she sighed. "I don't—"

"You don't have to say anything, Kate. I just wanted to be honest with you, that's all."

"Um, thank you." *Thank you? He practically tells you he loves you, and you say thank you?* She turned toward the window, refusing to look at him again. There was no denying that Rich was good-looking—and kind and sensitive and creative and talented and hot and.... Yeah, the list was practically endless. Nor could she deny how much she'd missed him yesterday. As much as she wanted to, she couldn't ignore the way those 'stolen touches' affected her too.

✕ ✕ ✕

Well, that was a surprising turn of events. She gets a call from her mother, something about Jesse going 'home' a week from Sunday, then he all but declared his undying love for her. *Dammit, Spencer, what the hell?*

Her response was like a slap in the face; a smile and a 'thank you' before she turned toward the window without another word. He had managed to make things more than uncomfortable for both of them. They were only minutes from the capital and this wasn't going to be pleasant.

You, stupid son of a...

"Rich," Kate said quietly, "I don't want things to be weird between us."

"I don't want that either." He chanced a look at her from the corner of his eye, and she had her arms folded across her chest, looking anywhere but at him. "I'm sorry."

"You don't have to be sorry. I'm flattered that you care so much." She sighed. "It's just important that you know how I feel as well."

This was either going to be really good...or really bad. "Of course." *Break my heart.*

"Rich, first and foremost, you're a married man." She laughed nervously. "Married to a lunatic, but still married." He nodded, unable to deny what she'd said. "Secondly, I'm with Jesse."

Kill me now! She wasn't telling him anything he didn't already know, but... *Damn!*

"I don't want to hurt you. You're a great guy, and you deserve all the happiness that life has to offer, but I'm not the girl for you. I'm sorry."

"Any chance I can change your mind?"

She was quiet for a moment then took his hand in hers. Warmth spread through his body as if he'd touched a flame. "I care for you. Please don't push this and make things awkward."

He ran his thumb over her knuckles in comforting strokes, and allowed himself to enjoy this moment.

"Never. I will be a great friend to you, Kate. Anything you need, I'm here for you—always."

Her plump lips lifted into a smile. "Thanks, Rich, that really means a lot to me."

He pulled into a parking spot, and turned toward her. "Let's just pretend I never opened my big mouth."

She smiled and shook his hand gently. "Deal."

"Now, let's go get our story."

Rich hoisted the camera onto his shoulder as they walked toward the two groups of people that were yelling at each other. A stab of anxiety hit as Kate headed into the thrall, microphone in hand. "What are you doing?"

"Getting my story. Come on," she hollered, urging him forward with a wave of her hand.

The voices coming through his earpiece were an intense echo as Kate put the microphone into the faces of some of the people willing to talk to her. A large man with an even larger protest sign muscled his way up to her, yelling, "Get good shots of all those illegals, then turn it over to Immigration so they can be sent back to *their* country."

"Hey," a heavily-accented voice yelled from over his shoulder, "we're just doing the jobs you're too lazy to do."

With that, things heated up—fast—and Kate stood right in the middle of the pressure cooker. The distinction between the two groups no longer existed, and fists began flying as well as anything else they could get their hands on. When Kate disappeared from view, Rich's body jolted into panic mode.

"Kate!" he screamed, searching frantically while trying to keep the camera on his shoulder. A pain ripped through his skull as something slammed into the back of his head. He reached up with his left hand to find a warm, sticky liquid. *Blood.* His vision started to blur and he dropped down to one knee.

"Rich," Kate's voice kept him from blacking out. "Are you... You're bleeding!"

"Yeah," he groaned.

Her eyes widened and she looked as queasy as he felt. She took the camera from his shoulder and sat it on the ground next to him, still recording. "Here," she said, handing him her jacket. "Put this on your head. It's good to have pressure on it."

His male ego wanted to argue with her, but she was right. He wasn't feeling all that great and took the jacket, holding it to the back of his head.

"Do you think you can walk?"

"Of course." *I hope.*

"Come on." She tugged at his arm and tucked herself under it. She lifted the camera strap over her shoulder, wrapped her arm tightly around his waist, and absorbed the weight he couldn't bear. "We need to get you to the hospital."

"I'm fine," he lied as his body swayed.

She snorted. "Yeah, real fine, Mr. Macho."

He loved that Kate cared enough to want him safe, and smiled through the humiliating pain. A friendship *was* a great place for love to start.

She got him into the passenger seat, the camera safely strapped into the back, and climbed into the driver's seat. She was already talking to someone on the phone. "Yeah, I'm going to take him to the ER right now." She paused. "I don't know. I didn't look at it. I don't do well with that sort of thing." Another pause. "Probably not. We weren't there long enough... Absolutely, send over a live truck and I'll slam out a vo/sot/vo for the five... Okay, I'll let you know more when we get there... Thanks, Dale. Bye." She dropped her phone into her bag, and put the vehicle into gear.

Through the blinding ache in his head, he couldn't help but smile at how Kate—his Kate—took control of the situation. He had no doubt that she would be the one editing the voice-over and stringing together the sound-on-tape. *Probably in the hospital parking lot*, he thought sarcastically, which caused him to chuckle lightly. "They're going to send a truck?" he asked for no other reason than to cover the laugh.

"Yeah, I kept the camera rolling, so we should have enough of the melee for a decent piece. Maybe I can interview you and show off your stitches."

He laughed even though a freight train ran

mercilessly through his head. "You don't even know that I *need* stitches."

Her phone rang and she dug in her bag that sat between them on the console. "You drive, I'll find your phone," he told her. Within seconds, he had the little pink device in his hand. The caller ID read 'Jesse'. His heart sank as he handed it to her.

She hit the speaker button, and sat it down on the dash, making it hands-free—and privacy-free. "Hi, Jesse."

"Hey ... how are you?"

"I'm fine. Just taking Rich to the ER."

"ER?" Jesse sound panicked. "Are you okay?"

"Jesse, I'm fine, really." She glanced at Rich and smiled. "Rich got hit by something in the back of the head. He's the one..."

"You're sure you're okay?" The guy didn't give a rip that Rich was injured.

"Yes, not even so much as a bruise."

Jesse chuckled seductively, and Rich fought a bout of jealousy—and a wave of nausea. "When you get home, I'll be doing an examination of my own."

Her cheeks flushed a gorgeous red as she bit down on her lower lip. Rich wasn't sure if it was what Jesse'd said, or the fact that he'd heard it, that made her uncomfortable. Her eyes shifted to him and she mouthed 'sorry'.

He leaned his head back and closed his eyes, ignoring the dull pain in his head and the excruciating sting in his heart.

"I need to go, Jesse. I'll call you in a bit."

"Sounds good. I love you, KC. Be careful."

"I will." She closed the phone and there was an awkward silence. He kept his eyes closed and concentrated on his breathing. "I'm sorry, Rich."

"Hey, don't be sorry. He's your boyfriend. I have to deal with that. I can't help how I feel, Kate, but then, neither can you. I want you to be yourself. Don't change just because of me." Another wave of nausea hit him, hard. "Um, can you hurry? I think I'm gonna be sick."

"Oh, sure, we're only a couple blocks away."

She pulled up into the ER drop off, and raced in while Rich waited in the car. She came out, dragging a guy dressed in scrubs, and opened the door. Kate's eyes were wide, her voice panicked. "I don't know how bad it is, but you really need to take care of him."

"Okay," he dismissed her, and looked at Rich. "On a scale of one to ten, how bad is the pain?"

"Seven."

"Can you walk?"

He wanted to play the He-Man, wanted to impress Kate with his superior manliness, but his legs felt like Jell-O. There was no need to insist that he was a man, only to pick himself up off the pavement. "I don't think so, I'm feeling pretty woozy."

"Let me grab a chair, and then we'll get you looked at." He turned to Kate. "You'll need to move the car. You can't leave it here." He rushed off toward the sliding glass doors.

"Oh, okay," she said, her eyes meeting Rich's. She smiled weakly and reached out to touch his arm. "I'm going to move this and then I'll be right in, okay?"

"I'll be fine."

She waited until he was in the wheelchair before running around the vehicle and climbing in.

"Wow, that girl cares a lot about you," the guy said quietly as the chair squeaked through the hospital waiting room. "You should have heard the fit she threw trying to get someone to come out to you. How long have you been dating?"

"We're not."

"Could have fooled me." He kicked the wheel lock into place. "Wait right here, I'll be back in just a bit with a nurse."

"Thanks," Rich mumbled. *Interesting.* Kate was freaking out so badly that she'd given them the impression he meant something to her. *You do, moron ... you're her friend.*

But was that all it was, a concerned friend? Or was it possible there was something more? Did he dare hope?

Yes, he thought, knowing that he would hold on to

that hope with both hands.

Eight

For the past week, Kate couldn't get Rich out of her head. It wasn't so much his declaration that had her mind reeling. It was her reaction to his being hurt that had him on the forefront of her thoughts.

The gash on the back of his head, that had her so worried and running around like a lunatic, was nothing more than a slight concussion and a simple cut that was all fixed up with some DermaBond and a Band-Aid. It was crazy how upset she'd been by the blood. The thought of Rich being hurt sent her into panic mode. She wanted to fix it, to make him better.

She understood that he had feelings for her. He'd all but come right out and said those three little words that would change their friendship forever. Her feelings, however, were a mystery—a mystery that scared the hell out of her. Jesse was still very much the man in her life, but Rich was slowly seeping into her thoughts, and she feared, into her heart.

"Hey, beautiful lady, you ready to go?"

She looked up and met Rich's intoxicating gaze. He already had his things with him, ready to walk out the door. She shook her head to clear her thoughts and blinked quickly. "Um, yeah, just give me two seconds."

"Where were you just now?" He chuckled. "It was as though you were a million miles away."

I wish! Being a million miles away from the guy—his tight blue Lucky's, covering his muscular thighs and tight rear, and navy sweater that hugged his chest, his aqua eyes twinkled and light brown hair she wanted to run her fingers through—standing in front of her was exactly where she needed to be. "I was just thinking."

His lips lifted flirtatiously at one corner as his eyebrow arched. "About?"

He was a little too cocky for her liking, and there was no way she was going to verify what he already *thought* he knew. She sighed deeply. "Jesse leaves on Sunday." His face fell, and she felt a small stab of guilt for throwing Jesse at him. "I'm just going to miss him."

"Of course you will." He smiled, but it didn't reach his eyes. The sadness in them made her consider telling him the truth.

Instead she grabbed her laptop, shoved it into its bag and placed it over her shoulder. "Let's go."

Although, they had agreed that things wouldn't be weird between them, they were. Kate felt like there was so much to say, but couldn't bring herself to open up Pandora's Box. Every time she got close, she thought of Jesse. Once she voiced how her heart was being torn in two, there would be no way to avoid hurting him. Ultimately, hurting herself.

And Rich was married, which made him off limits. End of discussion.

"You're doing it again," Rich said as he slid into the driver's seat.

She fastened her seatbelt and sighed. "I'm sorry, it's just that I'm..." *I'm what? I'm torn. I'm conflicted.* "Tired. I only got a few hours sleep last night."

"Oh," he sounded deflated, and she realized how suggestive her statement sounded, but didn't have the energy to clarify.

"How are things with Shea?

"Um, she's looking forward to meeting you tomorrow night."

Kate laughed but not with humor. "Yeah, I'm sure she can't wait to meet the woman she thinks has stolen her husband's heart."

"You didn't have to steal it. She lost it a long time ago."

"Rich," Kate warned.

"I'm just saying, besides I told her how much you love Jesse and that she had nothing to worry about."

"So she's going to be watching for proof of what you

told her?"

"Basically." His hands tightened on the steering wheel, his knuckles went white.

"Well, isn't that nice," she said through her teeth. She hated that her relationship with Jesse was going to be on display. "You have nothing to worry about," she snapped, "Jesse has no problem with showing his affection in public."

The muscles in his jaw worked as his teeth ground together. His eyes were focused on the road ahead, and even with his sunglasses on, she could tell that his look was fierce.

She felt a little guilty for pushing him. Her mouth opened to apologize, but closed again without uttering a sound. She glared out the window at the passing shrubbery. She couldn't go back and forth any longer. A choice needed to be made and she would have to live with the consequences. She hated that Jesse was leaving, just when she needed to have him here.

The day dragged on painfully slow as did the silence between the two of them. Kate was just finishing up the copy for the ten when Olivia plopped herself on the corner of Kate's desk. "So," she said incredulously, and Kate tipped her head to let her know she was listening, "what's going on with you and Rich?"

"Nothing," she responded, unable to look Olivia in the eye.

"Um hum." She raised an unbelieving brow. "I'd just like my story straight for Shea tomorrow night."

Kate's blood boiled in her veins. "What the hell is the deal with that woman? I don't care what she thinks." She slammed her laptop closed, stood up, and shoved it into the bag. She glared at Olivia. "What do *you* think's going on with me and Rich?"

"Um ... nothing."

"Good answer, Olivia." With fists clenched, she stuffed her arms into her coat. "For the record, I am in love with Jesse. Just Jesse."

And with that declaration, her mind and her heart had their decision. She had roughly thirty-six hours left with Jesse before he was gone for two weeks, and she would enjoy every single second.

As she walked through the parking lot, her thumb flipped open her phone, and she pressed the number two and held it to her ear.

"Hey, KC."

"Hi, I'm on my way home."

"Oh, good. Are you hungry? I was just leaving the shop. I'll swing by and pick something up. What are you in the mood for?"

"I'd love Chinese," she said.

"Done. I'll see you in a bit."

The phone beeped, signaling another incoming call. "Hey, I've got to get that. I'll see you in a few." She switched over. "Hello?"

"Kate?"

"Hi, Olivia." Anger raced through her bloodstream again. "What do you want?"

"I'm sorry, Kate. I'm a horrible friend. I shouldn't have said anything."

Kate took a deep breath and exhaled slowly. "It's okay, Olivia. You're forgiven." Kate knew she'd been hard on Olivia when she'd asked the very question Kate had asked herself more than once.

"Oh, good," she said with a sigh. "Well, I'll let you go. I just wanted to apologize for being rude."

"Olivia?"

"Hmm?"

"Why would you think there was something going on between us?"

"Um..." Kate could almost see Olivia biting on her lip.

"Olivia ... please."

"It's just the way you are together. And, he may have mentioned to Jordan that he has feelings for you. Don't you dare tell anyone I told you that."

"I won't." So not only had he more or less told Kate, he'd come right out and told other people. None of that mattered because... "He's married, Olivia, and I'm..."

"Very much in love with Jesse. Got it." She laughed. "It's okay, Kate. If you ever need to talk, I'm here."

Kate blew a breath out through her teeth. "Thanks. I

guess I'll see you guys tomorrow night at the party, then?"

"Yep. See you then."

Kate opened the door to the apartment, but it was dark. Jesse wasn't home yet. She walked into the bedroom to change clothes; a pair of workout pants and a t-shirt—braless, for Jesse's benefit.

"Kate," he called as the door closed with a slam. "Where are you, babe?"

"Right here," she said as she walked out to meet him. "Mmm, it smells good."

He sat the cartons out on the counter. "I didn't know what you were in the mood for, so I got a little of everything."

She laughed as the white boxes continued to multiply. "Did you leave any for anybody else?"

"Ha ha," he mocked, then grabbed a couple plates. "Dig in." He filled his plate with the contents of the various containers. "What do you want to do tonight?"

"Honestly, all I want is for you to hold me. To curl up in your arms, and maybe watch a movie or something."

His plate slid onto the counter and Jesse wrapped her in a hug. "Are you okay, KC?"

Tears burned her eyes and she hated that she was going to cry. "I know you have to go, but I'm going to miss you so much." She sniffed. "I'm sorry. I didn't want to do this."

His strong fingers were gentle against her cheeks as he brushed the tears away. "I'm glad that you're going to miss me. I'll miss you, too." He leaned in and pressed soft lips to hers, causing her to melt against his chest.

✕ ✕ ✕

It was only a matter of time before Kate arrived, and the anticipation was surely going to kill Rich. Shea was on her best behavior so far. Over the last week she'd kept her opinions to herself with regards to Kate. He assumed she was waiting to see for herself how things went tonight.

Nate had claimed a table, one big enough for four couples, off in a far corner of the banquet room that still had a clear view of the entire room. Kate had been on his thoughts all night. Rich knew that she was coming with Jesse—the man she loved—and dreaded her arrival as much as he craved it. And, then there she was.

Through the doorway she appeared like an angel from heaven. Her black cocktail dress was stunning next to her pale skin. The halter top and low cut back were so tempting. Rich wanted nothing more than to run his fingers over her exposed flesh.

"Don't you think, Rich?" Shea asked.

"Um, yeah ... whatever," he stammered, not taking his eyes off what was happening in the doorway. She was alone. His heart skipped a beat.

"What are you looking at?" Shea hissed. "Is *she* here?"

Her accusation snapped him back to his senses. "Jordan and Olivia just got here," he informed her as, by the grace of God, they walked in behind Kate.

They exchanged hugs, and then Jordan shook the hand of the man who came in behind them. Rich's throat closed off and his heart constricted in his chest as Jesse threaded his fingers through Kate's and lifted them to his lips. Kate looked up at him in the way Rich could only wish she looked at him—with total love and adoration. He smiled down at her, and mouthed, 'I love you' before leaning over to kiss her lightly on the lips.

Rich tried to swallow the jealousy that crawled to the surface, itching to get out, as the four of them made their way over to where he and Shea sat with Nate and Roxy.

Kate's eyes met his for only a moment as she acknowledged all of them. "Everyone, I'd like you to meet Jesse." He smiled and nodded to the group as he wrapped his arm around her shoulder, and she leaned comfortably into his touch. "Jesse, this is Nate and Rich and..."

"My Foxy Roxy," Nate supplied proudly.

All eyes fixed on Rich, though he only barely noticed.

Had Kate not even mentioned him at all? The man, who arrogantly stood there holding the woman they both loved, didn't even react to Rich's name as it crossed her lips. Although Rich couldn't say what he'd expected, a little semblance of jealousy would have felt good. He devoured Kate with his eyes, wishing she would let him simply stroke her cheek.

Shea cleared her throat, and every muscle in Rich's body tensed. "I'm Shea and you must be the infamous Kate I've heard so much about." Her tone was politely venomous. Kate's eyes widened and Jesse tucked her tighter to his side in a protective stance. "You sure mean a lot to my *husband,* Kate," she snarled.

Jesse stiffened. His face turned hard, his eyes angry. Interestingly enough, he was looking at Rich, not Shea. Olivia gasped. Roxy choked on her chardonnay. Jordan suddenly found the clock on the wall very fascinating, and Nate wrapped a beefy hand around Rich's forearm to keep him grounded.

Kate blushed, but in the subdued lighting of the banquet room, it was almost unnoticeable. She looked up at Jesse with adoring eyes and smiled weakly before glancing back at the group. "Rich has become a good friend to me, too." She took Jesse by the hand. "I think we're going to mingle. It was good meeting you."

As soon as Kate disappeared into the crowd, Rich turned on Shea. "What the hell was that?"

"What?" Her blue eyes were filled with an innocence Rich knew she wasn't even capable of.

The four people around them quickly found other places they desperately needed to be, vacating the vicinity like rats off a sinking ship.

"Don't you play innocent with me, Shea," he hissed, leaning closer to her. "You know damn well what you were insinuating. I told you there's nothing going on between us." He swallowed hard and continued, "Didn't you see the way she looks at him? Does that look like a girl in love with *me*?"

"No," she said quietly, her eyes flashed, "but that doesn't mean that my *husband* isn't in love with her."

"Shea, please, no more theatrics tonight."

"Fine," she huffed before standing. "I'm going to the ladies room."

Shea was right. What she'd said was spot on. Kate wasn't in love with him. She clearly loved Jesse. Rich tipped back another swig of the amber liquid that burned all the way to his stomach. It was barely taking the sting off seeing Kate in the arms of another man.

They were on the dance floor now, and Jesse held her close to his chest, his large hands slowly moved over the bare skin on her back. He leaned down and whispered something in her ear that caused her to blush and giggle before she melted into his embrace.

As painful as it was to watch, Rich couldn't bear to look away. His heart broke again and again as he witnessed firsthand Kate interacting with the man she loved. One song faded into the next and still he couldn't bring himself to stand up and leave the room.

Nate slid into the chair next to Rich. "Kate sure looks pretty tonight."

"Um hum," Rich answered, but didn't meet his gaze.

"Rich."

"Hmm?"

"Look at me." Their eyes met. "Rich, what are you doing?"

"What do you mean?"

Nate snorted. "Dude, you haven't paid attention to anything except Kate all night. You've got a serious case of pissed off, man. You're wound so tight, I'm surprised you haven't tried to start something with Jesse just to get rid of some of that frustration—or should I say jealousy?"

Rich narrowed his eyes and tried to look innocent. "I don't know what you're talking about."

"Listen, man, I get that you've got a thing for Kate, but I'm not the only one who's noticed. At least *pretend* you don't have feelings for the girl."

Well, that was easier said than done.

Out on the dance floor, Jesse wrapped his arms around Kate and lifted her up so that their faces were even. Their lips met ever so slightly then he set her back on her feet, his fingers playing with the curls at the end of her hair. He pulled her closer, not even leaving room for air between them. Dark eyes flicked over, remaining locked and unblinking on Rich's even as Jesse smiled and leaned down to press those smug lips against her neck.

"I have to get out of here," Rich snapped. With each beat of his heart, jealousy spread through his veins like acid, consuming him.

"Where are you going to go?"

He motioned his head over toward the balcony. "Don't let Shea know where I went, please. I really don't need her attitude right now."

"I got your back. Take as long as you need."

"Thanks, Nate." Yeah, Rich was sulking. His heart felt like it was breaking into a million pieces as Jesse lived up to Kate's promise of showing his affection in public.

The door opened with a hiss and a blast of cold winter air hit him. There was a group of girls standing off to the side, huddled together, sharing a cigarette. "Hi, Rich," Monica said.

He tilted his head to acknowledge her. "I just needed some air."

"We'll leave you to it. We were just finishing up." She lifted the cigarette to her lips for another quick puff before dropping it, extinguishing it with her black patent-leather pump. She leaned in to her friend. "With any luck, there's trouble in paradise. Do you think *all* of him is that perfectly...breathtaking?" Monica's friends found humor in her statement and the group giggled like school girls.

"Damn, that boy's hot! Do you think Kate'd share?"

Rich's teeth clamped together and his hands curled around the railing. There was little doubt who they were referring to. It seemed that Jesse was going to haunt him no matter where he tried to escape.

"Would *you*?" Another high-pitched round of laughter filled the night air.

The door cracked open. *Thank you!* he thought, *they're leaving.*

"Hi, Kate," Monica said.

Kate, he inwardly groaned. *Great, just what I need.* A tug of war began within his body. He wanted to look at her, but didn't. He kept his eyes focused on the street below and listened closely to the conversation going on behind him.

"Were your ears burning?" Monica asked.

"You were ... talking about me?" He could hear the speculation in her voice.

A feminine giggle was followed by, "Well, not *you* really."

"Oh." Comprehension. Monica filled Kate in on their discussion with regards to Jesse. Rich could almost hear the blush he was sure was on her cheeks. "He is pretty amazing, but sorry girls, he's a one-woman man." Rich winced.

"Damn. Well, it was worth a shot." Another round of giggles disappeared as the door closed.

He released the breath he'd been holding and stared down at the hustle and bustle of the street below.

"Rich." His name on her lips was the soft sigh of an angel. His body warmed from the inside out. He leaned down so that his forearms now rested on the ice cold railing, but didn't turn around or acknowledge that she'd said anything.

The whispers of shifting silk and the crunching of her heels on the salted concrete was heard as she took a step closer to him. "Rich."

He took a deep breath to compose himself and turned to face her. "Kate, I..." His heart leapt into his throat and kept him from finishing what he was saying. She looked remarkable; a black shawl hung across her shoulders and wisps of hair blew in the light breeze. "You look absolutely amazing."

✗ ✗ ✗

Kate could feel the color tinting her cheeks at his praise. But it was the way he caressed her with his eyes that really made her self-conscious; like the delicate fabric of her dress didn't exist. Her hands itched to touch him and she wrapped them tighter around the ends of the cotton shawl to make them behave. Encouraging him would only make things worse—for both of them.

"So are you having a good time?" She took a step closer to him, but forced herself to stop before getting too close.

He looked at her like she'd just sprouted wings and said quietly, "Not really."

His answer shouldn't have come as a surprise. Had she expected him to lie? As far as she knew, he'd never done that, so why would he now? "Oh, I'm sorry."

"Like I said before, Kate, it's my problem, not yours." He sounded so deflated. "You didn't ask me to fall in love with you."

Fall in love with me. He's in love...with me? Dammit! A shiver started at her toes and worked its way up her body. He must have thought she was cold because the next thing she knew he'd shrugged out of his jacket and was placing it gently on her shoulders. His fingers made contact with the back of her neck, and it felt like he was touching her with a lit match. She hated that he had this affect on her. She wanted to stay away from him, needed to, but couldn't bring herself to do the smart thing.

"Are *you* having fun?" he asked, bringing her out of her thoughts.

"Not really."

His eyebrows furrowed and his mouth dropped open a little. Her answer had obviously surprised him. "Why?" he asked, his eyes searching hers.

"I hate that I'm hurting you." Kate's voice was no more than a breath.

He lifted her chin so that she was looking into his face. "You can't control how you feel, any more than I can. You love Jesse." His jaw clenched, the muscles in his jaw flexed, as he said the last three words.

Kate could read the pain in his eyes and despised herself for being the one who caused it. Her every cell ached to comfort him. Her hand reacted without permission and ran a finger from his temple to his strong jaw.

He leaned into her touch as his lips pulled into a tight line, meant to be a smile. "It sucks, and I have to get over it." His palm left the rail and was cold against her cheek as he cradled her face.

Her eyes drifted closed at his touch and her lungs stopped working. "Rich," she whispered what was meant to be a warning, but it sounded more like a breathless invitation. She tipped her head deeper into his hand, and his warm lips met the skin of her cheek. Kate's mouth opened and, before she could censor it, she was confessing to him. "I care for you too...more than I should."

She wrapped her fingers around the hand that was still holding her face, and pressed a quick kiss into the palm. Emotions of every conflicting kind were at war in her system. She had to remove herself now, before she did something, said something, she couldn't take back. She'd already said too much.

"I have to go. Thanks for the use of your jacket."

His breathing was heavy, and his muscular chest filled out the starched cotton shirt with every deep breath. She wanted to run her hands across the fabric just to feel him underneath. This was very dangerous territory. She couldn't—she wouldn't let herself do this.

"Mmm," she groaned which sounded just like the hungry sigh it was. "I really have to go...now. Goodnight, Rich."

As she turned, her heel got stuck in a crack of the sidewalk, sending her plummeting toward the ground. She squeezed her eyes shut and braced for impact, but it wasn't the ground she slammed into. Her heart beat out of her chest, but not because of her near date with the cement. It was Rich. He was holding her, rubbing his long fingers against the exposed skin of her back. She felt like she was on fire. He smelled so good. She took a deep breath just to fill her lungs with him.

"Are you alright?" His question was in stereo, above her head and next to her ear.

She broke out in nervous laughter. "Yes, I'm fine. I never should have worn heels this high. It's a good thing you were here, Rich, otherwise I would have been picking myself up off the ground." She gathered what was left of her dignity and smoothed out her dress.

His lips lifted mischievously at one corner, and she knew she was in trouble. "I'll always be here for you, Kate. Always. In whatever capacity you'll have me; friend, confidant—" He paused, his eyes meeting hers pointedly. "—lover..."

The air rushed out of her lungs in a gasp. *Did he really just volunteer to be my lover?* This had to stop. "Rich," she warned.

He raised a suggestive eyebrow, and she knew he was going to push it a little further. "Husband."

Yeah, well... "It appears you already hold that title," she reminded him softly. "Goodnight, Rich."

His face was emotionless as she turned, leaving him alone on the balcony. She cautiously tiptoed toward the door and, after a quick glance over her shoulder, opened it. The noise and heat hit her in a wave. She scanned the crowd for Jesse. Getting out of here was the best idea she'd had all night, and it couldn't come to pass soon enough. What had just happened with Rich was too much. She worked her way through the warm bodies, smiling and saying 'hi' to those who made eye contact.

Chills covered her skin as a voice spoke from behind her. "Hi, Kate."

Kate turned slowly. "Um, hello ... Shea."

"Beautiful Kate," she sneered as she reached up and brushed a lock of hair from Kate's shoulder. "I can see why Rich is so taken with you."

Kate just stared at her, praying that someone—anyone—would rescue her. She'd settle for an earthquake that would cause the ground to crack open and swallow her whole. But the crowd was oblivious to the drama unfolding.

Shea looked over Kate's shoulder then glared at her with vengeful eyes. "So where have you been off to?"

Kate's palms started to sweat. Shea was deadly calm, and Kate's terror was taking over. "I was just ... looking for Jesse."

She smiled, her eyes flashed with an emotion Kate didn't recognize. "Oh, yes, that Jesse of yours is quite a catch. Tell me—" She leaned in close. "—is Rich really better than your beloved Jesse?"

"Excuse me?" Kate nearly choked on the insinuation.

"Surely Jesse is that … muscular all over."

Kate's fear flew to anger in less than a second. Shea had crossed the line. "You know, Shea, Rich is a great guy. If you'd get over yourself, and cut him some slack, you might just find out how wonderful he is."

Shea seemed completely unaffected by Kate's words. "Are you in love with my husband, Kate?"

"Not that it's any of your business," Kate hissed. "But I am in love with Jesse, and he is the only man who has given me his heart."

Shea laughed. "You're wrong, my dear."

"Whatever," Kate snapped, taking a step away from her.

Shea grabbed Kate's arm. Hard. Acrylic bit into her flesh. "You can delude yourself if that makes you sleep better at night. But Rich does love you."

"Kate," Jesse's voice called from a few yards away. "Hey, baby, you okay?"

Shea stepped away from Kate and turned to smile at Jesse as Kate said, "Yeah, Shea and I were just *talking*."

He gave Shea a cautious glare, and smiled at Kate. "You about ready to get out of here?"

Kate nodded. "More than ready."

"Okay, I'll grab our jackets and be right back." He kissed her just below the ear. "Be careful, I don't like her," he whispered.

Kate weaved her fingers through his, holding on to him as a buffer against the brewing storm. "I'll come with you. Goodnight, Shea."

"It was nice to finally meet you, Kate. Jesse."

There was nothing *nice* about their meeting. The woman was a nasty human being. Tucked into Jesse's side, Kate's heart hurt now more than ever for Rich.

✕ ✕ ✕

"Well, this evening has certainly been interesting." The

voice of Nate's gorgeous fiancée, Roxanne Reynolds, stated the obvious. They were some of the few people who still occupied the room that only a few hours ago had been filled with party-goers and drama.

Roxy leaned into him, resting her head on his shoulder. "Rich has bigger problems than just divorcing Shea. Did you see the way he was looking at Kate?"

"Yeah," Nate grunted.

She lifted her head and asked the question with her eyes before she voiced it. "What do you know?"

"Nothing," he lied.

"Okay, go ahead and lie to me." Her fingers fiddled with the cloth napkin that she pulled from the table. "You could be blind *and* deaf and still know that he's in love with her."

"You think?"

She tipped her head, narrowed her eyes, and continued, "But that's not really his *biggest* problem now, is it?"

"What do you mean?"

Her lips brushed his jaw. "Come on, Nate, think." She paused. "*She* loves her boyfriend, it's written all over her face. And holy hell, what's up with Shea? If Kate didn't realize Rich had a thing for her before, she does now."

"Shea's nuts."

"That may be, sweetie, but there's no way she's going to let go of him without making him miserable first."

"I think he's aware…"

"Welll, if it isn't Naat-te with hiz bootifool laadee."

"You're drunk, Clayton."

"Of courssse, I'm drunk," he slurred. "Two wordz." He reached out to slap Nate on the shoulder, but missed by a mile, and his hand swatted awkwardly through the air. "Open. Bar."

Nate wrapped an arm around Roxy as she snickered and buried her face into his shoulder. "What? Don't they pay you enough to afford your own alcohol?" Nate knew he was encouraging him, but a drunk Clayton Tate was an animal worth provoking.

"Why buy what you cannn get for fwee." He swayed and grabbed on to the table to keep himself upright.

"You're not going to drive, right?" Roxy asked.

He raised his eyebrows and attempted an intoxicated smile, but even the muscles in his face were drunk. "You wanna piece of *thisss*?" He ran his hands down his chest and grabbed his crouch.

Roxy's eyes widened and she laughed out loud. Clayton wrapped his fingers around each side of this shirt and ripped it open, buttons flew everywhere. "Oh, yeah, baby," she encouraged him. The shirt came off and then he started with the pants.

The band, which had started to put their stuff away, stopped and began playing stripper music. A plastered Monica and her equally inebriated friends appeared out of nowhere and the catcalls began.

Roxy leaned into Nate. "This would have made Rich feel better." Nate laughed and pulled out his cell phone. Recording this for posterity was the least he could do for mankind—and it would be great blackmail.

The scene was surreal as Clayton climbed up on the table next to them and began with hip gyrations that weren't even close to the sexy he was going for. With his SpongeBob boxers and his black socks, his feet were wide and the booty drops nearly sent Roxy into hysterics.

"You like thaaat, sweeet thang?" Clayton mumbled.

"Give me more," she pleaded through her laughter. "I need *more*."

Another drop to the table, and he shimmied back up with his tie in his hand. He twirled it and then slipped it over his head like a headband.

"What the hell is going on in here?"

Their eyes shot to the doorway in a collective stare. "Damn," Nate whispered humorously to Roxy.

"Greg … Clayton!" Dale shook his head then scrubbed his face with his hand. "Get off that table right now! And where the hell are your clothes?"

Nine

The first rays of the morning poured through the cracks of the blinds. Kate fought against the realization that it was time to get up. Instead, she cuddled closer to the man who would be leaving in a few short hours.

A low laugh rumbled under her ear. "I will miss waking up to you, KC."

"Shh! If we pretend it's not morning, we can just go back to sleep, and then you won't have to leave." The burning sensation started in her eyes again. *Damn traitorous emotions!*

His arms pulled her tighter against him. "I don't want to leave either, but my dad..." His voice was thick with the emotion. He cleared his throat. "I need to be with him right now."

She rolled out of his arms and sat with her feet dangling over the side of the bed. "I'm sorry. I'm being horribly selfish and making this harder on you." She forced her lips into what she hoped was a convincing smile and turned to face him. "Have a good trip," her voice cracked.

He laughed and held out his arms. "Come here."

She tucked herself back in next to his body and sighed. "Hey, I'll make you a deal."

"What kind of deal?" She could hear the skepticism in his tone.

She lay on her stomach so that she was looking into his eyes. Her finger ran along his dark brow, down his nose, across his full lips. His eyes drifted closed and he kissed her finger. She giggled through a smile.

"While you're gone, I'll spend my time finding the perfect negligee for our reunion sex."

His brows shot up and a smile spread across his face. "Oh, yeah?"

She pressed her lips to his. "Do you have any requests?"

He chuckled. "The smaller, the better."

"Of course." Her lips found his again for a sweet kiss. "Would it be okay if... I need you to hold me."

Despite his excited, ready-for-some-action, lower region, he pulled her into an embrace and simply held her. He didn't react when the tears rolled from her cheek, down his bare chest, except to whisper, "I love you." His fingers were pure comfort as they ran through her hair.

The bright red numbers kept changing, noting the passing minutes, no matter how hard she wished for time to stop. "I really need to get up, KC."

"No," she groaned. "I've changed my mind. I don't want you to go. I'm selfish, and I want you to stay with me." The words spilled out in a frantic plea.

He kissed her forehead. "You're not selfish, and you would never forgive yourself if I stayed. Although, I must say that I love that you're going to miss me, and I will miss you more than I can even put into words. You mean the world to me, Kate Callahan." He pressed his lips to hers for a sweet moment before letting the sheet drop from his hips as he left her alone in the bed.

✕✕✕

Even though the airport was its normal crowded craziness, Kate refused to recognize any of that. She was where she wanted to be, wrapped in Jesse's arms. It was taking everything she had to hold on to some semblance of composure. He tipped her head up with his finger and pressed his lips to hers in a passionate kiss that made her knees go weak, every cell in her body begged for more.

"Have a safe trip," she whispered.

"Of course." He kissed each of her cheeks. "I'll call you when I get on the ground."

"Give Tony my best. Tell him I'm so sorry I couldn't

get away."

"He'll understand. He loves you."

"I love him, too." Her brain kept telling her arms to release the death grip they had on his waist, but it didn't do any good. He seemed to be the only thing holding her together at the moment.

Jesse pressed his lips to her forehead and reached around to take her hands in his. "I have to go—" He kissed her knuckles. "—or I'm going to miss my flight." His lips brushed hers for a moment before he pulled away. He blinked quickly, fighting his emotions too. "I'm going to miss you, KC. Please keep yourself safe. If you need anything, Josh said he'd be around."

She nodded, refusing to give in to the tears that wanted to fall.

He smiled tightly. "Don't forget that Josh will be around. Call *him* if you need anything. Call Josh."

"I will."

"I know you've got other friends at the station, but I'd feel more comfortable if you'd..."

"Call Josh. I got it." She leaned up on her tiptoes and pressed her lips to his. "Please come home as soon as you can."

"I promise." He kissed the top of her head and entered the rope dividers that would lead him to security. He turned one more time and waved before riding the escalator up to the gates.

When he was no longer in view, Kate melted into a chair and gave in to her overactive emotions. She and Jesse had been together every possible moment since high school—almost ten years. Even when she went to camp, Jesse snuck up to bring her a teddy bear. "I didn't want you to be alone," he'd told her, before running off into the woods. The memory made her smile.

Marriage would be easy with Jesse. He was the only real boyfriend she'd ever had—the only one she'd ever need. He was kind, loving, and sexy. *So sexy!* Warm fuzzy feelings bubbled through her, causing her to sigh. His smiling face, an eyebrow raised in a suggestive way, entered her mind. *Damn!* He wasn't even here and he could make her feel better.

Her phone beeped...

Hey, beautiful, I'm getting on the plane. I'll call you when I land. I love you more than you know!

She hit the reply button...

I'll be waiting. You forgot phone sex! Love you!

Wishing she could see the look on his face when he read it, she pressed send and got to her feet. She didn't really want to go home, but there wasn't anywhere else she could go since being social was out of the question.

Kate made her way to the parking garage and disengaged the security system on the car, slid into the driver's seat and turned the key. The CD changer spun to the next disk and a slow, sappy love song wafted through the speakers. She turned the volume down and leaned her head against the headrest.

This was going to be an excruciating few weeks.

She stopped at the grocery store and picked up some Ben & Jerry's before heading home. She stood in front of their movie collection and debated her choices. Drama or comedy? Wallowing in her sorrow would only make her feel worse, she decided.

Her fingers ran across the various titles and she smiled at the one with Kate Hudson and the ever delicious Matthew McConaughey, *How to Lose a Guy in 10 Days*. Just thinking about the scenes she'd seen more times than she could count made her smile and caused the giggles to start.

After donning a pair of sweats and one of Jesse's t-shirts, she curled up on the couch. Her phone beeped, signaling a text message. She glanced over at the clock and realized it was too early to be Jesse. Curious, she opened the message.

I'm sure you had a really hard day. Just wanted you to know I'm here if you need ANYTHING!

Rich was such a sweetheart. She sent back a reply...

Yes, it has been hard. Thank you for your offer.

In a matter of minutes, she had a response from him—not that she was surprised.

I mean anything. Fix a flat tire. Change a light bulb. Connect the DVD player. Check your oil...?

Shaking her head, she set her phone back on the table next to the couch. It beeped again...

Honestly, anything! Take out garbage. Shovel the walks. Snake your pipes...?

Kate laughed out loud at his obvious double meaning. He was proposing more than either of them were in a position to act on. She considered texting back, but simply dropped the phone on the cushion instead. There was no need to encourage him.

A few minutes later, it beeped again...

Anything you need... Orgasm?

Ten

Alone in the News17 parking lot with the car in park, Rich's fingers tumbled the cold metal of his phone while his other hand tapped the business card against his bottom lip. Could he go through with this? Yes, he had to, but not for Kate, he was doing it for himself. If Kate came around, then— An involuntary smile tugged at his lips. –then that was just an added bonus. He punched in the numbers and, as the phone rang, every muscle in his body went rigid. If someone touched him, he might just spring like a cable pulled too tight.

"Good morning, Reynolds and Stratton, how may I direct your call?"

Doubt flooded his conscious. Was he really ready to do this? To be divorced? To admit failure?

"Hello?"

"Um, is Claudia Reynolds in?"

"One moment, let me connect you with her assistant." Background music played in his ear while he waited. The thought entered his mind to hang up and put this conversation off—again. "Claudia Reynolds's office, may I help you?"

"Yes, is Claudia in?"

"May I tell her who's calling?"

"Rich Spencer."

"Will she know what this is regarding?"

"Yes," he said quietly.

The music that rivaled that of an elevator's theme song started again, but only lasted for a moment before a familiar voice answered. "Rich, how are you?"

"Fine, thank you. How are you?"

"Good. How can I help you?"

He hesitated, trying to find the right words. "Do you have a time when I could speak with you about ... about Shea?"

"Absolutely." She paused as if she were looking at her calendar. "How does Friday at 2:30 sound?"

"I have to work at 2:00. Do you have anything earlier?"

"You know what, how about 8:00 tomorrow morning?"

"That would be perfect," he told her, sounding a little too excited. "Thank you, Claudia, I'll see you then."

"Rich, if you want to discuss moving forward with a divorce, it's important that you don't talk about our meeting with anyone. We don't want her to find out what we're planning."

We. One little pronoun had never meant so much. For the first time, in a long time, Rich had an ally in the constant battle he was fighting with Shea. There was little doubt that Claudia would give him the advice he needed. Even more importantly, he trusted that advice—he trusted *her*—wholeheartedly.

His eyes drifted closed and he rested his head against the headrest. It would take a few minutes to compose himself before he could go into the office. His mind was racing through everything that kept him from sleeping; Shea, filing for divorce, and of course, Kate. Always Kate.

He'd definitely come very close to the line in the sand last night. The text messages were suggestive, maybe a tad desperate or pushy. She hadn't responded, good or bad. Seeing her today would tell him volumes about how far she would let him push things.

Jesse was gone. Not out of the picture, unfortunately, but Rich fully intended on taking advantage of Jesse's father's untimely health problems. There wasn't a worse time for him to be out of sight, out of mind. A worse time for Jesse. For Rich though...

A tap on the window caused him to jump. His already beating heart shifted into overdrive when he saw the face on the other side of the glass.

Kate. And she looked pissed.

His fingers fumbled with the window controls, rolling down the other three before finally finding the one that was right next to him. "Hi." All the apprehension of seeing her could be heard plain as day in his voice. He may as well have just told her he was nervous, that he'd been stupid.

Her eyes were hard and her normally full lips were pursed together in a flat scowl. "I got some rather *interesting* text messages from your phone last night. Shea didn't get a hold of it again, did she?" The unreadable face stared at him.

"No." The word seemed to stretch on forever as he tried to figure out where this conversation was going.

A twinkle flashed in her eyes as a smile spread across her lips which washed away his nerves like a light rain. "It was very thoughtful of you to offer to help me."

"I just..." His voice sounded like a frog had taken up residence in his throat. "I just figured there were certain things you might need a *man* for."

"Um hum." She arched a brow and a grin lifted one of her lips while her cheeks tinged pink. "Yeah, if I need my oil checked or my pipes snaked, I'll be sure you're the first one I call. As for the—" Her face flushed crimson. "—orgasm, what exactly are you proposing?"

His jaw dropped. He never expected her to broach the topic head on. "Um."

She waited, her smile growing as he shifted uncomfortably in his seat. "Well, Rich, are you offering your ... assistance with that?"

Wow! Was she really standing here asking me if I wanted to sleep with her? "Kate, I... I, um... Do you want...?"

She started to laugh, lifting her hand to stifle it. "I'm *so* messing with you."

He shook his head. "Kate, there is nothing I would love more than to *assist* you with that." It appeared as if she actually stopped breathing. Her eyes widened and she just stared at him without blinking. "I'm sorry. I've said too much and made you uncomfortable. There's just something about you that makes me want to tell you the truth, whether you want to hear it or not."

The wind blew an auburn curl across her face and she tucked it behind her ear. She took a deep breath and exhaled in a slow, long breath. "We'd better get to work," she said quietly, then turned and glided toward the building.

Rich set new speed records as he jumped out of the car to hurry and catch up with her. "Are you okay?"

"Yes." She didn't turn to acknowledge him, just pulled the collar of her jacket closer around herself. "I just hate when you do that."

"Sorry."

She stopped and whirled around to glare at him. After a quick glance of the parking lot to make sure they were alone, her eyes returned to his. "Do you have any idea what you're doing to me? How...*conflicted* you're making me. This little rollercoaster ride you've got me on is hell. It's killing me. I know that I love Jesse..."

He should've fought his smile. "But...?"

"But—" She started walking again. "—I love Jesse. Let's just leave it at that."

"If that's what you want. We'll leave it at that—for now."

"For always. I can't keep going back and forth. Dammit, Rich, you're married. That's a deal breaker for me, and it should be for you too. Until you're ready to do something about it, you need to just keep your feelings to yourself."

"I can't—"

"You can. Please, *I* can't continue to live in this turmoil." Her chest was moving with intense breaths. Her high cheeks flushed an exquisite pink and her eyes flashed between frustration and...love?

Standing so close, he wanted to take her in his arms, wanted to tell her about his conversation with Claudia and their meeting to eliminate the 'deal breaker'. But he had promised himself that he would follow Claudia's advice to the letter. *They* had a plan and he couldn't do anything to jeopardize it. Even if it meant keeping something from Kate.

Kate walked through the doors into the newsroom

and Rich was only a few steps behind her. Laughter was coming from the photographers' lounge to the right. He took a quick inventory of the room and noticed that Clayton was in Dale's office—with the door closed. That was never a good sign. Dale believed in an open-door policy, and so the only time his door closed was during contract negotiations or if somebody was in *really* big trouble.

"Kate, Rich, you guys missed it," Nate said through his laughter. Olivia and Jordan stood next to him, holding his phone and laughing hysterically. "Greg. SpongeBob. Stripping."

Those three words were enough to already have Rich chuckling. "What are you talking about?"

"There's no way to describe this. You have to see it for yourself." Jordan continued to laugh as he tossed him Nate's phone.

Kate and Rich put their heads together and watched Greg dancing, if you could call it that, on a table with his SpongeBob boxer shorts, pasty white legs, and black socks. He dipped into a bootie drop and Kate let out a hoot that melted Rich's heart. Hearing her laugh was the greatest sound ever. She grabbed onto his arm and buried her face into his shoulder.

Rich found it more than difficult to focus on the idiot dancing on the tiny screen. Kate was next to him, touching him. She smelled so good, like vanilla and coconut and ... happiness. He wanted to fill his lungs with her. There was an audience though, and he forced his mind to come up with some kind of intelligent sounding response.

"When did this happen?" Rich asked when Dale's voice on the phone began to reprimand Clayton for his idiocy. Kate was still smiling as she pulled away from him. The sense of loss was instantaneous, and he wanted to feel her touch again—soon.

"After you guys took off. There was only a few of us left, and he came over and was hitting on Roxy," Nate explained.

Rich shook his head and continued to laugh. "Does he have a death wish?" Jealousy was not an emotion

Nate was able to control very well.

"Are you kidding?" Nate threw his head back and belted out a boisterous belly laugh. His eyes jerked in the direction of Dale's office. "Look at him, would you be jealous if he hit on..." For a second Rich was sure he was going to say Kate, but then he said, "Hit on Olivia, Jordan?"

"Um, no, I guess not." Jordan's eyes registered that he'd been expecting Nate to say Kate too.

"Nate," Dale's calm voice said from the doorway.

All the eyes in the room turned to look at Dale. He was normally so collected, but he looked tired, frazzled—and it was only 10:30 in the morning. His hair was in disarray on his head, sticking up in various places as if he'd run frustrated fingers through it a thousand times—or gotten his finger stuck in a light socket.

"Yeah," Nate answered.

"I have a favor to ask of you, Nate. You can tell me no, although, I really wish you wouldn't." He even sounded tired. "Your phone is your own, and that video is probably quite hilarious."

"But..." Nate sensed what was coming.

"But, I have *his* image to protect, even if he doesn't give a damn about it. I can't afford for that to get out. I've told him that his reputation and the station's reputation are one and same." He looked disgusted over his shoulder, glaring at Clayton, who was pouting at his desk. "I *think* we have an understanding."

"What would you like me to do?" Nate asked.

Dale ran his hand over his face. "*Please* delete it. Let's just forget about his lack of judgment."

"Sure thing, Dale." Nate smiled. "Make no mistake though, I'm not doing this for *him*. If it weren't for the respect I have for you, this would be going on YouTube."

"Thanks, Nate, I owe you." Dale nodded to each of them.

"Hey, Dale," Rich said, tossing him the phone. "Wouldn't you like to see it first?"

Dale's lips turned up into an evil grin. He pushed the button and ... laughed. He closed the phone and tossed it back over to Nate. He turned to leave and said over his shoulder, "Nate, if you accidentally dumped that to the outtakes reel, I'm not sure that I'd be all that upset about it." Laughter broke out from everyone in the room. "Then, please, delete it."

✕✕✕

Rich arrived at Claudia's office at 7:55, and the parking lot was completely empty. After double-checking the time, he opened the door and headed toward the building, fully expecting the door to be locked.

His fingers wrapped around the handle and tugged. It opened easily and he walked into the dimly lit reception area. There was no one around; no receptionist, no clients, only a light coming from a room down the hall. He started walking toward it. "Claudia?"

She came out of the doorway, smiling. "Rich, I'm glad you could make it."

He glanced quickly toward the deserted reception area. "Where is everybody?"

She laughed softly. "Oh, the office doesn't open until 9:30, but I wanted to get you in as soon as possible."

"Thanks, I really appreciate that."

She waved her hand toward her office, inviting him in. "Shall we get started?" She walked behind her mahogany desk and sat in her dark brown, leather wing-backed chair. He sat across from her and waited for her to take control. "I have to ask you one question before we move on to your options."

"Okay." He suddenly felt as though he were in trouble, a kid in the principal's office for fighting on the playground.

"I can't stress the importance of your honesty. We're a team, Rich, and I need you to trust me." Her eyes were searching him, but searching for what?

"Of course," he said, "I do trust you."

She took a deep breath and asked, "Why are you getting divorced?"

His stomach flipped. "Um, I thought you understood *why*."

"Is there another woman?" She leaned forward as

her fingers threaded through each other and she rested them a little closer to the middle of the desk.

Damn, didn't see that coming! His teeth began to gnaw on his bottom lip. Her eyes didn't leave his face as she waited patiently for his answer. His mind was swimming as he tried to come up with what to say. Finally all he could do was go with the truth. "I don't know how to answer that."

She smiled. "Honestly, the *why* of things doesn't matter to me except that you are Nate's friend. If this girl is the reason—"

"Claudia," he interrupted, "this has been coming for over a year. I won't lie to you, Kate is a huge catalyst to getting my butt into gear, but she isn't the reason my marriage went to hell. Shea did that all on her own."

Claudia picked up a pencil and began scribbling something, notes he presumed. Her eyes met his again, and she asked, "So you don't think you're at fault at all?"

He swallowed hard. "I've been a good husband; loving, supportive, faithful."

"Completely?" she asked, pencil poised.

He nodded. "Emotionally, up until the last few months, but physically, yes, completely."

Her pencil moved across the paper quickly. "I'm guessing that Shea suspects you have feelings for Kate?"

A chuckle burst out before he could censor it. "Shea suspects the checker girl at Circle-K."

"Fair enough." More notes made their way onto her notebook. "How is she going to handle being served?"

"I can't say for sure."

"Of course," she said with a nod.

"But I can guess that it won't go over well. She's chucked vases at me just for coming home late."

Claudia leaned back in her chair and tapped her pen on her lip. A few minutes of silence went by, and he could almost see the wheels turning in her mind, the questions forming. "How violent do you think she could get?"

"When this all comes down, I'm nervous for how far she could escalate things. Not so much for myself, but…" He let the statement trail off.

She nodded and muttered something to herself that he didn't catch. Then all was quiet, except for the incessant scratching of her pencil against the paper. Finally she looked up. "Okay, here's what I think we should do… Do you feel as though you're in danger?"

"Well, I sleep behind a locked door," he whispered. "But other than that I feel relatively safe. She's never tried to come in, and I can usually defuse her when I'm awake."

"Our plan will require some patience."

Haven't I been patient enough? "Okay."

"I think it's wise to get an Order of Protection."

"I couldn't agree more."

Claudia leaned farther back in her chair and propped a pair of red-soled, black high-heeled pumps up onto the desk. "She's already done a number of things that qualify for just cause, but time has run out. You have to file immediately following the incident. I don't think we should wait until *after* she's been served and has a chance to come after you. My first priority is to make sure you're safe. We will have to wait until she does something else that would qualify as domestic violence, and then with her history, you could file for an Order of Protection."

"What about Kate?" He sound panicked, and hated it.

She didn't react, not so much as a twitch of an eyelash. "Unfortunately, there's nothing we can do unless Shea goes after her."

"But she'll blame Kate. She'll blame anyone and everyone but herself. And if she can't get to me…" His breathing was erratic as he considered the possibilities. "Claudia, I have to protect Kate."

There was a soft thud as her feet met the floor again. She leaned forward and smiled. "How closely do you work with her?"

"I'm her photographer, so when we're both working, I'm with her nearly the whole time."

"That's good. After the Order is in place, the safest place for her is with you."

Staying close to Kate was exactly what he wanted, but by the time this all came down, Jesse would be back. "She has a boyfriend."

"Oh." Claudia tapped her pencil on her lip. "Well, let's not worry about that right now, okay? You go back to your life and I'll get things started."

His body felt numb as he tried to process what was happening around him.

"Rich?"

He looked at her. "Um hum."

"You do realize that you can't tell Kate what we're doing. Under no circumstances can you tell her that you're filing for divorce. And you need to be careful how close you get to her until the papers have been served."

"I don't know if I can—"

"You can." Her voice was quiet and serious. "If you want to keep Kate out of this, you *have* to keep your distance."

"But—"

"I deal with this every day, Rich." She paused and then asked, "Is Kate the reason for this divorce?"

"No," he said adamantly.

"Regardless of the reason, people will blame her if they think you're in love with her." She raised a knowing eyebrow, and he knew that Roxy had filled her in on the lovesick act at the party. "So I'm going to *encourage* you to be on your best behavior. You don't want to give Shea or anyone else an excuse to use Kate as the scapegoat for what's coming."

Grateful that he was still able to work with Kate every day, he stood and shook Claudia's hand. "I understand."

"One more thing, Rich." She smiled. "You're probably going to need someone to talk to."

You think?

"Nate would probably be the best person for that. Let him know how important it is to keep this quiet. If you need me to stress that importance, I can."

Rich sighed in relief. Having Nate to open up to would be a great help. "Thank you."

"And you know that I can't discuss this with

anyone."

There was little doubt she was referring to Roxy. "I figured, but thanks for telling me that."

"I'm glad you called, Rich. I'll be in touch. Feel free to call me if you need anything else."

As he left Claudia's office, his emotions were running on overdrive—from relief to panic to dread. He hated the thought of cooling things with Kate, just when Jesse had decided to take himself out of the picture. But if it meant protecting her from rumors, from Shea, then he would gladly play it cool.

Grateful that today was a dayshift, he climbed into the driver's seat and turned the key. He hoped it wouldn't be long before Shea went on another one of her tirades that, this time, would release him from her forever.

He pulled into the station parking lot and cursed himself as he searched for Kate's car. Only a half hour since being in Claudia's office and, already, he had a hard time not needing to be close to Kate. This was going to be excruciating. He scrubbed his face and stepped out to make the walk into the building.

"Good morning, Rich." Kate's voice made him stop dead in his tracks.

His breathing ceased and his stomach jumped. He turned around and had to shove his hands into his pockets to keep from pulling her into his arms. "Good morning, beau- Kate. How are you this fine day?"

She smiled and his heart melted. "I'm surviving," she said on a sigh as she continued walking toward the doors where real life would take over. "How are you this morning?"

He chuckled. "I'm surviving too." *Surviving until I show you exactly how I feel about you.*

Her laughter filled his heart which dropped to his stomach when his phone rang. He flipped it open to reveal yet another accusatory text message from Shea. He shook his head and groaned.

"Shea?" Kate asked, already knowing the answer.

"Yeah. You know I just don't understand her sometimes. Just when I think she can't surprise me, she does."

"She *was* quite a piece of work. I couldn't believe..."

"What do you mean?" His brows pulled together. His stomach flip-flopped uncomfortably as he waited for Kate to verify his suspicion.

She stopped walking and turned to face him, her eyebrow raised. "Shea talked to me at the party?"

"No," he choked. "What did she say?"

Kate shook her head, a plastic, unfeeling smile on her lips. "Oh, she asked me if you were better than Jesse."

His heart pounded in his chest. His lungs stopped breathing and he felt light-headed. "Oh, no."

"And..." She opened the door and stepped into the newsroom, walking quietly to her desk. He followed her because she hadn't really given him a choice. She'd left the 'and' just hanging in the air without further explanation. Once her stuff was settled on her desk, she turned to him. Her face was emotionless as she spoke, "And she said that you loved me."

"She said *what*?" he choked.

"Never mind." She shrugged, looking nervous. "I guess it's not important."

Not important? There was nothing on this planet more important. Rich did love Kate. He knew it, and obviously Shea did too. This certainly complicated things. And that complication strengthened his resolve. He would back off. He would protect Kate at all costs, even if it meant ripping his heart out.

Eleven

Long distance relationships suck!

Jesse had been in Arizona with his dad for a little over two weeks. Tony was doing better and, despite the diagnosis, Jesse was talking as though he'd be coming home in time for Christmas. Kate missed him so much; his smile, his sense of humor, his gorgeous body. She couldn't wait to have him wrap his arms around her again. His absence had most definitely made her heart grow fonder. The phone calls, text messages and emails were fine, but having him with her, in the flesh, was something she desperately ached for.

"Morning meeting in five." Dale's familiar message made her realize that she was out of time and needed to put the finishing touches on her email to Jesse.

Give my best to Tony. Let me know when you have your ticket. I can't wait to have you home. I miss you SO much! Love you, Kate

Inside the conference room, everybody took a seat and chatted quietly while they waited for Dale. Olivia sat down next to Kate and leaned over. "So when does Jesse come home?"

Kate sighed and turned to meet the eyes of her friend. "I'm not exactly sure. Soon, I hope."

Dale walked into the room and grabbed a marker near the dry erase board. "Okay, we have a busy day." He scribbled a few various stories, then began filling in names next to them. "Kim, I'd like you to take breaking news." Greg snorted. Dale continued, "Karen, I'd like you to take that story you pitched last night and run with it. I'd like to lead with it."

She smiled and quietly said, "Sure thing, Dale."

"Clayton," Dale addressed the pouting child two chairs down. "You're going to PA for Olivia."

"*What*?!" Clayton slammed his fist down on the table. "I haven't PA'd since right out of college. That's so unfair."

"Don't do this, *Clayton*," Dale warned.

"But..."

"You brought this on yourself." He left the juvenile delinquent to sulk and turned his attention to Kate. "Kate, I'd like you and Rich to go out to the Children's Hospital."

A disgusted breath whooshed out from Clayton. "You have got to be kidding me."

Dale rolled his eyes, but didn't show any other reaction. "Well, that's it. Let's cover the black." Everybody jumped up and starting filing out the door. "Kate," Dale said and she turned around to face him, "would you track down Rich and meet me in my office in a few minutes?"

"Sure thing."

Rich and Nate had their heads together, deep in what looked like an intense conversation. They were each sitting in a chair opposite each other and their foreheads were practically touching. Nate's voice was low. "I'm glad you finally called her. She's the best."

Her? It bothered Kate that Rich was calling a mysterious 'her', but it bothered her even more that it bothered her.

"It sucks that you can't tell Kate though."

Kate stopped dead in her tracks, held her breath and listened, hoping to find out what he couldn't tell her.

Rich pressed his palms into his eyes and sighed. "Yeah, man, that's the worst part."

Silence dragged on between the two men, and when she couldn't take it anymore, Kate coughed quietly and both their heads jerked in her direction. "Hi," she whispered, lifting her hand awkwardly.

Rich jumped to his feet and strode over to her with forced patience. "How long have you been standing there?"

"I, um, Dale wants to see us in his office." Telling Rich that she knew he was keeping something from her, something that he didn't want her to know, would only make both of them uncomfortable.

"Oh. Do you know what he wants?"

She shook her head, avoiding his eyes. "No. You don't think he knows..." She let her statement dwindle, afraid of bringing up his feelings for her.

He tipped his head to the side, his eyes searched hers. "Think he knows *what*?"

Nate started to chuckle nervously, saving her from answering his question. "I've got to get going, and you two need to get into Dale's office. Have a good one." He slapped Rich on the back, hoisted his camera over his shoulder and headed into the newsroom.

There was no way Kate was going to stand around waiting for Rich's interrogation. He hadn't so much as gotten close to crossing the professional line since Jesse had left. Which surprised her. She'd fully expected an onslaught of suggestive texts, provocative conversations, and inappropriate declarations, but he'd been a perfect gentleman. She began wondering if she'd imagined the whole thing. It seemed quite ridiculous that Rich could have feelings for her and maybe, just maybe, he'd come to his senses.

"Please come in." Dale motioned toward the couch that sat against the wall, behind a couple of chairs.

Rich slumped into the couch and patted the spot next to him. She questioned him with her eyes. He smiled, shook his head, and she took the spot at his left. His hand reached toward her. He hesitated, and rested it on his own knee. He was mocking her. She'd get even later.

Dale came around the desk, turned one of the chairs around to face them, and sat down. "Kate, I just wanted to take a second to explain how important this story is. It's the annual sing-a-long. We are the only station that is allowed into the event and the kids, and our investors, really look forward to it." He looked at Rich. "I forget, have you ever covered this before?"

Rich nodded. "Only once, five years ago, before

Clayton made it his baby."

Dale chuckled, but quickly hid his amusement. "Yeah, well, he won't be covering it this year. I need your best work on this, you guys." He smiled. "Thanks, I can't wait to see what comes back. I have the utmost confidence it will be fantastic."

Rich stood and Kate followed his lead, right on his heels as they walked out of the office. "No pressure," he murmured under his breath.

She looked up into his blue eyes, and tried to force a smile. "Yeah, no kidding."

✕ ✕ ✕

The smell of cleanliness was overwhelming. The stench of antiseptic and disinfectant made Kate's stomach turn. A vanilla scented candle would do wonders for this facility. It's too bad that it wasn't really an option.

Rich and Kate walked up to the reception desk. "May I help you?" asked the lady with gray hair, wearing a candy striper smock.

"Yes, I'm Kate Callahan with KHB. This is my photographer, Rich Spencer. We're here for the sing-a-long."

"Oh good, they're expecting you." She picked up the phone and spoke to someone on the other end. "Um hum. I'll send them right over." She stood and leaned over the counter, pointing the way. "Follow the hall to the first set of double-doors on your right. Just go on in, they're getting the kids ready now."

"Thank you." Kate smiled and looked up at Rich to make sure he'd gotten the directions as well.

The room didn't look much like a hospital at all. It was filled with vibrantly colored murals on the walls. Tiny orange chairs were set up facing an oak, upright piano that was off to one side.

Slowly children of all ages began to fill the room— some on their own power, most with the assistance of an adult. Despite the difficulty life had dealt them, Kate had never seen a happier group of children. They were smiling. Even the ones with masks that covered most of their faces had eyes twinkling with excitement.

Once the children were settled, they waited. And waited. And waited.

A dark-haired woman with a hospital badge was on her cell phone in the corner. She was talking low, but her frustration was apparent in her exaggerated movements. She snapped it shut and approached Kate and Rich.

"Hi, I'm Rhonda, the Event's Coordinator. Thank you for coming, but it looks like we're going to have to cancel today's sing-a-long." She sighed and blinked quickly to keep the glistening of her eyes at bay. "I'm sorry to have wasted your time."

"What's wrong?" Rich asked quietly.

She huffed in frustration as her irritation returned. "The guy who was supposed to play the piano for us... *forgot.*" She waved her hand toward the group of antsy children. "How can you possibly forget a room full of angels that are looking so forward to this?" She shook her head. "I hate that I have to send them back to their rooms without this."

Rich's deep blue eyes sparkled. "You may not have to do that."

Her brows narrowed and she looked confused. Kate probably did too. "But there's no one to play the piano."

Rich smiled and Kate had to fight the urge to kick him. Nothing about this situation deemed a smile, let alone a sexy, knowing one like he sported. "Do you have a guitar?" he asked.

"I think there's one..." She placed her hands over her heart. "You mean you can play?" He nodded and she bit on her lip. "I don't have any music."

"That's okay. I don't need any, as long as they don't mind a few mistakes."

"Wait right here, Mr. Spencer. I will find you a guitar, even if I have to go to Wal-Mart and buy one." She rushed out of the room, only to return seconds later with a guitar in her hand. "It's not the best but..."

"It's perfect," Rich said with a smile, playing the first of many chords.

Rhonda laughed and all the children turned to see

what had happened behind them. She clapped her hands and walked toward the front of the group. "Children, I have some bad news." A collective disappointed groan filled the room. "Mr. Moore can't make it." A few of the children started to actually cry. "But ... Mr. Spencer from KHB is going to take his place. Can you all say hello?"

"Hello, Mr. Spencer," they said in unison, while some of them waved in their direction. All the sweet faces grinned from ear to ear. As much as Kate detested Clayton Tate, she understood why he enjoyed this assignment so much. The kids' excitement was contagious and she found a smile of her own spreading across her face.

Rich carefully placed the camera on its tripod before heading toward the front. "Okay, who's ready for some songs?"

The room erupted with varying degrees of enthusiasm as well as song titles being requested. His fingers were magnificent, caressing the strings, relaying familiar melodies which caused the kids to get even more ecstatic. A few cords sounded, only to pause for his beautiful tenor voice.

The children joined in, and sang the best rendition of *Rudolph* Kate had ever heard. *Frosty* was next, followed by *Jingle Bells*.

Instinct took over and she lifted the camera from the tripod and put it on her shoulder. Rich's voice was strong and, as she pointed the camera at him, he flashed her the smirk that always melted her heart.

Song after song, she captured the tiny faces that seemed to adore Rich. It wasn't a side of him she'd seen before; a side that endeared him to her. He was tender with the little ones, playing whatever song they requested.

"Mr. Spencer! Mr. Spencer!" A teeny little thing with blonde pigtails waved her hand from her wheelchair.

Rich stopped the concert and turned to her. "What is it, sweetheart?"

Kate zoomed in on her face, forever preserving her dark lashes that briefly hid her big blue eyes for only a moment. "Mr. Spencer, would it be okay if I sat next to you?" Giggles dotted the room and she ducked her head, embarrassed.

His cheeks tinged with a yummy shade of pink as he stood and walked over to her. The little girl's mother nodded and Rich bent down, resting one knee on the ground in front of her. "What's your name?"

"Sami."

"Well, Sami, I'll let you sit by me if you'll do one favor for me." Her little head bobbed up and down. "See that lady over there?" He pointed at Kate.

Sami's wide eyes blinked as she looked at Kate. "Um hum, she's pretty."

"Yes, she is," Rich agreed. The color rose in Kate's cheeks now. She pushed the record button and the red light went off. There was no sense recording this. His smile told her that he knew exactly how uncomfortable she was, and that he was enjoying it. "Do you think you could help make her jealous?"

Sami giggled. "Is she your girlfriend?"

They both looked at Kate, and she lowered the camera from her shoulder, unsure of why she was so intrigued by what his answer would be. Rich smiled. "No, but she does mean a lot to me." Kate didn't even realize she'd been holding her breath until it all flew out of her lungs in a whoosh.

"Mr. Spencer." The little girl held up one finger and motioned for him to come closer. He did and she kissed him on the cheek. She giggled and looked at Kate. "Did it work, are you jealous, Miss Callahan?"

Kate sat the camera down on the floor and walked over to where the two of them were and crouched down. "Horribly jealous." Kate winked at the precious little girl.

Sami clapped her hands and chanted, "Kiss him! Kiss him!" Within seconds, the whole room echoed with the phrase. "Kiss him! Kiss him!" Every child trying to out scream the one next to him. "Kiss him! Kiss him!"

Rich stood, offered Kate his hand and pulled her to his chest. "Well, Miss Callahan, what are you going to do? You'd hate to disappoint all these children."

She tipped her head to the side and looked into his

darkening blue eyes. "You did this on purpose."

He feigned offense. "I have no idea what you're talking about."

"Kiss him! Kiss him!"

She grabbed his chin and turned his head, then wrapped her arms around his neck. Closing her eyes, Kate puckered her lips and leaned on her tiptoes to peck his cheek. Rich's arms tightened around her and when her lips met his skin, it wasn't the rough, stubbly cheek she'd expected. Her eyes popped open in surprise and she gasped into his mouth, tasting him.

Their audience applauded and whistled.

He looked down at her and his eyes reflected the conflict she felt. "I'm sorry, Kate." His voice was quiet, barely a whisper. "I shouldn't have done that. Let's wrap this up so we can talk, okay?" He released his hold on her and leaned down to the little blonde who was bouncing in her wheelchair. "Come on, princess," he said as he unlocked the wheels and pushed her over to his chair.

Once they were seated, the dark-haired woman stepped up to the front and the children groaned. "It's time for our last song. Mr. Spencer, do you know 'I'll be home for Christmas'?"

"Sure do," Rich said.

Kate picked up the camera and began rolling again. The melody filled the air, pushing all thoughts of Rich out of her head, replacing them with Jesse—and a lot of guilt.

Rich's lips on hers shouldn't have made her toes tingle. His scent shouldn't have made her breath catch in her throat. The taste of him shouldn't have caused her legs to feel like they were made of Jell-O, and talking about any of those reactions wouldn't do anything but add to her already confused feelings.

The group finished singing, a few of the mothers wiped tears from their eyes, but instead of capitalizing on their grief, Kate turned the camera off and sat it on the floor then slumped down into a chair.

Emotionally she felt like she'd been through the wringer, even without Rich's kiss. Seeing all the children in varying degrees of illness was painful to witness. Then Rich stepped in to play the guitar, and made little Sami's day. Kate sighed. All of it only made Kate even more confused.

Confusion was dangerous.

Her stomach flipped as she thought about the conversation that Rich wanted to have.

"Let's grab a few soundbites and get out of here," Rich said softly. She looked up, expecting to see him gloating, but his face was contrite, his eyes pained. He frowned. "Kate, please say something."

"I don't..."

"Kate, Rich, I can't thank you enough for saving the day," Rhonda rushed up to them.

Rich smiled at her. "You're very welcome. I'm glad that we could be part of this great day. I hope we can come back next year. If it's okay, we'd like to interview a few of the kids."

"Oh, sure. Sami, would you like to be on TV?"

Within half an hour, they'd wrapped up the interviews and were in the car with an excruciating silence dragging on between them. Rich stared out the windshield, not even looking at Kate.

When she couldn't stand it any longer, she cleared her throat. He still didn't look at her. "Rich, did I do something wrong?"

"No," he grunted.

"Are you mad at me?"

"No."

"Rich, what the hell is your deal? You kiss me like that..." She couldn't stop the sigh, remembering what it felt like to have his lips on hers. "Please say something, even if I have to tell you not to say things like that."

He closed his eyes and opened them again slowly, his chest expanded with a deep breath. "Kate, I am so sorry. I shouldn't have done that, you deserve better."

So maybe he didn't feel that way about her anymore. Maybe the kiss was just some kind of sick joke to make the kids laugh.

"It's okay. At least the children found it humorous, right? We both know it didn't mean anything."

His face didn't register any emotions, nor did his voice. "Kate, I..." he paused, still not looking at her. He blew out a controlled breath. "I ... I'm sorry."

✕ ✕ ✕

The story turned out really good. Kate had proven to be Rich's equal; getting the 'money shots'. As much as he hated the story revolving around him saving the day, he loved the stuff with little Sami.

Sitting in the photographer's lounge with his head resting against the wall, Rich closed his eyes and tried not to think about what had happened only hours before. Having Kate's lips on his.... Just the thought of it caused his heart to race and his lungs to stop breathing. The way she tasted. He groaned. Flipping open his phone, he dialed the familiar number and waited for the answer.

"Rich?"

He knew that since Nate had been assigned to Clayton, there wouldn't be listening ears while he was in his vehicle. Clayton always insisted on driving himself to the story. None of them ever knew why, but it saved the sanity of the photographer, that was for sure.

"You gonna be back soon?" His voice was a pathetic whisper.

"Yeah. You okay?"

Rich groaned. "Kate kissed me today."

"*What*? Dude, that's so great...and so bad."

"I know." His response only validated the fact that Rich was a selfish jerk. "Do you have time to get a drink tonight? I really need some girly, share your feelings, time."

Nate laughed. "You got it, man. Lemme call Roxy and tell her I'll be with you for a bit tonight."

"Please tell me you're not discussing all this with her."

"No. Claudia explained to me how important it was that you have a confidant. She told Rox that if I was with you, she couldn't ask questions. Roxy's cool. I'll be there in about fifteen minutes."

Since apologizing to Kate, he'd tried to avoid her, but it was proving to be difficult. Her determination was quickly becoming her only annoying trait. She wouldn't let it go.

Through the windows that surrounded the photographer's lounge, he could see that she was heading toward him. The internal tug-of-war began; his heart told him to stay while his head screamed at him to protect her and run.

"Rich," she whispered as she walked slowly around the corner. Her beautiful eyes glistened and her gorgeous, full lips were pulled into a worried line. "Can we talk?"

He wanted to jump out of the chair, pull her into his arms, and talk to her about everything. *Everything.* His lips longed to kiss her again, a real kiss, one that could unleash all the passion he felt for her, removing any doubts she had about how he truly felt for her.

Instead he managed a controlled rise out of the chair and buried his head in his lock-up cabinet. "Um ... I really can't ... uh, talk ... right now. I'm supposed to..."

"Rich. Kate."

His head jerked up and slammed into the top of the cabinet, stars streaked across his vision. "Damn," he muttered under his breath as he rubbed a hand over the sensitive spot.

Dale smiled. "You okay, Rich?"

"Yeah, no blood." Rich smiled at Kate as they both remembered her overreaction the last time he had a head wound.

She rolled her eyes, unamused, and looked over at Dale.

"I just wanted to tell you two how great your story was. The best one I've ever seen. Quite emotional." He shook his head. "Rich, you with that little girl was fantastic."

"Thanks," Rich mumbled, embarrassed.

Dale laughed. "I've decided there's only one word to describe the way you two are." Kate and Rich looked at each other and then back at Dale. "Perfection. You are perfect together."

Rich choked on his saliva at Dale's response. His hand flew to his throat and the coughing continued while he tried to breathe easily. His eyes watered as they met Kate's, which quickly filled with tears.

"Thanks, Dale. Excuse me, I really need to get home." And with that, she turned on her heel and rushed out the back doors.

Rich forced his knee to the ground and resisted the urge to run after her, to explain. Of course she'd misinterpreted what had happened; he'd been deadly silent, then nearly choked to death. He'd have seen it as rejection if the roles had been reversed. At least that's what he hoped she thought, and not that the idea of them being perfect disgusted *her*.

Dale meant that they were a good team, that they worked well together. Perfectly. Rich agreed with him. They were perfect. *We are perfect.*

"Is she okay?" Dale asked, pulling Rich out of his thoughts. "I didn't mean to upset her."

"I'm sure she's fine." Hoped she was.

"Okay then, you have a good night." He walked back toward his office and Rich sunk into a chair, resting his head in his palms, to wait for Nate.

"Dude, what's up with Kate?" Nate was standing right next to Rich. "She's out in her car, crying. What the hell happened?"

"She's *crying*?" Rich really wanted to rush out to her and kiss her tears away, but he couldn't. He wouldn't do that to her. This would be for the best ... until he could always be the man to pick up the pieces of her broken heart. He ached to be that man. "Are you ready to go?"

"Rich, are you going to bother to fill me in?" Nate's normally calm demeanor was on the verge of frantic. "Did you make her cry? I thought..."

"Just get your stuff. We'll talk about this at Fuzzy's." Rich secured his lock-up cabinet, grabbed the few things he needed to take with him, and started for the door ... only to stop and turn around. "Um..."

"Oh, good hell!" Nate pushed past him, exasperated by the whole situation and the fact that he was still in the dark. "I'll make sure the coast is clear." Nate opened the door and stepped outside. "We're clear," he mocked in a voice straight out of an old James Bond flick.

Rich rolled his eyes. "I'll see you there in a few."

His mind raced as he drove the few minutes to the bar. It sucked to live in a world where choices actually had consequences. He wanted nothing more than to hold Kate in his arms, to continue his declarations, to slowly whittle away at the hold Jesse had on her heart. But he couldn't.

The phone in his hand beeped with a text message. His heart jumped in hopes that it would be Kate trying to open the line of communication that he'd successfully managed to cut. He flipped it open and frowned.

Do I need to worry about Sami too? She's a little young. Don't you think?

He closed the phone with a snap and tossed it on the seat next to him where it would stay until he was done speaking with Nate. Even if Kate did call, he needed to keep his head clear while talking things out.

Nate pulled into the parking lot behind Rich and parked two spaces down. They walked into the bar and found a table near the back. Luckily, the whole place was pretty deserted, just what Rich needed to discuss what was going on in his head—and his heart.

They sat down and Fergie came over to take their order, then left. Nate waited patiently while Rich picked peanuts from the bowl on the table. When the silence was too much for him, he cleared his throat. "What happened?"

Rich took a swig of his drink, a deep breath, and then relayed the events of the afternoon; the guitar, the sing-a-long, Sami, and the kiss.

"Wow, she really kissed you, huh?"

Rich nodded, fighting between elation and abhorrence.

Nate laughed. "I'll bet Jesse would love that." His eyes flashed and he smiled. "How was it?" His question caught Rich by surprise, causing him to laugh, and he threw a peanut at Nate, who dodged so that the nut hit the wall behind him.

"Here's the problem, Nate." Rich pulled the

conversation back into the realm of seriousness. "I don't want anyone to blame Kate for my divorcing Shea."

Nate burst out in laughter and slapped the table with his hand. "Are you kidding? Anyone who *knows* Shea won't question why you divorced her. Most people wonder why you've waited for so damn long."

"I don't want Shea to blame Kate."

Another bark of laughter. "If Shea doesn't blame Kate, she'll blame someone else. She certainly won't blame herself and all her twisted antics." Nate shook his head and took a drink. "Look, Rich, I get wanting to protect Kate from Shea. But I really don't think you have to worry that anyone else will blame Kate."

Rich's lips pulled into a tight smile. "Dale said we were perfect together."

Nate's eyes widened and he lifted an eyebrow. "Is that what had Kate crying?"

Rich ran his fingers through his hair, pulling just a little to torture himself. "Well, when he said we were perfect ... I choked." Nate laughed. "Yeah, a whole choking fit, actually. I'm afraid Kate might have misinterpreted my reaction. I couldn't agree more with Dale, but I have to be careful how close I get to Kate. Do you think..."

When Rich didn't continue, Nate asked, "Do I think what?"

"I'm going to ask Jordan to have you start working with Kate. Would that be okay?"

His brows pulled together in confusion. "Why would you want to do that?"

"I can't trust myself with her. Today proved that." He shoved frustrated fingers through his hair. "If she's with you, I'll know that you can watch out for her."

"Of course, but will Dale go for it? I mean, he just told you that you're perfect together. Do you really think he's going to want to break up a winning team?" Dimples developed on his cheeks. "I kinda doubt it." He paused. "But, if you can swing it, I'll work with her for you."

"Thanks. If you see Shea anywhere near her, you have to call Claudia right away. Don't even bother calling me. You call her first, do you understand me?" Rich didn't like the vulnerability or the panic in his voice, but Nate needed to understand the importance of the task he was being given.

Nate nodded. "I understand, my man. I see Shea, I call Claudia. Got it." He smiled and winked. "You talk to Dale and Jordan, and then let me know what you want me to do." He stood and threw some cash on the table. "I've got to get home to Rox. You okay?"

"Yeah, thanks." Rich extended his fist and Nate bumped his knuckles.

"I'll see you tomorrow, my man."

Could Rich really go through with this? Could he not be close to Kate, stealing *accidental* touches, hearing her laugh?

Before even turning on the car, he checked his messages. Of course he had text messages.

Are you coming home?

He deleted the message and moved to the next one.

Where the hell are you? Please tell me that you're not really with that CHILD. I was kidding before. Rich, are you? Call me!

"Do you not know me at all?" he questioned the silence. Did she honestly think he was capable of *that*? He had definitely made the right decision in divorcing her. He deleted her disgusting message and moved on to message three. Probably another rant...

Rich, What happened today? Please talk to me. The not knowing is killing me. Friends? Kate

He could feel her emotions as she poured them into each letter of her message. He had hurt her, and hated himself. But things were better this way. Weren't they?

With every ounce of self control he could muster, Rich forced himself to turn off the phone and drop it into the passenger seat. He wouldn't answer Kate's questions. If it meant that she was safe, he *would* leave her alone.

Twelve

Kate rolled over and slapped the snooze button. The other side of the bed was cold, empty. Tony had taken a turn for the worst, and Jesse had insisted on staying with him a little longer. All the dates for him to return home had come and gone, and it was beginning to wear on Kate's heart in a way she'd never expected. She needed him desperately.

Maybe it was that the decision had been made for her. Her intrigue with the new feelings she had for Rich had been dashed in a single moment, after a slight brush of their lips. The electricity she'd felt nearly melted her insides. But as soon as his lips left hers, he pulled away emotionally as well, leaving her even more confused than before.

Since that day two weeks ago, she forced herself to focus on Jesse. Only Jesse. Too bad her heart had a mind of its own.

The morning after Dale informed the two of them that they were perfect together, and Rich's choking fit, Kate showed up to work to find that she'd been reassigned. Nate was now her photographer and, although she was sure he knew why Rich stepped aside, Nate wouldn't say anything, playing dumb.

Today was supposed to be one of the happiest days of the year, but Kate highly doubted that she was going to walk out and find Jesse—or Rich—sitting under the Christmas tree with a big red bow on his head.

She dragged herself out of bed and into the shower, pulled on some clothes and made the journey to work. The ghost town had only a handful of people doing the work of many others. Olivia and Jordan were supposed to have been off but...

"Kate," Olivia sighed. "I'm so glad you're here." Kate smiled, wishing she could return the sentiment. "If it's okay, you're going to stay in-house. Dale would like you to anchor again today."

That was the first piece of good news she'd had in a long time. "Really? What about Clayton?"

"I don't think he's been forgiven of his stupidity yet." She giggled and pushed back a chair at the work station next to her desk. "You can sit here. It'll be fun."

"Okay," Kate murmured then her mind drifted off to where it always seemed to go these days. Rich.

"Kate?"

"Hmm?"

"What's wrong?"

"I just miss..." Kate stopped as her eyes caught sight of Rich striding across the newsroom in his tight black jeans and long-sleeved white t-shirt with News17 across the back. He paused to speak briefly with Jordan, but blatantly kept his gaze away from where she was seated. She shook her head to clear her thoughts, and continued, "I just really miss Jesse."

"I can only imagine how hard that must be." She looked over at Jordan and sighed. "Hey, what are you doing for Christmas dinner?"

"I don't know. Josh and Sophia invited me over to their house, but I'm thinking I'll just go home and nuke a Lean Cuisine and call it a night."

Olivia gasped as if the words were utter blasphemy. "Don't be ridiculous! You're coming with us."

"Olivia, no. Really, I just want to be alone," Kate protested.

"Nonsense. What kind of friend would I be to let you eat something out of the microwave for Christmas dinner?" She stood up so that she could see over the assignment desk. "Jordan, honey, it's not a big deal for Kate to tag along to Christmas dinner, is it?"

Jordan shook his head. "Nope. I'll call Mom and let her know to set a place for one more."

Rich's eyes met Kate's for only a moment before she

dropped her gaze. Those pools of shimmering ocean water had a way of seeing straight to her soul, and she didn't want him to know what he'd done to her.

It's better this way, she told herself. *He's married and I'm in love with Jesse. Nice and easy.*

But there was nothing *easy* about the conflict waging war in her heart. Kate hated that she ached to feel the touch of another man. She loathed herself for feeling *anything* for Rich. She loved Jesse, adored him, and would happily become his wife—someday.

"It's all settled, Kate, you're coming with us. Do you wanna stay the night at our house too?"

"Oh, no." Kate laughed although it sounded forced. "I'm a big girl, I can stay home alone."

"Kate," Rich said, his voice concerned, "you do make sure that everything's locked, right? I wouldn't want... *We* wouldn't want anything to happen to you. Maybe you would be better off staying with Olivia and Jordan."

She wasn't sure why his concern irritated her, but it did—big time. "Listen Rich, I appreciate that *you're all* concerned for my well-being, but Jesse has been gone for three weeks and Freddy Kruger hasn't shown up. I think I'll be fine."

Jordan and Olivia laughed, but Rich's face looked wounded for only a second before he composed it into an emotionless mask. "I was just..."

The vicious side of her wanted to go for his jugular, but she just took another quick stab and then retreated. "The boogeyman hasn't made an appearance either. But if it'll make you feel better, I'll check under my bed before I climb into it at night."

He forced a defeated smile and dropped his head. "Yes, that would make me feel better. Do you think you could double-check your doors and windows too?"

"Fine," Kate scoffed, rolled her eyes at him then stood. "Olivia, I'll be back. I'm going to the bathroom. Rich, would you like to do recon for me, first? Just to make sure it's safe." Her voice had just enough venom to be potent, but not enough to make her sound like a complete bitch. It was the only response she could have to Rich now.

His rejection stung and she couldn't stand to be around him. She felt like such a fool. Jesse's a great guy, who doesn't deserve a girlfriend who is pining away for a jerk that finds pleasure in screwing with her emotions.

When she finally locked the door to the bathroom, tears started to stream down her face. After putting the lid down on the toilet, she sat down and let the emotions she'd kept bottled up to flow. Her heart was pounding so hard, she was sure that at any moment it would start to rattle the walls. She was miserable. Jesse was gone. Rich was distant. And she couldn't decide which was worse.

× × ×

"...and fade to black. Roll commercial," the director spoke the familiar words in Kate's ear. *Fade to black,* her thoughts repeated the phase, the one that meant she could finally breathe, finally relax, finally enjoy a job well done.

Within a few minutes, Kate climbed into the back of Jordan's Mustang for the trip to his family's Christmas dinner. Olivia chatted incessantly while Jordan laughed. Both of them allowed her to stay quiet, for which she was grateful.

They pulled up to a beautiful brick house that had a long sidewalk and big, open fields of undisturbed snow on each side. It was easy to imagine the lush green grass that would be in its place come summer.

Jordan led the way and opened the door. "We're here," he yelled into the hustle and bustle.

A woman came running from the kitchen, rubbing her hands on her apron. She pulled Olivia into a hug, moved on to Jordan then wrapped her arms around Kate. "Kate, it's so nice of you to join us."

"Th- thank you for having me." Kate questioned Olivia with her eyes.

Jordan tugged at the arms that were crushing her. "Kate, this is my mom, Elise Greene. Mom, please...let go of Kate."

She brushed her hands over her hair, then called into the other room, "Elaine, the kids are here."

"Elaine?" Kate shot a glare at Olivia. "As in Dale's Elaine?" she whispered.

Olivia giggled and nodded. "Um hum."

"You had me crash *Dale's* Christmas dinner?" Kate groaned, wishing she could just turn and run all the way home. "Olivia, how could..."

"Kate," Dale's voice said.

She forced a smile and turned around. "Hi, thank you for having me."

"Absolutely." He motioned toward the living room. "Please ... come in. Another fantastic job today, Kate."

"Thanks." Any other house on the planet and Kate would have been more comfortable.

"I have to say that I'm a little surprised you're here."

Her body filled with nervous energy and she started fidgeting. "I'm sorry, Olivia invited me...and with Jesse gone..." Her eyes burned and she cursed her overactive emotions.

His brows crinkled "Where's Jesse?"

When Kate didn't answer right away, Olivia spoke up, "His dad's sick, so he's in Arizona. He's been gone since the day after the Christmas party and Kate's pretty upset about it."

"Olivia," Kate hissed, brushing the tears away from her cheeks. As if her misery wasn't hard enough, but now, her boss knew. "I'm sorry, Dale, this isn't something you need to worry about."

"Nonsense. I wish you would have told me sooner." He winked. "When is he coming home?"

Kate sniffed. "We don't know. He's been going to come home but then doesn't dare leave his dad."

Dale put his hand on her shoulder and squeezed gently. "How about I make you a deal?"

"A deal?"

He laughed. "Yeah." His smile was contagious. "If you'll cover the New Year's Eve celebration, then I'll give you two weeks in Arizona." His smile grew with each word he spoke. He knew he was offering a proposition she couldn't refuse. "You just have to be back in time for ratings," he added. Deal?"

"Let me get this straight. If I cover New Years', I get two weeks off?" He nodded, and she squealed, covering her mouth to stifle it. She brushed at the tears on her cheeks again as she jumped up and threw herself into his arms. "Deal, Dale, you're the best!"

Elaine snickered softly from the doorway. "What have you done now?"

Dale blushed and tried to remove himself from her excited death grip.

"You remember Jesse," Olivia started to explain. Elaine nodded. "He's in Arizona with his dad, and Dale just made a deal that will allow Kate to go see him. I think she's a little excited."

Kate could feel herself blushing as everyone around her chuckled at her expense. "Sorry about that. I didn't mean to accost your husband, Elaine. It's just..."

"You don't have to explain to me, dear." She looked adoringly at Dale as he stepped to her side and wrapped his arm around her waist. "Being separated from the man you love is not something I enjoy either."

Kate smiled at her—at them. "Excuse me, I need to call Jesse."

"Of course you do." Elaine smiled. "Please don't take too long, dinner is almost ready."

"Thank you so much."

Elaine and Dale left the room, hand in hand. Olivia gave Kate a thumbs-up and flitted toward the kitchen.

Jesse's phone rang twice before a female voice answered. "Hello?"

"This is Kate ... Um ... Who's this?"

Laughter rang out. "Kate, it's Terri. Merry Christmas."

"You, too. I'm sorry, but I only have a second... Is Jesse there?"

"He was just helping Dad in the bathroom. Hold on, and I'll let him know you're on the line."

"Thanks." Kate walked around the exquisitely decorated formal living room, looking at the pictures. There was one of Jordan and Olivia where she actually had long hair, down to her mid-back and one from their wedding day.

"KC?" Jesse sounded a bit panicked. "Is everything okay? I thought we were going to wait and talk tonight."

Hearing his voice caused her eyes to burn with unshed emotion. "Oh, Jesse," she sighed.

"What's wrong?"

"Nothing's *wrong*." She paused, thinking of the best way to mess with him. "How much do you miss me, Jesse?"

"You're kidding, right?" He chuckled. "I miss you so much, it's making me crazy." His voice was full of want and desperate need.

"When are you coming home?"

He sighed, and she could picture his long fingers running through his black hair. "I don't know."

"Well, you can't come home until at least the middle of January."

"Oh, you really miss me, huh?" he scoffed.

She laughed at his disappointed tone. "Because I'm coming to Arizona."

"*What!* Really, KC? You're coming *here*?"

His excitement made her smile. "Yep. I just have to cover the New Year's Eve celebration, and then I'll get on a plane on the first and be out there for two weeks."

"Merry Christmas to me!" He let out a holler. "Who do I have to thank for this present?"

"Dale. I just have to be back in time for ratings."

"May or July?" he teased.

She smiled. "February."

"Bummer."

"Surely, you'll be able to come back with me."

"Let's not worry about that right now." She could hear that he was still smiling. "Damn, this is the best news. Tell Dale thank you for me."

Olivia cleared her throat from the doorway. "Dinner's on the table."

Kate nodded at her. "Hey Jesse, they're holding dinner for me."

"They, who?" It sounded an awful lot like an accusation.

"Would you believe I ended up at Dale and Elaine's

with Olivia and Jordan?" Kate laughed.

"Anybody else from the station there?" His question screamed Rich. Jesse was suspicious. And despite her saying otherwise, he did have a jealous streak that could get nasty.

"Nope, just the four of us." Olivia cleared her throat again. "Listen, I really need to get going. I'll call you tonight."

✕ ✕ ✕

The house was completely dark as Rich pulled into the garage. The presence of the little red BMW assured him that Shea was home. Worry and relief hit him at the same time. If she was home, she couldn't be anywhere near Kate and with any luck, she was already asleep. As he walked into the house, he softly called for Shea.

A soft whisper of an answer came from the living room, "In here, baby."

Baby? He rolled his eyes. "I've had a long day," he said on the short trip toward her. "I'm just going to go..."

She smiled, twirling a lock of hair that was hidden underneath a red and white Santa hat. Her breasts were covered in a red and white bra and she wore matching panties. Her ensemble was completed with thigh-high stockings and red stilettos. "I thought you might want to open your last present," she purred.

His member jerked, but the wiser of the two heads won out. "Um, I'm ... ah..."

She stalked toward him with the beauty of a cheetah. The urge to flee surged through his bloodstream and he stepped backward. Her tongue tsked and the pouting began. "Rich, darling, you haven't made love to me for so long. I need you."

"That's a nice offer, but I'm gonna turn in."

She eased toward him and put her hands on his shoulders, ran them down his back and rested them on his ass. She squeezed and pulled his hips into her. "You want me to beg?" Her tongue ran over her cherry red lips. "*Please,* Rich."

He took another step backward, his back meeting

the wall. *Dammit!* "Thanks anyway, Shea, but I'm going to go to bed—alone."

She narrowed her eyes and stepped away from him. Her hands moved around to her back and ripped her bra from her body, tossing it across the room where it landed on an upper branch of the tree. "What's the matter, Rich, you don't like *these* anymore?" She took a breast in each hand. "You certainly paid enough for them. I would think that you'd like to reap the reward of your investment."

"Shea, I'm not in the mood..." His thoughts moved to Kate and a sigh escaped.

Tears filled Shea's eyes. "I knew there was another woman."

"Not this again." He groaned and ran his hands over his tired face. "There is no other woman. Never has been." *Until I'm rid of you.* "I am faithful to you, Shea."

He brushed past her, frustrated in more than one way. Shea's breasts were magnificent, Dr. Pretètiti made sure of that, but sleeping with her would have been wrong, given what he had in the works. Not only that but, strangely, having sex with his wife would have felt like cheating on Kate.

The den door closed and Rich turned the lock. He wondered if tonight would be enough to set Shea off—not that he was *trying* to upset her. His body ached for release, but not from the one Shea was offering. He wanted to be rid of *her* so that he could on to better things.

He flipped on the TV and watched the rerun of Kate anchoring in silence. Her intoxicating eyes looked so sad. The distance he'd put between them had seemingly had an effect on her. Or was it just wishful thinking?

Minutes went by before he heard the clicking of Shea's stilettos coming down the hall. He expected her to stop at the door and start another rant, complete with her hand hammering against the barrier he used to keep himself safe while he slept, but her bedroom door closed softly.

She was not reacting at all how he expected. Slamming doors, screaming fits, and careening objects was more her style. His eyes inspected the lock to make sure it was in the locked position before he let them drift closed and fell asleep.

The morning sun shone through the window, cheerful and full of promise. Rich ran his hands over his face, the whiskers scratchy against his palm. Remembering the events of last night, he stopped breathing to listen for any sign of Shea.

Only silence answered.

With shaking hands, he unlocked the door and slowly opened it. The expectation of something flying through the air at him had his nerves on edge. He peered down the hall in each direction before stepping out completely.

Still nothing.

He started a quick recon mission, searching for the crazy woman who would soon be his ex-wife. She wasn't in her bedroom. The bed was made. He couldn't be sure if she'd slept in it or not.

"Shea?" Even his voice was shaky.

Silence.

He walked through the kitchen and opened the door to the garage. Her car was gone, but where the hell had she gone—and when?

Thirteen

Tomorrow Kate would be back where she belonged, in Jesse's arms.

Rich's distance had proved to be an irritation and a comfort all at the same time. Kate took a deep breath and walked into the newsroom. Monica stood at the assignment desk and waved her over. "Are you ready for the fun assignment?" she laughed and looked down at her computer. "Nate's off today, so I'm going to have you go out with—"

Please don't say Rich.

"—Rich. He called a bit ago, he's running late."

Kate nodded. "Thanks."

At her desk, she organized her things and pulled out her phone. If she was going to be working closely with Rich today, she needed to keep Jesse on the forefront of her mind.

30 hours. I love you! Kate

A few minutes went by, but instead of the phone beeping with a text, it rang. She smiled and flipped it open. "Hey, sexy." A delicious gasp answered. "I can't wait to feel your hands all over my body," she said seductively. There was only silence, so she continued talking dirty to Jesse. "I *need* you to kiss me, to worship me with that talented tongue of yours."

His heavy breathing caused a smile to spread across her face, and she loved the power she had over him.

"Tell me what you're going to do to me," she whispered, her voice husky with desire. "Tell me what you want me to do to you."

"Um—" He cleared his throat. "—Kate."

"Rich," she shrieked. "I'm sorry, I..." Heat covered

her body, but not the kind she'd been experiencing only moments before. "I thought you were Jesse."

"Oh." He actually sounded disappointed. "I, um...I guess we're together tonight, and I just wanted to let you know that I'll be in shortly."

Great. Seeing him was going to be even more embarrassing. "Okay. I was just doing some...things."

"Yeah," he chuckled, "I kinda got that impression."

The heat rose in her cheeks again. "Well, I'll see you in a bit." She closed the phone and groaned. *Mental note: Always check the caller ID.* She dropped her head into her hands and rubbed at her throbbing temples. As if her relationship with Rich wasn't strained enough, now she'd gone and given him ammunition to mortify her forever. *At least he's speaking to me, right?*

An hour later, he strolled into the newsroom, a picture of a pure male beauty, complete with a smug, mocking smirk. When his eyes met hers, he raised an eyebrow and chuckled.

She hated that he was so arrogant in her humiliation. "Let's just go," she groaned, stuffed her arms into her coat, and threw her stuff over her shoulder before stomping out into the parking lot. Rich popped the locks and Kate sank into the passenger seat of the news vehicle, twisting so that her knees touched the door. Maybe if her back was to him he wouldn't...

"Kate, I'll leave it alone."

She blushed and allowed herself to relax just a little. "Thanks," she grumbled, still hugging the door.

A long, drawn out sigh blew between his lips, one she heard rather than saw because she couldn't bring herself to look at him, then he muttered softly, "Jesse's a lucky guy."

× × ×

Standing on the rooftop, Rich and Kate waited for the clock to strike twelve, welcoming another year. People around them partied it up with the ones they loved.

The crowd started to yell, "Three, two, one..." And then the big clock at the courthouse started to strike midnight. The loud chimes drowned out the screams of the excited people who filled the streets of Gateway Plaza. Rich was doing his job perfectly, turning the camera to get the action happening around them.

When the clock made its final bong couples kissed and friends hugged, and the familiar melody of 'Auld Lang Syne' wafted on the breeze. Kate stepped in front of the lens and smiled. "With Photographer, Rich Spencer, I'm Kate Callahan and, on behalf of the News17 family, we want to wish you a safe and happy new year. Good night."

"We're clear." Rich dropped the camera from his shoulder. The two of them stood side by side and watched the chaos below as it slowly dissipated. "I'm for waiting a bit. Is that okay with you?" He lifted a lock of her hair and twisted it around his long, slender finger. He turned to face her.

She looked around and realized that they were completely alone. *No, definitely a bad idea.* "Yeah, that'd be okay." With the cold railing against her back, she pulled her jacket tighter while Rich stuffed the camera into its padded case and tugged at the zipper.

Working with Rich today was no different than it had ever been. He was kind, funny, and certainly competent. She was afraid that the uncomfortable, barely-acknowledging-each-other phase of the past few weeks would have seeped in, but it didn't. Although Kate was bugged by his little avoidance act, she savored the time they were spending together, grateful he'd decided to be ... normal.

He stood and inched over so he was standing directly in front of her. He closed his eyes and inhaled deeply, holding the breath in his lungs then exhaled in a slow, controlled breath. "Kate..."

Her heart stopped as did her lungs, and her skin buzzed with the need to reach out and touch him.

His hands felt heavy as they gripped her hips. The heat of his body warmed her soul, his breath warm and minty as it blew against her cheek. "This awkwardness between us has been excruciating for me." She dropped her eyes and kept her hands busy by playing with the zipper on her jacket. If she touched him in this moment it would be all over. "Kate, tomorrow, actually later today, you're going to go to ... Arizona, and I don't want you to go without knowing that I *do* care for you."

"You ... you do?" Her eyes flicked to his.

He leaned forward until his lips were right next to her ear. His warm breath caused her skin to break out in goose bumps. "Every beautiful girl needs to start the new year with a kiss." His finger lifted her chin and her eyes closed as he leaned in closer.

Her body melted into his embrace when his lips pressed against hers. It started out sweet, soft and grew with intensity. Her hands slipped into his hair in a frantic attempt to pull him closer. His lips were soft, but gloriously firm as they moved gently against hers. She started to feel lightheaded and realized she wasn't breathing. She inhaled deeply, tasting his intoxicating flavor, and moaned into his mouth.

He placed another quick kiss on her lips then pulled away only enough to place his forehead against her. "Oh, Kate," he sighed. "I've wanted that for so long."

She pressed her hand flat against his chest. He released his hold, and she shivered against the cold night air. "Rich, I can't." Erratic breath rushed from her lungs, evident as she spoke. "You're married."

"What if I weren't?" His blue eyes were the most beautiful shade of cobalt. "Would it make a difference if I weren't ... married?"

"You are. So it's kind of a moot point ... unless there's something you're not telling me." She knew he was keeping something from her and wondered if it might have something to do with his marital status. Surely he'd tell her.... She forced her thoughts to stop.

He stepped back and ran his fingers through his hair. "Kate, I lo-... I'm ... um ... I just want you to know ... ah..." he stammered, followed by a juicy curse.

"Dammit, Rich! Spit it out. What do you want me to know?"

"I want you ... to be happy."

"With Jesse?" she spat the words, knowing they were as sharp as any dagger.

His face registered the direct hit. He shrugged and bent over to pick up the camera bag. "Let's get you home. You're going to need your rest so you're ready for Jesse's talented tongue." He cringed.

And so did she. "Rich." She took his hand and tugged just enough to make him stop. "I'm sorry. I didn't mean for you to hear that."

"I know," he said bitterly, "you thought I was Jesse." His face was composed in an annoying mask when he turned to face her, but his eyes revealed the pain he was feeling.

"What does it matter? Surely you're not *jealous*." Kate was playing a dangerous game, but his insinuations were enough to drive her insane. She needed him to lay it all out on the table. If he was giving her a choice, she wasn't sure what she would do with it, but she wanted to know.

He groaned. "Kate, there's so much to tell you. I wish..." He trailed off.

"I wish you'd stop stammering and just tell me what it is that has you so flustered. Dammit, you're so frustrating sometimes. You all but tell me you love me, only to totally back off and refuse to even talk to me. Then you kiss me like ... *that*." She took a deep breath trying to forget what his lips felt like. "Pick a stance and stick with it. Love me or hate me, Rich. Part of me wants to slap some sense into you."

That damn smirk of his made another appearance. "And what does the other part of you want to do?"

"What the hell is your freakin' deal? Ugh!" She turned from him and stormed off toward the elevator.

His footsteps were quickly gaining on her, and within seconds, his hand wrapped around her arm, spinning her around to face him. His expression was intense and his eyes were alive with desire. Butterflies raced around her stomach as he looked from her eyes to her lips and back again.

She prepared for his kiss—wanted it, craved it—and had to remind herself that she was supposed to be pissed. Her skin tingled, her entire body wanting another taste of what she'd had moments before, and it took everything she had to not throw her arms around his neck and press her lips to his. He cleared his throat and Kate shoved her hands deeper into her pockets and looked into his eyes.

His voice was rough when he spoke, "Kate, I want you. There are things going on in my life right now that I've been *advised* against telling you." His face was inches from hers. "I am *flustered* because tomorrow you're going to be with Jesse ... and it's killing me. Am I jealous? Hell, yeah, I'm crazy jealous because I lo-..."

She gasped, unsure of whether or not she really wanted to hear what he was about to say. She closed her eyes to regain some kind of composure over her out of control system.

He leaned down and pressed his lips just below her ear. "Huh-uh, I won't say that until I'm completely free to do so." His breath was warm against her skin. Her whole body trembled with desire for this man. He wrapped a hand around each of her arms and held tightly as he gazed into her eyes. "Make no mistake, Kate Callahan, I care for you ... deeply."

Her mind was swimming. Being so close to Rich, feeling every inch of his muscular body, caused her knees to give out. She reached back and held onto the wall for some support.

Her phone rang and she jumped.

Rich laughed without humor. "I'll bet I can guess who that is."

The elevator doors opened and Rich went in first, standing against the back wall. "It's okay, Kate, you don't want Jesse to worry."

"Hello?" Kate tried unsuccessfully to sound chipper.

"Happy New Year, KC." His voice had enough enthusiasm for both of them. "I wish you were in my arms right now." He chuckled. "Oh, what I'd love to do to you," he said in a seductive purr.

She laughed unnaturally and turned her back to Rich, trying to protect him while not giving Jesse a reason to suspect anything. "I'm, ah... Can I call you back in a bit? I'm just finishing up."

"You're not in the city alone, are you?" He sounded

worried.

"No. I'm with Rich. He's going to take me home."

There was a silence on the end of the phone that relayed more of his suspicions than any words ever could. "Well, then, um," he finally said, "call me when you get home." Kate could hear the tension in his voice.

The elevator dinged for the parking garage and Rich held the door open for her. "Thanks," she whispered to him. "Okay, Jesse, I'll call you as soon as Rich drops me off."

He blew out an annoyed breath, which caused the hair on the back of her neck to stand on end. "I trust you, Kate Vasquez," he all but growled.

Like hell you do. She hung back while Rich moved to the back of the vehicle to put the camera away. "I'll see you tomorrow," she whispered before closing her phone.

An engine turned over, and Kate looked up to see Rich sitting in the car with the parking lights on. His head was leaned back against the headrest with his eyes closed, his lips drawn into a grimace. She climbed in and pulled the seatbelt across. Rich put the car in drive and began driving in the direction of her apartment. "Is everything okay?"

"Um hum," she answered quietly. "Sorry about that."

He frowned. "Yeah, that was a little hard to take."

She stared at him in the darkness, unsure of what to say. So she resorted to silence. His profile was as handsome as the rest of him; straight nose, square chin, muscular jaw that kept jumping as his teeth clenched. Kate knew that he was fully aware of her appraisal—and that it was irritating him. She should give him a reprieve, but wanted to commit every inch of his face to memory.

"Why Casey?" he blurted.

"Huh?" Her brows pulled together.

"Why does Jesse call you Casey? I mean, Katie I could understand."

She laughed. "It's not Casey. It's KC, my initials. I moved to Flagstaff my sophomore year and when I got there, there was already another Kate on the basketball team. Everybody started calling me KC to distinguish between the two of us." She shrugged. "I guess Jesse just never gave up the habit."

Rich pulled the car into the lot of her apartment building, eased it into a spot, and cut the engine. She narrowed her eyes at him. "What do you think you're doing?" she asked nervously.

His eyes twinkled and a teasing smile appeared, like it always did when he was thinking something mischievous. "I was hoping..." She tipped her head to the side and raised her brows. He laughed. "Will you *please* let me just walk through your apartment? I just want to make sure you're safe."

She glanced back at the dark building, and although, she wanted to tell him that it would be okay, it did look kind of sinister. "Um...yeah, that'd probably be the smart thing to do." Probably not the best word choice, since her brain was screaming to leave him safely in the car at the curb.

He followed behind her quietly, keeping his distance. Her key slid into the lock and she turned it, opened the door, and allowed Rich to enter first. She dropped her keys in the basket on the counter and flipped on the light. Rich studied the picture in the entry where she was in Jesse's arms, and she cringed. "So, um ... this is home."

His eyes scanned the entry and he stepped toward the living room. "It's ni-... Whoa, what happened in here?"

"What?" Panic threatened. "What's wrong?"

He laughed. "It looks like your closet exploded."

Her closet *had* exploded and left its contents all over her couch. Piles of outfits scattered the floor, and the suitcase was wedged into the overstuffed chair. "Ah, yeah ... I'm in the process of packing."

He nudged the completely empty black suitcase with his knee. "Yeah, looks like you're real close to being done."

She rolled her eyes. "You want something to drink?"

"Sure, whatever." His eyes continued to scan the room.

"Coke?"

"Thanks." He nodded. "Do you mind if I take a quick look in the bedroom?"

She raised a suspecting eyebrow which caused him to laugh. She shook her head and pointed, unable to fight her smile. "Yeah, sure, it's through that door." She walked into the kitchen and tugged the fridge open, grabbed two cans and poured the contents into a couple glasses of ice.

Rich was still in the bedroom, so she sat the glasses on the table and started organizing the piles. She lifted the sweaters, one by one, that were lying on the back of the couch and pulled them off the hangers, folding them. She picked up the last one as Rich came around the corner.

"Everything looks safe. I worry about you here all alone." Concern showed in the angles of his brow and the purse of his lips.

She waited for the irritation from earlier to reappear, but it didn't. She liked that he worried. That he cared. "I'll be okay."

"Kate, if you need anything, you know you can call me."

"Yeah, I've heard that before."

"Touché." They both laughed, remembering his suggestive text messages. He leaned against the doorway, his forearms folded over each other. He took a long sip from the glass of Coke and looked completely comfortable being in her home. "But I mean it. Even if you're just scared. I can be here in fifteen minutes."

His offer both thrilled and scared the hell out of her. "Thanks, Rich, that really does mean a lot." He approached her, only to stop and inhale sharply. "Rich, what's wrong?" She jumped to her feet and rushed over to where he stood by the corner of the couch.

Agony reflected in his eyes when they met hers. He reached down and each of his index fingers twisted in the straps of the black satin and lace negligee she'd promised to bring Jesse. He held it out, examining it, the fire returned to his eyes. He closed them before he let out a guttural moan. "Holy hell, I wish you'd bought this for me. The thought of him..." His eyes squeezed shut tight, and his full lips pulled into a grimace. The muscles of his jaws flexed and released as his molars ground together. "Couldn't you just forget it?"

"You know that it won't matter, right?" she whispered. "He's going to expect..."

Rich's hand shot out and covered her mouth with his finger. "Don't say it. Damn, just knowing.... Kate, please don't take this to him. Now that I've seen it, I can imagine how you'd look in it, and I ... I'm sorry." He tried to smile and dropped his hand from her lips to run it through his hair. "Kate, breathe."

Somewhere through his monologue, she'd stopped breathing. She gasped in an attempt to fill her lungs with some much needed oxygen.

"I know that I have no right to ask you that. To ask you anything."

"It's okay. Well, it's not okay, but I'm trying to understand how hard this is for you."

He stepped closer and took her by the upper arms. His grip was tight, but didn't hurt. "You have no idea how difficult it is to let you go."

"It's hard for me too." She sighed, and tried not to think about the way his touch made her feel or the fact that she was breathless. "Much harder than it should be."

His whole body radiated tense, stressed energy. "Do you think you can avoid having s- ... *intimacy*?"

"Rich," she warned.

He chuckled. "It was worth asking." He cringed and lifted her chin.

Protests started in her head, but didn't make it out of her mouth. His cobalt eyes stared into hers as he lowered his face. They drifted closed at the last moment. His lips brushed softly against the corners of her mouth, then kissed her full on—hard. His arms wrapped around her waist, and he held her tight against his body, which was good because her knees had buckled.

"Have a safe trip. I promise not to contact you, but I'm only a phone call away if you need me." He took a deep breath. His fingers plucked a curl from her cheek and twisted it around his finger. "*Please* don't forget how much I ... *adore* you, Kate."

He kissed her one more time, a slow, lingering kiss that caused her toes to curl, and then, without another word, he left her standing completely alone.

Fourteen

"Kate." His gentle hand brushed the hair away from her face, tickling her cheek. "Good morning, beautiful."

Her eyes fluttered open, trying to focus on the face smiling at her. "Wh- what are you doing here?" She shot up, bringing her lips within inches of his.

He gave her a quick peck and chuckled. "Is that any way to greet the man you love?" His mouth was on hers. Her hands gripped at his shoulders in an attempt to melt herself into his muscled body.

His lips moved slowly against hers, matching every movement with perfect intensity. He crawled onto the bed, his knees straddled her hips. He urged her against the pillow with his perfect plump lips, supporting most of his weight on his arms as he hovered above her. His fingers swept the strap from her shoulder, only to replace it with a trail of fiery kisses.

Her body answered his call, consumed with heat from his every touch. She eagerly worked at the buttons of his shirt, anxious to reach the delectable morsel that waited beneath the fabric. "I need you," she whispered.

"Let me make love to you, Kate."

"Oh, Rich," she moaned. In a flash her brain came back on line, and she shot upright in the bed, breathing heavy. It all felt so real. "Rich?" She searched the darkness, hating the disappointment she felt when no one answered.

It was frightening that she could still feel his kisses on her skin. She rubbed her hand on her shoulder in an attempt to extinguish the sensation. Her heart ached for the separation it was going to experience soon. At the same time, she was so excited to see Jesse that just the thought of him caused her overactive heart to skip a beat.

Her feet shuffled their way to the bathroom where she faced the shame of loving two men. She splashed water on her face and patted it dry with a towel that, despite his being gone, smelled like Jesse. Guilt began to overwhelm her as she stared into the mirror, loathing the ungrateful wretch staring back.

Her phone rang and she jumped, trying to control her gasps for breath before answering. "Hi, Mom." Kate sounded disappointed.

"Are you okay, honey?"

"Yes, I'm, ah ... I'm just in a hurry to get to the airport."

"Okay, I'll be quick. Daddy and I just wanted to make sure you had a ride home."

"Yeah, Jesse said he'd be there. I haven't talked to him yet this morning, but I doubt plans have changed. I'll call you if they do."

"Please do." Her mother laughed nervously. "Well, call us when you're on the ground so we know you're okay. I can't wait to see you, Kate. Have a safe trip."

✕ ✕ ✕

The plane ride had been uneventful, but Kate's nerves were still on edge. She wondered if seeing Jesse again would wipe out all of her feelings for Rich. She hoped so. The baggage from her flight began its trip around the carousel. She stepped forward, searching for the bag with the bright pink ribbon on it—a trick she'd learned from her mother.

"Hello, beautiful," a deep sexy voice said near her ear.

Her heart jumped. "Jesse," she sighed.

Strong arms wrapped around her from behind and pulled her back into his chest. Her eyes drifted closed and she melted into his comfort. Although the feelings she had for Rich were still a soft flutter in her heart, Jesse's arms felt like ... home.

"How was your flight?"

Kate turned and leaned up on her tiptoes to press her lips to his. "I've missed you."

"KC, I have missed you so much." His arms tightened again and he lifted her into the air, spinning her around. "Let's grab your bag and get out of here." He set her carefully back on the ground and took her by the hand, leading her toward the luggage carousel. He stopped and started to laugh as an average, ordinary, run-of-the-mill, black suitcase came down the conveyer. On the handle was a florescent pink bow, one nearly the size of a cantaloupe. "I'm gonna guess that one's yours?"

"Hey, it's easy to spot." She shoved him playfully. "I guarantee there's not another one in this airport, much less on my same flight."

He shook his head and gathered the bag. They walked toward the car hand in hand. Jesse leaned down and kissed her forehead. "Can you do me a favor?" She nodded. "Call your parents and let them know that we're going to stay here in Phoenix tonight. I have a surprise for you."

"Um ... are you sure it's okay to be away from Tony?"

He perked an eyebrow and grinned. "I seem to remember that you owe me *something.* Did you forget?"

Her memory shifted to last night with the speed of an Indy driver; Jesse's special present hanging from the fingertips of another man, a man who had managed to capture a small piece of her heart, a man who had begged her to leave it home.

"Kate?" Jesse sounded disappointed. "It's okay if you forgot."

She shook her head, trying to rid her mind of anything Rich. "I didn't forget to *buy* it. I just can't remember whether or not it actually made it into the suitcase. I guess we'll both have to wait and see." Kate knew that the flimsy piece of satin was tucked safely in the suitcase. It was whether or not she'd wear it that was still up for debate.

"That's okay, KC." He grinned, and in a flash any sign of disappointment was gone. "The good stuff's underneath anyway."

Kate laughed and flipped open her phone to make the call to her mother, whose over-the-top level of excitement piqued Kate's curiosity. "Jesse." Kate tipped her head to examine his expression. "What do you have planned for this little rendezvous?"

"You mean besides showing you *exactly* how much I've missed you?" His eyes twinkled with desire. "And how much I've missed making love to you? I have a lot of time to make up for, KC."

× × ×

The hotel suite was beautiful. Jesse had gone all out, sparing no expense to make their reunion special. "A Jacuzzi?" Her fingers ran over the cold, black marble, dipping down into the steaming hot water inside. Someone had just filled it for them—recently.

"Why don't you go slip into something more comfortable, and I'll get things ready."

"What kind of *things*?" she asked, suspicious.

A grin filled his face, and he swatted at her bottom. "Just go change, KC."

Her laughter bubbled out into the room as she pulled the wheeled suitcase into the bathroom. It fit easily on the large counter. She unzipped the lid and flipped it open. At the bottom was the piece of fabric she was looking for.

After stripping out of her clothes, Kate lifted the negligee up by the straps. She held it up to herself and stared into the mirror. She slipped it over her head and examined her reflection. She had every right to wear it. Wanted to. Jesse had gone over the top to make their reunion perfect, the least she could do was wear a stupid little piece of black lace. Her hands flattened the fabric against her skin. She smiled, but even she wasn't convinced by it.

Images of Rich's handsome face marred by disappointment rushed into her head, his pleading to leave it home, to not be intimate with Jesse.

Her fingers wrapped around the hem and tugged the

lingerie over her head. She threw it back into the suitcase, carefully burying it on the very bottom.

With the fluffy white bathrobe around her, Kate opened the door and gasped. The only light was from tea light candles all over the room. Music played slightly louder than the quiet bubbling of the hot tub. Jesse was lying on the bed wearing only a pair of silk pajama bottoms. His feet were crossed at the ankles and he held a glass of champagne in each hand.

For a split second, Kate considered backing quietly into the bathroom and slipping into the little number he was so eagerly waiting for. But every time she saw it now, she thought of Rich. And Rich didn't belong here. She didn't want him here. This was for Jesse—and her.

He sat up, a smile on his face. "Hey." The disappointment was back. "I guess you forgot to pack it, huh?"

"I'm sorry. I'll make it up to you when we get home."

His tongue swiped over his lips. "Promise?"

"Um hum." She nodded and walked over to the bed.

He stood and offered her a glass. "At least you gave me something to unwrap. Come here."

She hated that Jesse was disappointed, hated that Rich had ruined the perfect surprise. She looked good in the little black nightie and Jesse would have loved peeling it off of her. The images of his hands removing the silky fabric sent a shot of erotic heat through her body. She closed her eyes, savoring all of it.

The glasses slid onto the table, and Jesse's hands were on her neck, his thumbs stroked her cheeks while his lips caressed her eager mouth. His tongue played an intoxicating game of cat and mouse. She moaned and felt him smile against her lips. He lifted her into his arms as his lips moved along her jaw to her ear. "I have missed you."

"Um hum," she sighed. This is exactly where she belonged.

They moved to the hot tub where Jesse placed a hand on each shoulder, just under the fluffy fabric. His fingers were warm against her skin, and her entire body reacted to his familiar touch. He leaned forward to kiss her shoulder, her neck, moving slowly down her body until the robe pooled at her feet. His kisses were eager yet so gentle.

Her head fell back as she reveled in everything that was Jesse; his touch, his scent, his rock hard body pressed against hers. Her hands moved up his sides, rediscovering every muscle, across his chest and back down his abs to the waistband of his silk pajama bottoms. She slipped her thumbs underneath.

He moaned. His head fell loose on his shoulders. "Kate ... you're killing me." He was breathless, his eyes onyx orbs of desire.

"Do you think you can avoid having intimacy?" Rich's pleas entered her head, and she froze.

"Kate?"

She stared into Jesse's eyes, smiled and let her hands continue their exploration. In one fluid motion, she dropped down, taking Jesse's pants with her. He gasped and she struggled to push Rich out of her head, unwilling to let thoughts of him ruin this for her. No matter what her feelings were for him, Jesse was where her heart was. Where her *home* was.

Jesse pulled her into his arms, lowering her into the hot tub, then pulled her into this lap. His lips roamed over every inch of her exposed flesh; loving her, caressing her, worshiping her.

She placed a hand on each side of Jesse's face and looked into his eyes, letting their souls connect. "I love you, Jesse." He responded with a kiss. She ran her tongue over his lip, tasting him. "It's good to be home."

✕ ✕ ✕

Having Kate back in his arms was even better than Jesse could have ever imagined. Her skin was so soft under his fingers as he stroked her back. She was draped across his chest with her hair fanned out on the pillow, lying unused behind her. Exactly the way things should be. He would gladly be her everything.

She'd been reluctant to stay the night, blaming it on his need to get back to Tony, and he couldn't shake the feeling that something might be wrong. That things might have changed between them. Some of his doubts had been removed when they'd made love again and again. Her gentle enthusiasm left him wanting more, needing more, but he couldn't shake the insecure jealousies that kept creeping into his thoughts.

Rich, his thoughts snarled.

She stirred under his touch. A sweet moan escaped her luscious lips as she wiggled against him. Her hand moved up his chest, investigating. Her eyes popped open in surprise and she blinked as she looked up at him; almost as if she were checking to make sure it was him. He couldn't help but wonder who she was expecting. *Rich?*

Her head jerked off his chest and she smiled. "Pinch me."

"You're not dreaming. We're finally together again."

She cuddled in closer to him, molding herself against his side. "I have missed waking up to you."

He kissed her forehead, trying to force any negative feelings out of his body. "Me, too."

Her face grew serious and she scooted up, taking his hand in hers. She lifted it to her lips and kissed it, then attempted a smile that was weak by any standard. Panic stabbed at his heart and nervous energy started in his toes, building as it made its way up his body. All the negativity came flooding back.

"You know I love you, right?"

He nodded, scrutinizing her expression. They'd made love all night, expressing their feelings for each another, but the way she was acting would make even the most secure man nervous. And he *was* secure, just suspicious of the asshole who was in love with his girlfriend.

"'Cause I do."

"What's going on, KC?"

Her eyes lifted to meet his. "Nothing's going on." She sounded defensive. "It's just that I want to make sure you understand just how much you mean to me."

"Kate, did something happen while I was away?" His mind had just turned in a one-way ticket to a scary place. Suspicion was a dangerous, relationship-ending emotion, and right now he had a truck load steaming through his bloodstream.

She took a deep breath and jumped as his phone started ringing from the nightstand. She paused and looked between him and the phone. He shook his head. He was not going to answer that call. Nobody was more important than Kate. And right now, it seemed she was trying to get something off her chest. He needed to hear what she had to say before he gave into his gut reaction and put his fist through a wall.

"Are you going to answer that?" Her eyes drifted to the phone again.

"No." He forced himself to watch her; the fidgeting fingers, the eyes that wouldn't look directly into his, the tense shoulders. Damn, this didn't feel right. "Please just tell me what the hell has you so nervous. You're freaking me out."

She smiled and it looked like a grimace. "Jesse, you really should answer that. It might be some news about your dad. Nothing matters except that I love you." She blinked and met his gaze. "Let's get you back to your dad," she offered as the phone finally stopped ringing.

"Kate, anything that has you this fidgety *does* matter."

She sat up, crossing her legs under the sheet that she tucked under her armpits. She took his hand and kissed it just like before. "Jesse Vasquez, there is one thing I'm sure of..." She paused and he dropped his eyes. "Look at me, Jesse." When he did, she continued, "The only thing I'm sure of right now is that I love you very much."

"I love you, too." He coughed and cleared his throat, stalling to actually voice the question running through his mind. "Kate," he croaked, "did something *happen*?"

Her eyes glistened. "It was nothing, really." His heart dropped to his toes, then shot up and threatened to fly right out of his mouth before settling back in his chest to thump wildly against his ribcage. "Someone kissed me at midnight," she mumbled.

His molars ground together and he jerked his hand

out of hers. "Who?"

"It doesn't matter."

Every muscle in his body tensed, already knowing the answer. But Jesse wanted to hear his name. He wanted her to admit that her lips had touched *his*. "Who?" The question came out as a low, breathy growl.

A tear rolled down her cheek. "Jesse, I love you. Only you."

He palmed his face, scrubbing to make sure this was reality. His feet swung around and he tested his weight on shaky legs before he stood. He stepped into his boxers and pulled them up to rest on his hips. Blood rushed through his veins and the whoosh echoed behind his ears. He paced on the side of the bed, trying to calm himself. No such luck. He whirled around to glare at her. "Dammit, Kate, I already know. Tell me... *Who* kissed you?"

"Rich," she whispered the name that sent his body into a deep freeze—and a boiling anger.

"That sonofa..." His fists clenched with the need to pound something—or rather someone. "Tongue?" He snarled the question he knew he didn't want an answer to, but anger prodded him to get *all* the details. Her hand flew up to her mouth as she gasped. "Come on, Kate, did he slip his tongue into that beautiful mouth of yours?"

"No," she whispered.

The water works started, and that pissed him off. Did it make him an ass that he enjoyed the panic in her voice? That there was real fear there, a fear of losing him? Jesse would never leave Kate. Never. Short of death, there was nothing that could keep them apart.

She crawled toward him. "It was just a kiss. He's only a friend."

He backed away from her. "Don't kid yourself, KC."

She blinked and tears continued to roll down her cheeks. "What ... what are you saying?"

A bitter laugh exploded into the room before he could stop it. "He's totally into you." Jesse looked into her eyes, hoping she wouldn't see the vulnerability and hurt in them. He dealt better with anger than he did with hurt. "At the party, he didn't even *try* to hide it. At one point, I thought he was going to rush out on to the dance floor and rip you out of my arms. So, yeah, I saw it. Hell, that crazy wife of his saw it too."

Panic registered on her face as a small gasp exited her mouth and Jesse wondered where her heart really belonged.

He rubbed at the sandpaper that would be shaved off as soon as he made it to the bathroom. "My only hope was that you hadn't seen it, that you didn't know, that you wouldn't care even if you did figure it out." He chuckled to himself at the irony of the situation. "I'm sure the fact that I was leaving to take care of my *dying* father gave him a hard-on."

"It's not like that," she defended the bastard. He rolled his eyes and gave a scoffing snort. "Jesse, you are my past, my present ... my future. I love *you*," she said the exact words Jessed wanted to hear, but they offered little comfort.

His eyes drifted over to where his suitcase sat on the floor. The pocket in the front held three months salary in the form of a promise. A promise he was now glad he hadn't asked her to make last night. "Come on, Kate, get dressed," an emotionless voice, he barely recognized as his, instructed her. "Let's get back to Flag. Do you even want to go there now?"

She just stared at him, which sparked his fury as if she'd tossed lighter fluid on an open flame.

The damn teeth grinding and fist clenching started again. "Say something, damn you. Don't think you can just drop this bomb on me and sit there and cry. Are you in love with him? Do you want to go home *to him*? That'd be one hell of a surprise for his *wife*." He took a deep breath to calm himself. *Yeah, like that's gonna work.* "Look, KC, just tell me what you want."

Her tear-filled eyes met his. "Jesse, I love *you*." She crawled out of the bed, and her pure, pale skin was so beautiful, it almost shimmered in the light. She came to stand in front of him, taking his hands and guiding them around her waist. She held them there for just a moment, until he linked his fingers together behind her back. "I know you're mad, and you have every right to be. I am *so* sorry." Her voice cracked as her sobbing began. She wrapped her arms around his waist and pressed her cheek to his chest. "I'm so very sorry, Jesse." Her tears rolled down his chest, disappearing into the band on his boxers.

He lifted her chin with his finger and gazed into her eyes. Looking. Searching. Finding love, sorrow ... and honesty. With anger still boiling just under the surface, he released his hold on her waist and took her cheeks in his palms, rubbing the tears away with his thumbs. "I love you, Kate. I will always love you."

A large tear began its descent down her cheek and he caught it on his finger. "I'm so sorry. I hate that you're so pissed at me."

"No, KC."

She raised a brow. "You're not pissed?" she asked skeptically.

"Oh, I'm pissed ... but not only at you. I knew the night of the party that Rich would try to win your heart while I was gone. I've been making myself sick thinking about what tactics he might try."

Now she was pissed. "Did you think I was that stupid?"

"Stupid, no. Naïve, yes. KC, you're too trusting." He wiped off her damp cheeks and kissed each one before brushing his lips against hers. He reached down to squeeze her bare bottom. "Now, get some clothes on so we can get home."

"I am sorry, Jesse."

There was still a lot that needed to be said, even more to leave unsaid. The diamond solitaire would have to wait until they could work through the uncertainty Rich had introduced into their happily ever after.

And Jesse would have it. He would stop at nothing to give Kate the fairytale ending.

After all, all is fair in love and war.

Fifteen

Rich. The piece of Kate's foolish heart that she'd opened to Rich begged her to reconsider. *He cares for you,* said the naïve, ever-trusting part of her brain. *Shut up!* She was grateful when the more rational Kate stepped in.

Jesse was right about Rich. He had pulled out all the stops, if only by pulling away to drive her crazy. Kate had no doubt that somewhere deep down Rich had feelings for her, real or imagined. Maybe it was just the fact that she was nice to him, that she didn't yell or belittle him.

She couldn't let this go on any longer, couldn't let her heart drift between two men. A decision had to be made.

The ride into Flagstaff was quiet, both of them lost in their thoughts. Jesse's eyes avoided hers as he concentrated a little too hard on the road he'd driven a thousand times. His right hand, the one that usually held her left one, was pinned under his thigh.

"Jesse?"

"Huh?" he grunted.

Her eyes stung with the tears she refused to let fall. She had created this situation. It was only fair that she deal with the aftermath caused by her actions. She reached for his hidden hand, pulling it free without too much resistance, and squeezed it.

He glanced down at where they were joined, but then his eyes returned to the road. As his fingers slowly wrapped around her hand, Kate allowed herself to ease out a sigh. "Jesse, are we going to be okay?"

The intensity of his onyx eyes was full of anger,

something she had never seen directed at her. Until today. He sucked in a breath through his teeth, nearly growling his response, "You tell me, KC. You're the one out there kissing other men." His eyes started to glisten.

She opened her mouth, but closed it again. There was nothing she could say that would make the intimate exchange with Rich okay. Jesse had a right to be angry. She wanted to say it was all Rich's fault, that she held none of the blame. The truth was, though, a piece of her did care very much for Rich. And no matter how hard she tried to deny it, the feelings were there—and very real.

"We're here, baby."

Baby, her thoughts sighed. Maybe things would be fine between them. Her fingers curled into the fabric of his shirt and she pulled him toward her until their lips were fused together. "I love you, Jesse."

"Kissing is as far as it went, right?" He stiffened, his hands forming white-knuckled fists on the steering wheel, but didn't look at her. "Now is the time to lay it all out on the table."

Guilt licked at her skin like fire. She couldn't tell him about the feelings she had for Rich. Feelings she would not let herself give in to. Feelings that *didn't* matter. *Couldn't* matter. She just hoped that when it came time to see Rich again, Kate would be able to keep her heart in check.

"Kate?" he whispered, his eyes boring holes through the windshield.

"Kissing is as far as it went," she assured him in a voice barely above a whisper.

"Jesse, Kate." Kate's mother's voice bubbled over with enthusiasm as she raced down the porch and across the lawn. "How was your trip?" She crushed her into a hug. "Let me look at you." She released her hold on Kate's body and took her hands, holding them out so she could examine her appearance. "How does it feel to be ... oh, um..." Her eyes were focused on Jesse over Kate's shoulder, silently asking him something.

Kate looked from her mother to Jesse and back again. They definitely had a secret she wasn't privy to.

"Kate. Jesse." Ken bounded down the steps, rushing to Jesse and shaking his hand. "Welcome to the..."

Jesse shook his head, his eyes communicating. "It's good to see you too, Ken. Anna."

"Well, hell," Ken mumbled under his breath. He tossed his arm over Jesse's shoulder and led him toward the trunk, their heads together in hushed whispers.

Anna pulled Kate by the hand into the house. "Are you and Jesse all right?"

"Yes." *No. Maybe. I hope.* "We're just fine." Kate stopped and turned to look at her mother, examining the much too innocent look on her face. "What's your deal?"

"My ... *deal?*" Anna chewed on her bottom lip, looking even guiltier with her innocent act. "I don't know what you're talking about." Kate rolled her eyes and stomped up toward her room with Anna hot on her heels.

"Kate, did anything *happen?* Is everything okay with you two?" Her questions were leading ones.

"Everything's fine, Mom," Kate huffed.

Anna walked over and tucked a piece of hair behind Kate's ear. "He's a great guy, Kate, and he loves you so much."

Kate narrowed her eyes at her mother, trying to ignore the sudden sting in them. "You think I don't know that?"

"Then why did you turn him down?" Anna tipped her head to the side.

Kate's brows pulled together. "Turn him down? What the hell are you talking about?"

"Oh, um ... ah..." Anna's hands rubbed together with nervous energy. "Never mind. I just thought..."

"Hey, KC, where do you want this stuff?" Jesse interrupted Anna's awkward stammering.

Kate pointed to the bed. "Just set it there and I'll get it unpacked."

"Well, we'll leave you kids alone." Ken took Anna by the hand and they closed the door.

Jesse walked over and slumped down into the chair by the window. He dropped his head into his hands and sighed.

With an armful of clothes, Kate shifted from the bed to the dresser and dumped them into the drawer. Her fingers brushed against the silky fabric that had been carefully stuffed under everything else.

"What's that?" Jesse's voice caused her to jump.

"What's what?" she asked, already knowing the answer.

His face and eyes were hard, skeptical. She smiled uncomfortably. He'd caught her in deception. How to smooth this over? Her fingers tangled in the straps of the negligee, which floated delicately in the air. "I guess I didn't forget it after all."

His dark eyes flashed, and he rushed over, taking her in his arms. "Lock the door." His anger was gone.

"Jesse, my parents."

His lips moved over the skin of her neck then a low groan of frustration rumbled as he paused. "I'll be damned if I don't respect the hell out of your dad. And since he wouldn't be exactly happy if I made love to you under his roof—" His lips brushed hers with a short, but very sweet kiss. "—I guess we'll just have to come up with a place for you to model that for me." He pulled back and pushed his fingers through his hair. "You're right, this isn't the place." Jesse paced the room, muttering as if he were trying to convince himself more than her. "We're grown-ups now. We shouldn't sneak around, having sex in a twin-sized bed while your parents think you're unpacking." His eyes contradicted the words that came out of his mouth. "I will get you in that sexy thing just long enough to get you out of it, but it won't be under either of our parents' roof."

All it took to get his forgiveness was the nightie. She smiled, relieved and nervous. "What do you have planned?"

"I don't know yet." The wheels were spinning in his mind. "Don't you worry about that. Just promise me that you won't lose it again." He closed the distance between them and pulled her into his embrace.

✕ ✕ ✕

One week.

Seven days of torture, of missing Rich. She'd forced herself to not call him—although she'd gotten as far as pressing all the buttons except 'send'—and part of her hoped he wouldn't live up to his promise of not calling her.

Seven days of comfort, of reconnecting with Jesse—walks through the park, hand in hand. Laughing, talking. Making plans for the future. No worries, no concerns, except for the man that wouldn't live to see Kate marry his son.

Jesse was talking in hushed whispers with the Home HealthCare nurse assigned to take care of Tony. She showed up every evening and stayed through the night. "Thanks, Nancy, I'll only be gone for a few hours, but if you need me..."

"I'll call you," she assured him. "Now, go, take that beautiful girlfriend of yours, and have a good time."

His eyes met Kate's and flashed as he held out his hand. "Ready, baby?"

"Um hum." She stood and wrapped her fingers around his outstretched hand. They walked outside and he got her settled in the car before going around to the driver's side and climbing in. "You okay with dinner and a movie?"

"Sure," she answered with a smile, "as long as I get to pick the movie. I don't really feel like an action flick."

He nodded. "Dinner first?"

"Yeah, I'm hungry.

His long fingers ran over his flat stomach. "Yeah, me, too."

The drive didn't take long and Jesse pulled into the restaurant—if you could call it that—and turned off the car. The place was a little hole-in-the-wall, but had some of the best Mexican food north of the border. Completely authentic. It was one of Kate's favorites and she was sure Jesse had brought her here for that reason.

They walked inside and the sound of Mariachi music echoed off the stucco'd walls and Saltillo tile floors. There were large pine poles that held the beams that ran across the ceiling in place.

Kate inhaled and filled her lungs with the smell of green chilis and onions. "I have missed this place."

Jesse laughed. "I stopped for take-out my first night home. I should have brought you here sooner."

Her stomach growled. "Yeah, you should have," she tossed over her shoulder as she stepped up to the counter and ordered a carne asada chimi with extra sour cream.

Jesse's hand came to rest on the small of her back as he stepped up next to her to place his order. The contact caused her to jump. "Sorry, I didn't mean to scare you," he whispered into her ear, then said to the girl behind the counter, "I'll have a beef quesadilla, a chicken burrito, a side of guacamole and a large Coke." He looked at Kate again. "What you drinkin', babe?"

"Dr. Pepper." As soon as the words left her mouth, she thought of the man she'd been trying to pry out of her thoughts and changed her mind. "Water. I'll just have water." She stepped away from Jesse, scanning the room for a table.

"Kate Callahan!" a male voice shouted.

Kate's eyes shot to a guy, clad in a police uniform. She narrowed her eyes at him. "Tom? Tom Phillips? Oh, my..." Her words were cut off as Tom scooped her up into a hug and swung her around.

"How the hell are you, KC? It's been nearly forever since I've seen you." He lowered her to the floor, careful to steady her before taking a step back. His finger stroked her cheek as he helped her remove a stray strand of hair.

She looked at Tom from his thinning brown hair, his eyes the color of cognac, his strong jaw that sported a goatee, down his trim, uniformed body, and finally to his black boot-covered feet. "Wow, you've changed since the days of detention," she stated, adding a wink to soften the insult.

He shrugged. "What can I say? I saw the light. But look at you..." He lifted her arms, a low growl rumbled in the back of his throat.

"Easy, Phillips."

Tom's gaze shot over Kate's shoulder, changing from

playful to irritated. "You always were a possessive prick, Vasquez. I was just telling your girl here how good she looks."

"And now you have." Jesse's arm moved around her waist, his hand formed a fist at her side. "Later Phillips," Jesse dismissed Tom.

Kate smiled apologetically and Tom shrugged. "It really was great seeing you, KC.

"It was great seeing you, too, Tom. I hope to see you around before I head home." When Jesse stiffened, she added, "Say hello to Maggie—and hug the kids for me, too."

"I will." Tom smiled at Kate, then shot an disapproving glare at Jesse. "Take care of yourself."

As Tom walked away, Kate whirled around on Jesse. "What the hell was that? He's happily married with three kids. Get a grip." She shook her head and stomped off in the direction of an empty table.

Jesse slid the tray onto the table and slunk down into the chair opposite her. She'd suddenly lost her appetite and that pissed her off. She loved this place, this dish, and didn't have the stomach to consume even one bite.

The phone in Kate's pocket started to ring. "Who is it?" Jesse asked as she fished it out and looked at the caller id.

"It's the station," she said, surprised. Jesse grunted his disapproval. "Excuse me." She stood, but he grabbed her arm and glanced toward her chair, effectively ordering her to sit back down. When she glared at him, he tightened his grip and tugged lightly. She sat, jerked away from him and answered, "Hello?"

"Kate."

"Dale? You're working late." She twisted sideways in her seat, bent her head away from Jesse, pretending like he wasn't desperately trying to overhear every word.

"Have you seen the news today?" Dale asked.

She suddenly felt like she was about to fail an important exam. "Um, sorry, I haven't. I've been..."

"It's okay, Kate. I'm sure you know who Senator Kelley is."

"Of course." He was a representative for the state she was currently sitting in.

"It seems he got caught doing inappropriate things with one of his interns," Dale explained.

"You're kidding." Kate was truly surprised by yet another example of a family man living two separate lives.

"No. So now to the reason I'm calling. Do you think you could spare a few days to cover the story for me?"

"You want me to fly to D.C.?"

"Actually, I was wondering if you could *drive* to Phoenix. The senator will be there tomorrow sometime to hold press conferences."

Her thoughts ran rampant, not even giving her mind time to digest one before moving on to the next. Dale was offering her a great professional opportunity. But...

Jesse had suspicion written all over his face as his fingers drummed irritably on the table. His other hand moved in a hurry-up motion before grabbing his fork to shovel more food into his mouth.

"Kate? Are you still there?" Dale asked.

"Um, yeah, sorry. I, uh..."

"I know you don't want to leave Jesse, and I'm willing to tack however many days you're in Phoenix onto the end of your trip. You just have to be back here in time for ratings."

"What about a photographer?" she hedged, not daring to hope and too scared to believe.

"I'll have one meet you at the Marriott in Phoenix. The reservations will be in your name, and I'll have the photog rent a car so there won't be any extra mileage on yours. Do we have a deal?" She'd never heard Dale excited, but now he sounded almost giddy.

"Okay, I'll leave in the morning." She sounded excited too. She was. An opportunity like this didn't land in your lap every day. This story could make her career.

"Thanks, Kate. I'll text you the address of the hotel. Have a safe drive and call me if you need anything."

She closed the phone and turned back to Jesse. He reached out and took her hand. "So, what was that about?" He was trying to keep the accusation and irritation out of the question, but it still bled into his tone.

Kate relayed what she'd been told about Senator Kelley and Dale's request for her to cover the story. "This is a fabulous opportunity, covering a political scandal like this could be Emmy material, not to mention how it would look on a resume tape."

Jesse shook his head. "You already agreed to go." It wasn't a question and he wasn't happy that he hadn't been consulted.

Kate knew she had to soothe Jesse, convince him, or it would be a battle. "I can come back for however many days I'm gone. Let's not fight about this, okay?" She took his hand and squeezed it. "I didn't feel like I could tell him no. He's been so good to me." She hadn't wanted to tell him no, but she'd keep that little tidbit to herself.

The heartbeat and a half of silence was agony. Then Jesse stood, lifted her to her feet, and pulled her into his tense chest. He kissed her head. "When do you leave?"

"Tomorrow. Can I borrow your dad's car?"

"Sure, my motorcycle is still in his garage. I'll ride that if I need to get anywhere."

"I think we should call it a night," Kate said, waiting for World War III to erupt.

"No movie?" he asked quietly.

"No, I've got some research to do before tomorrow."

"Okay," was his only response, making the drive back to her parents' house a quiet one. Kate could tell that Jesse wasn't completely comfortable with her going to Phoenix. "Who's your photographer going to be?" he whispered, trying to hide his disapproval.

"I don't know. Dale just said that he'd have someone meet me at the Marriott tomorrow afternoon," she explained in an attempt to make the whole thing as innocent as it was.

"That sonofabitch." Jesse's fist met his thigh.

She flinched. "Who, Dale?"

"No ... *Rich.*"

"What does Rich have to do with this?" Kate already knew the answer and had had the same suspicions.

Suspicions that both excited and frightened her.

"Come on, KC, you really don't think he's going to be the one at the hotel tomorrow?"

If Kate defended Rich, it would only cause a fight that she didn't want to have. If she pretended to disagree with Jesse, they'd both know she was lying. So, she went with the only response she could.

Silence.

He eased the car over to the curb in front of her house, and cut the engine. "Kate, he's already tasted you. That's something so delicious no man could ever resist it. I should know." He attempted a weak smile to soften the hard expression and harder words. "I don't trust that arrogant bastard, but...I trust you."

There were those words again. *I trust you.* Jesse's greatest form of manipulation. When he muttered them, Kate knew it was because he really didn't ... trust her. And she hated being manipulated.

"Good night, Jesse." She yanked the door handle and rushed inside without any further conversation.

Sixteen

"How's it going?" Nate pulled up a chair, his huge hand clapped Rich on the shoulder. "You look pretty pitiful, man," he noted as he sat down.

"I hate that she's with him." Rich's eyes glanced at his unringing cell phone for the millionth time today.

Nate clucked his tongue. "Dude, he *is* her boyfriend."

"Don't remind me," Rich groaned.

Nate laughed. "You probably don't want me to remind you that they're probably having sex right now."

A growl rumbled in Rich's chest. His hand flew out and slammed into one of Nate's pecs. "Don't take my thoughts there. I can't ... even consider that."

His lips pulled into a tight line. "Rich, you have got to get a grip. This girl isn't worth the misery you're subjecting yourself to. Besides, until you unload the current baggage you're carrying around, Kate's not even an option. Speaking of which, have you heard from Shea?"

Rich rolled his eyes. "Yeah, she's doing the whole 'I can't stand to be around you' bit again. She saw that I was working with Kate on New Year's and decided to move out for a few days."

"That sucks."

"Totally. This waiting for her to freak out on me is going to drive me to a rubber room and a straitjacket."

Nate let out a bark of laughter. "She'd just follow you there. That's exactly where *she* belongs. Damn, how did you ever get tied up with that woman?"

Rich's eyes narrowed into a glare. "She was normal enough when I married her."

"Normal?" Nate shrugged his shoulders. "I'll give you that she was hot." The cell phone tumbled in Rich's fingers, and he flipped it open to make sure it was on and had a signal. "Dude, why don't you just call Kate?"

"I promised that I wouldn't contact her." Rich shook his head, hating that he'd made such an absurd promise. "Dammit, I wish she'd at least text me to say she's okay."

"Maybe she's better than okay," Nate muttered as his brows rose suggestively.

Rich shot him with a warning glare, not trusting himself to make physical contact with his best friend, and tried not to let his thoughts entertain Nate's suggestions.

Nate held his hands up in surrender. "I'm just saying. How long have they been together?" Rich's shoulders lifted in a shrug. "A long time, huh. Be real, my man, you're not gonna be able to waltz in and expect her to throw away all that history."

"If she means that much to him, then why hasn't the prick claimed her by putting a ring on her finger?"

Nate shrugged. "How the hell am I supposed to know? Maybe…"

"Maybe he doesn't deserve her. Maybe she doesn't want him. Maybe she…"

"Rich," Nate interrupted. His head moved back and forth on his thick shoulders. "You're grasping at straws, my friend. Maybe he just hasn't asked her yet. You have no way of knowing the circumstances of why they're not married. Regardless, you can't do anything until you're not married too."

"I know that, Nate," Rich reminded him with a heavy dose of sarcasm. "I'm working on it. If only Shea would give in to her lunatic side."

"Hey, you two." Jordan sauntered in casually. "Dale would like to see the three of us in his office. Can you spare a few minutes?"

Nate and Rich glanced at each other then nodded in

unison. "What's going on?" Nate asked.

Jordan shook his head. "I'm not sure. He just called and asked if I could track you two down."

Rich's curiosity was certainly piqued as he followed his friends into the boss' office. Dale looked up. "Oh, good. Have a seat." After a few more clicks of his mouse, he cleared his throat. "I'm sure you know what happened with Senator Kelley." When the three of them nodded, he continued, "I'd like to have our own crew covering the story. So, which one of you two wants to go on a road trip?"

"I'll do it," Rich volunteered. If the choice really was only down to the two of them, there was no sense tearing Nate out of Roxy's warm bed and loving arms. A change of scenery would probably do him good. "When do you need me to leave?"

He picked up the phone and pressed some numbers. "Gladys, I need you to book a roundtrip ticket for Rich Spencer to Arizona."

Warning bells blared in his mind. A senator from Arizona had been caught doing inappropriate things in a men's room on Capitol Hill. Rich assumed that he'd be headed to the east coast. Instead it looked like he was heading to Arizona. To...

"Okay, Rich, your plane leaves tomorrow morning. Gladys has your itinerary."

"Um ... which reporter is going with me?"

"Oh, there won't be one going *with* you. She'll be meeting you in Phoenix."

"She, who?" he asked the question as his heart pounded with the answer, *Kate-Kate. Kate-Kate.*

"I spoke with Kate just a bit ago, and she will be meeting you at the Marriott in Phoenix tomorrow afternoon."

"Does she know who she's meeting?"

Dale looked dumbfounded for a moment before shaking it off. "Um, no. Would it make a difference if she did?"

Probably. "No." *I hope not.*

"Good. Now, get out of here. The next time I see you

will be on TV." He laughed. "Well, I guess I won't see *you*. Do me proud, Rich."

"Of course."

Nate's brows raised and his eyes asked the questions Rich knew would be voiced as soon as he could get away and dial his phone.

Sinking down in the driver's seat of the car, Rich debated on giving Kate fair warning. Offering her an out. But as he dialed the numbers, his thumb refused to hit that send button. His heart ached to be near her. His skin craved the feel of her. Every part of him missed her. Her silence scared the hell out of him. He had never felt so vulnerable in his entire life.

The phone buzzed in his hand. "Hey, Nate."

"You okay, man?"

"Yeah," he lied.

"Are you sure you don't want me to go? It might be more comfortable for her—for you."

"No!" Rich nearly shouted. "Sorry, I just…"

"I get it, buddy. I was just making sure you're not getting in over your head."

"Hell, I was in over my head months ago," Rich pointed out the obvious. "Dammit, my life sucks."

Nate chuckled. "Whatcha gonna do when Jesse shows up with her."

"Shut up!" He couldn't bring himself to think of that. If Jesse did show up, Rich was sure it wouldn't be pretty.

Nate's laughter continued as he tried to speak. "If you … need to talk … I'm here."

"Yeah, you sound really convincing, *friend*."

"Good luck, Rich." He was still laughing as the line went dead.

When Rich pulled into the drive at home, the house was dark. He went straight to his den and locked the door. He lay down on the couch, throwing an arm over his eyes. His thoughts drifted to Kate, and he didn't even attempt to persuade them to stop. How pitiful his life was. He had to create fantasies to keep himself from going crazy. What were the odds that she'd bring that nightie to wear for him?

A half laugh, more pathetic cough, came out of his body. *Yeah, right.* He slammed his fist into the pillow more times than necessary and rolled over, determined to get some sleep.

×××

Morning came with an annoying buzz of the alarm clock. Although he'd gotten little sleep, Rich was more than ready to hit the shower and start the day. It was almost as if every cell in his body knew exactly where he was going today.

He wrote a quick note to Shea and re-read it as he stuck it under a magnet on the fridge.

Went on an assignment.

Be back in a few days.

-Rich

That way if she came home, she couldn't accuse him of just running out on her. Further complications weren't what he needed right now.

Three pairs of jeans, a pair of slacks, boxers, socks, a half dozen shirts—two of which were the button-up kind she wears in his fantasies—and a pair of pajama bottoms were thrown into a duffel bag. After adding a Zip-lock filled with all his three-ounce toiletries, he was off to the airport, more than eager to get to his destination.

The plane couldn't land fast enough, and he was grateful he'd gone the "carry-on" route. Waiting for inept baggage handlers to take their time getting a suitcase to the carousel would have been more than he could have handled.

His skin buzzed when he eased the rental car into a parking space at the hotel. He grabbed his bags, walked through the revolving door, and stepped up to the reception desk.

"May I help you?" a cute brunette with big brown eyes asked.

"Rich Spencer from KHB to check in."

She typed for a second then smiled. "Here you are, Mr. Spencer." She handed him a keycard to room 1040.

"Thank you. Has ... um ... has Miss Callahan checked in?"

More typing. "Not yet."

Rich flashed a smile and picked up his bag, heading for the elevator with every intention of just being good and going up to his room. But he couldn't. Not when the woman he loved more than anything was going to walk through that door at any moment.

The bar looked really good right now.

"What can I get you?" asked a large man with muscled, tattooed forearms.

"Dr. Pepper, extra ice."

His brows pulled together as though he didn't understand the innocence of the drink. But being even remotely intoxicated when Kate arrived would not bode well. Rich needed to be in complete control. The glass made a light thud as it came to rest on the bar.

"Thanks," Rich muttered, not taking his eyes off the revolving door that was fed people into the hotel lobby.

With every tick of the clock, his pulse increased and his heart pounded harder in his chest. Anxiety and excitement intermingled in his bloodstream. If she didn't get here soon, something might just explode.

Then ... the glass doors started turning again. A woman with auburn hair pushed her way in, followed by a suitcase, and Rich's breath hitched. She looked out of sorts as she pushed her fingers through her hair. Rich watched the door continue spinning, praying that she was alone.

She was.

His body couldn't get out of the chair fast enough, knocking it backward. His hand flashed out and caught it before it hit the floor. He hurried to the lobby just in time to hear her pulse-stopping voice. "Hi, I'm Kate Callahan with KHB."

The girl pulled the same routine as she had with Rich. "Yes, Miss Callahan, here is your key. Room 1042."

"Thank you. Um ... has anyone else checked in from KHB yet?"

"Yes, he was here just a bit ago." Her cheeks tinged pink as she smiled. "He's really cute, too."

Kate winced and Rich cringed. "Do you remember his name?"

"Um..." Those brown eyes met his, and the check-in girl tipped her head toward him, smiling. "He's right over there."

Kate hesitated for a moment before turning around. Their eyes locked and her face remained emotionless. Rich raised his hand in a pathetic wave. "Hi." Refusing to give into the urge to rush over to her, to kiss her, Rich walked over slowly and tried to smile. "I've missed you."

She blinked, that same emotionless look on her face. "I've ... uh ... I'm tired and need to get to my room. Good night, Rich." Her eyes dropped to the floor and she pushed past him without another word.

Rich wanted to argue that it was 2:00 in the afternoon. Instead he opted for sulking behind her, fighting the need to hug her. Obviously that wasn't what she wanted. He stood in the corridor watching her, and as the large silver doors began to close Kate's eyes remained fixed on the floor beneath her feet.

Look at me, his thoughts pleaded. She didn't.

When the light went out above the elevator, indicating that she was on her way up to her room, his lungs released the breath he didn't realize he'd been holding. The rest of his body started to react to seeing her, being so close to her, and ultimately, being denied by her.

There was no doubt that Kate's time with Jesse had gone well. It seemed that her inner conflict was now over and that his chance had ended just as he feared it would. This was most certainly going to be an excruciating couple of days. And a painful rest of his life.

✕ ✕ ✕

Seeing Rich standing in the hotel lobby shouldn't have

come as a surprise. Kate was as certain as Jesse was that he'd be the one to volunteer for the assignment. Yet, seeing his handsome face again made her realize what a fool she'd been. He was married for heaven's sake. Married to a crazy woman, but married nonetheless.

Her inner dialog was screaming, causing her emotions to rage and her brain to ache. She was nervous to be alone—in a hotel—with Rich. She hated the sadness in his eyes, knowing she'd put it there. But mostly, she was angry—pissed, really—that she let him get to her.

She slid the key card into the lock and turned the knob when the green light flashed. A king-sized bed took up most of the room, with a small table and two chairs near the window. A television sat propped up on the dresser that was next to a door leading to an adjoining room. Her heart jumped at the thought that Rich might be sleeping on the other side of that door.

Just like Jesse, Kate knew that this reunion with Rich was going to be difficult, and she worried about how her heart would react. So far, so good. But unlike Jesse, she knew that Rich would respect her wishes, her decision to be with the only man for her.

Her phone rang, and she knew who would be checking on her—for the millionth time today. "Hi, Jesse."

"Hey, baby, everything okay?"

"Yeah, just got checked in, and I'm in my room, getting settled. The drive kinda wore me out, so I'm going to just hang out and watch some TV before turning in early." The truth was that the drive was only two hours and wasn't a big deal at all, but she didn't want to deal with Jesse's accusations *again*.

"So, um ... Is your room nice?"

"Yeah, it's okay. There's a king-sized bed that's gonna seem awfully lonely."

"Lonely is good, KC," he laughed, but she didn't miss the suggestive undertone.

In this case, you're probably right. At the little table, Kate turned on her laptop and logged on to the hotel's wifi connection. "So what are your plans for tonight?"

"I gave Nancy the night off."

"Oh.

"I thought I could save myself the money, since you're not here to keep me preoccupied."

"Sure, blame *me*."

His warm laugh flooded through the phone, making her smile. The laughter dwindled and he paused, his breath filling the silence. "Have you met... Who's your, um ... What time is the press conference in the morning?"

There was little doubt where his question was going before he shifted gears. If he was willing to avoid the subject of Rich, then she certainly was. "9:30. But I want to get there long before then, just in case something happens."

"Well, I'll let you go. Just remember that I love you."

"I love you, too."

"And Kate?"

"Yeah?"

"I trust you," he whispered just before the line went dead.

There was a soft knock on the door and she answered it not even wondering who would greet her. "Hi," Rich said with a forced smile. "I just wanted to check on you. Is everything okay?"

She tried to swallow her heart which had jumped into her throat. "Yes, everything's fine. I was just going to do some more research, so I'm ready for tomorrow."

He shifted his weight from one foot to the other and wrung his hands. "Can I come in?"

"I don't think that's the best idea, Rich." It was a horrible idea.

"Kate," he said as his eyes smoldered. "I'll be good. I just want to talk."

"*Talk*?"

He laughed, a real belly laugh. "Yes, Kate. Just talking ... unless you *want* more."

"Rich," she warned, starting to close the door.

His palm smacked against the wood. "I'm sorry. I

won't do that again. Please, I'd like to hear about how the last week went."

Kate sighed and resigned herself to the fact that this conversation would have to take place sooner or later. *May as well get it over with.* "Fine. Come in." She opened the door and closed it once he was in the room.

He walked over and sat down in the chair opposite her computer. "So I'm guessing things went well with Jesse then?"

Kate nodded, positioning herself in the chair across from him, with the table between them. "Things did go well with Jesse."

"Did you tell him...?"

"I told him what happened between us." Well, not quite everything, but any more than what had already been divulged would have only caused World War III.

If Rich was surprised that she'd told Jesse about the sweet intimate moments they'd shared, it didn't register on his face. "How'd he take it?" he asked quietly, his eyes focused on her.

Kate tipped her head and glared at him. "He wasn't exactly thrilled by the thought of you kissing me."

"You kissed me, too," he reminded her as his lips pulled into that trademark grin of his.

She shrugged, unable to deny that. She had been a willing participant. Her eyes avoided his full lips as he ran his tongue over his bottom lip. "Regardless, I'd avoid Jesse like the plague if I were you. Despite my part in what happened between us, he blames you."

A bark of laughter accompanied his huge smile. "Of course, he blames me. Hell, I'd blame me, too."

"Rich, I need to say this..." She paused and he nodded. "Please don't interrupt until I'm finished."

"Okay."

"I love Jesse." He winced, but didn't react further. "I won't deny that I had feelings for you, but I can't continue to let my heart bounce back and forth between two wonderful men. I had to make a choice." Behind the controlled façade, his eyes betrayed the hurt he felt and she loathed herself for causing it.

"Jesse's a lucky man," Rich whispered with a voice that cracked. "I won't make our working together more difficult than it already has been."

Guilt was an excruciating emotion. "Rich, working with you hasn't been ... difficult."

"You know what I mean. I won't tell you that I adore you, nor will I tell you that I wish things were different and that you were choosing me." His muscular chest lifted and fell with the deep breath he'd taken. "Well, goodnight, Kate." He stood and walked to the door. "What time do you want to leave in the morning?"

"I was thinking 8:00. Is that too early for you?"

"That'll be fine. I'll meet you in the lobby. You've got my cell number if you need anything."

The door opened and Rich stepped out into the hall. And then he was gone.

Her heart was relieved and pained at what had just transpired. She hated that she'd caused him any semblance of pain, but it was better that he got over his obsession with her now versus later when he came to his senses and *Kate* ended up being the one devastated by his nonexistent feelings. He would realize he didn't love her, that what he felt for her was nothing more than an attraction to a girl who was actually civil to him. But would she ever get over him?

The rest of the evening was spent trying not to think about Rich. She read all she could on the internet about what had happened with Senator Kelley, Googled the intern's name, and had gotten a pretty good idea of who he was.

Kate crawled onto the bed that was way too big for one person, grabbed the notebook from the nightstand, and jotted down some questions for tomorrow's press conference. Her eyes were heavy, and she finally gave into the exhaustion that was more emotional than physical, letting her lids drift closed.

Beep. Beep. Beep. The alarm went off at 6:30, and Kate rolled over, stretching. The room was still dark except for the red numbers on the nightstand. She flipped her phone open and dialed the familiar number.

"Mornin' baby." Jesse's voice was like gravel. He cleared his throat. "How's that big ol' lonely bed? Still lonely?"

"Yes," she groaned, choosing to ignore the insinuation. "I just wanted to call before I started my day. I'm not sure I'll have the chance to talk to you before tonight."

He cleared his throat. "That's okay, I'm not gonna be reachable today anyway."

"What are you doing?"

"I was going to spend the day with my motorcycle."

"Have fun. Call me tonight?"

"You know I will," he assured her before the line went dead.

After a quick shower, Kate blew her auburn hair dry, and applied a light coat of make-up. She dressed in a pants suit and headed toward the lobby. The elevator doors opened and Rich was waiting, just as he'd promised. "Ready?" he asked.

"I am, if you are."

He nodded. "Come on, the rental car's parked over here."

Kate followed him out into the parking lot, pausing while he unlocked the door. He held it while she slid into the passenger seat then closed her into the confined space. Rich was a gentleman to his marrow. He couldn't help it. It's just how he was, who he was.

They pulled up to the state capital, and the media frenzy had already started. Satellite trucks from all over the nation were parked out front. This could be tricky, but Kate liked a challenge. She looked at Rich. "Who's sending our signal back?"

"Dale bought some time with CNN's truck."

"Good. Let's go get our story."

"Go get 'em, girl." He winked and opened the door.

× × ×

Ten hours later Kate was tired and hungry, watching nothing in particular out the window on the way back to the hotel. Rich had been professional and quiet all day, which made her both irritated and grateful. Even now, she could feel the tension crackling in the air between them.

In numb continued silence they entered the hotel. "Would it be okay if I walked you to your room?" Rich asked quietly.

Her heart pounded at the thought of Rich anywhere near her room. She should have said no, should have told him to stay as far away from her room as the hotel would allow, but her mouth opened and, she said, "Sure, thanks." Minutes later, they stood at her door and Kate wondered where Rich's room was, but didn't want to ask. It was safer not to know.

He reached for her only to pull his hand back. "Goodnight, Kate. Sleep well," he said on a sigh.

"You, too." Kate walked inside and closed the door, grateful that he hadn't tried to do anything, because she wasn't sure she had the strength to stop him. Her cell phone rang. It was a number she didn't recognize, one with an 801 area code. "Hello?"

"Kate, it's Dale. I just wanted to thank you again for covering this story. The choice to have you do it was a good one. Great job today."

"Thanks."

"Tomorrow, instead of covering the press conferences, I'd like you and Rich to do a background piece. Find out what you can about Senator Kelley, his past, his family, whatever you can dig up...even if it turns out to be a fluffy, humanitarian piece. Okay?"

"Okay. I'll call you tomorrow and let you know which way it's going."

"Sounds good. Goodnight."

Kate sat the phone down on the nightstand and picked up the hotel's phone, dialing room service. A burger, fries, and a large Coke would be here in about a half hour. She would have just enough time to catch a shower and wash off the grit of a busy day.

Standing under the spray helped her to focus, to think. Even though Jesse had said he would be unreachable, and even though, she wouldn't have had a chance to talk to him even if he had called, she worried at the lack of contact. It was so unlike him.

After she toweled off and brushed out her hair, she walked out into the room and picked up her phone. If Jesse wouldn't call, then she'd just have to call him. His phone rang once then dumped her into his voicemail.

"I love you," was the only message she left.

Her body relaxed as she lay back on the bed with the soft pillow cradling her head. Kate was just about to drift into oblivion when there was a knock at the door. Her stomach grumbled in response. *Dinner.*

Kate would eat, then, if she hadn't heard from Jesse, she would call him again ... and again, until he picked up his damned phone.

Seventeen

Working with Kate today had been excruciating bliss. She was beautiful as always, and completely competent. Her ability to get to the heart of a story never ceased to amaze Rich.

He lay down on the bed and closed his eyes, refusing to think about her anymore, because thinking about her didn't do anything but drive the stake further into his heart. Knowing that she was in the next room, only two flimsy doors away, made things all the more tempting.

A knock on Kate's door caught his attention. His first thought was Shea. He tried to stamp it down, but his instincts forced him toward the door. It didn't matter that he was stepping out into the hall in only his boxers. Being buck naked wouldn't have stopped him from protecting Kate.

His heart pounded with fear and adrenaline, only to crash through the floor as Jesse pulled her into a hug, lifting her off the floor. Deep bass laughter resonated through the hallway. The white robe she wore pulled up to reveal a perfectly toned thigh. Her arms wrapped around his neck as he kissed her.

"I brought something you promised to model for me," he said in a husky whisper.

The door closed softly and Rich's hands sought the wall for support. He knew exactly what he'd brought for her to wear, and why he was here. Jesse had come to claim his prize; the priceless treasure that had been his all along, Kate's heart.

Rich walked into his room and could hear the

muffled sounds of the lovers talking, Kate laughing. Against his better judgment, he opened one of the two doors that adjoined their rooms. The action made their voices that much more audible, and he hated himself for the self-imposed torture.

Muffled laughter vibrated through the wall, and his body ached to be the one pleasuring her. His mind pictured her under him, covered only by a black negligee and his naked skin. His lips would kiss her shoulder as the fabric moved down her arm.

A masculine chuckle rumbled through the door.

Rich's stomach rolled and threatened to heave up the food he'd just put in it. He thought he would be okay with not having Kate as his. He thought he was okay with her loving another man. But actually having to witness that love, to hear it with his own ears was more than he could handle.

When another round of laughter filled the silence around him, Rich closed the door and locked it, vowing he would never open that door again. He prayed that Jesse wouldn't stay the entire time they covered the story. His already screwed up insides couldn't handle *days* of feeling like this.

In that moment Rich realized that he had two choices. One, he could lay there and endure the misery of waiting for the headboard to bang on the wall. Or two, he could go down to the bar and get a little liquid relief. At least if he was drunk off his ass, he wouldn't have to feel the excruciating reality.

Numb. Yep, that was definitely the option.

His eyes still stung as he shoved his body into some clothes. When he got on the elevator and checked his appearance in the silver doors, he was grateful that he didn't look as bad as he felt. At least his clothes matched. But it was hard to screw up jeans and a t-shirt.

The hotel's club was nearly empty as he stepped inside. Instead of sitting at one of the tables, Rich opted for a place at the bar with close proximity to the guy in control of the alcohol.

"What can I get you?" asked the same bartender

that had served him earlier.

"Jack Daniels. A lot of it." The glass hit the surface of the wood bar and amber liquid was poured into it. Rich lifted it to his lips, downed the contents, and sat the glass back on the counter. "Give me another one."

"You're throwing that stuff back like you got girl troubles," observed the bartender, filling the glass again.

"That obvious, huh?"

"Is it the one you were waiting for yesterday?"

Kate's smiling face entered Rich's thoughts. He downed another swig, trying to rid his mind of the image. "No offense, but I really don't want to talk about it."

"Hey, no problem, man." He made a quick swipe with his rag. "Just let me know if you need anything else." And he walked over to help a guy further down the bar.

Rich nodded then slowly nursed the drink in his hand. His system wanted to pound them, to eliminate the pain quicker, but he forced himself to drink enough to be numb and still be able to get himself back to his room under his own power.

One hour passed much the same as the last. The only excitement was the two girls who came in and offered him a three-way. Nate would be so disappointed that Rich didn't traipse right up to room 935 and get it on with total strangers...no strings attached. Except Rich knew that if he had, regret would have been the only thing he felt in the morning. Especially if Kate...

Stop that thought right there, chief! His head dropped into his hands, his fingers plowing through the front strands of his hair.

"Hey, my friend," the bartender said softly from across the counter. "Last call."

Rich looked up. "No more for me, thanks."

He took the glass. "I'm afraid you're not going to be able to hide out in here anymore."

Rich laughed bitterly. "Fair enough."

After paying his tab and giving his new BFF a hefty tip, Rich headed out into the lobby. The elevator doors opened with a soft ding and a man Rich recognized strolled off. His dark hair was disheveled and the smile on his face spread from one side to the other. Jesse walked like a man on a mission, but it confused Rich as to why he looked so happy to be *leaving* Kate.

Rich hoped Jesse would just keep right on walking and not go the route of gloating. The exact moment of recognition was obvious. Jesse's face melted from elation to hatred in less than a second. He stopped dead in his tracks and glowered at Rich. Rich watched the battle between the little angel and devil on Jesse's broad shoulders as he debated what to do about the fact that they were finally face to face. Rich had no doubt that Jesse knew exactly what Rich had tried to do with the woman he loves. The woman *they* love.

Jesse's jaw worked violently. His teeth audibly ground against each other. His eyes were full of loathing. His chest strained against the t-shirt he wore as he took breath after deep breath, then he closed the distance between them in three strides.

Rich's lungs filled with a cleansing breath, and he braced himself for the coming confrontation. Jesse stood in front of Rich, seething. He opened his mouth to speak only to close it again, not that Rich blamed him. Not at all. If the roles were reversed Rich'd be pissed too.

"I know exactly what you're trying to do, Rich," he growled.

"Do you?" Rich didn't mean to provoke the gloating bastard, but controlling his tongue wasn't something his brain could handle at the moment.

"You can't have her." Jesse cracked his knuckles. "The game's over. She's made her choice ... and you're looking at him. I *will* propose to her, soon. We will be married, and *I* will give her the happily ever after that I've always promised her."

Rich's eyes began to sting, and he hated that he was showing any kind of weakness to this man, his enemy, as they stood only inches apart. Rich stepped forward and Jesse braced himself for the receiving end of a punch. Instead, Rich offered his hand. "You're right, Jesse. You've won." His hand still stuck out awkwardly in the air, and he dropped it back to his side. "Heaven help me, I would love for things to be different ... for Kate to love me, to want me. If she were to change her mind, I would take her away from you in a heartbeat." He laughed bitterly. "Hell, it wouldn't even take that long."

Jesse tipped his head and scrutinized Rich through narrowed eyes.

"Not that I've given you any reason to trust me, but I give you my word that I won't push her anymore. I can't hurt her like that." Rich laughed bitterly. "Besides my ego can only handle so much rejection."

"I don't want to have this conversation again," Jesse growled.

"Yeah, me neither."

The corners of his dark eyes crinkled as an arrogant smile spread to his lips. "I still don't trust you, Rich. Never will."

"If I were you, I wouldn't trust me either."

"Good to know. If you'll excuse me." The man who held the heart of the woman Rich loved walked out through the revolving door of the hotel, and Rich considered going back up to his room until Jesse walked back into the lobby with an overnight bag firmly gripped in his hand.

Rich lifted his chin slightly in acknowledgement as he walked by.

Jesse mirrored the action. "Good night, Rich." His tall, muscular body disappeared back into the elevators and as he went up, Rich's stomach sunk through the floor.

There was now another set of options. He could stay here, go up to his room and eavesdrop on the lovemaking session that involved the woman of his dreams and another man. Or...

Rich walked through the revolving door and inhaled deeply. His eyes searched the street, and two-hundred yards to his left on the opposing side, was a big red sign. *Vacancy.*

× × ×

The stench of cigarette and other various kinds of smoke assaulted Rich's lungs as he opened the door to the roach motel. A meth-skinny man with a bald head on top and greasy, wispy locks down his back greeted Rich with a single-toothed grin. His unpatched eye was bloodshot and could barely focus behind the caged check-in hole.

"How long?" he slurred.

"Excuse me?" Rich asked, confused.

"How many hours will you be needing the room?"

"Uh ... what's the minimum?" He couldn't avoid asking the question simply out of curiosity.

"Thirty minutes."

"Oh. Well, I'll need it a little longer." Rich checked his watch, 1:30. "Five hours."

Slimey glanced at the X'd out VISA symbol. "Do you prefer to use cash ... or ah, cash?"

Pulling out his wallet, Rich said, "I think I'll go with cash. How much?"

"Our rate is $25 an hour," the guy said without even flinching. Surprise slapped Rich, but it was nothing compared to what was added next. "And, since you don't have a reservation, I'll have to charge you double."

"You want fifty dollars an hour?" Rich was stunned that his voice contained any semblance of control.

Slimey nodded. "One room for five hours—" His forehead crinkled toward his patch as he desperately tried to calculate five times five. "That'll be $197.67, please."

Rich stared at the man through the bars, completely dumbfounded. "Um, that's not exactly the same figure I came up with."

The man snorted and rolled his eye. "Well, duh. We have to charge something for cleaning."

"Of course," Rich agreed with a nod.

Slimey handed Rich a key that dangled from a penis keychain. "Room 369."

"369?"

"It's either that or 4569."

"There are only two floors," Rich pointed out.

Years of smoking were evident in his barking hack

of a laugh. "All our rooms end with sixty-nine." The three extra long eyebrows nearly reached the hairline that didn't exist as he perked the entire caterpillar. "Too bad you're alone."

"Yeah," Rich scoffed. It *was* too bad that he was alone, but the only girl he wanted to be with was otherwise preoccupied. This hellhole was better than trying to sleep, knowing what was going on in the next room.

The long corridor went on forever, it seemed. Moans and erotic screams echoed down the hallway. Only three doors in, Rich came to the room that would be his sanctuary for the next five hours. A warm shower and a soft bed would be perfect.

Rich slid the key into the lock and opened the door, flipping the switch. Nothing happened. After moving it up and down a few more times, there was still no illumination in the room. Thanks to the light from the hallway, he stumbled over to the bedside lamp. His fingers twisted the little screw that at one point had a knob, and a dank glow flicked on.

Something brown darted across the center of the room.

A scream broke through the silence and Rich whipped around, searching for the little girl who was shrieking. His eyes met a sad, bloodshot pair that made his tear ducts burn. "You, wuss," Rich told his reflection. "It's just a stupid little mouse."

The furry critter was no bigger than a cotton ball as it scurried over the various stains on the carpet to disappear under the bed.

Rich knelt down and pinched the bottom edge of the comforter between his fingers, lifting it slowly. The thing staring back at him was even more disturbing than what he was searching for. A condom. An involuntary shudder raced up his spine. The mouse was nowhere to be seen, but the still oozing piece of latex kicked his gag reflex into gear.

His fist wrapped around the comforter, yanking the bedding back. Rich leaned in close, hoping not to find what he was fairly certain he would. There they were;

short, black curlies resting on yet another patch of stains.

The strong urge to wash his hands—in bleach—hit him with a vengeance and he kicked the door closed and headed in the direction of the tiny bathroom. He reached through the curtain to turn on the shower, only to find that it was already occupied—by a nasty-ass plunger.

A shower would *not* be on the agenda for tonight.

His bladder was begging for relief, so he unleashed the fury of his kidneys on the porcelain bowl. The silver handle moved down beneath the weight of his fingers, but there was no movement of the water.

"Well, that explains the plunger," he grumbled, not even bothering to wash his hands. Whatever germs were on them were probably better than what might be contracted from the sink.

Someone knocked on the flimsy door causing him to jump. As he stared at the light seeping in from three of the four sides, he realized that nobody knew where he was. Which on second thought, probably wasn't the brightest idea. What if he never made it out of this rat-infested hellhole?

"Hello?" he called.

"Housekeeping," came the response.

So, that was a good thing.

The woman with unnaturally blonde hair was dressed in a short skirt and miniature t-shirt. She smiled, and strolled past him, her eyes taking in the room. "I'm sorry, I'm late."

"It's okay." It wasn't okay, but what was he supposed to say? "Um ... my biggest concern is the bathroom."

"I'll get right on it, daddy." She winked through false eyelashes that were falling off then closed the door to the bathroom.

The fact that she had no cleaning products should have been a huge red flag. But it wasn't until the door opened, and she stood there with nothing on but tasseled pasties on really large, really saggy breasts and an enormous black thong covering her lower half, that Rich realized she wasn't a maid.

He gulped as she held up a condom collection. "Sorry, I'm out of blue," she informed him.

"Oh, but I really wanted blue. Had my heart set on it. I guess we'll just have to…"

"I can get one." Her eyes moved up and down his body with a hunger that made him feel dirty just having that much of her touch him.

"That's okay."

"No, I'll be right back." She headed toward the door.

"Wait," he called.

She turned and smiled. "Did you change your mind?"

He shook his head so hard his vision swam. "No, but don't you think you should get dressed?"

A high-pitched giggle filled the room. "Oh, yeah, that would probably be a good idea."

Ya think? He nodded.

As soon as she was in the hall, Rich slammed the door and locked all three deadbolts, then slid the chain into place. That woman was not getting back into this room, at least not while he was still occupying it.

The little mouse scampered from under the bed to seek refuge under the dresser.

It looked like sleep wasn't going to be on the schedule tonight either. He took a porn magazine off the table and rolled it into a weapon, poising himself in the chair. If the little furry critter or any of his friends tried to come near him, he'd be ready for them.

Another knock. "Who is it?"

"Housekeeping."

He gulped. "Um, yeah, I've changed my mind. The room's fine."

"Oh. Well, can't you give me something for, um…"

"You didn't do anything," he reminded her.

Her sobs carried through the door. "If I go back empty handed, then Marco will…"

"Okay, here." He shoved the last of his cash through the crack in the door.

"Ten dollars?" She sounded offended.

"Sorry, it's all I have. Tell Marco that I was completely satisfied."

"Ten dollars?" Completely offended.

"You didn't do anything!" Exasperation oozed through his words.

There was silence on the other side. Hopefully, she'd gone to split the ten dollars with Marco, who would probably be the next person to beat on his door. Instead of a pounding on the door, his pocket was vibrating. Shea. He sent it to voicemail. Two seconds later it vibrated again.

"Ugh. What?" He snapped into the phone. "I'm really not in the mood for your crap right now."

She sniffed in classic Shea style, only to pull the bipolar act as soon as she spoke again. "I saw that you were with Kate. I'm going to kick her skinny ass."

"Well, you'd have to get through Jesse," he said bitterly. "He paid her a little visit and they're together right now."

"Oh," she purred. "Maybe I'll pay you a little visit too."

Yeah, that's totally what he needed. "I'll be home in a few days."

"Fine." She sighed. "Will you at least tell me where you are?"

He hesitated, but ultimately said, "I'm staying at the Marriott near the Capital."

Banging doors, men shouting, and women screaming erupted outside in the hallway.

"Um, I gotta go." Rich didn't even wait for Shea to reply before shutting the phone.

The door shook on the hinges as something hit against it, hard. With the second slam, the door fell at his feet. He jumped up, held the makeshift weapon over his head, and prepared himself to fight.

"Freeze! Police!"

"Oh, shit." The magazine hit the floor with a thud as his hands shot up in surrender. "There's been a misunderstanding. I'm ah, I'm.... Oh, shit."

The three officers in complete tactical gear stared at him, grinning. The closest officer laughed. "I'll take this one." The other two nodded and disappeared down the hall, yelling as they busted their way into other rooms that really were full of criminals.

Officer Friendly's face smoothed over and he glared at Rich. "So what's your excuse, Mr. Handnmypocket?"

"Look, it's not what it looks like."

He smirked and raised a brow. "And I've never heard that one before."

Rich ran his fingers through his hair and groaned. His little furry friend picked that exact moment to rush out from under the dresser and stop just in front of the officer. The large man let out a squeal, shooting off his Taser, which the mouse dodged then raced under the bed again.

The officer's expression was mortified. "That's our little secret."

"Sure thing, *if...*"

He raised his brows. "You're not exactly in the best position to be asking for favors."

"All I ask is that you let me explain why I'm here ... and what I've been through. I've had a helluva couple hours."

"Okay, sit tight for a bit. I have to get another officer as a witness if you're gonna make a statement. Don't move. If I catch you out of this room, I'll arrest your ass."

"Fine." Rich slumped back in the chair. It's not like he had anywhere else to be tonight. "Oh, and by the way, the mouse isn't the scariest thing under that bed."

The officer smirked then walked out.

Rich tried to relax as much as his adrenaline would allow. But, as people in various stages of undress were escorted down the hall, his heart continued to hammer in his chest. As the ten dollar maid came by with Officer Scaredofmice, she pointed and screamed, "Why's he not in cuffs? He paid me. He's a cheapskate, but he gave me cash."

The officer scowled at Rich and handed Miss Saggytitties off, coming to stand in front of him. The dark eyes were hard, his expression much the same.

"Let me explain," Rich stammered, realizing that any leniency he might have gotten was about to go the way of the wind.

"Good idea." The officer crossed his arms over his chest, his badge catching the dim light. His skeptical expression made Rich worry. "Why don't you start with your name."

"Okay." A deep breath filled his lungs, then he let it out and began the explanation in a rush of panicked words. "I'm Rich Spencer from KHB in Salt Lake. There's this girl, Kate. She's the reporter that is..."

"Um hum." He wasn't impressed with the story so far.

The rush continued. "She beautiful, talented, amazing, caring." Rich sighed. "Did I mention she's beautiful?"

The officer nodded. "No offense, but I don't care about this Kate person. How the hell did you end up in this dive?"

"I'm getting to that." Another deep breath, and then diarrhea of the mouth hit. Kate. Jesse. The bar, where he drank until they kicked him out. The confrontation in the lobby and...

The officer held up his hand. "Let me finish the story for you." His lips pulled into a thin, understanding line. "You came here because they're not making love in the next room."

Rich laughed without humor. "Pretty much. Believe me, I would *never* come here for any other reason. I didn't even dare wash my hands after I took a leak. That bathroom's disgusting."

He chuckled and glanced over his shoulder. "So explain one more thing to me."

"Anything to get me the hell out of here."

"Did you pay that ... ah ... woman?"

The diarrhea kicked in again. "She said she was housekeeping. I let her in, hoping she'd clean the damned bathroom. Instead, she came out nearly naked." Rich shuddered and the officer laughed. "I got her out of the room and locked the door. When she came back, I gave her ten dollars to make her go away. Look, man, I cover stories like this all the time, and I sure as hell don't want this face on the news. I don't want *anybody* to know the horrors I've experienced tonight. I'm going to try to pretend they never happened. Please, can't we..."

Officer Friendly smiled. "I have some paperwork to do 'cause technically you were caught in the sting. Let me grab the captain, and we'll take your statement. We'll probably have to issue you a warning." He stepped toward the door, but stopped and looked back at him. "Hey man, any girl who would cause you to endure all this—" His hand waved over exhibit A. "—probably isn't worth the trouble."

Eighteen

"Mmm," Kate moaned on an exhale.

The hard, warm pillow beneath her head moved and a growl sounded just before two arms embraced her. "Damn, it's so good to have you in my arms. I've missed waking up to you."

She nestled into him. "You woke up to me a little over a week ago."

"One night without you in my bed is one too many." His breath tickled the skin on her neck. "What time is it?"

She shifted to see the glowing red numbers on the nightstand. "6:30."

"What time are you supposed to meet...Rich?" He sneered the name through gritted teeth. His whole body tensed and fists replaced his hands at her back. "I just don't trust ... *him*. I hate that he's staying while I have to go home." He sat up, leaving her lying on the bed.

"He promised to remain professional," she said, moving her hand over the tense muscles of his back in a futile attempt to ease his worry.

Jesse wasn't buying what she was selling. His dark eyes flashed with animosity. "Dammit, Kate. He wants you so bad, I can almost taste it."

This situation had to be difficult for Jesse. Kate understood that, but his jealousy was irritating, and it hadn't been the only wedge between them. There had been physical contact between Rich and her, contact she couldn't ignore nor deny.

"I'm just gonna shower, then I'll hit the road. I'm sure you have a busy day today." He stomped toward the bathroom, grabbed his bag on the way, then slammed the door.

"Don't be that way," she mumbled to the empty room.

There was a dynamic difference between the two sides of the man who held a piece of her heart. Jesse was sweet and kind, handsome and loving, and jealous. Brutally jealous. And when he was jealous, he was mean. Over the years, he had said horrible, accusatory things that had Kate groveling for his forgiveness, even though she'd done nothing wrong.

When he came out of the bathroom, he was still fuming. His dark eyes were nearly black as they met hers for only a moment. "Your turn," he snapped, setting his bag on the dresser.

She gathered her things and retreated, closing herself in the tiled room. Thirty minutes later, her fingers curled around the doorknob. She wasn't sure whether or not Jesse would still be in the room, or what kind of mood he would be in. She took a deep breath and prepared for the worst.

He looked up from where he was seated at the end of the bed and used the remote control to turn off the TV. His hard expression softened, a smile curving his full lips. "I love that dress, KC."

"Thanks," she said, forcing a smile.

"Turn around." He made the little circle motion with his index finger and walked toward her.

She obeyed and his fingers slid under the fabric. His breath met the small of her back and it arched in response. "Jesse," she warned.

"Hmmm?" The zipper moved up slowly, pausing as his lips met her skin. He chuckled, and the fabric tightened around her waist. He kissed the space between her shoulder blades, then the zipper sealed it in. When the zipper was at the top, Jesse nuzzled her neck.

"Jesse, I have to get down to the lobby."

"To *him*." He spun her around and roughly grabbed her by the arms. He added pressure, and she wondered if there would be a bruise. "Why don't you just say it the way it really is, KC. You can't wait to get down to him."

"That's not fair." She jerked out of his hold. "I hate when you get like this."

"*You* hate it?" he yelled. "Imagine how *I* feel, Kate, always worried about the way other men look at you."

"Just go, Jesse. Just get the hell out."

He stiffened. "What did you just say?"

"You heard me," she whispered.

"Does this have to do with him?"

"I'm not discussing this anymore. You're being irrational..."

"This isn't over, KC. I will not lose you.

"I didn't say you were going to lose me. I only said that I have a job to do, and my *co-worker* is waiting for me in the lobby."

"Fine. I'll walk you down, and we can say our goodbyes in the lobby."

Kate wasn't stupid. With Jesse's hand gripped firmly around hers, they walked toward the revolving door. Tears burned her eyes, and her lids blinked rapidly in a pathetic attempt to keep her emotions in check. To people watching them, it would appear that they were lovers saying goodbye, but that was not the reason she was going to cry.

Jesse pulled her into an embrace, his chin moved against the top of her head. "Have a good couple days, and I'll see you when you get home." He placed a hand on each side of her face and kissed her, soft at first then more intense. "Bye, KC. I love you."

It didn't matter that she was glaring at him, he was looking at something—someone—behind her. One more chaste kiss, and Jesse disappeared through the revolving door. Angry tears made their way down her cheeks, and she wiped them away quickly as someone cleared his throat behind her. Another swipe across her cheeks, and she turned around to find Rich holding a tissue.

"I thought you might need this." He smiled. "Where we headed?"

Despite the clean clothes and always dashing I-meant-for-my-hair-to-look-this-way hair, Rich looked like death warmed over. Dark circles stained the skin under his bloodshot eyes, and a tired expression marred his handsome face.

"Are you okay, Rich?"

He sighed, then lied, "Yep."

If he didn't want to talk about it, then there was no need to pry. "You up for a little road trip?" He nodded and she continued, "Senator Kelley was born and raised in Casa Grande. I thought we could poke around a bit, see what we can come up with."

Rich's exhaustion disappeared as his eyes twinkled. A smile flirted with his lips. "Maybe we can find his kindergarten teacher." He tried to choke back a laugh.

"Ha, ha. You are just so funny." Her response only made him laugh harder. "I was hoping for his Sunday School teacher." The warm, roar of his laughter caused the giggles she'd been suppressing to come bubbling out.

✕ ✕ ✕

They'd spent the day in Casa Grande, sent their piece back to the station and fronted the live intro and tag. Rich was beyond exhausted as they entered the lobby of their hotel. His body would be asleep before his head hit the pillow.

The ride up in the elevator was quiet. His brain was already beginning to shut down. When the ding sounded for their floor, Rich followed Kate to her room unsure of how his body was even still moving. More than once today, he'd nearly fallen asleep. It was a good thing when Kate volunteered to drive home.

She stepped up to her door, slid in the key and opened it, only to pull it closed with a slam. "So, um, I guess this is good night." Her eyes looked panicked as she tried to get rid of him.

"Kate, what's wrong?"

Her cheeks tinged pink in the dim light of the hallway and her knuckles had turned white on the handle. "Um, nothing's wrong. Everything's just fine."

Rich's head tipped to the side and he felt a skeptical brow rise. "And I don't believe you, why?"

"Fine," she sighed, stepping aside while pushing the door open. On the little table was a bouquet of flowers, next to the infamous little black nightie draped over a chair. Rich supposed there was a note too, declaring Jesse's undying love.

Nausea threatened as his stomach rolled. "Looks like Jesse left a thank you for last night."

She turned on him, her eyes narrowed with accusation. "You didn't look surprised that he was here."

Rich was too tired to make up any excuses. "Yeah, I kind of heard him arrive."

Her delicate brows pulled together. "*Heard* him arrive? Where's your room?" As she asked the question, her eyes shot over to the adjoining door as if she already knew the answer.

"Yep," he said simply.

It was a good thing that pink looked good on her because she was sporting it again. "You didn't *hear* anything else did you?" With a great deal of effort, he was able to swallow the knot in his throat. His silence spoke volumes and she groaned. "I'm so sorry, Rich."

"Hey, I'm a big boy."

"Regardless, to hear us mak-..."

His hand flashed out and covered her mouth. "Please don't. It's bad enough I didn't sleep last night."

"You didn't sleep? We were *that* loud?"

"Ugh." His head felt heavy as it moved back and forth on his shoulders. "No, I left. I didn't sleep because I didn't lie down for a single hour last night. Exhaustion is about to set in. Goodnight, Kate."

Her eyes were wide as she stared at him. Just before he pulled the door closed, she whispered, "Goodnight, Rich."

He made his way into his room. And after taking a quick shower, he sat down on the bed, working up the energy to sift through his suitcase for some clothes. *I'll just rest for a second,* he told himself.

Every cell relaxed as his body made contact with the bed. Sleeping in a towel was going to....

His eyes popped open. *Was that knocking?* There was the sound again. He jerked upright and looked toward the door that went out into the hall. His feet met the floor and shuffled along while his fists prepared to pummel the fool who chose to wake him from the first shut-eye he'd had in over a day.

Before he could reach the door though, another knock caused his head to twist in the opposite direction. The rapping came from the door that adjoined his room with Kate's. The same door he'd vowed he would never open again.

"Well, hell," he grumbled. *Sucker!* His fingers plowed through his still damp hair then reached for the knob. The pounding of his heart echoed the rhythm of her knuckles against the door. He whipped it open. "Kate, what's wrong? Are you okay?" His voice sounded frantic.

"Yeah, um..." Her eyes drifted from his face, down his chest... "Oh," Kate gasped as she blushed. "I should probably..."

It was that moment that Rich realized there was only a fluffy white towel, low on his hips, between him and Kate. His body wanted her, desperately. His sleep soggy brain tried ineptly to stomp down the hunger. With hands that resembled fig leaves, he cleared his throat. "Did you need something?"

She chuckled softly, and the pink was back in her cheeks. "Sorry to bother you, Rich."

He took a deep breath. His heart was beating so hard, he was sure she could hear it. "No bother." He tried to smile, but his face was too tired.

Her beautiful eyes twinkled. Over her shoulder, as if mocking him, was the reminder of Jesse's visit. His thoughts took him to hell and back as they replayed the memory of Jesse saying goodbye to Kate this morning—and her tears at his departure.

"Rich?"

"Huh?" He shook off the horrible thoughts and cursed his lack of concentration. "Oh, sorry. What were you asking?"

Another round of pink cheeks. "I hate to ask you this."

"Kate, you know there isn't anything I wouldn't do for you." *Come on in. We can make love right now. Forget that I'm half asleep already. I'll sleep better with you in my arms, anyway.*

She turned and stepped back into her room, but left the door open.

He secured the towel, tucking the corner against his hip. *Would it be so bad if it fell off?* his thoughts chuckled. "What can I do to help you?" *Sleep in here?*

"It's just that I've tried to..." Her hands moved up and around her shoulders like she was trying out for a contortionist act. "It's stuck." Her breathing was heavy through grunts and groans before she finally sighed and her arms fell limply to her sides. "Will you please help with my zipper?"

"Sure, come here."

She stood in front of him, the zipper down the six inches she could manage. Her slender fingers wrapped around her auburn locks and pulled them to the side, revealing even more of her elegant neck.

The urge to press his lips to that smooth skin was almost more than he could bear. His lungs filled and he exhaled with a long, controlled breath.

Shivers started at her lower back and made their way up her spine. Goose bumps covered her flesh and she rolled her shoulders. "Could you aim your breath somewhere other than my bare skin?"

"Oh, sorry. I didn't mean..."

"It's okay. I'm the one imposing on you."

He pressed shaking fingertips against his cheeks to make sure they weren't too cold before sliding one hand under the fabric and used the other to tug skillfully at the zipper. This task was proving to be much more difficult than it sounded. His body's reaction to the sight before him promised to be his undoing.

As the small V grew, exposing her beautiful creamy skin, his breath caught in his throat. Her pink lacy bra appeared, then the flesh beneath it and the lace of her matching panties. His fingers stretched out to caress her, only to jerk away as if she were fire. The thought of touching her...

Rich sighed.

Unable to control himself any longer, Rich allowed

the back of his fingers to slowly move up her bare skin until they reached the top of the gaping material. His hands cupped her shoulders as his feet moved his body a step closer to hers.

She gasped, and his lips tugged at the corners as he leaned down to press them to her neck only to be stopped by her clearing her throat. "Um, Rich...."

"Hmm?" It came out a throaty moan.

Her body moved one step away from him. "Well, um, thanks for um..." She looked at him, her tongue slowly moving over her lips. Was that hunger in her eyes? "Thanks for taking my dress off." A laugh burst from her as color flooded her cheeks. "Well, not off..." She shook her head. "You know what I mean." He nodded and she smiled. "Thanks, Rich."

"I'm happy to help you with *anything*, Kate." And with that obvious implication, Rich retreated into his room. Her skin had been so soft, so flawless, and he wanted to touch it again—more of it. Soon.

She walked over to close the door to her room and smiled. Her eyes moved slowly down his chest. The movement was so precise, so deliberate, that it was almost as if her hands were touching him.

In that moment, Rich had only two options; say goodnight and close the door or take Kate in his arms and show her just how much he wanted to be the man in her life. Knowing he couldn't handle her rejection, he smiled. "Goodnight, Kate."

His heart actually clenched as his hand closed the door between them. If he hadn't been so damn tired, he'd have stayed awake stewing on it. Instead, Rich climbed beneath the sheets, minus the towel, and drifted into oblivion.

✕✕✕

Instead of the annoying alarm clock waking Rich up, it was the even more annoying ring of the cell phone. His muscles were stiff as he rolled over to snatch the phone off the nightstand. "If that's you Shea, I won't have to wait for a divorce because I'll just kill you," he threatened, knowing that he could never really cause any harm to the psychotic woman. His thumb flipped the phone opened and he growled "This had better be good" into it.

"Ah, Rich? It's Dale."

He sat straight up in the bed, the soft cotton sheet slipping to his hips. "Oh, uh, sorry, Dale. What time is it?" His hand ran over his face, trying to clear his eyes enough to read the clock.

"It's 5:30."

"Oh. What the hell are you doing up?"

"I'll just tell you this real quick." When Rich didn't say anything, Dale continued, "I'm thinking it's time for you guys to wrap it up."

His heart sank and his throat began to swell with emotions he didn't want to deal with, a reality he didn't want to remember. What Dale was really saying was that it was time to send Kate back to Jesse and for him to return to Shea. Neither scenario was an idea he liked. A shudder ripped down his spine and he bit back a groan. His mind began searching for a way to bring things to a different conclusion.

"I've got you booked on a flight tomorrow morning." Dale paused. "Do you think you could relay the message to Kate?"

"No problem." His hand ran back and forth across the stubble that had grown on his chin during the night. He couldn't change the fact that Kate was going home to Jesse. His stomach flipped as his name crossed his thoughts.

"Okay, well then…"

"Hey, Dale." But Rich could change his plans. "Are you in the mood for granting a small favor?"

"Maybe. What do you have in mind?"

"My parents live in Vegas. I was thinking of driving home through there, since it's half way." His heart thudded in his chest as he spewed out his request. "It's a lot to ask, and I know…"

"Go." Rich could hear the smile in his order. "Just a couple days though, okay?"

"Thanks, Dale."

Dale laughed as the phone disconnected. Rich slammed his fist into his pillow, fluffing it to just how he liked it, and settled in for a few more minutes of much needed sleep. His eyes had just closed, his body had just relaxed when someone knocked on the door.

"Go away," he yelled, yanking the blankets over his head.

"Rich?" Kate's muffled voice called his name. Her knuckles met with the wood again. "Rich, are you okay? Open the door." She sounded genuinely concerned.

At her request, Rich jumped out of bed only to realize he was naked as the day he was born. His eyes searched the room for something to wrap around his body. *The sheet. Yes, the sheet will work nicely.*With the soft cotton firmly wrapped around his waist, held in his right fist over his hip, he again opened the forbidden door.

Kate smiled, freshly showered and dressed for the day. Her eyes focused on the top of his head and she chuckled. "Rough night?"

His left hand ran through the hair that was sticking up in every direction, doing its best impression of a porcupine. "It's still night," he informed her with a heavy dose of irritation. Being awakened was not something he enjoyed, even if it was by Kate.

"Maybe on the other side of the globe." Her red lips pulled up at the corners as she tried not to laugh and her eyes twinkled, still focused on his out of control hair. "It's a little after 8:00 here in Arizona."

"*What*?" He whipped around, looking for validation from the clock. 8:07. "Dammit. I'm sorry. Come on in. Have a seat. I'll just grab a quick shower, and we'll be off."

✕ ✕ ✕

Rich ran around the room like a chicken with his head cut off, darting from side to side, grabbing various pieces of clothing. Kate couldn't help but wonder what he was going to forget. There was little doubt it would be *something*.

The bathroom door closed, the water turned on and Rich yelped.

Too hot or too cold, she wondered with a laugh.

Stacking the pillows up, Kate climbed on top of the bed and leaned back against them. One deep breath filled her lungs with a scent she had no right to recognize, let alone enjoy. Her thumb pressed the buttons on the remote, absently flipping through the channels.

Rich's phone started to buzz on the nightstand. Unable to stop herself, Kate picked it up; a blocked number. Her eyes drifted toward the bathroom door. The water was still running, and she didn't want to miss something from Dale or Jordan, so she opened the phone and said, "Rich's phone."

"Where's Rich?" the unfriendly feminine voice demanded.

"He's in the shower," Kate answered without thinking.

"*What?*" she shrieked.

Shea. Dammit!

"What the hell are you doing answering *my* husband's phone while he's in the shower ... naked?"

"Well, would you rather I was answering his phone, or in the shower with him ... naked? 'Cause that could be arranged." Kate's eyes squeezed shut as she realized that she'd just antagonized the crazy woman.

Shea's answer was a string of unintelligible screams with a few colorful words thrown in for effect, all of which ended with "two-timing whore".

Kate tried not to let the irrational rantings of a lunatic get under her skin, but the blood seemed to be boiling in her veins with the need to defend Rich. One cleansing breath and she opened her mouth for a rebuttal, "Look, Shea, I don't know what you *think* is going on here, but Rich and I have a completely professional relationship." *For the most part,* her thoughts added. "Rich overslept ... by himself ... and is now rushing to get ready to go." Kate paused only long enough to breathe, then tacked on, "Trust is an important thing in a marriage."

"Yes, it is, and thanks to you, I can't trust Rich at all."

"Thanks to *me*? Oh, pa-lease," Kate mocked her. "Even if I weren't in a relationship with another man, I doubt that Rich would ever stray from the vows he's made to you. He's too great of a guy. Damn, Shea, he's too good for you, you know that, right?"

"You little—"

Kate closed the phone before Shea could finish the statement. Part of Kate really regretted provoking Shea. The other part, though, *really* enjoyed it. Rich didn't deserve the crap Shea continually gave him. Kate didn't understand what possessed the man to stay married to her. Shea was a horrible person, unable to give Rich the kind of love and adoration he deserved. *I could love...*

Her dangerous train of thought skidded to an abrupt halt. She wouldn't go there. Couldn't go there.

Jesse. As mad as she still was at him, she couldn't let herself make decisions that would destroy the trust he had in her.

The bathroom door opened, and a brighter-eyed, bushier-tailed Rich sauntered out into the room wearing nothing but a towel. The skin of his chest and arms were red from the shower but the pink in his cheeks was different.

"What'd you forget?" Kate grinned, loving that she was right.

"Boxers, pants and one sock." He chuckled as he headed toward his suitcase. The muscles of his back moved with the beautiful precision of a large predatory cat. He certainly was a fine specimen of the male species. "I'll be right out." His voice shook her out of her analysis of the water droplets that were making their slow descent toward the terrycloth that covered what she could only imagine was a perfect rear.

She forced her eyes closed. "Jesse. Jesse. Jesse," she chanted softly.

"Did you say something?" Rich asked from the bathroom door.

"Um ... take your time." *Stupid.* She turned off the television, grabbed her phone and walked back to her room to gather all the things she'd need for the day. No need to continue to ogle a man that didn't belong to her. *What the hell is wrong with you? You love Jesse. Stop it!* As if her thoughts of him brought him to reality, the little pink device in her hand rang. "Hello?"

"Hey, baby, did you sleep well last night?" He acted as though nothing had happened between them in the minutes before he left.

And that bothered Kate. "Nope."

"Oh?" His question had more of an accusation than if he'd have gone on another tirade. He paused, seemingly waiting for Kate to defend herself, but when she didn't, he continued, "What you going to do today?"

Kate realized she didn't know. "I've got to touch base with Dale to find out. What about you?"

"Just hanging out with Dad. Oh, KC, he's doing so much better. You should see him." The excitement in Jesse's voice made her smile.

"I can't wait. Hopefully, it'll just be a few more days."

"Hey Kate," Rich called from the other room. "Kate."

She cringed, and she wrapped her fingers around the phone in hopes of shielding Jesse from hearing Rich call her name. No such luck.

Jesse cursed. "I gotta go, Kate," he grumbled, then the line went dead.

"Bye," she said to the silence, if only to make things appear normal to Rich.

"Sorry about that," Rich said as she closed the phone. "He's probably totally pissed that you're stuck here with me."

"Nope—" He wasn't *totally* pissed, at least he hadn't torn into her. "—he trusts me."

Rich laughed as he closed the door to his room, effectively locking them together in the same hotel room. "He certainly doesn't trust me." Two strides later, he stood right in front of her.

Her body reacted to his close proximity. "Should he?" she sighed.

His lips were right at her ear as he whispered, "Nope."

Her eyebrows shot up in response to his answer, and she jerked away from him. Her heart thudded violently against her ribcage.

His lips pulled into a confident grin as he winked then headed toward the door. "Let's get going, beautiful lady. Today's our last day together." Despite his efforts to look cheerful, there was a sadness in his eyes he couldn't disguise.

"What?"

"I forgot to tell you. Dale called at 5:30 this morning. We're to cover the conferences today, then we're free to go our separate ways tomorrow morning." He opened the door, using his hand to usher her into the hall.

"Oh." She hated that she sounded disappointed. "Well, that's good news." She watched the burgundy squares as her feet shuffled over them. She didn't want to look at Rich and see his emotions reflected back at her. Leaving him would be harder than she ever imagined.

Rich reached out and pressed the down arrow as they waited for the elevator to arrive. She wanted to touch him, to take his hand in hers, but forced her hands into the pockets of her jacket.

The lobby was full of people and they weaved their way toward the doors. She probably should have refused to stay tonight with Rich. The smart thing would be to leave tonight and drive back to Jesse. But, despite the urgency she felt to get to the man she loved, Kate couldn't bear the thought of leaving Rich.

That's screwed up! her thoughts informed her.

Screwed up or not, it was how she felt. Kate would continue to fight her feelings for Rich. They were ridiculous. Jesse deserved better than a girl in love with... *I am not in love with Rich.* She did not love Rich. He was just a co-worker and means nothing more. *Nothing more.*

"Kate?" Rich gently shook her arm. Her eyes focused on his face. Her damned heart skipped a beat at the pools of Caribbean blue looking back at her, and worried sincerity reflected in them. "Are you okay?"

"Um hum." She nodded. "Why do you ask?"

"You just stopped walking and started muttering to yourself." He laughed. "Where were you just now ... and why did you say my name?"

"I ... I said your name?" Panic raced through her veins.

His lips lifted smugly at the corners. "Yep ... twice. You daydreaming about me?" Her mouth dropped open, causing him to roar with laughter. "Come on." His hand wrapped gently around her arm and he led her out into the bright sunlight. "I'm going to enjoy every moment of our time together."

"We're working, Rich." She closed herself in the car and waited a few moments for him to climb in as well. When he did, his smile was so big she waited for his face to crack. "What?"

"You know what they say, right?"

Kate wondered which cliché he was going to throw at her. Her brows arched. "What do they say, Rich?"

"All work and no play makes Kate a dull girl."

"I am *not* dull." Her tone was defensive and caused Rich to laugh again. She huffed and stared out the window in silence. Rich was quiet too, probably plotting a way to make her less dull.

By the time they reached their destination, her irritation had reached new levels of annoyance. Kate could almost feel the negative emotions buzzing in her body. She threw open the door and headed into the crowd that was gathering. Rich was right on her heels, chuckling softly.

"Come on, Rich," she groaned. "Let's finish this last day together."

Nineteen

Rock bottom was an interesting place. Sitting in a hellhole, drunk off your ass with a heart that's been torn in two, you tend to get a new perspective on life. Rich had promised everyone—Kate, Jesse, and himself—that he was going to walk away. He'd promised to leave her alone, pull himself out of the picture.

Things change.

He had big plans for tonight. There was no way he was going to allow Kate to hole up in her room and hide from their friendship. If he couldn't have Kate's heart, he would gladly have her as his friend. Although, until the day came that she devoted herself to another man, he would fight for her, show her how happy he could make her.

They'd barely stepped into the lobby before she headed toward the elevator, and his hand flashed out to grab her arm. "Huh uh, Kate, no room service tonight. Let's sit down and have dinner in the lounge." There was skepticism in her eyes. Her mouth, however, didn't offer a protest. "Just dinner, Kate," he assured her with a smile.

"Can I at least freshen up first?"

He led her toward the elevators, leaning down to breathe deeply with an exaggerated sniff. "You definitely need to freshen up. You smell." *Delicious,* his thoughts amended.

She slapped playfully at his chest. "You could use a shower too, Stinky." She continued to tease him by holding her nose and making gagging noises as they rode up the elevator toward their rooms. Chuckles turned to full-fledged laughter by the time they reached his room.

She leaned in and took a deep breath. Her eyes drifted shut and an intoxicated look passed over her face before she camouflaged it with a scowl. "I expect you to smell so much better when you come out of this room in thirty minutes."

He raised a brow. "Thirty minutes?" Never in his life had he met a woman who could get ready in only half an hour.

Her lips lifted at the corners. "Unless *you* need longer. I've always thought you were kind of a pretty boy."

"Stinky? Now pretty boy? If I didn't know better, I might worry that you were hiding your true feelings for me behind insults." He didn't wait for her to respond, just walked into his room and shut the door. Let her stew on that for a minute—thirty, actually.

Rich didn't need the full thirty minutes. A quick shower and a change of clothes, and he was ready to spend the evening with Kate—as friends. He smiled at his reflection as his hands smoothed out the shirt. Was it wishful thinking to hope she'd take it off later?

There was a light knocking on the hall door.

With shoes in hand and his heart pounding out of his chest, Rich hurried over to the door, jerking it open. His breath rushed from his lungs in a whoosh. "Kate, you look..." His tongue stopped while his brain searched for the appropriate word.

Her hair was pulled back in a loose ponytail, wisps already falling down to frame her face. Her cheeks were tinted pink, whether from embarrassment or some kind of makeup, Rich couldn't tell. Either way, she was beautiful. Her plump, kissable lips were shiny with clear gloss.

His mouth watered with the anticipation of tasting it. What flavor would she prefer? Strawberry? Cherry? *Passion* fruit?

She fidgeted under his scrutinizing eye as her hands moved down her neck and over the V of her cream sweater. "It's the only casual thing I packed."

"No, it's ... you're ... you look really ... great, Kate."

The pink tint took on a redder hue and she giggled nervously. "You don't look half bad yourself."

His brain decided to finally check back in and he held up his shoes. "Thanks. I just need to put these on, then we're off."

"Good. I'm starving."

Rich plopped down on the corner of the bed and slipped on the shoes, sneaking a peak at Kate as he tied the laces. Those jeans were the perfect combination of tight and loose, hugging each curve without being too revealing.

"Ready?" she asked when she caught him looking.

His hands ran over the hems of his slacks, straightening them. "Yep, let's get out of here."

The short journey toward the lounge downstairs was a quiet one. His emotions were reminiscent of his very first date; nervous, excited, anxious. Even his palms were sweaty. Was there any chance of kissing her at the end of the night? *This isn't a date, Spencer.*

"Rich, are you okay?" Kate's soft voice asked as they stepped off the elevator into the lobby.

"Yeah, just fine, why?"

"You're so quiet. We don't have to do this. I'm fine with ordering something in my room."

"No." It came out a bit harsh. "I mean, don't be ridiculous, I've been looking forward to this all day."

"All day?" She perked a brow.

"Yes, I have been working up the courage to ask you to dinner all day."

"This isn't a date."

Where have I heard that before? "I know. Dinner, as friends."

She smiled and her eyes crinkled at the sides. "Friends." She extended her hand which he took, shaking it gently.

The lounge wasn't very busy, which would offer the privacy Rich wanted, yet had a scattering of people to make Kate comfortable.

Unwilling to break the contact with Kate, Rich traded hands and squeezed it gently. When she didn't tug away, he led her to a table kind of off by itself and pulled out a chair. "Why don't you have a seat and I'll go get us a drink from the bar. What would you like?"

"I'll just have a um, Dr. Pepper."

He didn't miss her request for the same soda he always drank, but decided it was better not to mention— or make too much of it. Instead he teased, "Don't trust yourself with alcohol around me?"

She rolled her eyes. That pink tint was back, and he suspected that he was closer to the truth than she wanted to admit.

The anxiety and nervousness was beginning to wear off as he got to the bar. This was just Kate. *My Kate.* There was nothing to be wary of. She'd never hurt him intentionally. *If she broke my heart, it was only because I'd put it out there to get slapped again.*

"Well, you look happier than the last time I saw you," the familiar tattooed man commented.

Rich smiled. "Yeah, I am."

"Is she the reason you were so miserable?" He jerked his head in Kate's direction.

"It's a long story."

Jesse was gone. It was just Rich and Kate, and he wasn't going to let *him* interfere with the last few hours they had together. This was going to be his last Hail, Mary before he sent her back into the arms of the other man who loved her.

Big and Beefy cleared his throat. "What can I get you?"

"Two Dr. Peppers please."

His forehead crinkled and he smiled. "Sure thing, friend."

Rich turned to lean back against the counter, resting his elbows on it. His eyes sought out the most beautiful girl in the room. She was chatting away on her cell phone, laughing while her fingers absently twisted at a lock of hair that had released itself from her ponytail. The delusional part of his brain convinced him that it was her mother, or a friend, that made her smile that way. The practical side knew full well that it was Jesse.

"Here you go."

"Thanks." Sliding some cash on the counter, Rich took a glass in each hand and wandered back toward the table where Kate waited.

She smiled as Rich put the glass in front of her. "Thanks," she whispered to him before talking back into the phone, "Hey, I'll talk to you later." A deep reply answered her. She grinned, and dropped her gaze. "You too. Good night, Dad." She closed her phone. "Sorry about that."

"It's okay." And it was. Kate had been on the phone with her *father*, a man he didn't have to be jealous of. The phone in his pocket rang, and he answered it without looking at the caller id. "Hello?"

"Rich, where the hell are you?" the voice demanded.

"You already know the answer to that, Shea."

Kate choked on her drink and verified, "That's Shea?"

Rich nodded.

"Do I?" Shea said with her usual doze of animosity.

Kate's hand wrapped around his arm. "I need to tell you something," she whispered.

Rich held up one finger and walked away from the table. "I'm on assignment."

"Are you?"

Her insinuations made his head hurt. "Stop talking in circles. I told you where I was, and that hasn't changed."

Silence came through the line followed by a long breath. "You said that you were staying at the Marriott near the Capital, but they have never heard of you."

His brows pulled together as the confusion was overridden by panic. "Where are you, Shea?"

"I am standing in the lobby of the Marriott near the Capital. The worthless child at the check-in desk has never heard of you and can't find you in their system. She said that there was no record of you ever having stayed here." Another frustrated sigh came through the line. "I'm going to ask you again, Rich Spencer, where the hell are you?"

His heart forced the blood through his veins at lightning speed. If Shea was standing in the lobby that was *way* too close to Kate for his comfort. Before he even realized it, his feet had brought him to stand in the lobby, careful to stay off to the side just in case Shea was actually here.

A quick scan of the foyer and lobby didn't show any sign of the woman who would soon be his *ex*-wife. He took a few more steps into the open, caution being of the utmost importance. "I am standing in the lobby of the Marriott, Shea. You are not here."

"Don't patronize me, Rich. I know where I am. You sonofabitch, you're with her, aren't you?"

"Who?"

Her frustration came through as a scream. "You are not at the Marriott in D.C. As your wife, I demand..."

Laughter wasn't the best way to handle Shea, but that's what happened as relief washed over Rich, replacing the fear and anxiety.

"Don't you laugh at me!"

"That's your problem, Shea. I'm in Phoenix. The capital of *Arizona*. You, my dear, are on the other side of the continent." His laughter continued, as did her tirade of expletives. Hadn't she noticed the locator font? She'd obviously seen Kate on TV. He couldn't believe that she'd made such a mistake, but was grateful she had. "Look, we're almost done here. Just go home."

In classic bi-polar Shea fashion, she was crying. "I just wanted to surprise you ... like Jesse did for Kate."

"I don't get it, Shea."

She sniffed. "Don't get what?" She sounded so innocent.

"You treat me like shit. You leave and I don't hear from you.... Never mind. Forget it."

The pressure of a small hand on his back sent tingles from the point of contact, spreading through his body like fire. "Rich?" When his eyes met Kate's over his shoulder, she smiled encouragingly. "Is everything okay?" She fidgeted with the hem of her sweater.

A hiss flowed through his ear. "She's there now, isn't she?"

"Goodbye, Shea." He closed the phone with a snap, muttering "crazyass bitch" under his breath. Forcing a smile through his frustration, Rich said, "Yes, Kate, everything's fine."

Kate wrapped her arms around his waist and leaned her cheek against his chest. "I am so glad. I forgot to tell you that Shea called earlier, and I..."

When she didn't continue, Rich placed a finger under her chin and tipped her face up so she was looking at him. "You what?"

She chewed on her lip. "I kind of..." The corners of her mouth lifted, Rich could see she was fighting her amusement. "I told her off. I didn't mean to cause any problems for you. She was so nasty, and I just hate the way she treats you. You're such a great guy, who deserves a woman who loves..."

Rich cut off her words by pressing his lips to hers, trampling the boundaries that had been set up.

Kate's mouth moved under his. Her body relaxed and a moan escaped. Then, as if she'd been slapped, she jumped back. "That wasn't exactly *friendly*."

"Sorry." Breathing heavy, Rich touched his fingers to his lips. "It's just so sweet that you would defend me to her." He forced himself to take a step away from her, just to be safe. "Come on, I'll be good. Let's finish our dinner. I'm starving."

Her stomach grumbled, and she wrapped her arms around her middle. "Yeah, me too."

Extending his hand to lead the way, they both walked back in and returned to their secluded table in the corner. "Thank you, Kate." She smiled, then her eyes narrowed at something over his shoulder. "What is it?" he asked, turning to follow her gaze, only to groan.

"Hey, stallion," one of the girls from the other night purred. "Is *she* the reason you wouldn't join the two of us?" When Kate gasped, the big-haired blonde winked at her and said, "Can you say ménage-a-trios, honey?"

A growl rumbled in his chest as something between mortification and revolution bubbled in his gut.

The giggling girls glanced at him then turned to look at the wide-eyed Kate. "I'll bet he's really good in bed. You can tell us."

Kate's answer wasn't what Rich expected. "Oh, he

is. The best lover I've ever had." She leaned forward and stage whispered to them, "He's hung like a horse and can go all night."

Botox-filled lips fell open and gaped at her.

"Come on, lover," Kate said as she stood and grabbed him by the hand. "I've decided I want dessert ... *now.*" Her tongue darted out and ran seductively over her lower lip.

Yeah, Rich was ready, too. He had to remind himself that this little production was nothing more than an act. But he would gladly follow Kate to hell and back if she were going to talk like that. *Talk about a turn on.*

As they got to the doorway to the lounge, Kate glanced over her shoulder and winked at their audience before grabbing a handful of his butt. Her action surprised him and he jumped. She tilted her head so her lips rubbed against his ear as she whispered, "Sorry."

He leaned in to reply softly in her ear, "You still want to go upstairs?"

She nodded. "Yeah, but only because I'm tired, not because..." She trailed off.

"Okay." With his hand on the small of her back, Rich guided her toward the elevator, but waited until they were safely alone behind the closed door before daring to speak. "Not that I'm complaining, but what the hell was that?"

"I'm sorry."

"Don't be sorry." Having her devour him like a dessert sounded like a great way to spend the last of their time together.

"You know, sometimes I have the overwhelming urge to protect you. Like with Shea this morning and just now with those two floosies." She was focused on his face and waited until he looked at her before she continued, "Did they really offer you a threesome?"

The elevator door opened, and he walked out into the hall without answering her question. What was he supposed to say? *Yes, but I'm so hung up on you that I couldn't do it.* He continued past his door and stood next to Kate's. "Would you like to order some dinner? We could still eat it together." *Dare I hope?* "Where would you be more comfortable, my room...or yours?"

"Mine, I guess." She slipped the keycard in and waited for the light to flicker green, then invited him in.

The flowers were still there, a glaring reminder of who had left only a few days ago. Thankfully, Kate had put away the little black piece of silk and lace. "I was thinking we could order room service first." With phone in hand, he asked "What do you want?" and plopped down on the bed next to the nightstand.

"Something light. I'm not really that hungry."

"Burger? Sandwich?"

"Sandwich, turkey, light mayo," she said over her shoulder as she walked into the bathroom.

Rich placed the order, and the pleasant voice assured him it would be 'less than a half hour'. "Kate?" His knuckles tapped lightly on the door.

"Hmm?" she called back.

"The food will be here in a half hour. I'm going to go..." The door swung into the tiny room, sucking his breath with it.

Kate stood in a tank top and flannel pajama bottoms. She'd washed her face and had pulled her hair out of the rubber band. It now rested on her shoulders. Her eyes dropped down over her ensemble then returned to his ogling gaze. "I hope it's okay but I just wanted to get comfortable."

"Um..." Shaking his head, Rich tried to clear out the x-rated thoughts that seemed to have crept in. "Of course that's okay. I was just going to go change into something—" He chuckled and shrugged. "—more comfortable."

"Okay."

"I'll be back in a few minutes then."

She nodded, and Rich walked through the adjoining door to his room. There was a real potential for an inferno in that next room. The lighter was in his hand, all he had to do was flick the little wheel. Kate was comfortable with him, and Rich believed somewhere deep down, she had feelings for him. Maybe she even loved him. *Maybe.*

Rich wouldn't let her go back to Jesse tomorrow

without at least acknowledging those feelings. Rock bottom was a brutal place. He outta know, he'd hit it the other night. Now, there was only one way to go, and that was up. Kate was worth it, she was worth all of the heartache.

As soon as he got back, Rich would make that call to Claudia. Waiting for Shea to freak wouldn't get him what he wanted, what he needed. Staying married to Shea wasn't an option anymore, and the clock was ticking on how long Kate would stay within his reach.

Soft cotton pajama bottoms slid over his legs and a t-shirt over his head, the hem coming to rest at his waist. Rich started toward Kate's room with his phone in hand, only to stop, turn off the ringer, and set it on the nightstand. Interruptions weren't welcome tonight. He would share dinner with Kate, and then he would tell her how he felt about her, leaving nothing unsaid. She deserved to make an educated decision.

The knock on Kate's door was clearly heard from Rich's room, and he hurried to pay the man with their dinner. "I'll get that," he said as soon as he rounded the corner, his wallet in hand.

Both sets of eyes sought him out. The tray was wheeled over to the table and the plates set on it. As Rich handed the bills to the room service guy, Kate began to uncover the food he'd ordered.

The door closed with a snap and she cleared her throat. Rich turned to see her glaring at him. "What?" Obvious confusion was in his voice.

"Cheesecake *and*—" She lifted a little silver lid. "—some really yummy looking chocolate brownie thing."

"Decadent Brownie Dessert," he informed her, "with fudge sauce."

"But..."

"Don't worry, they're both for me."

"Oh." Her face fell just a bit.

He fought a smile and offered, "I'll share."

She grabbed a fork and the plate with the oozing, still steaming, brown dessert and dug in. She sunk into the chair, resting her heels on the edge of the seat next to her bottom. Her lips wrapped around the fork, and she pulled it out slowly. "Mmm, oh my..." she said dreamily. "Rich, you have got to try this." The fork scraped against the plate, and before he could protest, she held it out. "Come on, I don't have cooties." She looked so beautiful, so intoxicating, and he wanted to kiss away the remnants of chocolate still on her lip. The tip of her pink tongue slowly wiped away exactly what he'd been fixated on.

Blinking quickly, he attempted to remain in the here and now. His hand gripped the chair on the other side of the table for support. "It's that good, huh?"

She nodded. "Here." Her arm moved forward, hovering over the table, extending the fork with it.

His eyes focused on hers as he leaned forward to take what she was offering into his mouth. Despite the anxiety, the defensive numbness oozing from every cell, his taste buds worked just fine. The dessert was delicious. "You're right, that is good, but shouldn't you eat your sandwich first?"

"Nope, I believe in eating dessert first...before I get too full." She took another bite and chewed slowly. "So, you never answered me."

"You didn't ask me anything." His mind began to spin, trying to recollect a question that Kate had asked, and staring into the deep green of her eyes. The plump perfection of her lips wasn't helping matters.

She smiled. "Yes, I did." Her fork dropped onto the plate, and she stared at him. "Those girls in the lounge—"

Crap!

"—did they really offer you a threesome?"

A huge lump formed in his throat and he swallowed hard. "Yes." Surely, Kate couldn't think he would...

"Why didn't you...? Never mind, it's none of my business."

Rich leaned forward in his chair and waited until she looked in his eyes. "Kate, casual sex doesn't interest me." His voice was quiet, but strong. "I believe in making love. And I only want to make love to the woman ... I love."

She didn't speak for several painful moments. Her

face was somber. "Right, you're married." Her fork plunged into the dessert, lifting another mouthful toward her lips.

"My wife is not that woman."

She stared at him, blinking, while his revelation began to sink in. The dessert teetered precariously in the air. Her face grew tense and her full lips pulled into a tight line. "I, uh ... Rich, I'm..." Since her mouth wasn't doing a very good job of communicating, she decided to opt for using her hands, sending the brown dessert flying toward him. It hit his chest with a splat, and Kate jumped to her feet. "Oh my goodness. I am so sorry." With napkin in hand, she violently smeared the glob into an enormous stain that now covered the entire front of his shirt.

He took her hands, stopping the movement. "Kate, it's okay. I'll just change." His fingers caught the hem of the shirt and lifted it over his head. "I'll get cleaned up real quick then we can finish our dinner."

Three steps into his room and his feet wouldn't move any further. His soul ached to tell Kate exactly how much she meant to him. His lungs needed to be filled with her scent as she melted herself into his embrace. His heart longed to tell her that he loved her, that she was the only woman for him, the one he wanted to make love to.

"Rich?"

How long have I been standing here? "Just give me one second." Rich tried to refrain from a full out sprint into the bathroom and ended up doing some galloping thing that probably looked even more ridiculous than it felt. But his mind was too busy to care what he looked like. His heart pounded with the excitement of finally being able to put a voice to the feelings that had been eating him up on the inside.

Tossing the dirty shirt on the counter, Rich picked up a washcloth, ran it under the water and quickly wiped the remnants of the dessert from his skin. He plucked at the chocolate in his hair with the cloth, doing the best he could to get it out of his hair. A shower would definitely be on the agenda later.

The door between their rooms was still open, and he could hear Kate quietly humming a tune he didn't recognize. When he got to the suitcase, however, he realized that Kate had managed to dirty his last clean t-shirt. A button-up would look stupid, not to mention uncomfortable as hell. Shirtless it was.

After sucking in a deep breath to calm his nerves, Rich started toward the woman of his dreams. *Well, this is it,* he told himself as he walked slowly back into Kate's room.

She was sitting at the table, picking at her French fries. The moment that she realized he was back, her eyes caught his, only to drift down over the exposed skin of his chest. The movement was so slow and deliberate, as if she were memorizing every inch. She gave her head a quick shake then managed a weak smile as her eyes jumped up to his face. "I thought you were going to put a new shirt on."

"Oh, yeah..." His hands ran down his chest in a nervous motion. "You ruined my last clean one."

"I *ruined* it?" She stood up and took a step toward him. "I am so sorry."

His teasing had lightened the tension he was feeling just a bit, but it all came back with a vengeance as the knowledge of what needed to be said crept back into the forefront of his mind. "Kate, I really need to talk to you."

Her eyes searched his. "Is everything okay?"

"No. Yes. At least, I hope so." His heart was a battering ram against his ribcage. He took her by the hand, hoping that his palms weren't sweaty, and led her toward the bed.

She laughed nervously but sat down on the corner. "It's that bad, huh, that I need to sit down?"

"I just want you to be as comfortable as possible." Comfortable, physically at least, since there was no way this would go over without a little uneasiness. He mirrored her position, sitting with one leg bent under the other, facing her. "Kate." It came out as a croak. After clearing his throat, Rich tried again, "Kate, do you know how I feel about you?"

"Oh, um..." Her eyes dropped to the comforter on

the bed and she played with a loose string, tangling it around her finger. "Rich, I don't think—"

"Don't think. Just feel." Taking his own advice, Rich inched closer to her and lifted her hand in his, pressing it to his chest. Her eyes followed the movement and were now glued to the point where they were connected. "Do you feel that, Kate?" he paused, just letting the wild thumping of his heart fill the gap in his declaration. Having her touch his naked flesh made his insides stir. Suddenly this became even more important than before. "Do you feel my heart?"

She nodded, but didn't lift her eyes from his chest.

"My heart pounds like that every time I'm near you, every time I see you, every time I even hear your voice. Kate, you make me feel things I haven't felt ... well, ever. You are beautiful and kind and loving and..."

"Rich, don't." She lifted her face and her eyes glistened with tears yet to be shed. "Please don't do this."

"Why?" The question came out a strained whisper. "There's little doubt that you know how I feel, but I need to tell you. I need to know that there is absolutely no confusion. You deserve to know exactly how I feel about you, how much I..."

"Rich." Her hand pulled away from his chest and out of his grasp. She stood and walked toward the window, sliding the curtains out of the way to stare out into the night for only a moment before her head drooped loosely on her shoulders. Her arms wrapped around her middle. "Oh," she said on a sigh.

Unwilling to let her just walk away from this conversation, he followed her and weaved his arms around her waist. His breath was held uncomfortably in his lungs until she leaned back into his embrace. Her hair tickled his bare skin.

"I'm not that girl, Rich," she muttered quietly.

He kissed the top of her head softly, feeling confused but happy that she was at least still speaking to him. "What girl is that, love?"

Her shoulders lifted with a sigh, and she turned in his arms, leaning back to support herself against his clasped hands. "I never thought..." Her eyes were full of confused pain while her voice was soft, shaky. "Rich, I've always been a good girl. I never even skipped school, not even one class. Never in a million years would I have guessed that I could be the girl that would fall in love with a married man." She pulled away from his embrace and avoided his eyes. "But here I am."

Her revelation had his heart soaring. She had finally said she loved him. "Oh, Kate, you really..."

She nodded slowly then began to speak again. "Rich, you *are* married. Shea may be crazy, but she is still your wife."

"She won't be forever," he assured her quietly.

"Even still, I'm supposed to be with Jesse, in love with only Jesse. He's a great guy who will make a wonderful husband and father. But my heart..." A tear flowed over her lid and slid slowly down her cheek.

Tipping his head down, Rich lightly kissed her tear away, and when she didn't pull away or slap him, he allowed his lips to meet hers. Electricity flowed through his veins, captivating him with emotions unfelt for years. The soft, full lips began to move beneath his and Kate moaned in pleasure as her nails bit into his shoulder blades. His tongue moved out and caressed her lips and ... ruined everything.

Kate's hands moved to his chest and pushed against him. "Rich, I can't."

Rich was disappointed, but only lifted his fingers to his lips, sealing in her kiss, and then stepped backward. "I promise not to make you do anything you don't want to do, Kate. I still need to tell you everything. Maybe it would be best if I laid it all out on the table, so to speak, then you can decide what you want to do with the information."

She sniffed and nodded.

"Come here." His hands wrapped around each of hers, and he again led her toward the foot of the bed. His palms were sweating as his temperature rose with every ounce of nervous energy. Even if she took his words and threw them back in his face, Rich needed to say them.

With her seated again across from him, he opened his mouth and poured his heart out to her. "Kate, you mean the world to me. I go to bed with you on my mind and wake up thinking about you. Some nights, you even spend the entire night loving me in my dreams. Tomorrow morning, you're going back to...." A groan communicated what he couldn't. "I can't bear to even think of it, let alone say it."

Her eyes drifted closed then floated open to peer deeply into his. She began to wring her hands together but stopped to reach out to take hold of his.

He took that as her encouragement and continued, "Kate, I want you to be *with* me, for you to accept *my* ring, to love only me. I want to be the one who gives you children, the one you grow old with." His heart was pounding so hard in his chest, it was actually painful. He'd said almost everything, but now it was time to completely reveal all his feelings. "Kate, I can't hide behind the pretenses anymore. This is time for no-holds-barred, Hail Mary's, whatever it takes to make you understand that I..."

She swallowed hard, her eyes burning back into his. Her hands tightened their grip, verifying that she knew what he was going to say next and wasn't going to stop him.

"Kate Callahan, I love you."

More tears slid down her cheeks, and he wasn't sure if that was a good sign or not, so he waited. And waited. Her nose turned red as did her eyes. The words hung in the air like a nuclear bomb just waiting to explode.

When he felt like he might spontaneously combust as well, he got to his feet. She opened her mouth but closed it again.

His eyes were focused only on the infinitely deep jade of her eyes as he said, "Kate, you now know everything you need to know." A small, unfelt smile tugged at the corners of his mouth. "I'm going to bed. I'll leave my door open. If you need *anything*, please know that you're welcome in my room, in my bed, in my *life*." Leaning down, he pressed his lips to hers, then moved them to just below her ear and whispered, "I love you, Kate. Please let me love you."

Kate didn't offer any kind of reaction other than to turn away from him. Her shoulders began to shake as she cried. Maybe he'd been wrong to tell her everything. Maybe she wasn't ready for it. But did he have any other options?

With his heart completely exposed, Rich turned on his heel and closed *her* door.

Careful to leave his door wide open, he went into the bathroom and turned on the water. His heart was breaking, causing real physical pain that consumed every inch of his chest cavity. If Kate didn't want to be with him, then...

"Oh, Kate," he sighed, pushed fingers through his hair and stepped under the spray. The temperature wasn't even noticeable since he'd given in to the depressed numbness that was saving him from completely losing it.

The water ran over his face, acting as the tears he wouldn't let fall. He'd done everything he could. The situation was now completely out of his hands. If he'd thought he'd felt helpless before, that was nothing. Giving into his emotions, he sank down to the floor of the shower, letting the water beat on his bare skin.

When it started to prune, Rich gathered what was left of his dignity and turned off the water. The steam was thick in the room and the mirror was completely fogged over, which was good. The last thing his ego needed was to actually *see* how pathetic he looked. Feeling it was enough.

A quick rub of the towel to dry his skin and he pulled a pair of boxers up over his hips then headed into his room. Wishing he could take something to ease the pain of his breaking heart, he eased onto the bed and leaned against the pillows. His thumb fumbled with the remote control, turning on the television for no other reason than to fill the uncomfortable silence.

Kate's door clicked and he quickly turned off the television. She appeared in the doorway. Her nose was red, as were her eyes, and her skin was splotchy. She'd obviously been crying since he'd witnessed those first moments of her breakdown. "Rich," she squeaked, only to start sobbing again.

Jumping to his feet, he rushed to her. "Kate?" His arms ached to hold her, but pushing her right now wasn't something he was willing to do. Instead his finger tipped her chin to urge her to look at him. "What can I do for you, Kate?" Her only answer was a sob. "What do you need?" Panic began to consume him as he waited for her to answer.

She blinked as she looked into his eyes. "Rich, will you please..."

"Anything, Kate. I'd do anything to make this hurt go away. I hate seeing you like this. Just name it. What can I do for you?"

Another stifled sob escaped her. "Please ... hold me."

"Oh, my love," he whispered against her hair, wrapping his arms around her, "that is the easiest request I've ever heard. Come here." She melted into his touch and he eased his arm under her knees, lifting her into his arms. He started toward the bed, but stopped as she shifted. "Are you okay if we..."

Her head moved against his skin as she nodded. "I just need to be in your arms tonight. Please."

That particular request was one she would not have to make more than once. Rich had dreamt of holding her in his arms while she slept. He eased her on to the exposed sheets then crawled in next to her. She snuggled in next to him, resting her head on his chest. Her arm lay across his waist and tightly held onto his body.

Rich sighed, feeling relaxed for the first time since arriving in Arizona. Tiny rivulets ran down his side as Kate's emotions continued to get the best of her. The occasional sob or hiccup let him know that she was still awake. His arms tightened around her and his lips found the top of her head. "I love you, Kate."

"I know," she whispered.

Although, he would have wished for those three words coming from her mouth, he was grateful for her answer. It would have to be good enough...for now.

Kate's breathing slowed, and the tears ceased as she drifted into, what he hoped, would be a peaceful sleep. She sighed and snuggled into him. Her hand moved up over his chest and she smiled against his skin before pressing her lips to it. She was still for a few minutes then began to violently shake her head back and forth. "Jesse, please..." she said in a strangled whisper.

Rich's teeth ground together at the sound of his name on her lips.

Her body stilled, and her breathing steadied as she found sleep again.

Rich tried to relax, but could only think of Kate saying Jesse's name in her sleep. She was pleading with him. Why? What was she dreaming? Rich's focus was on the features of her face; the cute dusting of freckles on her small, straight nose and cheeks. Dark eyelashes rested against the skin of her pale cheek. She looked so peaceful now, so content, so innocent. Her lips pulled into an intoxicating smile and her arms tightened around him. She flipped her leg over his thighs, pulling herself closer to him, almost as if she were trying to fuse their bodies together.

In response, Rich tightened his grip on her, enjoying every moment of this side of her. This was something he'd been craving. The feel of Kate's skin against his sent an electrical current running through his veins.

"Oh," she moaned as her leg moved up and down his thigh. Rich tried to extinguish his excitement when Kate began crawling up his body, and his eyes closed. She pressed her lips to his neck and sighed, "Rich."

Yes! Rich fought the urge to holler in victory. She may have said Jesse's name, but she'd said his too. And, she was kissing Rich while she said it.

She relaxed, easing her body against his. "Oh, Rich," she said in an erotic whisper.

"Oh, Kate," he answered then with a smile on his face, Rich allowed his body to follow her lead and drifted into the happiest sleep he'd ever experienced.

Twenty

Fuzzy visions still flooded Kate's mind as sleep started to release its hold on her. The skin against her cheek was moving steadily as the chest expanded with each intake of breath. Kate snuggled deeper into the warm body, needing the solace that only he could offer. Her fingers explored the smooth, toned muscles that rested just under the skin.

"Mmm," she moaned, filling her lungs with the calming scent that was frighteningly familiar. The pounding of her heart was violent, banging against her ribcage. Her lungs ached for more of the delectable aroma it had just experienced and sucked in a deep breath, only to pause, savoring it. Her skin buzzed where it touched his. Hiking her leg up over his thigh, Kate pulled herself even closer, giving into the desire of her soul.

The man starring in her dreams tightened his hold on her. Strong arms wrapped themselves around her. His long fingers traced circles on the bare skin of her back, just under the hemline of her shirt. A growl rumbled beneath her ear and she turned to press her lips to his soft chest. His heart stuttered at the intimate contact.

Her heart matched his, beat for steady beat. As the heat built between her thighs, her stomach churned in glorious anticipation. She allowed her hand to travel across his tight abdomen then used one finger to follow the narrow line of hair that would lead to delicious things.

The sharp intake of breath, followed by a hiss as he

exhaled, caused her to smile. The fact that she had that kind of effect on this man was such a turn on. His soft hands tickled their way under the waistband of her pajamas and he firmly filled his palm with her ass. He kissed the top of her head then used his hand to urge her up his body. He spent a few moments worshipping each new inch of her face as it came within his reach. The corners of her mouth lifted as he moaned his enjoyment. His lips made contact with each side of her smile before unleashing his passion on her mouth.

Tingles and more heat surged through her bloodstream as he teased her with his lips and tongue. Short pants of breath were all that she could manage as the war raged in her mouth.

"Oh, Rich," Kate moaned, "I need you."

Rough hands gripped her face, shaking her awake. Her eyes flew open and were met with the cobalt ones that belonged to the man she'd been fanaticizing about. They were suddenly very real and burning with the desire her own reflected.

"Oh, Kate," he muttered in a husky whisper before his lips crashed into hers.

Caught up in the moments of her erotic dream that were fast becoming an even more passionate reality, Kate responded to his touch. Their mouths moved in perfect unison. His hand moved back down to clutch her bottom.

Rich's soft fingertips teased and tickled their way up her sides, slowly removed the straps of her tank top and quickly replaced them with gentle kisses. His tongue moved from her shoulder to her ear, leaving a trail of fire in its wake. "Are you sure you want this, Kate? 'Cause if you let me go much further, I don't think that I'll be able to stop." His breaths left his lungs in short puffs, escaping through parted lips.

Her fingers weaved their way into his hair and tugged his head back gently so that they were looking into each other's eyes. Uneven breathing filled the room around them. "Rich," she panted, "don't think, just feel." His eyes sparkled and that damn sexy smirk of his sealed her fate. "Make love to me."

Now was not the time to think. Kate wanted to feel Rich, only Rich. Her heart needed him to love her. Her body needed him to *make* love to her. And her soul needed him to fill the empty feeling she had when he wasn't near her.

Rich sat up and urged her to follow his lead. His hands slid up her sides until they firmly held her face. His eyes smoldered, turning from aqua to the darkest navy, as he stroked her cheeks with his thumbs. "I love you, Kate. More than I have ever loved any woman in my life."

A knot formed in her throat at his declaration. Although she had feelings for this man, stronger feelings than she dared admit to herself, she couldn't seem to voice the words that her heart had been chanting for far too long. "I know," she whispered.

His frustration was expressed in a groan while his hands made the messy hair on his head stand up on end. "Kate," his voice was heartbreaking, "can't you just say the words? You love me. I know it. You know it." A gentle finger rested just beneath her chin and tipped her face upward so she was looking into the blue pools of need. "Tell me what you feel, Kate ... *please.*"

Confusion swam in her mind. She loved him. There was no way she could deny her feelings any longer—at least to herself—but she wasn't ready to tell Rich that she loved him

"What do you feel?" Rich croaked, breaths causing his chest to move as the air rushed in and out of his lungs.

"I feel you," she whispered, her lips caressed his slowly.

Dark lashes rested on his cheeks as the muscles in his jaw clenched tight. His strong face was that of pure confusion, torn between eager contentment and overwhelming desire. "Kate," he moaned as fingertips wrapped themselves around the hem of her shirt. His eyes opened, silently asking permission one last time.

She nodded and lifted her arms over her head. Self consciousness caused her to bite her lip. What if he didn't like what he...

"Kate, you are beautiful." His hands moved slowly over the newly exposed skin as he sucked in a breath through his teeth. "So very beautiful."

Rich dipped his head down and pressed his lips to her tender skin, causing her to gasp. Threading her fingers through his hair, Kate urged him to continue his exploration. Gentle kisses started on their path up her chest then turned frantic when they met her lips.

Her hands drifted down his back, pausing at the cotton that would be coming off this time. She slid her fingers beneath the fabric. His skin was soft and the muscles of his rear were firm under her touch.

Strong, eager fingers eased her pajama bottoms off and her panties soon followed. He grabbed her hips and stroked her stomach with his thumbs. His head lowered and she leaned up to meet his lips, willingly accepting all the passion in his kiss and releasing every ounce of the desire she'd ignored for so long.

Their tongues battled for position as his arms wrapped her in a tight embrace, molding her body into his. In one fluid motion Rich took control, reversing their position with such ease it was barely noticeable. His kisses continued to devote attention to every inch of her neck and chest, bracing himself above her on his arms.

His movements were slow as he made love to her. His soulful eyes stared at her with so much love that her own eyes started to water, overcome with the emotion flowing between them. *Oh, Rich, I love you.*

This was more than a coming together of their bodies. It was a culmination of their hearts, their very souls. She closed her eyes and forced any thoughts from her mind. She wanted to concentrate on only one thing. Rich. Making love to him—with him—was perfect, a true joining of their spirits.

Bliss consumed her in waves and she trembled beneath him, savoring his touch. Rich's breathing stopped. His broad shoulders bunched, every muscle tensed, as pleasure shook him. He slumped over her for a moment, his breathing staggered. He lifted his head and his navy eyes smoldered while he leaned down to press an intense kiss to her lips. He slowly lowered himself to Kate's side, cradling her against his body, kissing the back of her neck and bare shoulders. Heavy breaths against her skin caused a shiver to run down her spine and back up again.

"You okay, love?" he asked huskily.

"Um hum." She snuggled even closer to him and crossed her arms over his. "That was incredible." Her eyes closed as she tried to memorize how every inch of him felt against her.

"I thought so, too. We won't wait nearly as long for the next time."

Next time? Her heart jumped into her throat and tried to pound its way out. There was no way she could live without a next time, but... *Jesse. Holy hell, what have I done?* She closed her eyes and let Rich absorb some of the weight she was feeling. A sigh escaped her lips. She was content and contrite all at the same time.

He shook her gently. "Come on, love. We'll never get out of this room if you go to sleep because I won't have the heart to wake you. As far as I'm concerned the real world could disappear forever, and we could stay in this bed until the end of time." She could feel the smile on his lips as he pressed a kiss between her shoulder blades.

She rolled toward him, allowing herself one more chaste kiss before begrudgingly pulling herself from his hold, taking the sheet with her. "I'll be in the shower," she mumbled.

Steam started to billow over the top of the shower. After letting the sheet pool at her feet, Kate stepped under the hot water. The spray cascaded down her body and she poured some shampoo into the palm of her hand. Rubbing her hands together released the scent that was usually so relaxing.

I trust you. I trust you. I trust you. Jesse's words slammed into her like a battering ram.

As the fluffy, white bubbles found their way to the drain, Kate's intestines tied themselves into a knot. Her stomach threatened to heave the nothing that was in it, and her lungs refused to accept or release any air. The pounding of her heart was painful and she could almost feel it tearing in two, accentuating the horrible weight of what had happened bore down on her shoulders and caused her knees to wobble.

Using the back of the shower as a guide, Kate slid down to rest on the floor, hoping to be able to gain some semblance of control. None came. She gave in to the excruciating emotions and let them have her. Wrapping her arms around her knees and pulling her legs into her chest, Kate sobbed.

Her heart had been successfully divided. She was consumed with the guilt of what she had done to Jesse and how much her actions would devastate him. But remembering the stolen moments with Rich and imagining what a future could hold with him meant more to her than she dared even hope for.

The shower door opened with pop, and Kate didn't even look up as Rich stepped inside. His hands gripped her arms softly and he guided her to her feet. "Kate, I'm so sorry," he whispered.

Another sob broke free and her eyes met his. "And what exactly are you sorry for, Rich? Are you sorry you fell in love with me? Are you sorry we made love?"

Comforting arms embraced her, and soft lips kissed her wet cheeks. "I am not sorry for loving you. Making love to you is something I want to experience again and again. I'm sorry you're hurting. I would take it away if I could." He kissed her lips.

Rich simply held her as she cried out every last tear that wanted to fall, then he gently and devotedly washed every inch of her body, concentrating on her hair. His fingers massaged her scalp, easing the lather out of her hair. Turning off the water, he reached for a towel and wrapped it around her body.

Kissing her nose and each cheek, he soothingly gave her a soft peck on her lips. "We'll get through this, Kate. I'm here however you need me. I'll let you get dressed." He glanced down at all of his bare skin and smiled. "I need to get dressed too. I love you, Kate. I do not regret what happened between us and pray that you don't either." Another quick kiss, and then she was alone in the bathroom.

Kate quickly got dressed and tried to do her hair and makeup without looking at the reflection of the guilty woman that would be staring back at her.

Her phone rang, and she found herself praying that it wasn't Jesse. After the wonderful night sleeping in Rich's arm, not to mention the glorious hour she'd spent making love with him, having to pretend that everything was normal would be excruciating. Kate wouldn't be able to hide her infidelity for long. Jesse knew her better than she knew herself sometimes and would sense that something was horribly wrong.

"Hello?"

"Is this Kate Callahan?" The authoritative tone made her heart nearly leap out of her chest. There was something recognizable about the deep voice speaking to her, and Kate knew she should recognize it but couldn't place who it belonged to.

"Yes. Who's calling?"

"Kate, it's Reggie Brown."

Knowing the who of things allowed her to relax—a little. "Good morning, Chief, what's up?"

"Actually, um ... Kate, I don't..."

An uncomfortable half laugh burst out. "Come on, Reggie, it can't be that bad."

"Well, it's your apartment..." He paused again.

"Dammit, Reggie, spit it out. What the hell is wrong with my apartment? Did it burn down?"

"Someone broke into your apartment, Kate." His words rushed out, and she could see him, in her mind's eye, rubbing his hand over his stubbly chin.

"Oh." Well, that wasn't too bad. It certainly wasn't good, but possessions could be replaced. "How bad..."

"Kate," he interrupted her, his voice soft and serious, "do you have any enemies?"

"Enemies?" The question came out a strangled groan.

"There was some ... vandalism."

"What kind of vandalism?"

"It seems to be a crime targeted at you...a crime of ... passion," he whispered as if he were embarrassed to be discussing this with her.

"Reggie, I'm a big girl. Please just give me the details."

A deep breath resonated through the line. "It seems that the only things that were touched in the apartment were your, uh—" He coughed softly. "—your lingerie."

The air left her lungs in a small gasp. *Shea*, her thoughts screamed. *Holy hell!*

"It was shredded, all of it, and every mirrored surface in the place has the word 'whore' written across it in red lipstick. As far as we can tell, there's nothing missing, but we'll need you to verify that. How soon can you meet with me?"

"I was planning on coming home in about a week."

"Can it be quicker than that? The sooner we get going on this, the better...within the next forty-eight hours would be best."

Blood boiled in her veins, her heart ready to explode with the heat of it. *Damn, Shea.* "I'll see what I can do. Let me make a few calls and I'll let you know."

"This is my personal cell phone, call me back so that I can make arrangements." The line disconnected with a click.

Kate stared at the phone for a moment, caught up somewhere between numb and completely pissed off. Her finger pressed a few numbers, and she waited for Jesse's answer, while her stomach twisted in guilt-induced knots.

"Hey, baby."

"Hi, I have to get back." No need to pussy foot around the subject.

"Why?" She could hear the disappointment in his voice—and the worry. "What's wrong?"

A sigh rushed from her lungs. "I got a call from Chief Brown this morning, and someone broke into our apartment just to destroy stuff."

"I'll strangle the sonofabitch."

"I don't know how bad it is. I have to get back and do a walk through with them as part of their investigation. But I don't know what to do about the car, and there are still clothes at my parents' house." The words rushed out in an emotion-filled rant. She hoped that Jesse would just chalk it up to the break-in and not the fact that she had completely betrayed his trust.

"Kate, sweetheart, it'll be okay. Dad is doing so much better, and I was going to suggest that we both go home this weekend. I'll go get the clothes at your parents', then work something out with the guys to get the car back." He paused, probably formulating a plan in his head. "When I fly out of Sky Harbor, I'll have the guys drive up to take the car back. We'll work it out."

Another hardcore doze of guilt swept through her. "Okay. We'll talk soon."

He replied in the affirmative and the line went dead. Replaying all the events of the last few minutes over in her head unleashed an onslaught of emotions. Kate was relieved that she had put off the inevitability of breaking Jesse's heart for a few more days. She was overwhelmed by the intimacy that she had shared with Rich, furious with herself that she couldn't muster a single ounce of remorse, and completely pissed off that his crazy wife had been in her apartment destroying *her* things.

Giving into her anger, Kate closed the phone with a snap and threw it onto the bed. Seething irritation began to take over. Her eyes focused on the white door in the middle of the beige wall. She threw it open, satisfied when it slammed against the wall with a glass rattling bang then repeated the action with Rich's door. "Rich Spencer!"

The sound startled him, and he jumped, whipping around to face her. His eyes were wide, his mouth was open in a gasp, and his fingers were still stuck to the buttons of his open shirt.

"Do you have any idea what that psycho woman you're married to has done?" Fists formed at the bottom of her arms and slammed into her legs. "Dammit, Rich, she was in my apartment. My *apartment!*"

"*What?*"

Her blood ran cold as a shudder ripped down her spine. "How did she know where I live?"

"How the hell am I supposed to know?" His head shook back and forth on his broad shoulders as his hand grabbed at a lock of messy, caramel hair.

"This is your fault, you know?" Truthfully, there was no one to blame but herself. A fact she knew, but couldn't bring herself to accept.

"My fault?" he squeaked. "How is this *my* fault?"

"She knew you loved me." It came out as a whisper.

"Love, Kate, present tense. I love you." In three strong steps, he crossed the room and took her into his arms. "It will all be okay. Here, sit down."

Kate's feet moved absently, following him to the bed. She leaned into the arm that was still around her waist, needing desperately to feel the strength and love emanating from him. Easing down on the bed, she watched him as he stood and took the cell phone from his pocket, pressed in a number, and held it to his ear.

Anxiety spiked and fear threatened to consume her. If not for the smile on his face and his intense stare, she might have given into the churning of her stomach and vomited all over the floor.

"Claudia Reynolds, please." He paused, winking at Kate. "Rich Spencer. Thank you." The phone tipped away from his ear, and he smiled. "It will be okay, Kate."

"Who are you talking to?"

"It's my ... Yes, Claudia. Fine, thank you. Shea has gone too far now." He explained to the Claudia person what had happened with Kate's apartment and the suspicions of who had caused all the damage. "No, no proof at this point. I don't care. I need to go through with the divorce, *now*."

Divorce? Kate heard herself swallow.

"No, I'm not willing to wait anymore. I can't. I need to move on with my life. How soon can you serve the papers?"

Holy crap! Rich was speaking to his divorce attorney, requesting that Shea receive the papers. Rich was getting divorced. Divorced. He'd soon be free. Her mind was reeling with what that meant, with the possibilities. Was this because of her, because of what happened? She couldn't allow that.

"Thank you, Claudia." Rich sighed. "That is such good news." He closed the phone and rushed over, kneeling in front of Kate. His hands wrapped around hers. "Do you know what this means, love?"

"You're getting divorced?" came the monotone question.

"Yes. Which means...?" he drawled out the last word, encouraging her to finish the thought.

Kate knew what he wanted her to say, and although they'd just experienced the most amazing sex, she still wasn't sure what to do. Kate did love Rich, but she'd loved Jesse. She had promised Jesse her life, her heart, and her soul. But, somewhere along the line, Rich had crept his way in taking all three of those things.

"Kate?" Gentle squeezes to her hand brought her back. "You okay?"

"Rich, you can't bank on what happened between us. It was amazing, and—" Her eyes drifted closed, and her body began to react to the memories of his hands exploring every inch of her body. "—and everything, but ... Jesse is..."

Strong, soft fingers flashed out and covered her lips stopping the rest of her words. "There are a lot of differences between *him* and me, I get that. But has it ever been like *that* with Jesse?" He kissed her gently. "Let me love you, Kate. You will never want for anything. You think he's safe, he's comfortable, and, right now, I'm the frightening unknown. But with me, you'll always be loved, always be safe. Always."

"Rich." She sighed and then let the words rush out. "I can't kick the little voice in the back of my head that keeps trying to convince me that I'm nothing more than the rebound girl. You can't get divorced because of me. It's bad enough that I'm crazy in love with you. That you're all I think about. That I'm supposed to be getting engaged to another man, and it's you I want to wake up to every morning. " Her fists slammed into the bed at her sides. "Dammit! My life is such a mess." Tears burned her eyes and her throat began to constrict with emotions she didn't want to feel.

He chuckled softly as warm arms comforted her. "Kate, I can assure you that you are not the rebound girl. You are the *only* girl. That first day, when you stepped into the newsroom, I felt drawn to you. Then each moment since has been just another second that solidified how much I need you in my life."

"But you're getting divorced because of me," Kate blubbered.

"No, love, I am getting divorced because Shea is a horrible person who gets off on being mean and nasty. Not to mention the fact that she hates me. Our loveless marriage was over a long time ago. The papers have been prepared for over a month."

"A month?"

He nodded, taking her hands in his. "Kate, I was waiting in hopes of being able to get a protective order ... to protect *you*. The station would be listed on the order as off-limits, which would mean that while you were working with me, you would be safe. Then if I slept out in front of your house, you'd be safe while you were home."

Her head moved back and forth as his words sunk in. "Rich, you were planning on sleeping in your car ... in front of my apartment?" A nervous laugh escaped as she contemplated the absurdity of the thought. "That would thrill the hell out of Jesse to find you in the parking lot of our apartment complex."

"Kate, I couldn't care less what Jesse thinks or feels. You are the only thing that matters. I love you. Since the moment I met you, part of me has loved you. You are like air to me. I need you to survive."

"I hate that I have to hurt someone that I care so much about, but that seems to be an inevitability at this point."

His tongue swiped along his bottom lip, spreading moisture as it went. "I guess the question is...who do you see yourself with forever?"

Kate's heart answered the question right away. Her mind took only seconds to confirm the answer, but it took a few beats of her heart for her to have the courage to voice it. She thought of all the times he'd starred in her dreams, all the times she ached for his touch, and missed him when they were apart. She'd tried—really tried—to fight the feelings she had for him, but in the end she'd only tortured Rich—and herself. And now was the time to offer him what she should have given him in the beginning.

She launched herself off the bed and into his arms, knocking them both into the floor. She kissed his cheeks, his neck, his mouth. "You, Rich."

"Me? You're sure?"

"Rich, you are the one in my dreams. I need you in my life. When you're not around, my whole body aches. I can't survive without you either. Are *you* sure?"

He nodded and pressed his lips to hers.

Kate had one last request and prayed this wouldn't ruin everything. Her hands moved up between them and pressed against him. He pulled away, his blue eyes searching her face for answers. "I have to ask you one thing. It's really important me."

"Anything, love." His smile consumed his face, his eyes twinkled brightly.

"You've already waited so long, been through so much heartache, and I hate to ask you this, but I need more time. We can't be together until I break things off with Jesse. This isn't fair to him, and I hate that I'm hurting him. I do still love him."

His Adam's apple bobbed as he swallowed hard while considering the difficult request. "For you, I would wait forever." The corner of his lip lifted. "But please don't make me wait long. It feels like it's been an eternity already."

She kissed him then laughed. "Come on, we'd better go if we're going to make our flights."

His brows pulled together. "Flights?"

"Oh, yeah. I have to go home to meet with Reggie Brown about the break-in. So finish getting your stuff so we can be there in plenty of time. Maybe we can rearrange the seating so we can sit together on the plane." A smile was the reaction to that thought.

"Kate, I cancelled my flight so that I could spend a few days in Vegas with my parents."

Disappointment soaked her like a bucket of cold water. "Oh," she mumbled, fighting tears. Now that Kate had given into the desires of her heart, she never wanted to be away from him.

He kissed her cheek. "You know what? I'll just drive straight through and probably beat you home."

"You should at least stop in and say hello." She wrapped her arms around him, loving the way they seemed to fit together like two pieces of a puzzle.

"Yeah, I probably should. I'll be home by the weekend, I promise." He sealed the vow with a quick brush of his lips across hers. "And if you need me, I'm only a phone call away." He pulled her close, his arms encasing her in a hug. "We'll be together soon enough. Forever."

Stretching up on her tiptoes, she pressed her lips to his. "I love you, Rich Spencer."

Twenty One

"...Leave a message and I'll get back to you as soon as I can," Rich's sexy voice said for the millionth time today.

Fear and frustration bubbled violently in Shea's stomach as it clenched into an uneasy knot. She tapped the sparkle-covered Blackberry against her red hued bottom lip before chucking it against the wall above her bed. Upon impact rhinestones and pieces of plastic flew in every direction. "Dammit, Rich, where the hell are you?"

When she'd first started calling three days ago, after humiliating herself by surprising him in the wrong city, his phone rang incessantly before shifting to voicemail. But now, it would ring twice, maybe three times, before his voice would repeat the same message. His phone was on, it had to be, and he was avoiding her calls. *Damn caller id!* She didn't even want to think of whose calls he *was* answering.

Her fingers curled into fists, acrylic nails dug into the palms of her hands. She scowled at the woman staring at her from the mirror. "I'm his wife!" she screamed at her reflection. Fury hid just behind the unshed tears of aggravation.

Rich was having an affair. There was no other explanation. She recognized the signs. Hell, she'd *lived* the signs.

Cheating on Rich was the biggest mistake of her life. In those moments of unbridled infidelity, she'd thrown away any chance of true happiness. Her lungs filled with air, only to release it in a sigh. When Reese had rejected her, she'd had no choice but to return to the husband who loved her only because he didn't know about her betrayal.

Shaky hands rubbed violently at the tears that now rolled down her cheeks. She would not cry. Tears meant irrational behavior and she needed to be rational. She needed her wits about her, if she was going to figure this out. There had to be a way to win him back. She'd held his heart once. Winning it back might be difficult, but surely, it wasn't impossible.

Shea slid perfectly pedicured toes into a pair of black strappy sandals and walked out into the living room. Despite the chilly late January weather, she wanted to look great when Rich finally came home. And since he wasn't answering her calls, she would have to always look fabulous.

The television was already on from when she'd been watching it while drinking her morning screwdriver. Alcohol consumption first thing in the morning was something that Rich detested, but she'd learned long ago that what he didn't know wouldn't hurt him.

It has orange juice in it, she thought smugly before lifting the glass to her lips for another sip, only to spew the contents all over the room.

The bitch was back.

"...With photographer Nate Hughes, I'm Kate Callahan reporting for KHB." She flashed a smile, making her eyes twinkle and her face practically glowed. The bitch mocked Shea.

Rage began to build in Shea's gut, plaguing her bloodstream with a seething venom that seemed to scorch as it flowed. Her hand tightened painfully around the glass in her fingers only to feel it slipping from her hold. It fell to the floor and shattered upon meeting the tile.

Glass crunched under the soles of her shoes as Shea stomped through it to get to the medication that would take away all of these negative feelings. If she was going to get through this, she wouldn't be able to do it without a little drug-induced help. The prescribed dosage was only one pill, but given what she'd just learned, she shook a few more of the little white pills into the palm of her unsteady hand.

The waves of irritation at the mess of broken glass that had once contained her drink were washed away as her lips wrapped around the bottle of vodka. She tipped her head back and let the liquid burn its way over her tongue and down her throat. One gulp successfully did the trick, but Shea took another one for good measure.

"Just a few more minutes and you won't feel anything," she comforted herself.

Picking up the phone, she dialed the only friends she had left in this entire world. With desperation she tried to fight against the tears that were building but ended up sobbing through the tirade to her annoyed sister.

"Shea, calm down. I can't understand a word you're saying," Sharlice said into the phone before screaming at ShyAnne, "Get in here. Shea needs us."

Another line connected with a click. "What is it, darling? Please tell me it's not that no good husband of yours again."

"ShyAnne, you're not helping," Sharlice chided, then her voice softened, "What's wrong, Shea?"

"It's *her*," Shea hissed. Another intense wave of fury caused her skin to heat, the tears sizzling away. "Turn on your television. She's back."

"What are you talking about?" ShyAnne snorted.

"When I spoke to Rich on Tuesday, he said he was coming home in a few days. Well, it's Friday and *she's* home. So where the hell is *my* husband? Home! That's where he is. He has to be with her. I just know it." Her voice cracked as the final words of the rant left her mouth and her throat constricted with the emotions of that knowledge.

"You don't know that. Maybe he's..."

"He's what?" Shea interrupted. "Having a sleepover like some kind of child? Come on, don't patronize me. You have said all along, ShyAnne, that you thought this Kate girl was trouble. Do you not remember the text messages at Thanksgiving? Now I have proof that's he been using that little slut for the sex he's not getting from me."

The doorbell rang, and Shea's heart jumped into her throat. "Hold on, girls, that might just be him." Her hurried pace was accentuated by the clicking of her heels on the oak hardwood. She hurried down the few stairs to get to the door, excitement replacing the worry that had been eating at her. Maybe he did still love her.

As she dropped the phone from her ear, she heard Sharlice mumble, "Wouldn't he have a key?"

After taking a deep breath, her enthusiastic hands smoothed down the front of her blouse, then ripped the door open as her body prepared itself to jump into the arms of her husband. But everything skidded to a halt when a man she didn't recognize was standing on the porch. His dark blue jacket was halfway zipped, his starched white shirt barely visible underneath as he shifted nervous weight from one foot to the other. He smiled, his white teeth standing out against his olive-toned skin. "Shea Spencer?"

"Yes." Surprise struck, radiating through her like the vibrations of a tuning fork.

The man she'd thought was a salesman knew her name. "This is for you." He handed her an official looking envelope. "Please sign here," he said, extending his clipboard.

Shea scribbled her signature then, in a completely dazed state, closed the door. Her heart hammered in her chest, knowing what the manila envelope contained and not wanting to see the white and blue papers that would mean the end of her marriage. She'd worked for a law firm and recognized being served. Cotton replaced her tongue and, despite the incessant urge to vomit, she couldn't find the saliva to moisten it.

Numb fingers slid beneath the seal and slid the contents out. It was exactly what she'd expected; Rich wanted a divorce.

The room started to spin and her mind couldn't focus. As her knees began to give out, she gave into the laws of gravity and sank to the floor just as tears flowed down her cheeks. Anguish took over and her shoulders shook with sobs. This wasn't happening. Not again. She would not let another man walk out of her life to leave her for a woman they found more attractive or more interesting or whatever the hell Rich saw in the pale-skinned, mousy Kate Callahan.

The thoughts only added to the jealousy and anger that were quickly overtaking the pity, sadness and fear.

"Shea! Shea!" The muffled shouts from her sisters came from the phone that had fallen to the floor next to her. "Shea, are you there?"

Shaky hands fumbled with the phone, somehow managing to find her ear. "Yes," she whispered.

"Who was it?" Sharlice asked.

"Yeah, since we're guessing it wasn't Rich," ShyAnne sneered his name.

"He wants a divorce." Shea sounded so surprised, and honestly she was. She and Rich had a great marriage—once. They had both had their share of infidelity, but they had worked through it. She had forgiven him for sleeping with Kate months ago, and well, he never knew about hers, so it was as though it never happened. Her lips tipped upward at the corners. *He really is a fool to not have noticed. Did he think I'd taken up a vow of celibacy in the months Reese and I had been working so many hours of overtime? I didn't want to have sex with my husband and cheat on my lover.*

Just thinking about Reese had her body overheating with the desire he always sparked in her. With his sleek black hair and intoxicating steel gray eyes, and a body that belonged in a magazine, he had her from the first smile of his perfect lips.

Despite all that, Rich belonged to Shea. He had a kind heart, a sexy body, and had vowed to give her both … until death, do they part. *Death, do us part. 'Til death, do you part.*

"Girls, I've got to go," Shea told her sisters. Their voices asked a thousand questions she didn't have time to answer, interrupting the thoughts that were quickly becoming a plan of revenge and retribution. "Listen, I really need to do something. I'll call you later."

"Shea," the tone of Sharlice's voice was a warning, "don't do anything stupid."

"You know me," Shea reminded them.

"That's what has us worried," ShyAnne said under her breath.

Shea chose to ignore the snide comment and focus on what needed to happen in the upcoming hours. If she played her cards right, she would be completely vindicated by tonight—and that two-timing bastard, she once called her beloved would get what was coming to him. The corner of her lip curled into a smirk. *With any luck, his whore will be with him.*

The smile on her face grew as the plans began to come together in her mind. She knew exactly what she would do. The events unfolded in her mind just as though the future was revealing itself.

After changing into something more comfortable—and more conducive to her plans—Shea made her way over to the scene of Rich's betrayal. She'd seen this little apartment before, even parked in the same spot in the parking lot. The same elderly man with his poodle passed her in the hall as she walked toward the lock that would be so easy to pick again.

Reese had taught her that little trick too, every time they went to his wife's family's little cabin that sat completely secluded up the canyon.

The older gentleman smiled, and Shea returned the gesture. The white furball cradled in his arms growled at her, but the sound was quickly muffled by an age-spotted hand. "Sorry, miss, he's usually so friendly."

"It's okay," she mumbled, then continued her journey.

Standing outside the familiar door, she revisited the satisfaction of a few days ago when she easily shredded the various pieces of satin, lace, and feathers that once had adorned the spindly body of that hussy. The slut did have good taste though, nothing off the Wal-Mart clearance rack in that girl's panty drawer. It seemed to have all been from Victoria's Secret, Frederick's, or some online lingerie peddler. Shea hoped Rich wouldn't recognize the expensive, all leather bustier and panty combo she didn't have the heart to shred.

The door was open in a matter of seconds, and Shea

again crossed the threshold into the den of sin. It was quite different from what she'd left behind. The picture in the entry—the one of the man-stealing hussy on the back of her poor unknowing boyfriend—no longer wore the mark of her cheating. Shea frowned. *It had looked so much better with 'whore' written across it.* But someone had carefully cleaned off the red lipstick.

"Well, that just won't do," Shea whispered, pulling the tube out of her purse and raising it to fix what someone had destroyed. *But if Rich cleaned it off...* Her hand paused midair. She certainly didn't want to give any warning that something was amiss. If Rich had been the one to wipe the stain from the face of his mistress and her boyfriend... *He's an even bigger fool than I thought.*

The tube slid easily back into her bag and she continued to survey the scene that had been returned to order. Inside the bedroom, curiosity got the best of her, and she slid the drawer open to find only a black nightie occupying the spot that had once been overflowing. Her fingers slid over the fabric, and she could imagine the dark lace against her pale skin as Rich's hands eagerly removed it. He had a way of making the process of unwrapping his lover more erotic than the actuality of making love.

Her tongue slid over her bottom lip before teeth bit it, she anticipated the reunion and redeclaration of their undying love for each other. She tossed the black lace over her shoulder and continued her search of the tidy apartment.

The bathroom was lit by the late afternoon sun that poured through the glass block windows. Her feet carried her further into the room only to pause in front of the mirror that nearly covered the entire wall above the sink. Big blue eyes widened, horrified by the unbecoming outfit.

"Drab does not suit you."

If she was going to win Rich back from the little whore, this boring, all black cotton and denim get-up would not bring him running into her arms. Shea reached for the hem of her t-shirt and ripped it over her head, exposing a black bra.

The counter that had been empty when she visited last was now full of the lotions and perfumes that had been a key to gaining her love's heart. On the edge of the bathtub was a bottle of shampoo and bubble bath that must have also been in Arizona with the home-wrecking slut. One swift flick of her thumb, and her sinuses were overcome with the sickeningly sweet scent of coconut. Her initial reaction to the hideous smell was punctuated by a sneeze, and she closed the lid, setting the bottle back down on the edge of the tub before turning the knobs to start the water pouring into the large, white basin.

After adding a dollop of vanilla scented bubble bath, Shea turned back toward the counter and ran her fingers over the various bottles arranged there. A spray of perfume dissipated into the air, and Shea sniffed, inhaling the scent that Kate had been wearing the one time she had been close to her. Another exaggerated sniff and her body suddenly ached to bathe in the scent of the woman who had stolen her husband's heart.

As the tub filled with water and bubbles, the scent of vanilla wafted through the air. Shea quickly shed the rest of her boring clothes, stuffed them into her bag then eased down into the hot water and relaxing foam.

"Mmm." A moan escaped her lips. "I have to give it to her, Kate has great taste in men and bubble bath." Rapid heartbeats sent anxiety speeding through her bloodstream, and she filled her lungs with a vanilla-coated breath and tried to relax by reminding herself that the skank still had hours before she'd even be leaving the station. Her eyes were suddenly very heavy and drifted closed despite her best mental arguments. Her head rested against the cold porcelain.

Shea awoke with a start. Cold water caressed her skin in bubbleless waves. The dim light proved that it'd been more than just a catnap. She jumped out of the tub, grabbed the towel off the rack, and quickly dried off her pruned skin. A few swipes of the putrid lotion that smelled like a florist's shop, and she slipped the lace and satin over her head. Turning from one side to the other, she admired the beautiful woman staring back at her.

"How could he not love this?" she whispered through a smile as her hands smoothed the satin over her flat stomach. *Heels. I need to find a pair of heels.*

Fifteen steps back into the bedroom brought her into a pathetically small closet where the perfect pair of shoes was lying haphazardly on the floor; black, four-inch, patent leather platforms that would bring her lips even closer to Rich's.

Holding the door jamb for support, Shea slipped her toes into the beautiful shoe. It was a tight fit even without her heel in the pump. *There's a price for beauty, Shea!* A thrust and a groan later, and her feet were completely encased in their shoe-shaped vises, which sent cramping pains up her calves.

With cautious, painful steps, she walked toward the bed, suddenly very curious as to what kinds of things Rich's precious whore kept in the nightstand next to her bed. A notebook, a pen, and a remote control.

What, no condoms? Was the hussy trying to trap Rich with an 'unplanned' pregnancy? Before he came back to Shea's bed, a blood test would have to be taken, to prove that he hadn't contracted anything from the little tramp. A shudder ran up and down her spine at the thought of what Kate might have given him.

Absent-minded hands thumbed through the notebook, finding only empty pages. Her heart skipped a beat as a picture fluttered toward the floor. Every jealous cell in her body recognized the glimpse of the man. Rich.

She picked up the picture between her index finger and thumb to verify what she already knew. He was seated casually in a chair, facing the camera, with his hands resting on his thighs. His eyes were twinkling right through the paper, flirting with her, loving her while his lips pulled into his signature smirk. All the relaxation of her bath vanished in a flash, replaced by fury. Turning it over exposed familiar handwriting that nearly brought her to her knees.

Never forget that I love you.

Her hand wrapped itself around the photograph, crushing it into a ball before she threw it back into the drawer. She then made her retreat to the kitchen. The clicking of the shoes was annoyingly loud as they met the tile near the stove.

"What to use...? What to use...?" The unnatural sound of her voice caused the hair on the back of her own neck stand on end. But a case of goose pimples was not going to keep her from a bit of revenge.

Her hand wrapped comfortably around the handle of the largest knife in the butcher's block just as a key slid into the lock. Now was the moment she'd anticipated. A glance over her shoulder revealed a closet that meant her only chance at a surprise attack.

Shea snuggled in against a jacket, which surely would have fit a Neanderthal, and sniffed the glorious smell of leather mixed with the natural cologne of the man who owned it. A stab of pain nearly brought tears to her eyes as she thought of the other scorned side of this horrible situation. Poor Jesse didn't deserve what he was getting. If things didn't work out with her and Rich, she would volunteer to comfort Jesse's pain away.

Through the crack in the door, Shea could see Rich as he entered the apartment carrying roses, a paper bag, and a bottle of wine. The smile of his gorgeous face was breathtaking as he put the wine in the refrigerator and the vase of already blooming red roses on the table.

The first couple of buttons were open on his shirt, showing off the strength and sculpted perfection of his chest. The white of his shirt was a striking contrast to the black slacks that clung to all the right parts of his muscular legs and rear. He had been the most handsome man she'd ever seen, and the day he married her was one of the best of her life.

Crinkling paper brought her out of her ogling, and she watched while strong hands gently spread rose petals from the front door toward the bedroom. Anxious, sweat covered her body as if someone had doused her with water as her mind's eye pictured the scene in the bathroom. The tub was still full and her bag still sat in the middle of the floor spewing the clothes she'd been wearing.

Water rushed through the pipes in the wall behind

her, and deductive reasoning wasn't needed to know that Rich had pulled the plug. She prayed he didn't look too closely at the contents of the bag.

A happy little tune in the form of whistling came into the room before Rich did. When he came into view from her vantage point, he was just pulling something out of his pocket. Her curiosity piqued. She strained her eyes in hopes of seeing better. When the ring box came into view, vomit crept its way up the back of her throat.

Tears burned her eyes. *I'm such a fool.* Her fingers gripped the handle tight preparing to make her attack. *We're not even divorced yet.*

"Oh, Kate." The masculine sigh stung her heart. He sounded so happy. "I will make you mine tonight." He pressed the ring to his lips and stuffed it back into his pocket. His next movements were quick and concise, lighting candles and making the apartment the most romantic place she'd ever seen.

Rich's proposal to Kate was going to be so much more romantic than the quickie, Vegas wedding Shea got. After spending three and a half years at UNLV, she coaxed a proposal and wedding out of Rich. The timing had to be perfect. She'd waited for an alcohol-induced, passion-filled weekend when his parents and Nate weren't around to object. Would he have even married her if she hadn't dragged him in front of the King while he'd been so heavily intoxicated?

Self pity was not an emotion she wanted to feel in this moment. Anger was. Shea concentrated on the events unfolding in front of her eyes. If she hurried, she could do a little slice and dice, get her revenge by taking away the man Kate loved, killing the two-timing bastard who had committed a betrayal.

Her hand pushed gently against the door but when it squeaked, she paused. This would have to be quick. A deep cleansing breath stretched her lungs and she prepared to attack as soon as his back was turned. The wood in the palm of her hand was warm from being held so long. She switched hands, wiping off any sweat that might be there.

They say the first cut is the deepest and she

intended to make hers count. He would know what hit him, and he would know who had delivered the fatal blow. She would do to Rich's heart what he had done to hers—leave it broken and unable to function.

A key in the lock caused Rich to pause, his shirt expanded to capacity as his lungs filled with air. He was obviously nervous, but not for the thing he should be. The slut would say yes—if Shea gave him the chance to propose.

The door opened and his lips pulled into a smile when he saw her. Kate gasped, her hands flew up to her face and the soulless pits where her eyes should be glanced around at all the work Rich had done.

"What ... what are you doing here?" Kate stood unmoving just inside the door.

He rushed to her, taking her into his arms. "Don't tell me you're disappointed." His lips met her cheek and a tear rolled down Shea's. "I told you I'd be home this weekend."

Kate's hand stroked his jaw from hairline to chin as she smiled. "Yeah, but it's only Friday. I didn't expect you until this *weekend*, like tomorrow or Sunday." Her arms moved around his back and she melted herself into his chest.

A deep chuckle rumbled, muffled by her body pressed against his. "I wanted to surprise you. There's something I've been dying to ask you." He pulled her into the apartment, and there was a loud thud as his shoe forced the door closed. "Come here, I want to do this right. You know I have loved you since almost the first moment I saw you."

Kate nodded, her eyes filled with tears to match the ones flowing freely down Shea's cheeks. As Rich made the motion to kneel, a sob sounded in stereo—Kate's and Shea's. The noise caused them both to turn around.

Shit! So much for the element of surprise. Shea threw the door open lunging at them. She was quick enough to sink the blade firmly into his chest. "You son of a bitch!" she screamed, withdrawing the steel as she pulled back.

His eyes widened in surprise, and it almost sickened Shea to realize what she'd become capable of. Almost.

He deserved what was coming to him. The white shirt he wore began to turn red as the blood gushed from the wound.

Kate screamed and caught Rich in her arms as he stumbled. "What have you done?" She dug through her bag and retrieved her cell phone. Three numbers later, she spoke to an operator. "We need an ambulance, now!" With the phone held in the crick of her neck, she rattled off the address and started to remove her jacket, stuffing it against the deep gash of his chest.

"I can't allow that," Shea whispered, taking the phone out of Kate's hand and throwing it across the room. "You both deserve what's happening now."

"What are ... you ... talking about?" came the gurgled question. "I never ... did anything ... to you."

"Shut up, Rich!" Shea slapped him across the face with the back of her hand, sending him further into Kate's embrace. "I know you slept with this whore."

"You don't ...know what—" He coughed, grabbing his chest. "—you're ... talking about."

"Shh." Kate's voice was a soft whisper in his ear as tears dripped from her chin onto his cheek. "It will be okay." Her hand softly stroked his hair as she continued to comfort him.

It was quite a tender scene, if one enjoyed watching two adulterers lie to each other.

Kate leaned over him to press a tender kiss to his lips. "Don't you die on me, Jesse."

He looked at Shea with hatred festering in every line of his face. He held her hand as tight as his dying body could. "Kate would ... never ... betray me. I ... trust ... her." He gave her a weak smile and his eyes drifted closed as his shallow breaths became strained.

"Jesse!" Kate shrieked, her voice emanating the exact pain Shea had been hoping to cause. "Jesse Vasquez! Don't you leave me!" She shook his motionless body. Her face was dampened with the tears that flowed steadily down her cheeks.

"Stop calling him Jesse. Do you think I'm stupid?" Shea hissed, still gripping the knife in her hand.

"This *is* Jesse, you psychotic bitch!" Kate slowly

stroked her fingers over his pale, masculine features. "It'll be okay, Jesse."

The words combined with the sirens that were getting closer by the second caused Shea to shake herself back to reality. Her head moved back and forth as the realization of what she had done struck her. She dropped the knife, grabbed the vase, and hurried toward the distraught whore, smashing the glass into her head as her legs were pinned under the weight of her dying lover. Kate collapsed in a heap on top of him.

Shea took one last look at the wounded man Kate didn't deserve. "I'm sorry, Jesse, truly I am. I never meant to bring you into this." The toe of Kate's shoe—the ones that looked better on Shea's feet—met her side in one more act of vengeance. "Blame yourself for this Kate, dear. There is no one else to blame." Then Shea ran into the bathroom, wrapped her fingers around her bag, and escaped out the bathroom window.

The choices Shea had made tonight would be irreparable. Rich still deserved to die—even more so now. And, with a little help from her family, Shea would have time to accomplish that. Eventually.

Twenty Two

Kate was pretty sure her head was being assaulted by a meat cleaver. The constant throbbing and massive headache affected her stomach, making it churn and threaten to heave at any moment.

Without opening her eyes, she cautiously lifted her hand toward her head only to be stopped by a painful tugging sensation. The other hand wasn't an option because something warm was holding it in a gentle, unrelenting vise.

She peaked through her lashes to see Rich's hand wrapped around hers. His arms were crossed and his head rested on his forearms. His chest expanded and contracted with deep breaths as he slept.

Through the pain in her head, she tried to piece together where she was and what had happened. The white sterile environment and the IV, that had been the source of the tugging, were a good indication of a hospital, but why…?

Frantic sobs ripped from her throat as the memories rushed at her, pummeling her like a swimmer lost in the middle of the ocean during a hurricane. Just as she thought she resurfaced, another round or horrifying images slammed her beneath the surface. Her lungs burned with the need for oxygen, and her body began to thrash around in fear.

Rich jumped to his feet. "Kate." His voice registered all the panic she felt, as did his eyes. "You're okay, Kate."

Her frantic breaths rushed in and out of her lungs, and all kinds of beeping started around her. Warm hands rested on each side of her face, Rich's eyes stared into hers. His voice was calm as he spoke, "Kate, you need to calm down. You're okay, that's all that matters, right now."

Kate took a deep breath and concentrated on Rich's face and nothing else. A strained smile crossed his lips as gentle fingers moved the strands of her hair away from her forehead. He leaned down and kissed her. His eyes were kind, yet worried, as he smiled again.

"Tell me what you remember, love."

Her mind began to spin as the throbbing continued. As though it were a movie rewinding, memories flashed through the background. "I remember," she began, pausing to clear her scratchy throat. "I remember that you only stayed one night with your parents—" She squeezed his hand trying to ease her nervous energy. "—because you couldn't bear to be away from me."

He smiled, but it was only an echo of what he was capable of. "True enough, being apart tears at my heart, love. This is important though. I need you to remember exactly what happened after that."

She put her hands on each side of her head, trying to stop the pounding. Whatever medication they had her on wasn't working on the pain, but was certainly effective in keeping her loopy and unable to focus.

"Okay, give me a second." Kate closed her eyes and slowly shook her head from side to side. Whether the movement was to clear her thoughts or to avoid the pain of the memories her subconscious knew were coming, she couldn't be sure. "You kissed me goodbye at the station." A smile spread across her face at the memory of his intoxicating caress. "You were going to go change at Nate's so that we could go to dinner."

He nodded, his expression serious which caused an onslaught of butterflies in her stomach. "Then what?"

"Then..." She paused, forcing her mind to focus. "I went home." Horrible fear and apprehension flowed through her bloodstream as sweat covered her cold skin.

Soft lips met hers, but his eyes were full of cobalt intensity as he urged her to continue. "What happened, love?"

Breath rushed from her lungs in short, frantic bursts as the various pieces of machinery began beeping to match the erratic beats of her heart. Her eyes burned with tears that suddenly battled for release. A sob erupted and she buried her head in her hands, fiercely trying to avoid the horrific memories that assaulted her thoughts. Through tear-filled eyes she searched for Rich's face. His eyes reflected the pain she felt as his thumb stroked over her shaking hand. "Shh. What else do you remember?"

"Shea," Kate breathed the name as if it were the vilest word in the English language. "She was in my apartment, Rich. She rushed from the closet wearing my negligee and stabbed Jesse." Another sob took over, causing her to shake under the intensity. "Oh no. No. No. No. No. Jesse!" A voice she didn't recognize burst out of her throat. It was full of an agony that caused her numb body to shake.

People started to rush around the room checking her vitals and injecting various syringes into the IV. The hysterics that were on the verge of consuming her were quickly numbed, leaving her barely coherent—for the moment.

"I don't think now is a good time, Reggie." Kate heard Rich say through the fog.

Chief Brown was here. "I heard her scream. Is she okay?" He paused then said softly, "You know I need to get a statement from her, Rich. She's the only one who knows what happened. Maybe she saw who did it."

Rich's voice was full of guilt and grief when he spoke, "Reggie, she said it was Shea."

"Shea?"

"My ... wife."

"Oh." Reggie's tone lacked the judgment Kate deserved. "Well, that gives us a place to start. I'll leave an officer in the hall. Let them know when she's ready to give a statement."

When the door closed Kate forced her heavy lids open and searched for Rich in the room. She knew he wouldn't leave her when she needed him so much, but she needed the verification.

The crotchety nurse turned to glare at Rich. "I'm going to have to ask you to leave, Mr. ....."

"Spencer," Rich supplied his name. "But I am not leaving her. Ever."

"Are you her..."

"We've been through this." Rich's voice was acidly calm as he addressed the nurse. "I am not leaving this room unless Kate tells me to." He looked down at Kate and smiled reassuringly. "Do you want me to leave, Kate?"

Her head moved, creating a scratching sound against the pillow. "No," she said in a weak whisper, "I need you."

"Fine," the annoyed nurse snorted, "but if you upset her again, I'll have security remove you."

"It's not my presence that's upsetting her," Rich retorted. "She has been through a lot the last few weeks."

Whatever cocktail the medical professionals had sent into her bloodstream was taking control and, despite all the willpower she had, her eyes drifted closed and the voices around her sounded like they were miles away—and drifting.

"Mr. Spencer." The nurse's tone was irritated, and Kate's mind's eye pictured the stout woman with her hands on her hips glaring at Rich. "I will not have you upsetting this poor girl. It's bad enough that the boy she came in with ended up in the morgue."

Morgue! her thoughts screamed. Tears flowed out from under lids that refused to open. Jesse was dead. Her Jesse was gone...and it was her fault. She'd allowed herself to fall in love with a married man who was married to a mentally unstable, murdering bitch. She moaned through the drug-induced haze then, unable to help herself, gave into the nothingness that awaited her.

× × ×

Anger boiled through his veins as Rich glared at the plump woman who stood in front of him. "How dare you," he snarled.

Her squinty, dull gray eyes blinked innocently. "I'm sure I don't know what you're talking about."

"There are more tactful ways to tell someone that the person they cared about didn't make it." Rich checked to make sure Kate was finally peaceful before continuing. "What if she heard you?"

She snorted and took a step backward. "She'll know soon enough, Mr. Spencer."

"How about you work on your bedside manner, and *I'll* work on helping Kate get through this." His teeth bit down on his tongue, making it behave, and he turned toward the beautiful, broken girl in the bed.

His only concern was Kate. She was the most important thing in his life and, come hell or high water— or a man with handcuffs in cahoots with a feisty nurse— Rich was not going to leave her side.

The tranquilizers had finally taken their desired effect and the agonized expression on Kate's face had faded into peaceful, relaxed lines. Her breathing was steady, although despite it all, tears continued to flow from under her lashes.

He could feel the scrutinizing gaze on him as he moved the chair back to the side of Kate's bed. The door closed with a quiet pop, signaling that they were finally alone.

Gratitude nearly overwhelmed him as Rich watched Kate sleep. Tears came to his eyes as he studied the contrast of deep auburn against the stark white of her pillow. Her pale skin was beautiful, in spite of the fact that she was trying to recover from an injury that never would have happened if he would have just followed her home like he'd wanted.

His fingers moved along the delicate features of her face. She sighed and turned toward his touch. "I love you, Kate." He pressed his lips to hers in a gentle kiss. "I will do everything in my power to help you get through this." Rich fought the urge to climb in next to her. Instead he simply took hold of her hand and laid his head on their clasped hands and drifted to sleep.

A heavy hand on his shoulder woke Rich out of a fitful sleep. His head jerked up to meet Nate's supportive half smile. "You okay, my man?" He tightened his grip. "Everybody's really worried—" He tilted his head toward the still sleeping beauty, then his gaze returned. "— about both of you."

Roxy smiled as she set a bouquet of flowers on the little table next to Kate's bed. "You look like hell."

"Thanks." Rich's legs were asleep and nearly gave out as he stood. He leaned against the wall and stuffed his hands in his pockets. "Who covered it?"

"Clayton." Nate said the name Rich expected.

A groan of frustration and irritation came from Rich's lungs. "Of course, he did."

"It was actually really good." Roxy smiled as Rich scoffed. "No really, it's true. He said something about how you all spend every day covering the news, and that it's with great sadness that he's reporting on a member of your own family, who has become the story."

"I'll bet he *loved* that he could smear me publicly. I can hear it now." His voice rose, taking on a mocking tone, "'Our very own Rich Spencer brought the retaliatory wrath of his crazy wife on reporter Kate Callahan and her unsuspecting boyfriend.'" His tone returned to normal. "Am I close?"

Nate's warm chuckle rumbled over the quiet beeping of the machines. "Is that the guilt talking, Rich?"

"Damn straight," Rich muttered, turned his back to him and returned to his love's side. "I'd be a heartless bastard to not feel guilty. My actions brought about the murder of a man who'd done nothing but love Kate. I am just as guilty of that crime as he was. Dammit, I wish I could go back and change things."

Nate slipped into his periphery and held his hands up in surrender. "Easy, tiger."

The door opened, then closed and Rich turned to see that Roxy had left. Rich shoved his hands roughly through his hair. "I did this to her, Nate." He took hold of her small, lifeless hand and slumped back down in his chair.

"You can't blame yourself for this, Rich. *You* didn't bash Kate in the head with that vase and *you* didn't stab Jesse."

"I may not have been holding the knife, but I pushed Shea too far. I knew she was dangerous and..." He took a chance and let his eyes seek out the judgmental look of his best friend.

Nate was shaking his head. "Honestly, Rich, are you that stupid?"

His mouth moved, but Rich couldn't seem to form any words and he stood, bracing himself to take the criticism straight on.

"Shea is crazy, has been for years. This is not your fault. Did you make mistakes? Hell, yeah. The biggest of which being the fact that you waited so damn long to divorce the psychotic bitch." He paused. "I'm the last one you'll find judging you for following your heart. If Kate's what you need to feel complete, then don't give up on her. She's going to need space, time, love, and *a lot* of understanding. Be patient with her, my friend." He took a step forward and offered his hand. When their hands were clasped, Nate pulled Rich into a hug with their hands between them. "Call me if either of you need anything."

"I will. Thanks."

Nate smiled and handed Rich a DVD. "I don't know if Dale had a hand in this or if Clayton just chose not to be a dick for the first time in his pitiful life, but..." He laughed. "Well, check it out if you want. I burned you a copy of the air check."

The rest of the night was complete with phone calls from Dale, Olivia, Jordan, and even Claudia, who called to say that she had pushed through a protective order for Rich and Kate. Some friends of Kate's, Josh and Sophia, had stopped by and through gritted teeth Josh informed Rich that her parents would be here tomorrow morning.

Nurse Nasty tried to make Rich leave, giving him the excuse that visiting hours were over and there were rules that needed to be followed.

"Do what you have to, but I am not leaving," Rich told her in a harsh whisper.

She rolled her eyes, then her shoes squeaked against the white tile floor as she left in a huff, her irritating, nasally voice muttering something about the 'poor girl's obsessive boyfriend'.

When the door opened a little while later, Rich's whole body tensed in preparation for another round with the old bitty that didn't want him in Kate's room. He wasn't even going to give her the satisfaction of even acknowledging her presence. He brushed a lock of hair from Kate's cheek and kissed her softly.

"Are you Rich Spencer?" came the quiet question. He turned his head to meet the deep blue eyes that were an exact match for the scrubs on the pretty, young nurse. Her long, dark curls were swept up in a ponytail. "Rich?" she asked again.

"Yeah." He sat up straight. "Um, yes, I'm Rich."

She smiled. "I don't know who you know, but somebody with some clout made some calls on your behalf." She opened the door further to reveal a roll-away bed. "Are you tired, Mr. Spencer?"

His feet met the floor with a thud and were practically running over to help her with the awkward contraption.

Once they had it all situated just a few feet from Kate's bed—a problem easily fixed as soon as the nurse left the room—Rich thanked her and asked the same question he'd asked every new person to walk through the door. "So when can she go home?"

Nurse Nice smiled, her eyes focused only on the chart she flipped through. Rich wondered if she had even heard his question until she spoke. "Hmm..." She tapped her lip with her finger. "It looks like she might get discharged tomorrow, as long as she comes off the tranquilizers okay."

His lungs filled with the first relaxed breath in hours.

She looked up and offered a feigned gasp of surprise. "Oh, I didn't realize you were listening." A smile tugged at the corners of her red lips as her eyes twinkled mischievously. She winked over her shoulder. "Good night."

× × ×

Morning light poured into the room, and Rich woke to the gorgeous eyes of the woman he loved staring at him. He scrubbed his eyes with the back of his hand.

"You're still here," she whispered in disbelief.

"Of course." He kissed her forehead. "Only you have the power to keep me away. I am here by your side forever."

The door opened again and the man he knew as Kate's doctor walked in. "Good morning. How are you feeling?"

"Okay. A little tired. Can I go...?" She paused.

"I'll discharge you as soon as I make sure everything's okay." He did a quick once over. "Looks good. I'll send the nurse in with the paperwork and have her get this out of your hand." He patted the IV softly.

Kate waited until the doctor was gone before she looked at Rich through tear-filled eyes. "Rich, is Jesse..." She didn't finish the question.

He sat down next to her on the bed and pulled her into his arms. She relaxed and her cheek rested against his chest. Her hand wrapped tightly around in his shirt. Tears started to fall, dampening the cotton. "Yes," he answered her, "Jesse is gone. I am so sorry."

The tiny rivulets ran down her cheeks with a greater intensity as her shoulders shook with a sob. His hands moved over her back, desperately trying to ease her pain.

Nurse Nice cleared her throat in the doorway. "I just need a few minutes."

Kate pulled against his embrace and wiped at her wet face.

The nurse made quick work of the IV, and had Kate sign away her firstborn before gathering the papers. "Do you have a ride home?"

"Yes," Rich answered for her, "I'll make sure she's taken care of from here." When Kate and Rich were alone, the tears started again. "What's wrong, love?" It was a stupid, insensitive question, but he hoped she'd just answer it without too much analysis.

"I don't have anywhere to go. I don't have anything

to wear, except *this*." She tugged at the blasé cotton covering her. "With the exception of a few pictures, there is nothing I want from the place I used to call home."

"I'll take care of it—of you. You won't have to worry about anything."

She sniffed. "I just need to go home."

Rich didn't understand her contradiction. "I thought—"

"To Flagstaff, Rich. I need to take Jesse, and go home."

"I'll call the airlines and make the arrangements. We'll get Olivia to bring you some things to wear, and then we can go—"

"No!" she shouted. "You can't. Jesse didn't know that I betrayed his trust, and I won't dishonor his memory by showing up at his funeral with my lover." She may as well have reached out and slapped him, the sting of that statement was the same. "I have to do this on my own."

"Whatever you want, love. If it's okay, I'll call and make arrangements with Olivia for you to stay with her and Jordan."

She shook her head and met his eyes through her tears. "I think I'll stay with our friends, Josh and Sophia. They'll want to come home to the funeral."

Our friends? With that one statement, she successfully shut Rich out of her life. He prayed that she wouldn't do it forever.

Twenty Three

It'd been four days since Rich had watched, like some kind of pathetic spy lurking in the shadows, as Mr. and Mrs. Callahan escorted his broken-hearted Kate through the airport terminal. Four gut-wrenching days since Kate had told him, in no uncertain terms, to let her do this alone. Four excruciating days since he'd been able to look in Kate's beautiful eyes and tell her how much he loved her.

Worry plagued him. Kate was strong, but she shouldn't have to do this on her own. He shook his head to bring his thoughts to the here and now. He would be there for her. Always.

Jordan drove the rental car into the parking lot of the little white church in Flagstaff, Arizona. The sky was overcast, and the sidewalk was still wet from an earlier rain. A black hearse—a painful reminder—was waiting to take Jesse the last few miles that his body would ever travel.

Rich's eyes burned under the dark Oakley's that wouldn't leave his face—unless Kate requested that specific thing.

"Rich," Olivia's somber voice asked, "you ready?"

Am I ready? For what, to strut in there, disrupt their mourning, and piss Kate off for not honoring her request? To break his own heart all over again as he watched the woman he loves devastated over the death of another man? "Ready or not, as they say," he mumbled, jerking the handle on the Honda Accord.

The air was so damp that it was even more difficult to breathe. A gust of ice cold air stung his cheeks and glued his pants against his legs. Rich stuffed his hands deep into the pockets of his black wool overcoat, and Olivia slipped her arm through his.

"We're here as much for you as we are for her, Rich. This has to be—"

"I don't want to talk about it, Olivia."

"Okay." She slipped away from Rich and fell into step with Jordan, who was walking just behind him to the left.

The heavy wooden doors were closed, keeping out the rain, cold—and unwanted guests. If not for the fact that Kate was on the other side, Rich would have turned around and waited in the car. Jordan reached around him, tugged the door open, and walked past him. The heat from the quaint little chapel flowed over him, causing his body to break out in a sweat underneath his clothes. It wasn't that he was hot, though; it was seeing Kate.

She was standing with a group of people near the front, and behind her was the closed casket with a large spray of red roses on top. Jesse.

One of the men turned around and walked slowly down the aisle toward Rich and his friends. Kate didn't even turn around. The tissue in her right hand was balled up and periodically moved up to wipe at her face.

"I'm sorry, but the service doesn't start for two hours."

"Oh, we know, we're just a little early. I'm Jordan Greene from KHB and was asked by our News Director, Dale Morris, to come with my colleagues here to show our support for Kate at this horribly difficult time."

The older gentleman offered his hand. "It's nice to meet you. I'm Ken Callahan, Kate's father."

A huge knot formed out of nowhere in Rich's throat, making it even harder to breathe. The man in front of him was the same one he would ask for Kate's hand in marriage someday, and Rich wouldn't wait nearly as long as Jesse had.

Time was a precious thing, especially when it involved Kate.

Jordan continued the introductions, "This is my

wife, Olivia. And this is Rich Spencer. He's worked quite a bit with Kate. We all care very much about your daughter, Mr. Callahan."

Ken's hand was strong and callused as he gripped Rich's, shaking it. "It would seem so, if you'd travel this far just to support her." He looked into Rich's eyes, trying to study them behind the dark glasses.

"She means a great deal to me," Rich answered.

Ken offered Rich a strained smile, his eyes puffy from the tears that he had shed for the man who might have been his son-in-law. "Excuse me, and I'll let Kate know you're here." The dress shoes he wore shuffled softly across the carpeted aisle. He took Kate by the arm and leaned down to speak into her ear.

Kate's body shifted then turned completely to face them. Rich's heart thundered in his chest and he held onto the oxygen in his lungs, afraid that he might never take another breath if her reaction wasn't a good one. She stood silently, just staring at them for the longest moment of his life.

"Kate." Her name was only a breath on his lips.

A sob shook her entire body and Rich worried that her knees could hold her in such a fragile state. Instead, she straightened her spine, wiped her nose with a tissue, and walked toward them. Three steps into the journey, she broke into a sprint. Tears streamed down her cheeks and all his muscles tensed in preparation of her small body crashing into his.

It wasn't Rich she ran to, though. "Oh, Olivia." Kate wrapped her arms around their tiny friend and held on for dear life. Her tears disappeared into Olivia's black hair. She moved to Jordan and the scene replayed itself, except Jordan's tie mopped up the salty water from her cheeks.

When she finally slipped into his arms, Kate let her arms slide around his waist and pressed her face to his chest. "Thank you for coming, Rich." She squeezed and he returned her snug embrace, unwilling to release her.

"You're not mad?" Rich asked into her hair, wanting so badly to make all of her pain go away.

Her head moved back and forth against his white

shirt. "I should be, but no, I'm not. Please keep your distance, though, no one can..."

"Kate?" a woman's voice asked, and Kate practically hit the ceiling, she jumped so high. "Who are your friends?"

"Mom, this is Jordan Green, KHB's Assignment Editor." She attempted a soggy smile. "His wife, and producer extraordinaire, Olivia Greene, and my favorite photographer—" She squeezed his hand quickly before dropping it. "—Rich Spencer. Everybody, this is my mom, Anna."

Anna was an older version of Kate. It was easy to see whose genes were dominant in the makeup of their daughter. Anna smiled, and they all voiced polite hellos. Kate stepped to stand at her mother's side. Anna nodded then turned to speak with the minister, following him toward the casket.

Kate wiped underneath her eyes. "Can I get you anything? Are you hungry?"

Olivia reached out to Kate. "Honey, we're here for you, not the other way around. We'll go find somewhere to get a bite and be back in time for the services." She gave Kate another hug then said quietly, "Do *you* need anything?"

Tear-filled eyes searched his face, the answer clear as day. Kate needed Rich, wanted him, but didn't want to *disrespect Jesse's memory with the presence of her lover.* Kate's words echoed through his mind. His heart skipped a beat with the painful revelation that would forever haunt him. She finally tore her eyes from his and twisted the tissue in her hands. "No, I'm fine. I don't need anything."

Liar. Rich wanted to scold her, wanted to force her to ask him to stay, but guilt seeped back into the picture. This was ultimately his fault. Rich couldn't pawn that off on anyone else. It was the fact that he had fallen in love with Kate that brought this whole horrible scenario to fruition.

Olivia took Rich's hand in hers, squeezing it. "Well, then, we'll be back in a little bit."

"Thanks for coming, you guys. It really means a lot

to me—and Jesse."

The mention of *his* name on her lips caused a flame of jealousy to flicker through Rich's veins. He swallowed hard, trying to extinguish the sensation. It was ridiculous to harbor feelings like that for the deceased, especially when it was his fault Jesse was about to be put six feet under for eternity.

A gentle tugging on Rich's hand made him stop and look at Olivia. Her lips were pulled into a tight smile. "Let's go, *Rich.*"

"I think I'll just stay here for Kate."

"No, I think you should come with us. You need to eat, just like we do." Olivia had read the expression on Kate's face, the deer-in-the-headlights-with-an-oncoming-semi kind of look, when he mentioned that he wanted to stay.

Dammit, this situation was impossible. Kate needed him. She needed *him,* not a church full of sympathy-givers. It was his comforting embrace she wanted, his touch that would ease her pain...but not her guilt.

How could she even stand to look at him after what he'd done? Hell, Rich couldn't stand to be alone with his thoughts. Was she having the same ones? Did she hate him, resent him? Could she ever forgive him? He wasn't sure that he could ever forgive himself.

In all honesty, Rich wasn't sure how he'd gotten from Kate's side at the church to the little diner where he was now seated across from Olivia and Jordan. The two of them were talking softly amongst themselves, probably avoiding his downer attitude. Rich was depressed—even for someone attending a funeral.

The food on the plate in front of him had been moved around so much that it no longer resembled the chicken-fried steak they'd brought him. It tasted like cardboard, and he was pretty sure that had little to do with the chef and more to do with that his tongue that felt like sandpaper.

Every time his thoughts drifted back to Kate, standing next to the casket, his eyes burned. At one point, he had to excuse himself to go outside, stand in the drizzling rain, and regroup. Kate's pain was very much his own. Her guilt, his guilt. And her wanting him at an arm's length tore his heart out. If she continued to push him away, his heart would surely break in two.

What if she didn't want him anymore? Had this changed her feelings for him? The list of questions went on, thousands of them it seemed, all of which needed answers. Today.

Jordan's hand clamped down on his shoulder. "You ready, man?" Rich jerked around, his hand fumbled in his pocket for his wallet. Jordan smiled. "I got it." He chuckled softly. "Actually, Dale got it."

"You're sure?" Rich mumbled, rearranging his coat.

"Yep, Dale said to treat it like a business trip. You okay?"

"Me? Yeah, I'm fine," Rich lied. "Where's Olivia?"

"She's in the ladies room. She said to just wait in the car." He continued rambling about women having to check out every restroom they ever come in contact with, but Rich wasn't really listening.

The wheels in his mind raced, trying to come up with the how—and when—to ask his questions of Kate. If she needed him to, Rich would gladly take up residence at the Motel 6 in this sleepy little town. But then that had the potential of bringing Shea here. No one knew where she was. Rich's guess was that she wouldn't stop until she had killed him—or Kate. He couldn't let either happen. Kate's heart couldn't handle losing another man she loved, and Rich couldn't handle losing her.

There were far more cars in the parking lot as they pulled in this time. Jordan found a space and they walked in together, taking the pew in the very back. Jordan took the aisle—probably to block Rich in so he couldn't make a fool of himself—Olivia took the middle. Rich sat next to an older Hispanic woman and, what he guessed were, her children.

As the last few people filed in to stand in the back, the minister stood at the pulpit. Rich didn't really pay attention to the eulogies, the guilt-building speeches about what a great man Jesse was, how this was a tragedy that never should have happened.

His stomach twisted into knots. Bile made its way up the back of his throat. If his guilt was eating him alive, Rich could only imagine what it was doing to the love of his life. He watched her closely as her shoulders moved gently with her emotions.

"...And as they say, the good die young," Kate's father said. "They didn't come better than you, son."

Son? Ken Callahan viewed Jesse as a son. Would he ever honor Rich with that name? He could only hope—and dream.

"We'll miss you. Rest in Peace."

The organ began to play, and a group of men stood to make their way to the casket, flanking its sides. They lifted it in unison and the procession began out the back door. Josh was at the corner closest to Rich, and he blatantly avoided looking anywhere near him. Two of the others, however, glared at him with eyes so full of pain—and animosity—his heart clenched.

These men loved Jesse, that much was easy to see. But how much did they know about his suspicions when it came to Rich and his feelings for Kate? He could guess that they knew more than any of the other mourners in the church.

Kate was right behind them, a white rose in her hand, followed by her parents. Next, an older version of Jesse in a wheelchair, oxygen tubes running into his nose, was being pushed by a woman who had to have been Jesse's sister. They were all crying softly and Rich's heart broke for each one of them. They had lost a son, a brother, a friend, all because of him—and his actions.

He certainly felt like a selfish bastard.

Jesse's death had been horrific, but he was gone. Rich was left to pick up the pieces of Kate's broken heart, a position he would gladly fill, but wished he didn't have to.

The rest of the unknown faces passed quietly, and soon it was their turn to follow the crowd and pay respects at the gravesite. A woman cleared her throat and tapped Rich lightly on the shoulder. Rich smiled at her, mumbled an apology, then closed the gap between him and Olivia. The air outside was damp, but the sun had come out from behind the clouds almost as if it, too, needed to say goodbye to Jesse.

The short drive to the cemetery was quiet. Jordan and Olivia politely left Rich alone with his thoughts. Three country blocks went by quickly, even at the slow processional pace. Watching from near the end of line, Rich cringed as Kate stepped out of the limo and took her father's arm for support. Oh, how he wanted to be the one she leaned on.

The ceremony at the gravesite was over after only a few minutes, then Kate, along with Jesse's family, graciously accepted the sympathies from everyone. Olivia and Jordan approached the group, offering handshakes and hugs. Rich stayed off to the side, watching, fighting the tears that burned his eyes.

Rich would have to pull himself together if he was going to have a conversation with Kate. He needed to be the strong one, the one she could lean on, the one to support her. Her eyes searched for him over Olivia's shoulder and her lips lifted slightly when she found him standing in the tree line.

Olivia and Jordan went to wait in the car while Rich remained hidden and out of the way. He waited—and waited—until every last person had left to go back to the church for a dinner in Jesse's honor. The burial crew tried to convince Kate to leave, but she dropped to her knees and refused to move. Even Ken couldn't persuade her to leave with them.

So, standing between her parents, Kate watched as they lowered Jesse into the ground and filled in the grave. Rich could see her shoulders shaking as new sobs overtook her. It was difficult to watch, even more difficult to stay away.

Kate begged her parents to leave her, to let her mourn in peace. Whether or not she knew Rich was waiting, he couldn't be sure. It took a while, but finally her parents did as she asked and took the limousine back to the church.

The tires crunched against the gravel road until becoming nearly silent when they hit the asphalt. At almost the same moment, Kate fell to her knees, her whole body shaking with sobs. "I'm sorry, Jesse," she slurred the words, "so very sorry. This is all my fault." Her whispers carried over the silence, breaking what was left of the remnants of Rich's heart.

The leather of his dress shoes slowly moved toward her, hushed by the drizzling rain that had started back up only moments ago. He dropped to his knees just behind her and took her by the shoulders. "Shh," he comforted her, "this is not your fault, Kate. I won't let you take the blame for any of this."

Her limp body fell back into his embrace and he pulled her into his lap, holding her as she cried. His lips kissed the tears from her cheeks. After a few minutes, when she had gained a bit of control over her emotions, Rich helped her to her feet and led her toward the tree line away from any prying eyes, to a place that might shield them from some of the moisture.

With her hands tightly in his, Rich kissed her knuckles. "Kate, are you okay?" *Stupid question.*

"I will be."

"I'm here, love. We'll get through this."

She took a step away from him and held up her hands in surrender. "I can't do *this*, Rich." Her hands waved between them. "Don't you get it? Jesse lost his life because of me, because of *us*. He had faith in me right up until the very end. I can't dishonor his memory by jumping right into your arms. He deserves better than that."

"But you love me, Kate."

"Shh!" she hissed, her eyes flashed with an infuriated intensity that caused Rich to take a step back. "Don't you say that. Someone might hear you." She looked over her shoulder at the empty cemetery for eavesdroppers. Her face softened as the tears continued their descent down her cheeks. "Rich," she whispered, "I need some time."

"Of course, love, I'll help you."

"No." She shook her head, and his stomach jumped into his throat. "I have to work through all of this on my own."

"I will do whatever you ask, Kate. I owe you that

much." Taking her hand, he pressed it to his erratically beating heart. "You feel that, Kate? You are the reason my heart beats. You're the reason my lungs breathe. You, Kate Callahan, are my reason for living. Just answer me one question before I honor your request."

She nodded and eventually teary eyes met his.

"Do you love me, Kate?"

The tears broke the banks and slid steadily down her cheeks. "Yes," she croaked, "heaven help me." Her head moved back and forth in an agonized motion. "I do love you, Rich. That's what makes this all so damned hard. Please let me work through my feelings. I'm just asking you for a little time."

"How much time?"

"I don't know." Her answer was barely audible.

"When are you coming home?"

"Rich, I *am* home."

He placed a hand on her cheek, and she leaned into his touch. "When will you come back to me?"

Her hand covered his as she sighed. "I don't know." She broke contact with a single step backward. "I'm sorry, but I just ... I don't know."

Taking the last chance he had, Rich closed the small distance she'd created and wrapped her in his arms letting his feelings for her seep through their bodies. His lips crashed into hers then paused, waiting for her to respond. When she did, he increased the intensity, moving his tongue along her lip. She opened to him, and Rich was able to taste her. Everything about her captivated him. He loved *everything* about her.

Rich broke the kiss, leaving her breathless. "Kate, I will walk away but only because you are asking me to. My heart is breaking. There is nothing I want more than to spend every second of every day showing you just how much I love you." His head dropped down to press a kiss just below her ear. "Kate, please don't ask me to leave. *Please....*"

Her voice cracked as she spoke the words he knew were coming. "Rich, I'm sorry." Tears flowed down her cheeks without any barriers. He could see the pain in her eyes, feel the pain radiating in her voice.

Grateful for the dark glasses that hid his own emotions, Rich bit his lip, blinked back his own tears, and kissed her for the last time. "Goodbye, Kate. Don't you ever forget that I love you." Then, with no other choice, Rich turned on his heel and walked away from the only thing left in his life that mattered.

Part Two

Moving on

✕ ✕ ✕

six months later

Twenty Four

"Hi Jesse." Kate sank slowly to her knees beside the headstone that read *Jesse Vasquez. Beloved son, brother and friend.* "So I'm probably a little late with the information since he's most likely standing right there next to you, but your dad passed on. I stayed after you ... left ... to be here for him—just like you wanted to be."

The late June sun beat down on the back of her neck. Her fingers brushed across the cold granite before smoothing a tear away with an icy touch. "It's been hard without you, Jesse. You didn't deserve this. I'm sorry. I'll probably be leaving soon, especially if Mom has her way. I will never forget you ... no matter what happens in the future. I loved you, Jesse." Pressing a kiss to her hand, Kate touched the headstone then struggled to get to her feet. Her face lifted toward the sky and she smiled into the clouds. "Hey, Tony, do a jig for me." The wind kicked up around her, and Kate could have sworn Tony's laughter was on the breeze.

The walk home was slow, only because Kate couldn't force her feet to move any faster. Decisions had to be made. Her parents weren't going to sit around and let her coast through life forever. Utah *did* hold a lot of things for her; a promising career, a new house—purchased sight unseen—a man, who, despite her best efforts to push him away, refused to give up on her ... and guilt. A lot of guilt.

Hiding out in Flagstaff, Kate could pretend that her perfect life hadn't fallen apart. That Jesse hadn't been murdered because of choices she'd made, and that at the time she was desperately in love with another man.

Nobody here knew the truth. In Utah, though ... they all did. Olivia, Jordan, Nate, Roxy. Hell, Dale probably knew too. And Rich...

Her heart clenched at even the thought of his name. Kate missed him so much, but couldn't bring herself to even answer his calls anymore. The crazy bitch, that was now his ex-wife, had already taken the life of one man that Kate loved. Maybe if she stayed away from Rich, Shea would leave him alone. And if she didn't... Well, the distance Kate had created between them would make it so his death wouldn't hurt quite so much.

The sun was fading in the sky making the temperature perfect. A bird sat in a tree over the sidewalk singing a happy, carefree tune. As Kate rounded the corner, her parents' house came into view. Her mother sat on the porch with a vase of familiar flowers next to her. Kate groaned. Anna was preparing for the exact conversation Kate was dreading.

Anna jumped up and ran over to Kate, taking her arm. "Kate, I've been so worried about you. Next time, please, take your cell phone so that you can call me."

"Oh, Mom, stop being so ... motherly." Kate kissed her cheek and wrapped an arm around her waist. "I'm a big girl and I can take care of myself."

Anna matched her pose and they walked toward the porch, daughter resting her head on her mother's shoulder. "So, um, today's Friday...flower delivery day." She picked up the vase in her hand and carried it into the kitchen. "It seems that there's at least one thing waiting for you in Utah."

"Mom, there was nothing..." Kate lied ... again.

"Kate, I don't care if there was *something*—" She coughed, cleared her throat and smiled. "—between you and Rich then. The point is that he obviously cares about you *now*."

"He may care now, but will he *still* care when he finds out that I betrayed him?"

The vase slid across the table with a scratching sound. "Katie, I think you should have a little faith in him."

Silence filled the space between them as Kate filled

a glass with water and slowly drank it. There was little doubt that her mother could be—and would be—horribly persistent. It didn't matter that going back to Utah was the best thing for Kate. Seeing Rich again scared the hell out of her.

"Kate," her mom said softly, waiting until she looked at her. "A man doesn't send you flowers every week for six months just because he doesn't have anything better to do with his money. How long has he loved you?"

Kate's stomach tightened into a knot, and she considered lying, denying that Rich loved her, but that would have been far too painful. "It doesn't matter."

"Fine, it doesn't matter. The fact is that he does, am I right?" Kate opened her mouth to scold her mother again, but she held her hands up in surrender. "Sorry. We won't talk about Rich. I do want to talk about you, though. Hiding out here in your mother's home like a scared little girl isn't working anymore. You have a life to get back to. How long do you think your patient boss is going to hold your job? It's already been six months."

"I know, Mom." Her voice sounded just like it did in high school when Kate was tired of hearing her mother's reprimand—especially when Kate knew she was right. "How 'bout I make you a deal?"

"I'm listening." Anna raised a brow.

"I'll stay for the July 4th celebration then I'll go back to Utah."

Tears filled Anna's eyes and she rushed to hug Kate, her arms pulled her tight. "Katie, I know this time has been really hard on you. I can only imagine, but you don't have to do it alone. We'll only be a phone call away. The people at the station care about you. Josh and Sophia have already done so much and would do anything else you asked."

Josh and Sophia *had* gone above and beyond the common courtesies one offered a friend. They'd completely cleaned out her apartment; selling, donating, or trashing everything but pictures. They'd dealt with the apartment manager, convincing him that letting her out of the lease was the only decent thing to do. Josh had even bought out Jesse's half of the garage, paying

Kate the proceeds. "To move on," he'd said. Kate tried to protest but he wouldn't hear of it, stuffing the check deeper into her fist. "Kate, it's what Jesse would have wanted." Those words did it, and she accepted the money with the promise to put it as a down payment on a house.

The very next day, her phone rang. "Hello?"

"Miss Callahan?"

"Yes." It was always an eerie feeling when someone addressed her so formally on her cell phone.

"This is Joyce McNary with National Life Insurance Company. I'm sorry for your loss."

"How did you…"

"Miss Callahan, I'm sure you have a lot of questions, but we'll make this as easy as possible."

"I'm sorry, but what are you talking about?" Kate stammered.

"Mr. Vasquez's life insurance policy." Her tone was a tad irritated, which added to Kate's confusion.

"Jesse had a—"

"—had a life insurance policy that named Miss Kate Callahan as his sole beneficiary."

"But—"

"Would you like me to mail you the check, or is there an account you'd like the money wired to?"

Kate's head was spinning so fast there was no way she could wrap her brain around what this woman was telling her. She dug her knuckles into her temples trying desperately to rub the confusion away. "Can you stop talking for a second?" She stopped immediately. "I don't understand any of this. Why would he…?"

"He wanted you to be taken care of in the event he couldn't do it anymore."

Guilt-induced tears flowed freely down her cheeks. Kate didn't deserve his love, his trust, or the money that would only be hers in the event of his death. A death that never would have come if she…

"Kate?" Her mom's voice brought Kate back to the here and now.

"Yeah." She shook her head. "I'm going to go upstairs and call Dale."

Her mother hugged her. "You'll get through this, baby girl. Eventually your heart will mend. Don't lock it up forever."

Easier said, than done, Kate thought as she left her mother in the kitchen. She wondered how long it would take Rich to find out that she was coming home.

× × ×

The ice cold bottle was welcome in his hand, a sorry excuse for antiseptic that would never fully numb the pain that was his constant companion. There was nothing, except for Kate's return, that could heal the pain Rich felt. He lifted the bottle to his lips and tipped the last bit of Guinness down the back of his throat.

"Dude, you look like hell," a familiar voice thundered from behind him. Nate pulled out a seat next to him and plopped down.

"What can I get you, Nate?" Fergie, the waitress that kept the alcohol coming every night, asked as she rubbed her hands on the white towel that was stuffed between her tight belly and short shorts.

"I'm good, Fergie, thanks. Just checking on my drunk buddy here."

"Let me know if you change your mind." She turned around and flirted with a group of college guys at the next table.

"So..."

"I don't want to hear it, Nate." The words were more slurred than Rich would have liked. His tongue was obviously intoxicated, but the rest of him had barely registered the dulling effect that had been his goal.

"I'm just trying to get my facts straight. How long has it been?"

"Five months, two weeks and three days."

Nate bit on his lip and moved his head up and down in an exaggerated nodding motion. "Replay things for me."

Air rushed out of Rich's mouth, dousing Nate in an alcohol soaked breath. "I really don't want to relive it. The first time was hard enough."

"Humor me."

"Fine," Rich growled, his mind returned to Valentine's Day as if it were yesterday.

Rich pulled the rental car up in front of Kate's parents' house and cut the engine. There were no cars in the driveway and no other signs of life coming from the house. A lump formed in his throat, and suddenly Rich had serious doubts with regards to the surprise he had. Maybe *he* was going to be the one surprised.

He sucked in a deep breath and yanked on the door handle. He stepped out, his back and legs stiff from the two-hour drive. The journey to the door was only a few short steps, but seemed to take an eternity. He raised a fist to knock, considered the doorbell for a second then finally let his knuckles meet wood.

Seconds passed, but felt like years.

He rang the doorbell then shifted nervous weight from one foot to the other. "Damn," he muttered, preparing to return to the car for his phone.

"I'm coming!" a sweet voice called from the other side of the door.

Relief washed over him as the locks were flipped and the door opened with a soft squeak.

"I'm sorry, I..." Her big green eyes widened. "Rich!" she squealed, launching herself into his arms. Her legs wrapped around his waist as her arms took his neck in a death grip.

"I have missed you," he whispered in her ear.

As if his voice woke her, she gasped, wiggled out of his embrace, and gawked at him. "What are you doing here?" she asked, tugging him inside and closing the door.

"Happy Valentine's Day, love." He held up his hands when she opened her mouth. "I know you're uncomfortable having me on Jesse's turf. I've got us a room in Sedona."

She smiled and looked so beautiful in her black and red plaid, flannel pajamas. Her normally sleek locks were pulled back into a disheveled ponytail that sat more to one side than the other. Dark lines marred the perfection under her eyes, remnants of the mascara she'd worn to bed.

"Sleeping late?" he teased.

Horrified eyes looked down at her appearance. She crossed her arms over her chest, and Rich was sure there wasn't a bra under that long sleeved t-shirt. "Give me um, give me a minute." She turned on her heel, took two quick steps toward the stairs, stopped, whirled around and ran back to him. He opened his arms, welcoming her. It felt so good to have her soft body pressed hard to his. "I love you," she said before her warm lips gently kissed him.

✗ ✗ ✗

Their getaway had been perfect, a communion of two souls. They'd played hard and loved harder. He couldn't even begin to count the times he'd made love to her—with her. Then he'd returned to the ice and snow of Salt Lake just in time to have her shut him out a week later.

She'd gradually stopped answering his calls. Her parents said she was fine when he'd called the house. "Just give her time," Anna had instructed him. And he did, over five excruciating months.

"So there's the recap," Rich bit out. "Thanks so much for making me revisit that oh, so enjoyable time in my life."

Nate wiggled his eyebrows. "That's what friends are for." He leaned forward and Rich glared at him across the table. He pulled away, but continued his speech. "Listen, buddy, you're killing yourself from the inside out. She may never come home."

"She loves me."

"If she can stay away from you for this long—" Nate shook his head, and Rich dropped his gaze. "—she doesn't love you, my man. I'm sorry. The truth does more than hurt, it sucks, I know. But this has got to stop." He chuckled and Rich looked up just in time to see him puff out his chest. "I'm gonna sound all fatherly, but if you can't pull your act together, you can't crash in the guestroom anymore, my friend. Roxy's actually getting ulcers worrying about you."

"I'll find a new place," Rich grumbled, not wanting to inconvenience anyone with his misery.

"Dude, that's not what I'm saying." Nate scrubbed his hand and blew out a frustrated breath. "We're worried about you. And it's not just Rox and me. Olivia and Jordan are too."

As if his ears were burning, Jordan's name showed up on the caller ID. Rich groaned and sent the call to voicemail, wondering if his reaction just now was the same one Kate had when he called her. His stomach suddenly felt violently sick.

"You boys okay?"

Nate nodded, but Rich raised his hand and said, "Bring me another one, Fergie."

She and Nate exchanged disapproving glances, but she gathered up the empty green bottles and walked away without saying another word. "I guess I'll see you at home soon?" Nate asked as he stood.

"Yeah, soon." *Whatever, just leave me alone.* How sad that it was not even 8:00, and there was more than a comforting buzz working on the pain of his broken heart.

Nate's large hand landed on Rich's shoulder with a thud. "Roxy and I are going out to a late dinner with her folks, so we might not be home when you get there. Just... well, just so you know. Later."

Nate's steps faded as he walked away, but another set got closer. Fergie's face was determined as she grabbed a chair and spun it around. She sat down, straddling it, her arms across the wooden rail that ran across the top.

"Where's my beer?"

"I'm cutting you off."

"But I'm barely buzzed." Completely shit-faced had been the goal when he sat down a few hours ago.

"Listen, Rich, I am sick and tired of watching you come in here every night to drink yourself stupid."

"So don't watch." Rich tried to stand, but stumbled, and fell back into his chair. "Better yet, I'll find a new place tomorrow night."

"That's not what I'm suggesting, you moron." She

leaned in closer to him, intensity blazed in her determined eyes. "Do you not realize how hot you are? Hell, if I didn't know how pathetic you are, I would try to get you in my pants ... and I'm *married*." She looked over his shoulder and smiled at Fuzzy. "You're the whole package ... or you *were* until you let that..."

"Careful," Rich warned, scowling at her.

"She wouldn't know a good thing if it bit her in that cute little ass of hers." She flashed a sarcastic smile. "I'm serious, Rich. You have a decision to make. Either fly out there and drag her back by her hair, or get on with your life. Look around."

Without a conscious decision to do so, his head moved from side to side, noticing for the first time all the women in the bar—some of which had noticed him.

"Yeah, they ask about you. Some of them have become regulars in hopes of being the one to crack your soggy exterior. Most nights you're the best looking guy in this dump."

Rich raised a brow, playing along. "Most nights?"

"Well, yeah, when my husband isn't here. He's the hottest man I know." She looked over his shoulder and blew a kiss to the man behind at the bar.

A strange, unfamiliar sound burst from Rich's body. A laugh. It felt good to really laugh. That was what Rich loved about Fergie, she could make him laugh even when he felt like shit. Which is the way he felt ... always. The phone in his pocket vibrated again and Rich just let the buzzing continue.

"Come on," she said, holding out her hand, "give me your keys and I'll drive you home."

Rich considered protesting for only as long as it took to realize he was more than just buzzed, but not quite plastered. Either way, he was in no position to drive. The keys dropped into her hand with a clank and she smiled victoriously as her fingers wrapped around the pieces of silver.

On the short drive of only a couple miles, Fergie kept her opinions to herself, singing along to the radio. Her husky voice was only sexy when she spoke, the girl couldn't carry a tune in a bucket. The screeching hurt his ears but broke the grimace he'd been wearing for months. He smiled, a real smile.

They rounded the corner and the headlights glanced off a dark green Volkswagen Jetta. Somewhere in the back of his mind was a voice screaming that Rich should recognize it, that he knew it from somewhere, and that it being here was relevant—and *really* important. But instead, Rich listened to Fergie's horrific rendition of Toby Keith's, *I Wanna Talk About Me.*

"Well, here we are, Mr. Spencer." She eased the car to a stop.

"Hey, thanks, Fergie. Do you realize that tonight is the first time I've really laughed in months?"

She nodded. "I would have guessed as much."

The light came on in the car as she opened the door, and the sudden illumination hurt his bloodshot eyes. The damn cell phone buzzing in his pocket was going to drive him insane. *Damn, Jordan!* His head pounded as Fergie closed the door with an unnecessary slam. Rich cautiously opened his door with a quick jerk of his hand.

Fergie stood next to the car, waiting to escort her intoxicated friend to the door.

"I can do this alone," Rich informed her, only to stumble as he stood to his full height.

She laughed, making him smile. "Yeah, you look like you're as steady as … a kite in the wind. Hold on to me, and I'll get your drunk ass to the doorstep, but that's as far as my obligations to you go, my friend. As hot as you are with your clothes on, I can only imagine what you look like…." She shook her head and bit her lip, groaning as if the thought of having sex with him really was something she'd considered. She was mocking him. There was no real seduction in her words. "My imagination is quite active, and it's best to leave you fully clothed in my thoughts." She wiggled her brows and tried to look sexy.

"Wow, you're a real charmer. I can see why Fuzzy married you."

Her head flew back and she erupted in a contagious laughter that had him clutching her to keep from falling. The porch light was on, and she slid the key into the lock, turned it, and opened the door. She leaned up on her tiptoes and pressed a friendly kiss to his cheek.

"I mean it, Rich. Please take a long look at things. This is no way to live. Hell, you're not living, you're not even surviving. If she comes back..." She squeezed his hand and rephrased her statement. "*When* she comes back, is *this* what you want her to find? Come on, dude, you're just pitiful...even for a hottie."

Rich pressed a kiss to her forehead. "Thanks, Fergie, you told me the same thing Nate's been saying and... Well, it must have been your creative delivery of the message, because I get it. I can't promise I'll be all smiles and sunshine and shit, but I promise to try and be better. Good enough?"

The sides of her lips lifted. "Good enough. 'Night, Rich." An engine started, as she stepped off the porch and walked back to Fuzzy, who had just pulled up in their car.

The Jetta purred as the driver urged the pedal toward the floor. *Damn, why do I know that car?* Rich tried to focus as it drove away, but that only made his head hurt worse.

Fergie waved from the curb and Rich returned the gesture then stepped inside. The house was dark, except for the hall light that, as a rule, was left on if coming home after dark. He hung his keys on the hook and headed in the direction of the kitchen for another beer before he gave into his promised sobriety.

His phone buzzed again. "What?" Rich growled.

"Where the hell have you been?"

"What's it to you, Jordan?"

"Fine. Whatever," he snorted. "I have just been trying to get a hold of you all night to warn you..." His statement drifted off.

"Warn me? Why?" Riddles didn't have a chance of getting solved in his current condition.

"Dale called, and Kate starts back tomorrow. I wasn't sure whether or not you knew, but I just wanted to give you a head's up. Being blindsided by that..." He sighed. "Well, I guess we'll see you tomorrow." The line disconnected without waiting for a response.

Of course there was no response. Kate was back in town, coming back to work, and hadn't even bothered to call him. Unless...

His mind raced back on track, the pieces of the soggy puzzle sliding into place. The green Jetta—Kate's Jetta. *Shit!* She had been so close and Rich was too drunk to know it. But why hadn't she stayed, and what the hell would she have said anyway? There was only one way to find out.

Intoxicated fingers fumbled with the speed dial. The phone rang twice before a familiar voice answered, "Hey, man."

"Nate, do I sound drunk?"

"Um, no."

"'Kay, thanks." And without any further comment or explanation, Rich hit the big red 'end' button. His heart pounded ferociously against his ribcage and his lungs struggled for breath.

What did all of this mean? It bothered him that she hadn't talked to him about coming home. She hadn't even answered any of his calls in the last month. *Maybe she wanted it to be a surprise*, he tried to delude himself. Sweaty palms made dialing her number difficult. The phone actually hit the floor once.

Rich finally dialed the numbers that were second nature to his fingers and waited for the ring, praying that this would be the time she would actually answer. Four rings. Five. And then, her beautiful voice spoke the all too familiar phrase, "You've reached Kate. Leave a message." Rich closed the phone without leaving a message. What was the point?

The butterflies that fluttered in his stomach only moments before were now gone, replaced by some really big predatory bird, hell bent on shredding his insides. She was in town, coming back to work, and didn't even have the decency to answer...

A buzzing sound nearly stopped his heart. Kate's number was on the caller id and the butterflies were back. He cleared his throat and answered, "Hello?"

"Sorry I didn't get to the phone fast enough. I was in the bath-... Well, anyway, hi." She sounded so ...

normal.

"Kate?" he asked, unable to believe it really was her.

She laughed. "Has it been that long?"

Relief tried to push away the fear and anger, but ultimately the booze in his veins wouldn't let her comment go without a response. "Yes, Kate, it has been that long. Why in the hell haven't you—"

"Rich, please, I don't want to fight." Her voice was quiet.

"I don't want to fight either," he admitted. "I love you, and—"

"Rich," she interrupted him again, "please let me talk."

"Fine—" The talons were back, clawing at the lining of his stomach. "—talk." He didn't really care that he sounded harsh and cold—not too much, anyway.

"Rich, I came by tonight."

"That *was* you."

She giggled nervously. "Of course it was me. I wouldn't just waltz back into the newsroom without giving you some kind of warning."

Rich didn't want a warning. He wanted for her to need him, to want him. "How thoughtful of you, Kate." The compliment oozed sarcasm and he could almost hear her wince.

"I guess I deserve that." She paused and her breath was the only sound between them. Rich waited—impatiently—refusing to give her any kind of reprieve. "I, um..." She stopped again.

His tongue ached from the pressure his teeth issued. The tinny taste of blood filled his mouth and he snapped. "Why did you come by, Kate? It's not like you've been dying to talk to me. Hell, it feels like you've done nothing but continually push me away."

"Rich." Tears invaded her speech. "Oh, Rich, I am so sorry. I can only imagine how hard... You know what? I really wanted to do this in person. Can we meet for breakfast in the morning?"

Yes! Hell, yes! "I can't. How 'bout lunch or maybe dinner?" Yeah, it was a pathetic attempt at playing it cool.

"Dinner it is." She sighed. "I have missed you, Rich. Well, I'll see you tomorrow." There was hesitancy in her voice.

"I've—"

"I'm happy for you ... that you've moved on, I mean. Bye."

She missed him. *That was good.* She wanted to 'do this in person'. *That was bad.* She was going to dump him on his pathetic, shit-faced ass. And she was happy that he'd moved on. *What the...?*

Fergie!

Shit!

Twenty Five

When the alarm went off at 7:00am, Rich was already awake, staring at the ceiling. The DJs announced the time, made some stupid insignificant jokes, and tossed to commercial. Did they not realize that today would be life altering for him? Of course they didn't. Did Kate?

Thanks to the suped-up air-conditioning, the room was cool as he whipped the blanket off his nearly naked body. He dug his toes into the bath towel-soft carpeting. Rich rubbed at his temples, praying that the little man inside his head would turn off his jackhammer. The pounding was loud, incessant, and really painful.

A quick shave, shower, and change of clothes later, Rich stood in front of the mirror examining, scrutinizing exactly what Kate would see. The unruly hair that had never bothered him in his life was suddenly an enormous irritation. His eyes were puffy, bloodshot, and felt like they were full of rocks. And who the hell gets a pimple at thirty?

He certainly was a sight to behold. Fergie was right. Kate had come back, and he was a lush. *Exactly the kind of man she was looking for,* his thoughts taunted.

After running his fingers through his hair one last time, Rich headed toward the kitchen for some breakfast. Three Advil sat in his palm while he reached into the refrigerator for a beer to wash them down.

"Breakfast of champions?" Nate laughed from the doorway. "What are you doing, Rich?"

"Oh, come on, Nate, you know the best cure for a hangover is another beer."

He nodded. "And a greasy burger." His arms folded

across his chest. He leaned against the door jam and attempted a smile. "Jordan called."

"So?" Rich shrugged.

"So ... don't let her do this to you, man. You deserve better."

"Yeah, 'cause I'm such a keeper." He popped the pills into his mouth, cracked open the can, and took a swig.

Nate responded with a dramatic eye roll. "I like Kate, I really do. But dude, she's killing you."

Rich's hands flew up in warning protest. "I appreciate your concern, *I really do.*" Nate winced as Rich used his words. "I love her, Nate, and I'm going to fight for her. If she dumps me on my ass today then you can lecture me some more, okay?" His stomach rolled, and he tried to keep the emotion hidden from Nate.

"Okay," Nate said softly, stepping out of the doorway as Rich stormed past. "We're just worried..."

"Save it. *Please.*"

Nate's concern would have been touching if it hadn't been so damn annoying and made Rich feel like such a loser. Safely inside the news vehicle, Rich allowed himself a few moments to dwell on his situation. He'd kept up a brave face, but his friends had seen right through his act. They knew him too well. Rich hated it; their worry, their concern...their pity.

The thought of seeing Kate today had his heart alternately racing and screeching to a halt. His lungs refused air only to gasp from the lack of it. His emotions were on overload. Rich wanted to scream in joy and curl up in a ball to sob like a baby all at the same time. Kate meant everything to him, even after all this time. What if she didn't want him?

Forcing the thought out of his mind before any kind of emotion could break through, Rich started the engine and headed in the direction of Kate. A Krispy Kreme caught his attention, and his stomach growled at nearly the same time. Having only alcohol in his system wouldn't do anything beneficial, he needed something to absorb it.

"A dozen glazed and a dozen assorted," he ordered.

He may as well share.

"Anything to drink?"

"Um, yeah, give me a large Dr. Pepper."

The female voice gave him the total and asked him to pull around, which he did. There wasn't a line, and he pulled right to the window. The young blonde handed him the boxes just as his phone rang.

"Good morning, Olivia." His voice was flat, more of a statement than a greeting.

"Rich, are you coming in today?" she asked after a long hesitation.

"Yeah, I'll be there in about ten minutes."

"Oh, um ... well ... I don't..." Her tone was frantic, panicked. "Rich, I need to talk to you. It's um ... It's about Kate."

Rich pulled the car into a space of the Krispy Kreme parking lot, threw it into park, and heaved an annoyed sigh into the phone. "Olivia, I am going to say this once, so listen good. I don't want to discuss Kate with you—or anybody else. Got it?"

"But Rich—"

"No! I'm not budging on this. Goodbye." And he snapped the phone closed, tossed it onto the seat next to him, and opened one of the red and white boxes, pulling out a glazed donut. He chewed slowly. The sweet, sugary texture melted on his tongue. His stomach gurgled as the food reached it, growling for more. After devouring the first one, he polished off another then took a huge swig of his drink.

The phone rang again and irritation consumed him. If it was Olivia again, he would really lay into her this time. Nope. It was Jordan. "I already told Olivia..."

"Shut up and listen to me," Jordan snapped.

"No, *you* listen to *me*, Jordan. You and your well-meaning better-half just need to butt out. This isn't your concern."

"Yeah, well, it might not be your concern either," he retorted.

"What the hell is that supposed to mean?" Rich yelled.

Jordan took a deep breath. "How 'bout you just

meet Clayton downtown for a press conference with the governor?"

"Is Kate there?"

"Rich, I think—"

"Is she there?" Rich demanded.

"Yes," Jordan whispered.

"Then I am not going to meet Clayton. I am coming to the station." As if there would be a debate.

"I'm not sure that's the best idea."

"Why?" Silence was his only response. "Why, Jordan, what's going on? Dammit, you were so eager to talk before. Spit it out. You know what? Never mind. I'm just around the corner."

"Rich—"

Rich closed the phone, successfully cutting off any further protest. Nothing could keep him away from the station now that he knew Kate was there. The familiar green Jetta was parked near the fence and, as he pulled in, his heart sank to his toes only to jump into his throat. The pounding made it hard to breathe. What was he doing?

Another ring made him jump. "What do you want, Nate?"

He was breathing heavy. "Have you gotten to the station yet?"

"Just pulled in." Rich eased the car into a space and cut the engine.

"I'm about seven minutes away. Why don't you wait for me, buddy?"

"*Buddy?* What the hell is going on, Nate?"

"Um ... I just think—"

"You know what, you all need to stop thinking. Stop trying to know what's best for me. I need to see Kate. Now." He was excited and nervous as hell.

"Rich, there's something that Kate needs to tell you," Nate said quietly.

"And you know this ... how?"

"Jordan and Olivia."

"Of course." Rich was done playing games, done waiting. This day had been on his mind for the last six months and he was not waiting another minute.

"Dammit, Nate, I'm a big boy. Nothing she can say can hurt more than the limbo I've been in."

"I wouldn't be so sure about that." Nate sighed into the phone. "Listen, I'll be there in five minutes. Wait for me, huh?"

"Drive faster, sunshine, I'm getting out now." Rich grabbed hold of the handle and jerked the door open, closing it with a slam. He left all his gear in the truck and headed toward the building.

"Rich, please wait—"

Rich hit the power button and let the phone slip into his pocket. Through the plate glass door he could see Kate sitting behind her desk, chatting away with Olivia. Kate threw her head back and laughed, her hand covered her mouth.

Warmth spread from his heart to every cell in his body. To see her happy and well meant everything to him. It was what he'd always wanted for her. Rich searched for the courage to actually wrap his fingers around the handle and put himself that much closer to her.

The gate opened and he saw Nate pull through. Rich would not let his friend talk him out of this. Seeing him was all the encouragement Rich needed. Without another thought, his hand tugged and cool air washed over him.

"Rich," Nate's voice called just before the door closed.

Olivia and Kate looked in his direction, and Rich tried to force a natural looking smile. Olivia jumped up and ran over to liberate the donuts from his hands. Her eyes were full of panic—pity, which added to the anxiety that was making his stomach roll. She gave him a supportive smile then hurried off in the direction of the assignment desk. Rich's eyes were locked on Kate's. He forced his feet to slowly walk in her direction, careful to watch for any signs that he needed to change direction or stop all together.

"Rich." His name was only a whisper on her lips. She stood, smiled, and slowly made her way over to him. Going up on her toes, she kissed him on the cheek. "I have missed you so much."

His mind was swimming. She had changed—drastically. His friends' phone calls all made sense. They'd been worried and concerned, and their urging him to not see her for the first time in a public place was because of those dramatic, life altering changes.

"I, uh ... you look ... good, Kate." His voice cracked as her name glided over his vocal cords.

Something really painful slammed into his chest; a dagger, maybe, he couldn't be sure. His heart ripped in two. He crossed his arms over his chest to hold it together. His teeth gnawed on the inside of his cheek to keep the tears that stung his eyes from making an appearance.

"Thanks." She reached out to touch him and Rich jerked away, taking a step back to put more space between them. She frowned and ran her hand over her pregnant belly. "I should have told you."

"No, this is the perfect way to find out." Emotion seeped into his voice and Rich hated that. This was not the place to fall apart. "I, um...I have to get to my assignment. It was good to see you." He turned without letting her say anything more and headed toward the door, nearly plowing into Nate, who followed him outside.

"How could she?" Rich's fist slammed into the hood of the nearest vehicle. The alarm protested the contact and Rich kicked the tire for good measure before walking further away from the building. "Pregnant, Nate. She's *pregnant* and didn't even bother to tell me!"

Nate shrugged. "So, she's carrying Jesse's baby."

"It could be mine." Rich hedged a glance back at the building.

"*What*!?" Nate smiled and hit Rich in the arm with his fist. "You dog! I can't believe that all this time I've been giving you shit about pining for this girl, and you were keeping this from *me*."

"It wasn't just sex, Nate, and it wasn't a mistake. We are meant to be together. I'm sorry that Jesse died, but I am not sorry about what happened between me and Kate. And now she's carrying my baby."

"You don't know that." Nate's hand clamped down on his shoulder. "You need to slow down just a bit. Get your facts straight. Maybe the baby isn't yours—or Jesse's."

Rich's eyes narrowed at the insinuation.

Nate held up his hands. "I'm not saying that she's a slut or anything. But Rich, come on, you haven't seen her for months. She hasn't even spoken to you in the last thirty days. There's got to be a reason for that, man. I don't want to see you devastated when there's another daddy waiting in the wings."

Rich didn't realize that his teeth were grinding together until he placed the obnoxious noise resonating through his head. "Fine. I'll talk to her. I'll get my facts straight then I'll claim my baby."

Nate's head moved back and forth on his thick neck. "Dude, be careful, that's all I'm saying. *Be careful.*"

"I will."

Nate stiffened and concentrated on something over Rich's shoulder. Rich turned to see Kate coming in their direction. "I guess it's me and you today, Nate," she said with her eyes focused only on Rich. "Can you give me a minute with Rich first?"

"Sure thing. I'll be in the truck." A warning flashed in Nate's eyes as his head moved in a supportive nod.

And then there was silence. Lots of uncomfortable silence. Rich stared at his shoes, kicking at the rocks that had worked loose from the asphalt, and waited for her to start the conversation. She cleared her throat, and he fought the urge to look into the beautiful green eyes that he'd missed so much. He lost the battle before it had even begun.

She took a step toward him, her head tipped to look at his face. "Rich, I'm sorry I didn't tell you about the baby."

"Why didn't you?" he asked in a whisper.

"I wasn't sure how to—"

"This was the perfect way, Kate." It pained him to step away from her but, somehow, he managed it. "Dammit, how could you hurt me like this?" His hands balled into fists. Anger was better than the pain right now.

"I came by to talk to you last night. It's not my fault you were otherwise occupied," she huffed, her eyes intense.

"What the hell are you talking about?" He met her intensity with irritation.

She sighed and rubbed at her slacks. "I'm glad that you've moved on. It's good, actually. You shouldn't have to be tied to a baby that isn't yours."

A two-by-four to the gut would have forced less air out of his lungs than that statement. "It's.Not.Mine?" The question came out in breathless puffs.

"Of course not. He's Jesse's." Her answer made him feel like an idiot for even asking.

He's Jesse's, his thought taunted. "He?" She nodded, rubbed her round belly and smiled. It pained him that she was so happy, but only because she wouldn't let him share in her joy. "And you're sure of that because—"

"Rich, can we do this later?" She looked over her shoulder when Clayton laughed out loud as he was talking to Tommy.

"I've waited months. What's a few more hours?" Rich replied sarcastically.

Her small hand wrapped around his arm. "Rich, please, you still mean a lot to me and I..."

"Whatever, Kate." His arm burned, in an intoxicatingly delicious way, but he still forced it out of her grasp. "We'll talk whenever you can find the time."

She sniffed, and Rich looked up to see her wipe tears from her cheek. "Dinner tonight?" she verified their date.

"Fine." He kept up the angry façade. It was either that or join her in the blubber-fest. "I'll meet you here after our shifts. Later, Kate." With great difficulty, Rich forced his feet to move, each and every step more painful than the last.

"Hey, Spencer, wait up." Clayton's obnoxious voice called as he jogged toward Rich. "I need to ride with you today."

This day just keeps getting better and better.

Turning the key, the engine came to life. Rich eased the volume up on the radio, sending an unspoken message to Clayton that he wasn't up for any kind of communication.

Clayton's fat, manicured fingers pushed the knob, cutting the music all together. "So," he said, looking in Nate and Kate's direction, "do you think they planned it?"

Rich pulled out onto the street as he responded, "Do I think *who* planned *what?*"

Clayton's head jerked in the direction of the parking lot. "Do you think Kate planned on having Jesse's baby? Before your crazy ex-wife murdered him, I mean. It must be really hard—"

Rich's foot smashed the brake to the floor and the vehicle screeched to halt. Clayton's head jerked forward then met the headrest with a satisfying thud. "What the hell?"

"We. Are. Not. Discussing. Kate. Today," Rich informed him through clenched teeth.

An annoying laugh was followed by an even more obnoxious question. "What's the matter, Spencer, you got a thing for the MILF?"

Rich ground his teeth, the muscles in his jaw flexed. "You talk about her again, and so help me, you'll be walking."

"Fine. Whatever." Clayton shrugged and turned the radio back on.

This is going to be a long *day.*

× × ×

Clayton must have taken the threat seriously because he hadn't brought up Kate's name again since Rich had promised to make him walk, but that changed as they pulled into the parking lot.

"Mmm, mmm, mmm," Clayton groaned. "That is one mighty fine piece of ass—even if she has a big ol' belly. At least that'll go away." His tongue ran across his bottom lip as he entertained sexual thoughts about the woman of Rich's dreams. "How long do you think it'll take before she's got that smokin' hot body back?"

Rich's teeth ground together. His knuckles turned white around the steering wheel. He pressed his foot down on the gas and the engine roared in protest. Screeching tires caused Kate and Nate to look in their direction.

Clayton grabbed onto the 'oh, shit' handle, his face white under a panicked expression. "Rich, what the hell is your problem?"

Adrenaline rushed through his veins as Rich concentrated on keeping his hands on the wheel. If they were given the chance, they might not be able to stop before ripping Clayton's arms off and using them to beat him until his filthy mouth was closed permanently.

Nate smiled, his shoulders moved with laughter as his head shook back and forth in a knowing motion. Clayton was an ass on a good day, and today was turning out to be one of his best.

Rich circled the parking lot before exiting again and pulling back onto the street. Five blocks and a lot of whining from the imbecile in the next seat later, he pulled into a Circle K, threw the transmission into park and waited.

Clayton's eyes were the size of dinner plates. "What the...?"

"Get out!" Rich ordered without acknowledging him further.

"You can't—"

"Get out!" Rich repeated, fighting to keep his voice semi-calm, looking straight ahead.

"I'll tell Dale—"

"You do that." Rich popped the locks. "Get out!"

"Why...?"

"I warned you. I always follow through with my promises." His voice was flat, frighteningly calm. "And now, you get to walk."

"Is this about Kate?"

"You do not even *think* her name." His vision turned red as fury built in his bloodstream, blood hammered in his ears.

"Hey man, she's just a girl."

"Maybe. But *she's just a girl* who happens to mean a lot to me." Rich turned to his head to glare at Clayton. "Get. Out!"

Clayton just stared at Rich, pulling the wide-eyed goldfish routine.

"Close your mouth." He did. "If I have to come over there and drag your ass out of this vehicle, I will."

Plump fingers frantically grabbed for the handle then Clayton scurried out into the heat. "This isn't over. You can pull the protective caveman crap while we're alone, but Dale..." His threats faded as Rich drove away.

"Passenger door ajar," the mechanical voice informed him. The door gaped open as he turned right around a corner. *"Passenger door ajar."*

He pulled into another parking lot, out of Clayton's line of sight, and forced himself to breathe through his fury. The little prick was right—he had been acting like a caveman, but couldn't bring himself to act any differently. It was his job to protect Kate. *No, it's not.* He groaned, crammed his fingers through his hair and sucked in deep breaths, sending the air through clenched teeth in a whistle.

When his blood pressure had returned to pseudo-normal, he headed back for the station. Nate and Kate still stood in the parking lot when Rich slowly moved through the gate. They approached as he pulled into a space and turned off the car.

Nate found great humor in Rich's anger. "What'd you do with him? You weren't gone long enough to bury him."

"He's alive. Pissed, but alive," Rich grumbled as he stomped toward the building.

"What did he do that made you so upset?" Kate asked, completely oblivious. Nate looked at her in disbelief.

"It doesn't matter," Rich told her, hurrying toward the door in hopes of avoiding any further interrogation.

Her footsteps stuttered behind him as she hurried to match his pace. "Rich, you're upset, and that matters to me."

Rich stopped and whirled around to face her. She

bumped into his chest then stumbled backward. "Does it, Kate? You care that I'm upset?" Out of the corner of his eye, Rich noticed that Nate had discretely disappeared behind a car. "You didn't think for one second that strolling back into my life today might upset me? That the fact that you're pregnant wouldn't have any effect on my mood? Come on, Kate, you're a smart girl. Why do you think I'm upset with Clayton?"

Her eyes were glassy, filling with tears by the second, as she blinked wildly. "I'm..." She cleared her throat. "I'm so sorry. This isn't at all how I wanted this to go."

"How did you expect *this* to go?" Rich added a tad more sarcasm. "Oh, Kate, honey, I'm so glad you're home. Thanks for breaking my heart, leaving me an emotional basket case, and keeping the fact that you're pregnant a secret."

She reached for him but pulled back before she made contact. "I didn't want to..."

"Rich Spencer, please come to my office," Dale's voice resonated over the loud speaker in the parking lot. It contained a hint of humor which meant that Clayton had made it back.

"I've gotta go." Rich took a step toward the door before stopping. "Oh...one quick question." She nodded, then he asked, "When's the baby due?"

"October 5th, why?"

"Never mind. I've gotta go." *October 5th. October 5th.* That date would forever be ingrained on his heart.

Inside Dale's office, Clayton paced, livid beneath his sweat-drenched Polo shirt. His pits were soaked and his thinning hair was plastered to his head. His tiny eyes were full of fury under brows that were pulled into a deep V. His fists clenched as Rich walked into the office where a disgusting cross between Obsession for Men and his BO polluted the air.

Dale was the first to speak. "From what I understand there was a *situation* between you two. Would you like to tell me your side?" He was trying really hard to not express the humor that shone in his eyes.

"I told him that certain topics were off limits, and that if he brought them up, he'd have to walk back." Rich delivered his explanation with careless flippancy. "I guess he didn't believe me," he added with a laugh. "I'll bet he won't make that mistake again."

Dale leaned back in his chair, folding his arms behind his head. Clayton didn't respond, except to pull the drenched shirt from his armpits, shuffle his loafers on the carpeting, and grumble unintelligently under his breath. The clock just ticked away in silence as he ran stubby fingers through sweat-drenched hair, making it stand on end.

"Is that true?" Dale asked, then allowed the uncomfortable silence to continue. His eyes bore holes through Clayton until he finally looked up and nodded guiltily once before glaring at Rich.

"Thanks, Rich." Dale tipped his head toward the door, dismissing him.

Rich nodded and walked out of the office just as Clayton began his protests, "*What*? You can't..."

A smile spread across Rich's lips as he imagined the lecture Dale was giving to Clayton. He deserved more than what Rich had given him, but hitting the girly man could have ended with Rich's unemployed butt in jail.

"Are you ready for dinner?" the sweetest voice on earth asked from behind him. Kate was sitting in Gladys' chair, doodling on a sticky note. She stood and stepped toward him. "Ready?"

"Um, I guess. If you want."

"I *don't* want to leave things the way they are. I hate this tension between us. I still..." She dropped her eyes to concentrate on the hem of her blouse. "Do you have somewhere you want to go?"

Rich had honestly thought that after his tirade in the parking lot that dinner would be out. Obviously, he was wrong. "Yeah, I know the perfect place. It's near Nate's. You wanna follow me or—"

"I'll follow you. Just let me grab my stuff." She walked off to her desk and Rich looked toward the door.

Nate was holding up the wall with his shoulder. Rich walked over and Nate laughed. "So, how'd it go with

Dale? Are you fired?" He already knew that Rich wasn't in any kind of trouble. Rich rolled his eyes and continued out the door, with Nate hot on his heels. "You headed home?"

"No," Rich grunted.

"Where you going?"

"Are you my father?"

Nate's hand clamped around his bicep, pulling gently to stop his stride. "Rich, be careful."

"You sound like a broken record."

"You forget that I've watched what she's done to you. I just don't want—"

"Rich?" Kate's voice caused Rich's blood to run cold. How much of their conversation had she heard?

Nate gave a squeeze then released his hold. "I'll catch you later. Bye, Kate," he said without even looking at her.

She bristled. Tears were in her eyes when they met Rich's. "We don't have to—"

"No, I want to." Rich inwardly cringed at the eagerness in his tone, dropping it to the harsher one he'd been using earlier before he continued, "I've got a few questions for you."

A weak smile eased the corner of her lips up as she wiped the tears from her cheeks. "I'll answer anything you want—as honestly as I can."

"Honesty would be nice." His response dripped venom. She winced, and he apologized, "I'm sorry, Kate."

Damp eyes looked up at him, and she sighed. "I know."

His fingers wrapped themselves around the flesh of her upper arm. "Come on, let's not do this here. Let me buy you dinner." Rich attempted a smile of encouragement, unsure of how successful it looked, since it felt like an utter failure.

They were quiet as they made the short trip across the parking lot to her car. "So I'll follow you." She awkwardly sank down into the driver's seat, her belly nearly touching the steering wheel. Her eyes flicked up to his, full of pain and sadness that broke his heart.

His eyes started to sting and he knew that this was

not where he wanted to breakdown. Stepping away, his hand assisted her in closing the door with a pop. She looked at him through the glass, and it caused actual, physical pain to take the few steps back across the parking lot to his vehicle.

The drive to dinner went quickly. His foot pressed the pedal to the floor. More than once Rich had to remind himself to slow down. Nervous energy had taken over and settled deep in his chest. His heart pounded out the beat of her name.

She followed him into the parking lot and chose the spot next to him. She was getting out of her car when he came around his. She looked up at him and laughed. "Nice place," she said sarcastically.

The little 'club' was a bar, complete with neon signs and motorcycles in the parking lot. Its brown wood frame and black shingled roof were quaint, but it certainly didn't have the feel of a five-star restaurant.

"There's a reason I brought you here." He shrugged. "I really want you to meet someone."

"Oh?"

"Yeah, *she* works here," Rich added, hoping for the reaction she gave him.

Her face fell before she quickly tried to hide her reaction. "That's nice. I can't wait to meet your girlfriend."

Rich didn't feel the need to correct her. There was a certain amount of satisfaction in the fact that she was bugged by Fergie. He just prayed that Fergie would behave. She had a way of being a little too honest for some people's liking. Cursing himself for not giving Fergie warning, Rich opened the door and ushered Kate inside.

After a quick scan of the bar, Rich found who he was looking for. Fergie and Fuzzy sat against the wall to his left. Fuzzy was in a chair with Fergie straddling across his hips. His enormous hands held her hips in place as his fingers stroked the bare skin of her back. They were only talking, but the pose was uncomfortably intimate for onlookers brazen enough to watch.

Kate stood at his side, shifting her weight from one

foot to the other. Her discomfort made his skin tingle.

Something caught Fuzzy's attention and he whispered to Fergie just before she turned around, curiosity on her face. She shook her head and stood, shaking out her unnaturally red hair that was dyed blonde at the flipped ends. Her tongue clicked against her teeth as she approached. "Well, if it isn't my favorite lush."

Rich fought against the cringe and tried to convince himself that this was actually good. He wanted Kate to know how miserable he'd been without her. There was nothing left of his pride when it came to Kate—no need to pretend.

"Who's your friend?" Fuzzy's deep voice was hard, unfriendly, his expression the same.

With his hand on the small of Kate's back, Rich brought her to his side. "I'd like you to meet Kate."

"Kate? *The* Kate?" Fergie asked, her eyes moved to Kate's belly. "It seems she kept more than just her distance from you, Rich."

Kate tensed under his touch. Fuzzy stepped forward, extended his hand, and Fergie's name flexed on his upper arm. "It's nice to meet you, Kate. Does this mean that you're going to take away our best customer?" Kate appeared completely numb as she shook Fuzzy's hand. "Your favorite table's open. Have a seat and Fergie'll set you up, my treat. You hungry?"

Fergie glared at her husband, but he smiled and warned her with his eyes, something he would certainly catch hell for later.

"A couple of burgers, fries and something to drink."

"You want your regular?" Daggers flew from Fergie's eyes as she glared at Kate. "I'm guessing *she* doesn't, since alcohol can harm a baby. Is it even—"

"Fergie, why don't you come with me," Fuzzy instructed, successfully cutting off the question that had been swimming through Rich's head since seeing Kate for the first time. "A couple of Cokes?"

Rich nodded. He'd expected Fergie to be protective, but her hostility had come as a shock. "This way." Kate and Rich moved toward the corner table, each taking a seat. His hands itched to take Kate's and his heart nearly jumped out his chest when her soft hands touched his arm.

"Rich," she whispered, her voice full of emotion, "I really am sorry for everything. I just... Well, I didn't know how to tell you about any of this." She motioned toward her swollen midsection.

"You could have just told me. Is that why you ... avoided my calls?" It felt like the temperature in the room had risen by a hundred degrees.

She nodded. "I've been avoiding this discussion because I knew it would hurt you...that I'd betrayed you."

"Betrayed me?" His face crinkled in confusion. "How did you betray me?" Thoughts of another man touching Kate intimately made his stomach roll.

"The baby. I thought that..."

A relief induced laugh burst from his chest. "Unless you're going to tell me that the baby isn't mine—or Jesse's," he added when she tipped her head to the side, wrinkling her brow, "then you haven't betrayed me."

Tears formed in her jade eyes, and she tightened her grip. "Rich, this baby is Jesse's. It has to be."

"You don't know that," he retorted, a little sharper than he'd intended. "It could be—"

"Here you go." Fergie plopped a couple glasses on the table in front of them before she turned quickly and stomped away.

"Your girlfriend really doesn't like me, does she?"

"Do you really think that she's my girlfriend?" Rich asked, needing to clear up any kind of confusion.

"Well, you said you wanted me to meet someone, I assumed—"

"I did want you to meet Fergie and her husband, Fuzzy."

Her eyes widened. "Oh."

"Kate, this little table is where I've spent nearly every night since you started avoiding me. I refuse to sit here and pretend that I don't still love you, that I don't want to be the man in your life. I have been a miserable excuse of a person since you've been gone, drinking myself numb because I couldn't stand to feel the pain."

She winced, tears in her eyes. "I can't saddle you with a baby that isn't yours, Rich. That wouldn't be fair to you. And someday you would hate me for it. I couldn't bear to have that." Her eyes flicked up and she stopped talking just as Fergie was back with the food.

"I'm sorry I was rude before," she said coldly. "What happens between you and Rich is, well, between you and Rich."

Thank you, Fuzzy.

She leaned down so that her face was only inches from Kate's and whispered, "You destroyed him, little girl. You broke his heart and we all had to watch him soak the pieces in alcohol, trying to survive the heartache. Hurt him again, and I'll be the one you answer to. Got it?"

Kate's big eyes blinked as she nodded slowly. "I didn't mean—"

"I don't want to hear it," Fergie said as she straightened, then she turned to him. "I love you, Rich, like a brother."

"Thanks," Rich told her, smiling, "but if you ever speak to Kate that way again, Fergie, I'll be the one *you* answer to."

White teeth appeared from under her tight lips as they formed a smile. "Got it." She looked at Kate, smile still in place. "Sorry."

"I understand," Kate said, her whole body seeming to relax right before his eyes as Fergie walked away. "Wow, she really cares about you."

"You spend every night for months in a place, you get to care about the people you're around."

She nodded again and began to pick at her fries. After dumping some ketchup on her plate and slathering a fry in it, she popped it into her mouth. Rich could only watch as she took a bite after bite of her hamburger.

She took a long sip of her drink, cleared her throat and asked, "Aren't you hungry?" Her eyes moved from his face to the still full plate in front of him to the nearly empty one in front of her.

"I can't believe you're really here."

She smiled, uncomfortable with his obvious appraisal of her. Rich needed to get this conversation back on topic before the gurgling in his stomach turned into a bleeding ulcer. "Kate, you said that my hating you was something you couldn't bear."

She nodded, wiping at her mouth with a napkin. Her eyes were focused on him as she swallowed hard, almost as if she was anticipating where the conversation would go next.

"I have one question for you. It's the most important one. Your answer will mean everything, so don't answer too quickly. Okay?"

"Okay."

His heart was pounding so hard, it actually hurt. Leaning forward, he took her hands and filled his lungs with a deep breath in preparation for the answer he prayed she wouldn't give him. Rich concentrated on a slow exhale then asked, "Kate, do you love me?"

Her eyes widened, she blushed. "Rich, I..." She paused and took another sip of her drink. A loud slurp sounded.

"Yes or no?" he pressed. "Do you still love me?"

"Yes, but..."

His fingers flew up, covered her mouth, successfully cutting off her words. "No buts, Kate. If you still love me, then nothing else matters. We can work through everything else."

"Even *this*?" She pointed at her large stomach. "Can you honestly say that Jesse's baby growing in my belly doesn't hinder your feelings for me?"

Rich couldn't answer that question yet, so he countered with, "What if it's not his, Kate? That baby could be mine—ours—and *that* would make me the happiest man on Earth."

"It's Jesse's, Rich." Tears filled her eyes and slid elegantly down her cheeks. She dropped her gaze and her voice. "It *has* to be Jesse's." There was a desperation in her voice that broke his heart. "Rich, we're a package deal, the baby and me. Whether or not I love you doesn't matter if you can't love him, too." She stood and tossed her napkin on the table. Tears still dampened her cheeks as determined footsteps headed for the door.

Rich dropped some cash on the table then rushed after her, finally catching up next to the familiar green Jetta. "Kate."

She stopped, but didn't turn around. Her shoulders shook with a sob, and her whole body tensed when his hands gently took her by the back of her arms.

"Do you love me?"

Her head moved in a nodding motion as another round of sobs assaulted her.

Rich turned her slowly until she faced him then tipped her chin so that their eyes met. "Do you love me?"

"Yes," she whispered. "I could never stop loving you."

His hands shook as they rested on each side of her face. Love reflected in her shining eyes. His burned with the emotion of that knowledge. Her lips were soft under his and she accepted his kiss with a sigh before pulling away too soon. She nervously bit on her lower lip before dropping her head to rest against his chest.

"I should go."

"Good night, Kate."

The lights flashed as she disengaged the locks, then she opened the door and slid out of his embrace and into the driver's seat.

"I love you, Kate."

Her eyes swam as she looked up at him, smiling. "I love you, too."

Twenty Six

As Rich watched the bright red taillights put distance between them, his heart was soaring. The heavy weight that had been strapped around his neck, weighing down his shoulders, and dumping him into a depression that wouldn't release him, had been lifted. A great desire to spread his arms out, just to see if he really could take flight, struck him. Rich fought the urge to jump in the air and click his heels together. But only because Kate might be watching in her rear view mirror.

Screeching tires, flying gravel, and then the smell of burning rubber caused the joyous beats of his heart to become frantic as a red BMW tore out of the parking lot. It raced over the pavement in the same direction that Kate had gone.

His blood ran cold.

Shea.

His body jumped into action before his brain had even fully come back on track. Rich slid into the driver's seat and gave chase. There was now more at stake than just Kate—although, she was enough. That crazy bitch of an ex-wife would not be allowed anywhere near his son.

His headlights lit up the back end of the shiny, red car ahead of his. It didn't have Shea's vanity plate, and Rich allowed himself to hope. Light from an overhead streetlight exposed the driver, and unless Shea had shaved her head and had a sex change, it wasn't her.

For the first time in minutes, Rich was able to take a relieved breath. "Kate's safe," he said in an attempt to calm the frantic beats of his heart and the vivid thoughts plaguing his overactive imagination.

The little red sportscar flew right around a corner, nearly slammed into a tree, then corrected and disappeared into the night. Kate's car was clearly visible now. She stopped at a red light, and he slowed hoping to buy enough time to have the light turn green.

He felt like some kind of stalker as he followed Kate at a distance to her house. She pulled into the driveway of a rambler. In the darkness it looked beige with a nicely manicured yard. The garage door went up, then back down, sealing Kate into the safety of the place she called home. Lights turned on in the front window, but thankfully, there were no shadows that could be picked up by a maniac waiting to pounce.

The window of his car slid down almost silently and the heat from the July night poured inside. Having it up with the air-conditioner running would make the temperature more comfortable, but he wanted to hear what was happening in this *Leave it to Beaver* neighborhood, and listen for any sign that Shea was after Kate.

Rich eased the car away from the curb and drove down the quiet street. When he got to the end, he turned around and slowly drove to the other end. After five or six passes, the lights were out in her windows and he pulled into the driveway before cutting the engine.

It's going to be a long night, he told himself. The seat was already back all the way, and he reclined the seatback as well. His knees were cramped, his legs uncomfortable. He leaned his head against the headrest and closed his eyes. A warm breeze blew through the car, caressing his cheek.

A sound, soft yet out of place, caused his head to jerk toward the house. He squinted his eyes, searching for the source of his distress. There, in the shadows, was a person; by the size and shape, a woman. She was dressed from head to toe in black.

Rich grabbed the handle of the car and tugged roughly. It refused to open. Rich popped the locks and tried again. Still nothing. The damn door wouldn't budge. Using his shoulder and as much body weight as his position would allow, he tried to force it open.

His eyes searched for the intruder, finding her near a front window. Her hands moved slowly, with the deadly grace of a cheetah. Something caught the moonlight and reflected it in his direction.

A knife.

The battle to get out of the vehicle became even more panicked. The window was down and Rich seriously considered pulling a Bo Duke routine just as her head turned toward him. A vicious smile pulled at her lips revealing teeth so white they glowed in the darkness. Long lashes closed over one eye as she winked.

"It's a race, Rich. How fast can you run?" Then Shea disappeared around the corner of the house.

Rich awoke with a jolt and sat straight up in the car. His breathing was abnormally quick, his heart raced as though he'd just run the Boston Marathon, and a sheen coat of sweat covered his entire body. Sweat that had nothing to do with the heat.

He prayed that what he'd just seen was the nightmare he thought it was. Shaking hands rubbed over the stubble that had grown since he'd shaved this morning then scrubbed his sleepy eyes. His heart still pounded with no sign of stopping until he made sure that Shea was nowhere near this house.

One quick jerk opened the door. *Well, that's a good sign*, he thought.

Crickets chirped happily as he cautiously made his way to the exact place he'd seen Shea. The grass was damp and it wasn't long before the leather of his tennis shoes allowed the moisture through to his toes. Rounding the corner, Rich found a six-foot wall covered in climbing roses. The odds of a person tangling with those thorns wasn't likely.

The rubber soles of his shoes squeaked softly as he walked back across the grass. He couldn't help but laugh, thinking about what he must look like. A stalker? A psycho? A crazy obsessed man?

Two out of three, he thought, biting back another laugh.

As absurd as it was, his inspection had done little to calm his fears. There was only one thing that could do that. Kate. It would be her sweet voice saying that she was okay, that would do the trick.

Once in his car, he turned the key just enough to let him roll up the windows. He pulled out his phone and pressed the speed dial that belonged to Kate.

"Hello?" She sounded tired. "Rich? It's really late."

"I know. Sorry. Are you okay?" He winced at the pathetically frantic sound of his voice.

"Yes. Are *you* okay?"

"I was just..." He didn't want to upset her, but it was important that she understood the danger still lurking. "Shea's still out there." *Subtle.*

"I'd heard that," she said as if she didn't have a care in the world.

"Did you lock your doors and check all your windows?"

"Nope. They're all unlocked and wide open with a neon sign telling Shea to come right in. I even have the guest room made up for her. And I bought some more lingerie for her to shred. I'm hoping she'll like them, maybe add them to her collection." She was mocking him and that pissed him off.

"That is *so* not funny."

"You calling me at 2:00 in the morning is *so not funny.* Do you have any idea how hard it is to sleep these days?"

"How far along are you?"

"Twenty-eight weeks ... almost twenty-nine," she answered then continued as though she hadn't been interrupted, "I was asleep, Rich." A car alarm went off in the driveway next door and he could hear the stupid thing in stereo. "Oh good hell, Rich, please tell me that you're not outside."

With a quick flick of his wrist, the engine turned over, and he hoped that she hadn't heard as he made his cowardly retreat. "No, I'm not that big of a loser."

Kate's laughter tickled his ears. "I saw you, Rich."

"I'm just worried about you—and *our* son."

Her only response to his suggestion about the

paternity was a breath that rushed into the phone. "I know you're worried. I love that you care, but you should really go home, get a good night's rest."

"But—"

"I have the best security system money can buy." Her revelation made him feel a little better. "I'm fine. *We're* fine. I just hope I can get back to sleep."

"Sorry."

"It's okay."

"Sleep, love. I'll see you tomorrow."

At the end of the street, Rich made a u-turn and headed back for Kate's driveway, not caring whether or not she thought he was a lovesick fool. Why deny it? He was completely in love with her.

A good night's sleep wasn't on the agenda tonight because the driver's seat of a Ford Explorer didn't have much room. It wasn't like his Jeep would have given him any more comfort. He closed his eyes and prayed that another nightmare wouldn't wander into his brain.

Morning sunlight and the buzzing of a weed eater woke him out of a dead sleep. He rubbed a hand across the drool on his chin and sat up, running the other hand through his hair. The car turned over with one turn of the key and he was off.

The drive home was uneventful. Talk radio filled the silence, not that he was listening to their debate. His mind was devoted to Kate. It was spinning with thoughts, anticipation and fear. His whole future, his entire happiness hung in the balance. Kate had the ultimate power over his heart. If she were to turn him away again, his heart would never mend. He would be broken forever.

Rich pulled up in front of Nate's house, cut the engine, and debated whether or not going inside was a good idea. His best friend had a way of being infuriatingly honest. Rich didn't want to be ridiculed, but was in desperate need of a shower, a shave, and something to eat.

Nate was sitting at the kitchen table eating a bowl of Cap'n Crunch, watching the morning edition of KHB's newscast. He looked up and smiled. "Morning, sunshine.

You look like crap."

"I feel like crap." His hand unconsciously rubbed at the crick in his neck. "I didn't get much sleep last night."

Nate chuckled as he used the spoon to dig into the bowl for another bite. "Good to hear. I knew she'd come around."

Rich rolled his eyes, making sure Nate saw the action then crossed the kitchen to find something to eat. "It's not like that."

"Oh, of course not," Nate said sarcastically.

Turning on his heel, Rich started for the door. Even though he'd known that this was exactly how the conversation would go with him, he couldn't stand it. He'd rather starve.

"Hey," Nate called, "where you going? I thought you were hungry."

"I lost my appetite," Rich said without turning around.

"Sorry."

Rich grunted, pausing in the doorway.

Nate laughed and kicked the chair opposite him. "Now, sit, have some breakfast. The Cap'n is really good this morning." The little yellow cereal nuggets clinked as they hit the ceramic surface of the bowl. Rich poured some milk over the top and then put some in a glass. "It's good to see you've graduated from beer for breakfast," Nate noted before scooping another spoonful of cereal into his mouth.

Rich used a quick swig to punctuate the observation. The cool liquid was a refreshing change— not that he would admit that to his best friend.

"So how'd it go with Kate last night?"

Rich glared at him.

"I don't want *sexual* details." He wiggled his brows and flashed a cheesy grin. "I'd just like to know ... well, whatever you're willing to tell me."

The sweet, sugary cereal crunched beneath his teeth, and Nate's interrogation caused the subtle chewing to turn to grinding. "She insists the baby is Jesse's."

"It's possible, isn't it?" His voice of reason was

irritatingly correct.

"Of course it's possible, but—" Rich put another spoonful of cereal into his mouth.

Nate watched him then as he chewed asked, "But...?"

"But ... it could be mine. We didn't use any kind of protection." Rich's skin tingled as he remembered the moments Kate had spent in his arms. He ached to have her there again—soon.

"Was she on the pill?" Nate asked before shoveling another heaping spoonful into his mouth.

"I don't know. I would think she and Jesse used some kind of protection, but I don't know." Rich shuddered at the thought of *him* touching her intimately.

"But the pill—" Nate's face scrunched with concentration. "—well, that would have... You wouldn't have gotten her pregnant either."

"Hey!"

"Those little pink puppies would have stopped Superman's swimmers too." Nate laughed. "At least that's what I'm banking on."

"You're Superman, huh?" Rich raised a brow.

Nate blew on his fingernails and rubbed them on his t-shirt. "Somebody had to take the job." Then he leaned toward him and whispered, "You have to keep it a secret though. I wouldn't want it to get out. I have other things to do besides saving other people's asses all the time."

"You're a saint, Nate Hughes."

"I know," he said as dimples appeared.

Rich finished his cereal, polished off the milk, then rinsed the dishes and set them in the sink. It was a good thing that he was working the late shift today, because his body was exhausted. And, now that Kate was safe at work, he could allow himself to sleep, to rest.

The bed was soft under his body, and as soon as his head hit the pillow, his eyes closed.

✕ ✕ ✕

Kate hummed softly as she waited for her computer to

power up so she could log on to the station's network. A smile tipped her lips as she remembered the concern on Rich's face last night. She had been able to get back to sleep, only to dream of Rich.

Was it actually possible for a man to love another man's baby? It wasn't fair to expect that of Rich. He was a wonderful man who deserved children of his own, not to be saddled with one that wasn't in any way his responsibility.

Kate had resigned herself to the fact that she would raise this child on her own. Jesse's son would have everything Kate could give him. The only thing lacking would be a father, and she wasn't willing to give him that. She couldn't.

She just couldn't.

A tear slid down her cheek as she thought of pushing Rich away—again. He didn't deserve that either. This whole situation was impossibly unfair. Jesse's son would grow up without a father. Rich would be on the receiving end of heartache. And Kate... She sighed. She would have to learn to live without the man she wanted more than anything in this world.

Her heart belonged to Rich. And if she were being honest with herself, he had captured it long before she'd allowed herself to realize. She'd wasted so much time. This baby could have been his. Jesse would still be alive, heartbroken but alive. And she wouldn't have again wasted time cowardly avoiding the consequences of her actions.

"Kate," Olivia asked, "are you okay?"

Kate sniffed, grabbed out a tissue, and wiped her nose. "Damn hormones."

Olivia laughed. "Yeah, I've heard they can be a bitch."

Kate looked into the eyes of her friend, and asked, "Why didn't you tell me?"

Her dark brows pulled together. "Tell you what?"

Kate attempted a smile. "Olivia, I met Fergie last night." The statement in and of itself explained everything, and Olivia bit on her lip. "I'm surprised you and Jordan—and Nate—didn't just kick me out on my ear. I would have deserved it."

Olivia covered Kate's hand with her own. "Listen, Kate, Jordan and I have decided that what happened, or what will happen, is between you and Rich. That doesn't mean I agree with your actions, but we're going to try and stay out of things."

Kate laughed. "Did Jordan have to write that down for you to memorize?"

Olivia smiled, but didn't disagree. "It's been hell trying to keep my opinions to myself, Kate. Especially when you show up...a little bigger than you left." She bit her lip, did a quick scan of the newsroom for Jordan's whereabouts, then leaned in. "I do have to say, though, that letting Rich find out the way he did was ... well, it was really chicken shit, Kate. He deserved better than that."

Kate nodded. "Rich deserves a lot better of a lot of things. I hate the way things are between us, that this baby—as much as I love him—is a wedge that will never go away."

"You don't give Rich enough credit."

"You give him too much," Kate retorted. "I can't ask him, nor will I, to accept a child that isn't his. He deserves better than a constant reminder of Jesse. I love him too much to put him through that."

"Rich or Jesse?"

Kate's brows crinkled. "Huh?"

"Who do you love too much, Rich or Jesse?"

"Morning meeting in five."

Saved by the PA.

Olivia smiled. "I guess it doesn't matter to me, Kate, but it sure as hell matters to you—and to Rich. And believe it or not, your son deserves a father, even if it's not his biological one."

"I guess we'll just have to disagree on that, won't we." Kate stood and picked up her notebook. "Come on, let's get me a good story.

✗ ✗ ✗

Rich opened his eyes when the annoying blare of his

alarm insisted that he should. He needed more sleep. Geez, this situation had disaster written all over it. There was no way he'd be able to keep up this pace for long. Kate needed to be protected, but Rich needed his sleep.

He somehow made it to the shower, got dressed, and stood with his keys in hand. The drive to work should be interesting since the only thing his mind could concentrate on was Kate. Always Kate.

She'd been on his mind for months, and now that she was back, she was an even more permanent fixture. When he closed his eyes, it was her face on the back of his eyelids.

He walked through the door of the station and, of course, his eyes scanned the familiar room in search of the familiar face that made his whole world complete. Jordan tipped his head in a hello then shook it. Rich groaned, knowing that the whole world knew just how whipped he was over the pregnant girl who had chosen to show back up in his life.

Something else had been on his mind. *October 5th*. He sat down at an empty computer and hit the internet connection. Within seconds he had 'conception date' entered in the search box. Sweat broke out on his forehead and he nearly gnawed a hole in his lip in the seconds before he pressed 'enter'.

Three clicks later and he had a calendar on the screen. The conception dates were when they were in Phoenix. That was good. It gave a range of three days; the day Jesse showed up, the day Rich confessed everything, and the day Kate finally accepted him.

In other words, Rich thought with a groan, *it could be either of ours.*

But it was still a possibility. One he wouldn't give up on until he was forced to. He sighed and clicked the close button, erasing his pathetic search.

With his head held high, Rich crossed the room to the assignment desk. He propped his elbow on the chest high desk. "Busy day?"

Jordan looked up and smiled. "Not much going on. Mostly just coverage of the Pioneer Day festivities. I've got Kate and Nate at the Horse Parade downtown." He paused then said, "I need you to join her there for the actual newscast. Nate has to...go to another assignment."

Rich fought the urge to kiss his longtime friend. "Sure thing. When should I..."

"Now. Get your ass down there...*now*."

Rich tossed him an I'm-not-buying-it look. "What have you done, Greene?"

"Moi?" He feigned innocence.

"Yeah, you. What are you trying to pull, Jordan?"

"Get your ass down to the parade," Jordan growled through his teeth, glancing over his shoulder to look at Olivia, who smiled.

Rich didn't wait to be told twice. He snorted and walked back toward the Photog's lounge, and as he did, Olivia said, "I thought we were going to stay out of it, Jordan."

"Great," Rich muttered. He didn't stand a chance of escaping this catastrophe with his heart intact with those two playing matchmaker.

✕✕✕

"Oh good, you're here," Nate said.

Kate turned just in time to see Rich walk up. Her heart stopped. "What are you doing here?" It wasn't meant as an accusation but sure sounded like one.

Nate answered instead of Rich. "I have to meet Roxy in twenty minutes. Thanks for covering the 5:00 for me. I owe you, buddy." Nate clapped Rich on the shoulder and whispered something in his ear before tossing Kate a smile. "Great working with you today, Kate. I forgot how much fun you are." He winked and was gone.

Kate watched Rich, who watched over his shoulder as Nate vacated the premises on a near run. She wasn't sure if his story was fact or fiction. It seemed a little convenient. "So do you think it was his idea?"

"That depends—" Rich turned to face her. "—did Jordan call him or did Nate call Jordan?"

"Jordan ca-..." Kate's eyes narrowed and Rich

smiled, raising a knowing brow. "Ew, Jordan." She said his name as a curse.

"Can you say matchmaker?" Rich groaned under his breath.

This new little bit of information made Kate angry. How dare Olivia—how dare *they* interfere. She promised that they wouldn't and, in classic Olivia form, she was butting in. *And* there were three more long months before the baby would be born. "I wish Olivia would just keep her..."

"Olivia?" Rich's brows knitted together. "What does Olivia have to do with this? Did she—"

"Let's just get this story finished, okay? I can't think about this right now."

"What's to think about?" There was an edge of angry frustration to his voice, one that he tried unsuccessfully to hide. "I love you, you love me. End of story." Rich stepped forward and Kate matched the action by retreating.

"That's not the end of the story." She rubbed her hand over her ever growing stomach. "There's so much more to the story. A little boy, who has a story that hasn't even begun, Rich. *That* is...." Her voice grew thick with emotion as she talked about her unborn son. She cleared her throat. "I can't do this, Rich. Please don't—"

"I'm sorry, Kate." He stepped forward and took her hand. "You love me, right?"

She wiped roughly at her cheeks, and snorted.

"Right?" he encouraged.

"You know I do," she said without looking in his eyes.

He tipped her chin with his finger. "Don't ever forget that I love you, too. Always."

Her hand again moved over her son. "It's not enough, Rich. I'm sorry." She walked away from him, glad to have the crowd swallow her up. Yes, she loved him. Adored him. Couldn't imagine her life without him in it. But it wasn't enough.

Twenty Seven

They finished their story and were headed back to the truck when Rich stopped. "You can't ignore me forever, Kate."

"Who said I was ignoring you?" she asked without looking at him—or even slowing her pace.

Let her walk, Rich thought smugly, reaching into his pocket to palm the keys. Eventually she might stumble onto the locked vehicle and then she wouldn't have any other choice than to wait for him.

It didn't take long though. When she realized that her puppy had slipped its leash, she turned. Rich shrugged. "Nobody had to tell me, Kate, your lack of words is telling enough. Hell, if you hadn't *had* to speak to me today, you wouldn't have. I'm not a complete idiot."

She crossed her arms over her chest, where they rested on her belly. "I never said you were an idiot."

"You've sure as hell done your best to make me feel like one," he muttered under his breath.

Kate rolled her eyes and huffed with irritated audacity. Her arms were still folded tightly across her front as she turned her back and walked away. She stomped three steps, then stopped.

Rich slowly moved to her side but didn't stop, just walked past her. He snorted. "You don't know where the truck is, huh?" he mocked.

"You think you're so funny, don't you?"

"No, not funny," he said with amusement oozing through the words, "I just really like being right." He couldn't hide the smug smile, not that he tried.

The two of them were quiet as they walked the few blocks to where the white Ford Explorer was parked. Rich hit the locks and the lights flashed. Kate slid into the passenger seat and closed the door with a poignant slam. Rich put the camera in the back, a whistle on his lips. He climbed behind the wheel and turned the key. The truck's engine came to life, and Kate reached for the radio, turning it up to an uncomfortable volume before she turned toward the window.

"I'm guessing you don't want to talk?" Rich yelled over the music. Her only response was to turn it up even louder. Rich turned the radio off. Kate tensed, but offered no other reaction. "Kate, we can't continue like this."

"You're right," she said to the window.

"I'm what?"

She turned her head only enough to glare at him then turned back to the window. "This can't go on this way, but we have to face the facts."

"The fact is that I love you. That, my love, is something that will never change." Rich expected a tender emotion in her eyes, but when she looked at him, she sported an intense one he didn't recognize, nor did he like.

"The fact is, Rich—" Kate whirled in her seat to face him. "—that your ex-wife would like nothing more than my head on a spit. That fact is that I have guilt flowing through my veins, eating at me." She squeezed her eyes closed, but continued her rant. "The fact is that a piece of me really misses Jesse." She paused, and looked at him, tears in her eyes.

Rich tried to hide the emotions that Jesse's name brought up in him. He hated that Kate missed *him*. Hearing her say so caused his hands to tightened on the steering wheel. He forced in a deep breath and reminded himself that it was ridiculous to be jealous of a dead man.

"The fact is ... that Valentine's was the last time I felt..." She let the words drift off, blushed and dropped her eyes to where her hands rolled the hem of her blouse.

"Passion?"

"Yes. No!" She shook her head, color continuing to flood her cheeks. "I was going to say, it was the last time I'd felt normal. Happy."

Rich couldn't help the elation he felt. Kate hadn't been touched by another guy since he'd made love to her. The possessive male instinct kicked him in the ass, and he bit his lip to keep from grinning like a fool.

"And the fact is, Rich," her voice cracked, "the cherry on top of the shit sundae is that...*I'm pregnant.*" She was nearly shouting through her sobs, her voice a higher pitch than normal.

Rich stared at her, watching in bewilderment as she melted into a puddle of tears right before his eyes. "Kate, are you...?"

"I'm fine," she snapped. "I don't want your sympathy, Rich. I'm. Fine."

"Okay. You're fine." Rich nodded, wanting to argue, but knew better than to provoke her. "Are you hungry?"

She shook her head, only to stop and nod. "Yeah, I am."

"What do you feel like?"

A sob broke the silence. Kate sniffed. "Why are you being so nice?"

"Kate, I love you. I am not just being nice. I want to take care of you. Both of you."

"Please leave my son out of this." Her tears flowed steadily down her cheeks, and she wiped at them with little hope of drying them.

"Our son," Rich corrected.

"*My* son," she snapped, her eyes flashed a warning. "On second thought, just take me back to the station. I'll eat when I get home."

"I'd love to take you to dinner, Kate."

"You don't need to bother." She turned back toward the window, putting as much distance between them as the car would allow. "I just want to go home."

Rich was smart enough to know that he'd lost this particular battle with Kate. But he had no intention of losing the most important war of his life. He loved Kate, and she loved him. All he needed to do was help her remember how much.

× × ×

Kate wasn't sure if it was her recurring nightmare or the violent kicking of her baby that had woke her. The little guy in her belly always took the times when she was stretched out to show her just how strong he was. Sometimes she felt like there was an alien growing in her belly. The way it moved and shifted all on its own was eerie—and exciting.

She stumbled into the kitchen and tugged open the fridge. She poured some milk into a glass and slowly doused the acid that had bubbled up in the back of her throat. As if the four months of morning sickness hadn't been bad enough, now she couldn't sleep and was closely approaching the size of a small barn.

Something outside caught her eye and she pulled the curtain back to get a better look. She yelped, dropped the curtain, only to pull it back—a tiny bit—and looked out again. There was a car parked in her driveway. A car she recognized. *Rich.*

She should have been really pissed, but was too tired and uncomfortable to let it get to her. With her robe pulled tight around her, she padded out to the sleeping man in the car.

"Rich," she whispered. He made a soft snoring sound, but offered no other indication that he'd actually heard her. With her index finger, she poked him in the shoulder, but he didn't move. "Rich," she whispered a little louder. "I love you, Rich," she breathed the words. It felt so good to say them. She wanted to scream them from the rooftops, but couldn't bring herself to lead him on. There was no real future for them.

Rich shifted in the seat, and Kate panicked that he had heard her. He mumbled something unintelligible then settled into another soft snoring pattern. His long lashes rested against his cheek, his strong jaw relaxed, and his full lips looked so kissable even in his sleeping state. She reached out to touch them only to pull her hand back. She would not allow herself to remember how they felt against her lips, against her skin.

Her heart started to beat with the memories and she took a long breath. Her hands moved over her swollen belly, and the baby kicked as if to punctuate the importance of keeping Rich at a distance.

Kate watched Rich for another moment before deciding that she couldn't just allow him to sleep in her driveway. She reached her hand out and pushed his shoulder. "Rich." He didn't react, so she shook him again.

He jerked awake, wiping his hand over his eyes. He blinked, stared at her as if he were seeing a ghost, and blinked again. He was looking at her, but she wasn't sure that he was actually seeing her.

"Hey, sleepyhead," she said with a smile. Oh, how she loved this man.

"Hi," he said sheepishly. He tried to sit up, using the seat back to help in the effort.

Kate could see the disorientation swimming in his eyes and had to giggle at the absurdity of his efforts. It was obvious that he felt the need to protect her. It was also obvious that he was in no shape to do anything but sleep. "Would you like to tell me why you're sleeping in my driveway?"

"I, um ... I was worried ... about you." He looked so cute half asleep.

"Are you planning on spending every night right here?"

He nodded as he rubbed at his neck. "Yes. At least until Shea's caught."

She laughed and tugged at the handle on the car door. "Come on, Rich. I can't have you sleeping in my driveway. Somebody might call the police, and I'm not up for filling out a bunch of paperwork."

He looked even more confused by her offer. His brows pulled together in question.

"You can sleep on my couch tonight."

"Are you sure? I don't want to..."

"Shut up, Rich. I'm tired and..." She laughed softly. "Haven't you learned that it's not wise to argue with a pregnant woman?"

"I'm tired, too," he admitted, using his hand to stifle a yawn.

✕ ✕ ✕

Kate disappeared down the hall, and returned a few minutes later with a stack of blankets and a pillow. "It's a pretty comfortable couch. I've fallen asleep on it a couple of times."

"Thanks," Rich muttered as he helped Kate spread the sheet over the cushions. "You don't have to do this."

"I know, but I don't feel good about having you sleep in your car. The least I can do is give you my couch."

"Well, thanks. My body thanks you, too." He ran his hand over the knot in his neck that had been aggravated by the few hours he'd slept tonight.

She laughed lightly. "Good night, Rich."

"'Night." He smiled, watching her cute, little, very pregnant body turn to disappear down the hallway. "I love you, Kate."

He couldn't be sure, but he thought he heard her whisper that she loved him too. With a smile on his face, he slipped his shirt over his head and his jeans off his hips then slid beneath the blanket in only his boxers.

Everything smelled like Kate; the sheet, the blanket, the pillow. He sighed. She smelled so good. He wanted to hold her in his arms and inhale the real thing. When he pulled into Kate's driveway tonight, after the day he'd had with her, he never would have imagined that she'd show up and invite him in.

He closed his eyes and concentrated on nothing, except letting his body relax, to get a good night's sleep. Something he hadn't been blessed with for a very long time.

"Jesse!" Kate's shriek brought Rich out of his sleepy haze.

His ass hit the floor, and Rich scrambled to his feet before running to where he could hear Kate whimpering softly.

"Kate?" He approached her slowly, not wanting to

freak her out. "Are you okay?"

She nodded, but Rich didn't believe her. She was sitting up in the bed, her entire body shaking from the trauma of her nightmare. Her white cotton nightgown clung to the cold sweat that drenched her skin. Rich walked to her and sat on the edge of the bed closest to her. When she scooted closer, he opened his arms and she nearly crawled into his lap.

"Will you—" She sniffed. "—hold me 'til I get back to sleep?"

He wanted to jump up and do a little dance, but somehow managed to play it cool. "Sure. Slide over." She didn't hesitate, just lay down and rolled so that he could crawl in behind her. He wrapped his arms around her expanded belly suddenly nervous about the intimate contact. "Oh, is this okay?"

Kate tucked her body closer to his. "Yes, better than okay. Thank you, Rich."

"My pleasure," he sighed into her hair.

"I'm glad you're here," she said softly.

"Me too, love. Me too." Rich listened to Kate's breath as it slowed and steadied. He wanted nothing more than to stay right where he was, holding her in his protective embrace, but she had asked him to stay only until she was asleep. And now she was. Rich probably could have gotten away with sleeping next to her, but didn't want to push things. Being in her house was close enough—for now.

He pressed a light kiss to her shoulder and removed himself from Kate's bed, Kate's room. The couch was comfortable, just like Kate had promised, and it only took a few minutes for his body to relax into a deep sleep.

× × ×

Rich didn't know how he knew, but he knew Kate was up. She was in the kitchen, and if he hurried, he would soon be standing in the same room as she was. He rubbed the sleep out of his eyes and turned, placing his feet on the ground. Kate's sweet humming floated in from the next room. A smile spread to his lips and he sauntered toward her.

Kate was standing with her back to the door when Rich entered. He leaned against the door jamb and crossed his arms over his chest. It occurred to him in that moment that he was bare-chested, and his bottom half was as close to bare as was possible. He was just about to turn and get his pants when Kate gasped.

"Oh," she said softly. "I hope I didn't wake you." Her eyes moved slowly over his torso, then moved down until she'd consumed every inch of him to his toes.

Rich moved his hands in front of him to cover his lower half and smiled. "No, you didn't wake me."

Her eyes met his and she blushed then pulled her robe tighter around her. The satin that used to fit perfectly now gaped around her middle due to its ever increasing size. "Are you hungry?"

"Yeah, whatcha got?"

She shrugged and pulled a dissatisfied frown. "Not much I'm afraid. I'm not really a breakfast eater. I do have some Raisin Bran."

Not one of Rich's favorites, but it was better than nothing. If it meant not hurting Kate's feelings, Rich would have choked down a bowl of straw. "Sounds good. What time do you need to be in?"

She glanced over her shoulder at the clock on the microwave. "I'm early today. What about you?"

Rich really wanted to be early today, but the fact was he didn't have work at all. Not until working with Kate had he ever cursed a day off, but that was usually the case these days. If he wasn't at work, then she was unprotected. And Kate being unprotected was unacceptable. Completely unacceptable.

"Rich?"

"I'm, uh ... I'm off today."

"Oh," she said while fishing a spoon out of the silverware drawer. "What are you going to do today?" She leaned up on her toes and took a bowl out of the cupboard. The bowl slid onto the table with a soft scratching noise then the chair screeched as Kate pulled it away from the table. "If it's okay, I'll join you for breakfast."

"I'd like that." He sat down and began to pour some cereal into the bowl. With a spoonful of cereal in his mouth, he chewed slowly. Kate watched him intently, her eyes focused on his every movement. "Is everything okay?" he asked, feeling like a hamster under glass.

"Yes, I just ... I didn't think you'd be eating breakfast in my kitchen so soon after I got back." A pathetic, humorless laugh leapt into the air between them. Her teasing jade eyes met his. "You work quick."

He took another bite, chewed, and swallowed. "Seems to me, Miss Callahan, that *you* were the one who invited *me* in last night."

She smiled, her cheeks tinting a beautiful shade of pink. "Yes, I guess you're right." Her teeth bit down on her bottom lip and she dropped her eyes. "Thank you, Rich."

"You're welcome. But what are you thanking me for exactly?"

Her eyes started to fill with tears, and she rubbed at them. "You really helped me last night. I have ... nightmares."

"I figured. You know they're just nightmares, right?"

"I know, but they're so real and..." She sniffed.

"You have them every night?" he asked quietly, taking her hand in his.

She nodded.

"I'm sorry. I wish ... I'm just glad I could be here for you." An invitation to sleep with her every night would have been nice, but Rich wasn't going to suggest that. He knew better. He'd made progress, closed the Grand Canyon sized gap between them, and there was no way he would jeopardize that.

"Well, I guess I'd better get in the shower."

"Kate, you do have a protective order, right? For Shea?"

"Do I look like an idiot, Rich? Of course I do." Another soft scratching sound signaled Kate's retreat from the table. "Please make yourself at home. I'll be out in just a bit." At the kitchen doorway, she turned and flashed him a quick smile before disappearing into the other room.

✕✕✕

Getting ready for work couldn't happen quickly enough. Kate had found herself alone in her house with Rich, the one man she vowed would never set foot here. As if that wasn't bad enough, he had actually been in her bed—with her. Kate shook her head. How could she have been so stupid?

The way she felt about Rich was frightening enough. Giving in to those feelings terrified her. She took one more look in the mirror, smoothed her hair, pursed her lips, and took a deep breath. There was no doubt that Rich was still in the house.

The door opened and she could hear the television. In one more step, Kate would be able to see the couch—and Rich. She paused and worked up the courage to take that final step. Except she didn't have to. Something bumped into her. Hard.

Air rushed from her lungs as her back met the wall. "Rich," she gasped as his arms wrapped around her, steadying her on her feet. She was breathing heavy, but not from the near death experience. It was being in such close proximity that had her gasping for oxygen.

He chuckled softly. "Sorry, Kate. I was just coming to check on you." She forced her hands into fists, making them behave. What they really wanted to do was pull him close, clasp his face and kiss him, the way he deserved to be kissed. "If you don't leave soon, you're going to be late," he told her.

She forced herself to blink, to focus, and not on the beautiful man who was currently pressed against her body. "I'm uh, you can take a shower if you'd like." Her comment had nothing to do with what he'd said, but it was the first thing that popped into her head. Except it was a dangerous thought. Rich in her shower, water and soap running over every...

"It's okay." He kissed her forehead. "My stuff is at Nate and Roxy's, I'll just head over there to clean up. You ready to leave?" His eyes were full of questions, probably all of them relating to her strange behavior in the last few minutes. She'd shot right from acceptably normal actions to the realm of bizarre and incoherent.

"Yeah, I just need to grab my stuff. You don't have to wait."

"It's okay," he said with a smile. "I'd be happy to walk you to your car." She also heard the rest of his statement even though he hadn't said a word of it. Rich would be happy to do anything for her. *Anything.* He'd once offered all kinds of household chores, and she had no doubt that he would hang the moon for her if she asked him to.

There was no argument. Kate only stepped past him and gathered her things from the entry way. "Are you ready? You have everything?"

He nodded. "I have everything I need...except one thing."

"Rich don't." *Please don't.* Fighting off his advances was proving to be more difficult than she could have ever imagined. She thought for sure that when he saw she was pregnant, he would have run for the hills, never to even glance over his shoulder. Boy, had she been wrong. He seemed even more determined to be a part of her life now that he knew there was a baby growing in her belly.

"Sorry," he grunted, moving his hand out to cover hers which was caressing her stomach. "How big is he now?" There was an awe in his voice that nearly brought Kate to tears.

"I would guess about a pound, maybe two. There's still a lot of growing he needs to do before he's ready to make his grand entrance."

"Wow, it really is a miracle," he breathed the words. Kate eased her hand out from under his, and Rich moved his hand in a loving caress over the rock hard belly. "Does he have a name yet?"

He did, but Kate wasn't ready to tell Rich—or anyone. His name was something that would be kept a secret until the day his little eyes greeted the world. Then, when the dust settled and after Kate saw who was still standing, she would name the baby. "I haven't decided."

"I can think of a good name." His eyes flashed mischievously.

"Yeah, I'll bet you can." Chances were, it was the same name she was thinking. But she didn't dare hope. "I have to get to work."

Rich took hold of Kate's bag and followed her out to the car. She opened the garage while he placed her stuff in the backseat. "Have a good day. If you need anything all you have to do is call me."

"Thanks." She loved—and hated—that he cared so much. The emotions running between them would only make it harder for both of them, when this baby came out looking just like Jesse. "You have a great day." She slid in behind the wheel, her belly nearly rubbed it.

He smiled, leaned down and kissed her cheek. "I love you, Kate." Then he closed the door and walked away.

"I love you, too," she said to the silence. In her rearview mirror, Rich offered a final wave before he pulled out of the driveway. Her hand moved unconsciously to her belly. "Baby, I love you more than anything in this world." She could hear the tears in her voice. "No matter who your daddy is, you need to know that you were conceived in love." Her eyes looked in the mirror and she squeezed them closed. "How pathetic! What kind of woman loves two men, and doesn't even know who her baby's father is?"

Her phone rang, and Kate jumped. She attached her Bluetooth and answered, "Hi Mom." The car moved out of the garage, and the door went down slowly.

"Kate, are you okay? You sound like you've been crying."

An overreaction from her mother was not what Kate needed right now. She was having enough trouble dealing with her own overactive emotions. "I'm fine. It's just been a couple hard days." Kate pulled out onto her street and began the commute to work, passing a red BMW parked against the curb.

"How's Rich?"

"Subtle, Mom. Real subtle."

"Well?" Anna was not going to let this go.

"He's fine. Persistent, but fine."

"Persistent?" Kate could hear the smile in her mother's question. "That's good. I liked him."

"You don't know him."

"I met him," Anna disagreed. "He seemed very nice. And he's quite handsome."

"He is very nice." A little too nice for his own good. That was how Shea had been able to hurt him so badly, and how Kate was going to ultimately break his heart.

"How is our baby? Is he still moving like crazy? How are your nightmares?"

Kate laughed. "One question at a time, Mom. The baby is fine. Yes, he moves a lot, especially at night. And I don't think the nightmares will ease up as long as Shea is still out there. She scares me, but more for what she might try with Rich than for myself."

"You worry about Rich?"

"Of course, I... Don't, Mom. I know what you're trying to do and it's not going to work."

Anna giggled softly. "Okay, fair enough. Well, I'll let you go. I just wanted to check in on you. Call if you need anything."

"Would you believe that's not the first time I've heard that this morning?" Kate muttered under her breath.

"Really?" There was a hopeful tone in Anna's response. "Just make your decisions carefully, Katie. Even with Jesse gone, you and his child deserve to be happy and loved." She paused, and Kate could imagine her twisting a lock of hair around her finger. "We just want you to be happy."

That was key, wasn't it? Happiness. There was nothing Kate wanted more, but right now, it seemed to be something just out of her grasp. Was it something she would ever truly experience again?

✕✕✕

Shea pulled off the dark wig and fluffed her matted

blonde locks. Fury fueled the fire in her gut. Hatred boiled through her veins. It was bad enough to know Rich was playing detective, staking out what she'd believed was Kate's house, but to actually see them together, to see him walk out of her house first thing in the morning, put her in her car, and kiss her goodbye. That wasn't the worst of it though, Kate was pregnant!

Her stomach rolled.

She shook her head, unsure of how much more pain she could take. Revenge was the only thing that kept her going. She'd managed to stay hidden, but wasn't sure how much longer she'd remain lucky. *Vengeance is mine!* She would form a plan and execute it—and Kate—sooner rather than later.

Twenty Eight

The day had been excruciatingly long, probably due to the silence of the man who was still ignoring her. Nate finally cleared his throat, and Kate actually jumped at the unexpected sound. She turned to look at him, but he wasn't looking at her. He stared pointedly out the windshield. "Hey Kate, can I ask you something?"

Butterflies invaded her stomach, and she knew she wasn't going to like his question—or her answer. "Yeah," she mumbled, unable to tell him no for some absurd reason.

"I would just really like to know what the hell you're thinking." He ground the words out through his teeth, the muscles in his jaw worked overtime.

"Excuse me?" She fought the urge to slap him so that maybe he'd turn to look at her.

"You are doing everything you possibly can to push Rich out of your life." He threw his hands up as though it were the only way to punctuate his exasperation. "Why?"

"That's none of your business," she snapped, her anger—and guilt—spiked.

"Maybe. But it sure as hell is Rich's." He turned to look pointedly at her stomach.

She ignored the insinuation with the hope that she'd read it wrong. "Maybe. Maybe not."

"What are you going to do when your son is born and looks just like his daddy? Huh? What then? What are you gonna do when you have successfully pushed him out of your life."

She gasped, mortified. "He *told* everybody?"

Nate glanced at her, his face a combination of frustrated irritability. "No Kate, he didn't tell *everybody*. It slipped out yesterday when you decided to waltz back into his life with a baby growing in your gut. A baby you didn't bother to tell him about. Do you know how much that hurt him?"

Kate's eyes burned as she again thought of the look on Rich's face when he saw her for the first time. There was a pain registered in those crystal eyes that she never wanted to see again, but seemed too inevitable. Every time she spoke with Rich she seemed to hurt him all over again. She bit on her lip and focused on that physical pain instead of the emotional kind that was overwhelming.

"He believes that baby is his," Nate added an explanation.

"It's not," she whispered, running her hand over her belly.

"Maybe." He used the word like he didn't believe her. "Here's the deal, Kate. I like you—a lot—but I love Rich. He is the brother I never had. His happiness is second only to Roxy's." He yanked a tissue out of the box in the console and handed it to Kate. She took it and rubbed at her nose. "Just give it some thought, Kate. He loves you, and is more than capable of loving your son."

"You must hate me for the way..." She broke off when her voice cracked.

"No Kate, I don't hate you. Nobody does." He chuckled. "Well, maybe Clayton, but he's not got the best judgment." Nate flashed her a smile, exposing deep dimples. "My advice, take it or leave it, don't push him away until you're absolutely sure you don't want him in your life. Ever."

"I can't—"

"You can't what? Honestly Kate, do you have such little faith in the man you love?" He watched her closely for her reaction, and whatever flashed in her eyes, on her face, made him smile. "It's obvious you love him. You can't hide it, Kate. Stop trying."

She opened her mouth, prepared to tell him where he could go and exactly how he could get there, but closed it again. How could she possibly dispute anything he'd said? She couldn't. She knew Rich loved her. She loved him. And despite her arguments to the contrary, she knew there was a very real possibility that the baby was Rich's. She had her reasons for wanting the baby to be Jesse's. All of them were completely selfish.

"Be gentle with his heart, Kate. He's done the cold-hearted bitch, who doesn't-give-a-shit thing. He deserves a good dose of love." Nate let out a dramatic breath and tightened his grip on the steering wheel. "Okay, I've said my peace. This girly-feeling shit is more than I can handle."

Kate laughed. A boisterous sound bellowed from next to her. "It's good to hear you laugh, Kate."

× × ×

It'd been a long, hard week of sleeping in Kate's driveway, and Rich was exhausted. That first night had been wonderful, sleeping on her couch, but he'd tried to be a little more subtle with his guard duty. He waited until just after midnight before pulling into the place he would try to get some shut-eye. All the lights were off, except for the porch light, which flashed as soon as he extinguished the headlights. He tried to swallow the knot that had suddenly leapt into his throat and reached to restart the engine.

He would have raced off into the night, if not for Kate, who was already out the door and crossing the lawn. Her robe flapped at the ends as she hurried toward him. Her lips were pulled up in a smile, and her head was moving back and forth. With his foot on the brake, Rich rolled down the window.

She laughed, continuing to shake her head. "I've been expecting you."

"You have?" Of course she had. He'd told her flat out that he'd be here every night to make sure she was safe.

Her tiny hand reached through the window and came to rest on his arm. "Please come inside, Rich. You need a good night's sleep...and so do I. I'll never be able to sleep knowing you're out here." She stepped back, opened the door, and took his hand. "Come on."

He rolled up the window and again turned off the car. Through his complete confusion, he followed her inside. The blankets were already laid out on the couch, waiting for him. Not only had she been expecting him, she'd prepared for him. He stomped down his excitement. Kate was known for just being nice, and his heart couldn't expect any more than that. If he allowed it to, they would both end up broken.

"So, um, I'll see you in the morning," she said, suddenly eager to get out of the same room. "Good night, Rich. Make yourself at home."

"I love you, Kate."

She smiled, her eyes closed for a long moment then she looked at him, a gaze he felt in his soul. "You too, Rich."

He waited until her back was turned, and she had made her way to her room, before stabbing his fist into the air.

"Yes!" he said quietly. It was only a fraction of what he wanted to do. He wanted to jump up and down, do a full-fledged song and dance, and shout from the rooftops. With a great amount of self control, Rich slipped out of his shoes and socks, pulled his shirt over his head and took off his jeans.

His mind was still whirring, spinning with the events of the last few minutes. Kate had said she loved him. Well, almost. Rich would take what he could get. He used the remote to flip the television on and then settled against the pillows, his arms resting behind his head.

It hadn't been very long since Kate had left to go to bed, but she was screaming with a frightened intensity. Being awake didn't ease Rich's panic as he raced to Kate's side. Just like last night, she sat up, breath rushed in and out of her lungs, and sweat coated her skin like she'd just run the Boston Marathon.

"Kate, honey?" She turned toward him, the light from the hall exposing her distress. Her frightened eyes blinked back her tears. "Are you okay?"

"I'm sorry." Her voice broke, her legs scissored under the sheets. "I didn't mean to wake...."

"Slide over," he offered, and she accepted without any verbal acknowledgement. She slid to the middle of the bed and waited for him to pull her into his arms. Her entire body relaxed against him, and he wrapped his arms around her. Her back was pressed snugly to his front, his hands rested on the mound that moved under his touch. Then moved again. "Is that...?" he said in awe.

"Yeah." Her hand slid up to hold Rich's tight against her stomach where the fluttering continued. "He moves a lot at night, especially when I wake up from my nightmare."

"You have it every night?"

"Yeah." She snuggled her head deeper into the pillow. "I'm glad you're here, Rich. I know you'll scare the boogeyman away."

He smiled against her hair, pressing a kiss to the back of her neck. She had once used the boogeyman as a way to discredit his worry. And now here they were all these months later with Kate in his arms, and she was glad that he was exactly where he was.

She relaxed even further, all of her weight seeming to sink into Rich, which he gladly absorbed. Her breathing steadied and Rich again was torn between what his head said he should do and what his heart desperately wanted to do. He lay there in the silence, listening to her shallow breaths and the strong, steady beats of her heart.

Ultimately Rich knew he would leave her in the bed, and finally he had to fight the urge to go to sleep and eased his arms from around her. A soft groan, followed by a louder moan escaped her lips, and she rolled toward him, hitching her leg over his hip. "Don't leave."

"Kate?" He waited until her eyes fluttered open. "Are you sure?"

She nodded, her head moving against his chest. "Yes." He relaxed against the sheets and pulled her into his arms again. She stayed facing him and rested her forehead against his chin. "Thank you, Rich. I really needed you tonight."

Her muscles tensed and his responded, becoming taut as bow strings. "Do you want to talk about it?"

"It was you," she whispered.

"Me?" He was confused.

"In my nightmares, I relive the night Jesse was killed, but tonight..." She tugged him even closer. "Tonight it was you."

"I'm not going anywhere, Kate. I won't leave you." He kissed her head. "So please stop trying to push me away." She didn't respond, not that he expected her to.

× × ×

A beeping brought Rich into the realm of consciousness. As he lay there and listened to the obnoxious sound, he cursed the fool who seemed oblivious to the damn thing. It wasn't until he shifted against the soft sheets that his body sent the message to his brain as to where he was and with whom... *Kate!*

He sat up with a jerk, his head pivoted wildly on his neck, searching for her. Holding his breath, Rich listened to any telling sounds in the room—the house. Silence called from the bathroom. And the rest of the house didn't offer any clues as to where Kate had escaped.

Rich blew out a sigh just as the silence was disturbed by a crash. He jumped to his feet and rushed in the direction of the noise. He raced down the hall, through the living room, and hurdled the couch to arrive in the doorway of the kitchen.

Kate stood barefoot, in her red satin bathrobe, amongst the shards of a broken plate. Her focus was on the floor as she began to tiptoe through the mess.

"Don't move," Rich ordered. Her big green eyes shot up to him, and she offered a half-hearted smile. "Don't you dare move. I'll be right back."

She nodded. "Okay. I'll stay right here." Her hands popped up on her hips as if she was annoyed by his request, but she stayed in place.

His feet moved almost as quickly as his heart as he

ran into the living room. He stuffed his legs into his jeans and his bare feet into his tennis shoes, then ran back to save Kate. He couldn't move fast enough because Rich knew she was just stubborn enough to try and walk through glass to rescue herself.

Thankfully, when Rich raced back into the kitchen, Kate was standing in nearly the same position she'd been in when he left, except that her hands had moved from her hips to rest lovingly on her belly. "I'm sorry about this." She motioned to the mess at her feet.

"There's no need to be sorry." Glass crunched under the soles of his shoes as he approached her. He wrapped his arms around her waist and pulled her against him. With an arm under her knees, he scooped her up, cradling her against his body. She gasped softly and rested her head against his shoulder.

It was in that moment that Rich fully took in what Kate had done here in the kitchen. Strong scents of freshly brewed coffee, citrus, and bacon swirled around him. His eyes scanned the room verifying what his nose had told him. Kate was cooking breakfast—for him.

There were two sets of silverware, two glasses of fresh-squeezed orange juice, but only one coffee cup. At the head of the table. She'd placed him at the head of her table. That knowledge made his heart skip a beat.

He carefully placed her in the seat where just the orange juice sat. "Where's the broom?"

Just as he expected, her head moved back and forth, beginning her protests. "You don't have to..."

"Kate, let me do this." He held up his hand to halt her arguments then lifted his foot. "I already have my shoes on. Now, where's the broom?"

Irritation flashed in her eyes, but she motioned toward the refrigerator with her head. "Right there."

Rich walked over and pulled the broom from the small space between the fridge and the wall. He snapped the dustpan off, and swept the glass into a pile. Kate grinned and with a defiant glint in her eye she stood and walked over to the cupboard. Rich shook his head, but said nothing as he brushed the pile into the dustpan and deposited the remnants into the trash.

Kate stretched up on her toes and reached for another plate. She wobbled, caught herself, only to stretch up and fall back, nearly toppling herself to the floor.

Rich rushed over and, with hands on her shoulders, steadied her. "How 'bout you let me get those." It wasn't a question. He eased her out of the way then, without the effort of reaching, pulled down two plates. "Where do you want 'em?"

She held out her hands, and Rich walked over to where she stood near the skillet on the stove. "How many eggs do you want?"

"Just a couple would be great." He smiled as Kate went about cracking two eggs into the skillet. She looked up at him in question. "Over easy, please." Rich leaned against the counter.

Kate bit on her lip and concentrated on the eggs sizzling in the pan. The spatula moved in the pan. "So, um … these are ready." She picked up a plate and placed the eggs on it, then opened the microwave to reveal a plate of cooked bacon. "Would you like some?"

"Sure, thanks." He followed her to the table, but just stood near his chair when she turned and walked back over to the counter. She plucked the coffee pot from its brewing perch, and then she returned and sat down in the chair to his right. "Wow, everything smells great. Looks great, too." He bent and sucked in an exaggerated breath, while plunging his fork into the eggs.

Kate lifted the coffee pot and poured some into his cup. She added the perfect amount of sugar then slid the cup back over in front of Rich. She was quiet, reflective. And Rich ate in the uncomfortable silence, the clatter of his fork brushing against ceramic was the only sound around them.

After what felt like an eternity, Kate cleared her throat and brought her eyes from the familiar sights of her kitchen to focus on him. "So, do you really think that you can spend every night in my driveway?" She didn't wait for him to verify her question. "I've been thinking about our situation."

"Our situation?" Anxiety slammed through his

bloodstream. "I didn't know we had a *situation.*"

A nervous laugh burst from her and she brought her hand from her lap and laid it on the table, palm down. "Rich, you and I have a very complicated situation. Don't try to deny that fact."

"We're back to facts now?" he said with a smile and what he hoped sounded like an amused laugh.

Her head tipped to the side and she shot him a glare. "Yes, we're back to facts. You insist on sleeping in my driveway to protect me, right?" He nodded, and she continued, "You're worthless out there in your car. I could have driven right past you, and you wouldn't have even batted an eyelash."

His wounded male ego flared. "I would have..."

Her laughter cut him off. "You wouldn't have done anything." She smiled. "It's okay. I've just been thinking that we need to come up with a better plan." Rich felt his brows pull together. Kate's hand slid across the table. When it neared his hand, she lifted it to reveal what she'd been hiding. A key.

Rich wasn't sure what to think. It was a key, there was no disputing that. But did he dare even entertain the possibility of the lock it would open?

"If you're going to insist on sleeping on the premises, the least I can do is offer you a nice, warm bed." Rich wasn't sure what the look on his face was, but it must have registered the surprise of her offer because Kate started to laugh, and added, "The guest room, Rich."

He tried to hide his disappointment, but he was pretty sure it was written on every cell in his body. "The guest room, of course." He added a nod to emphasize his understanding of her offer. "Are you sure about this?"

Her lips tipped upward and her green eyes sparkled. "Yes, Rich, I'm absolutely sure of this. Having you in my home the last few nights has been such a comfort. I can't even tell you how much better I've been able to sleep."

Not only had Rich spent the last few nights in her home, last night he had spent it in her bed, with her encased in his arms. That was the difference, and his smug side couldn't deny the elation brought on by her statement. She recognized that having him here was a good thing.

A very good thing, Rich thought.

"I was also thinking that since we're both off today we can move your stuff in." She paused and cocked her head to the side. "Where's your stuff?"

Ah, his stuff. "The only stuff I have is at Nate's."

"Do you have any furniture?"

He shook his head. "No, only clothes. All the furniture is still in that damned house I can't sell. It has too many memories, bad ones. I haven't been able to go back since all this went down. Most of it wasn't something I liked anyway and I don't want any of it now."

"Fair enough. I don't want any of that bitch's stuff in my house." She sat back in her chair and rested her hands on her belly. "Well, I think we should go shopping then, get you a bed and a dresser. Maybe we'll get you a television too."

Her mention of a TV brought to mind the awesome flat-screen that was still mounted on the wall in his old house. "I have a TV, and it does not belong to the bitch. We'll swing by and pick it up."

"Deal," she said with a laugh. Her fingers picked up the key and held it out to him. "Take this, Rich, attach it to your keychain and use it. I want you to feel at home here."

Home. Kate. The terms were interchangeable.

"Thanks, Kate. I already feel very much at home." And he did. He was in Kate's home, Kate's life, and hopefully, Kate's heart.

Her beautiful green eyes sparkled as her full, pink lips pulled into a smile. "I'm glad." She turned her back to him for only a moment before whirling back around. "Thank you, Rich. I'm glad you're here." Her teeth nibbled on her lip. "Well, um, I'm gonna go take a shower so we can get going. Finish your breakfast." She stepped toward him, only to pause, turn and flee.

Rich scooped a fork full of eggs into his mouth, barely registering the taste of it because his mind raced with the events of the last few minutes. He picked up the key and tumbled it in his fingers. This little gold piece of metal, as small and insignificant as it seemed, was life altering. It meant that he would now call Kate's house, home. He slid it into his pocket and hurried to devour the rest of the breakfast that had been made by Kate's loving hands.

× × ×

Kate fluffed her hair and swiped some Chapstick over her lips. She'd stalled for long enough. The skeptical part of her still couldn't believe she'd actually followed through and given Rich a key, an open invitation to live in the room across the hall. There had been elation shining in his baby blues, and it made Kate second guess her choice.

Rich didn't deserve to be led on. He deserved so much more than she could give him, but.... But. Kate loved him. She wanted him in her life. She wanted him to love the little boy who would need a father no matter who he looked like. Nate was right, not that she would ever tell him so.

A soft rapping brought Kate out of her thoughts. "Kate, honey, you ready?" Rich's deep voice asked as the door opened.

She stepped out of the bathroom and smoothed the shirt over her belly. Self-conscious was an emotion she felt a lot these days. She loved the baby growing inside her, but hated, absolutely loathed, her ever changing body.

Rich, who had showered and changed clothes, must have sensed her apprehensions because he said, "You're beautiful, Kate. Pregnancy suits you." He crossed the room in four large strides and took her face in his hands. "I can't wait until next time when I can watch your body grow from the very beginning." Then he kissed her.

Kate's body reacted to his touch, her lips firming against his mouth. She wanted to enjoy the moment, but his words had rubbed her wrong. "Next time?" she asked against his lips. "Are you really that confident that there will be a next time?"

His hands still held her face. He rested his forehead against hers. "Aren't you?"

"I don't know what I am right now. I can't promise anything more than I already have, least of all a future with you—or anyone. My priorities are kinda limited to the little person who will soon consume my whole life." She sighed, feeling an overwhelming sadness she didn't want to acknowledge. "I'm sorry, Rich." She blinked hard against the tears. "I'm really sorry."

Rich kissed her, hard, and Kate could feel his every emotion conveyed by that simple intimate contact. "I will take whatever you're willing to give me. I'd love your whole heart but realize you're not ready to give me that much. It's okay." Her hands moved up from her sides and rested on his hips. "I love you, Kate." He kissed the tip of her nose. "Forever."

Forever, she thought with an inward sigh. She wanted to believe that was something she could have with Rich. But this baby was a huge factor in that equation, the big X desperately needing to be solved. She would follow Nate's advice, and try—really try—not to let her heart get too involved. The baby could be Rich's, and until she knew differently, she wouldn't push him completely out of her life. When the baby was verified to be Jesse's, she vowed she wouldn't hate Rich for walking away.

The thought made her heart clench in her chest, and tears sprang up behind her closed lids. She felt Rich's thumbs move gently over her cheeks, his lips brushed over the damp skin. "Don't cry, love."

"I hate hormones," she tried to explain them away.

He chuckled softly, then kissed her lips again. This time it was soft, loving. "I'm not going anywhere."

"Not yet," she whispered, looking into his deep, intense eyes.

"Not ever."

✕ ✕ ✕

Kate stepped away from him, and Rich let her. He loved her too much to push her, and was too afraid that she would put even more distance between them. His point had been made clear. He couldn't afford to be coy, to pretend she didn't affect him the way she did. That would make him an even bigger fool than he already was.

He followed her out the door, used his new key to lock the front door, smiling like an idiot. Kate had actually given him a key. A key to her house, *their* house. He'd not mentioned the possibility of them becoming roommates. She'd conceived the idea all on her own.

"Are you coming?" Kate grumbled, standing next to the truck.

"Yeah," he answered, still smiling. He popped the locks and Kate climbed inside. Rich hurried to the vehicle, got in and started the engine. "Where to?"

"Let's check out RC Willey then if we don't find something we like, we can try Granite's. Sound good?"

Of course it sounded good. Rich could have spent the day dumpster diving, and it would have sounded good. He was with Kate—and they weren't on the clock. Today was personal. This date with destiny was personal. Completely personal.

Rich reached for Kate's hand as they entered the store. The beds were toward the back, and they walked through the maze of furniture to their destination. A blond-haired woman, who could have easily been either of their mothers, approached. "I'm Mona. Can I help you find something?"

"We're looking for a bed," Kate told her.

"Right this way," she said as she led them in the direction they were already going. "We've got some really nice pieces. Are you looking for a king or a queen?"

"Queen," Rich answered.

At the same time Kate said, "King." Rich raised a brow at her and she shrugged. "I was just thinking that the more space..."

"King it is," he told Mona. "Whatever she wants, she gets." He smiled and Mona sighed.

Mona's eyes were caring when she turned her gaze to Kate. "I remember what it's like those last few months. It's so hard to get comfortable, and a new bed might just do the trick."

"Oh, it's not..."

"Yeah, that's exactly what we were thinking," Rich interrupted. He squeezed Kate's hand and guided her in the direction of the first row of bedroom furniture.

Kate let go of his hand and began to peruse the various beds. "Too big," she muttered, passing by one that looked like it had tree trunks for legs. "Too tall" was the one that she would easily need a step stool to get in to. "Does this come in natural wood?" Kate asked of one that looked like a little girl would be right at home in it.

"No, I'm sorry. This particular one is from our Juvenile line."

Rich cocked a brow and Kate laughed. "Okay, I'll keep looking." She walked a little further and stopped in front of a set that was masculine, but not enormous. Natural wood, as she'd asked before, with a large slated headboard and smaller uniformed footboard. The dresser had a similar design. "Do you like the one with the mirror or the taller one with no mirror?" She bit on her lower lip, her eyes moved from one to the other, as she debated the question she'd just asked.

Rich smiled, not missing just how adorable she looked with her hands draped across her midsection. "It doesn't matter, love, whatever you think."

She thought for another minute then turned to Mona. "We'll take the taller one."

"And you want the bed in a king?" Mona asked.

"Yes, and we'll want it delivered." Kate smiled as Mona nodded. And when she was gone, Kate looked at Rich. "Are you okay with it? I was thinking it could be good when this little boy is ready for a big boy bed."

"Where will I sleep then?" he teased, thinking it was just a bit enormous for a 'big boy bed', and she blushed as she sputtered an incoherent answer. "It's okay, love, I'm sure before he's ready for a big boy bed, I'll have found another bed to sleep in." He just hoped that it would be the one Kate currently slept in. "Should we go pick out a mattress?"

"Oh, yeah," Kate whirled on her heel and headed off in the direction of the mattresses that were just a little further down the aisle. She sat down on one, bounced a little, bounced a little harder, then giggled and blushed as her eyes lifted toward his.

It wasn't hard to imagine what she'd been thinking, and Rich was thrilled at the prospect of using the new mattress for just that event. To make love to Kate again would be...

"Find one you like?" asked a voice from behind Rich. Kate's eyes shot up and Rich turned to see Mona standing there with a clipboard. She smiled. "Sorry, I didn't mean to startle you." She paused, and when nobody said anything, she asked the question again, "Do you like this one?"

"Oh, um, I don't know." She scooched up to the top and laid her head down on the pillow. "Rich, why don't you see what you think."

He quickly complied, lying down next to her. She smiled as he rolled to face her. "I like it," he said, "but are you comfortable in it."

She scowled, her voice barely a whisper to keep Mona from hearing her. "I won't be..."

"Please Kate, you don't know that you'll never end up sleeping in this bed. I just want to make sure you're completely comfortable in it."

She closed her eyes but didn't argue anymore. Her lips pulled into a tight line. A deep breath was sucked in through her nose, causing it to flare a little. She held the air in her lungs for a long second before she blew it out. The air was warm against his cheek and he felt his eyes close, wanting to burn the memory into his thoughts. Rich was caught completely off guard as Kate rolled over, into his arms. He wrapped his arms around her, out of instinct more than anything.

She sighed. "Yes, this mattress will work very nicely. We'll take it."

Mona scribbled a few things on her clipboard, then offered it to Rich. He stood and took it. He quickly read over the paperwork and signed it. "So delivery will be..."

"Excuse me," Kate interrupted.

Rich turned to see Kate wrestling to get out of the clutches of the enormous bed. She was rolling from one side to the other, using her hands to gain leverage against the beast eating her. He laughed. She glared. He held out a hand. "Let me help you, love."

"I really wish I didn't *need* your help, Mr. Sensitivity." She blew a stray lock of hair out of her face.

"Sorry." He bit back another laugh, then, with Kate safely steady on her feet, he reached into his back pocket and took out his wallet handing Mona a card.

"Wait. No, Rich," Kate protested, tugging at her purse.

Rich nodded to Mona, who took the card and walked away. "I want to do this," he told Kate.

"But it's going in my house and someday..."

"Someday," he sighed, and pulled her into his arms. "Don't worry about someday. Just think about right now."

She relaxed against him, resting her cheek on his chest. "I wish I could."

"You can, Kate." His muscles tensed against her. "Damn, I wish you'd believe that." Her belly was hard against his abdomen and he loved the thought of his child growing inside Kate's womb.

"You're all set."

Kate jumped and stepped away from Rich. He was flooded with an unavoidable sense of loss which was extinguished as soon as Kate took his hand. He lifted their hands and kissed hers.

Mona handed him the paperwork, completely oblivious to the tender moment she'd just interrupted. Rich signed it, wrote down the address, and took his copies after Mona tore them off. "Delivery tomorrow, between noon and 4:00."

"Great. Thanks, Mona."

She offered a nod then left them alone. Kate squeezed his hand and Rich looked down at her. She smiled. "You're sure you like the bed? I want you to feel at home."

"Stop." He hushed her by pressing his finger to her

lips. "It's fine, all of it is fine." He replaced his finger with his lips. "I was happy with the couch." A smile plucked at his lips and she cocked her head. "But what I really enjoy is waking up in your bed."

Her beautiful brow arched while her eyes twinkled. "Yeah, I'll bet you did."

Rich was still smiling as she tried to pretend she didn't enjoy sleeping in his arms. She'd told him she did, had actually asked him to stay. This new bed was nothing more than window dressing for the guest room. If it made Kate feel better to think he had his own bed, so be it.

× × ×

The drive to Rich's—and Shea's—house was really long despite only being a few miles. Kate's mind raced with the skeletons that might still reside inside. Shea's ghost haunted Kate every day. Not so much the murderer, but the woman who had captured—and broken—Rich's heart. It was one thing to hate the psychotic, murdering bitch who had devastated Kate's world, and quite another to be jealous of her for being loved by Rich. For sharing his home. Taking his name.

Mature trees lined the quiet street. He pulled the car into the driveway of a red brick, split level. The yard was meticulously manicured, the only thing that appeared out of place was the 'for sale' sign planted in the middle of the front lawn.

"Wow, who takes care of the yard."

"I do," he said with a shrug. "It's something I like to do. You want to come in?" he asked as if either answer wouldn't come as a surprise to him.

Her brain screamed no, but her mouth opened and said, "Yes." The out of body experience continued as her hand reached for the door handle, jerking it open. She stepped out of the safety of the vehicle and was struck with an overwhelming wave of nausea.

Rich stepped up behind her. "You don't have to..."

"It's okay. I'd like to see your house." Only part of that statement was true. She was actually far more scared than curious.

Rich took her arm and guided her up the steps. He slid the key into the lock and opened the door, holding it for her to enter. She muttered a thank you and stepped in onto the tile of the entry. She wanted to run, screaming back to the car and lock the doors, but found her feet carrying her up the stairs to the living room.

It wasn't like anything she would have expected in the home of laid-back, easy going Rich Spencer. This room was filled with fancy furniture and frou-frou accessories. The statues and vases looked expensive and above the fireplace was a hand-painted portrait that nearly caused Kate's heart to stop; Shea was sitting in a chair with Rich kneeling next to her. Bile rose up in the back of her throat. She hated that he actually looked happy, and breathtakingly handsome.

Large hands came to rest on her hips then moved around her waist, easing her against his body. "I have always hated that painting."

"I don't like it either." She leaned into his warm body and enjoyed the sound of his heartbeat. His hands rested on her stomach, easing her tension with slow, loving circles. There was magic in his touch. Always had been.

Despite being so close to Rich, Kate couldn't shake the nervous feeling eating at her. The hair on the back of her neck stood on end, and Kate tried to shake the feeling that she was being watched. She hated the constant sense of paranoia that plagued her. Shea was a danger that seemed to stalk Kate at every turn. Kate hated her—wanted her caught and rotting behind bars where she couldn't hurt anyone anymore.

Rich cleared his throat and spoke low in her ear. "I just want to grab a couple of things." As soon as he broke contact, a shudder wiggled its way up her spine and she hurried to follow him.

The den was much more Rich; a large leather couch against one wall, a flat screen television on the other. He rummaged through a dresser drawer and pulled out a picture, setting it on the small table next to the couch. A snapshot; one the subject didn't realize was being taken.

It was of her; smiling, happy. She couldn't be sure when, or by whom, it was taken except that it was before her world had been turned upside down.

Rich made quick work of disassembling the expensive plasma TV and lifted it from the wall. "This is the only thing I want from my old life." Kate followed him out of the room and down the hallway. "My life began the day you admitted you loved me." It was said as matter-of-factly as 'the sun is shining today', but the statement brought tears to her eyes. She blinked quickly hoping to keep them where they were.

Rich muscled the awkward high-tech rectangle down the stairs and out the front door. Kate opened the car door then hurried around to the other side to help guide it into the backseat.

"I'm just going to lock up. I'll be right back."

Kate nodded and closed the rear passenger door before she climbed into the front to wait for Rich to return.

It took only a few seconds for Rich to come out of the house. His face was pale, as if he'd seen a ghost, and he was running toward her. He whipped the door open, his eyes frantic as he did a visual inventory of her well-being. "Are you okay?" The tone of his voice had her worried and the hair on the back of her neck stood on end again. As the phone landed in her lap, he ordered, "Call Reggie."

"Rich, what's wrong? What's going on?"

His hands shook as he jammed the keys into the ignition and turned the engine over, then slammed the car into reverse. Tires squealed and the transmission moaned as he shifted into drive, then the smell of burning rubber assaulted her nostrils as he drove away.

"Rich!" Kate screamed as she frantically punched in the number to the police station. "What the hell happened in there?"

He grabbed his cell phone from her hands. "Reggie Brown," he said into the phone. "Rich Spencer. It's about Shea."

Kate turned in her seat to look back at the house they'd just left. There was no sign of anybody there, but something—someone—had Rich freaked. And because of his reaction, Kate felt her nerves jolt to life. Her stomach rolled and the baby living within kicked in protest of her anxiety.

Rich rattled off the address into the phone then relayed what had him so spooked. "I came back down the hall and the portrait above the fireplace had a huge slash across my face." He shook his head in response to whatever Reggie had asked. "No, we looked at it only a few minutes before and paintings don't just shred themselves. She's close, Reggie. Shit, do you realize...?" He blew out a breath and nodded as Reggie spoke to him. He took Kate by the hand. "I won't let anything happen to her. Yeah, we'll be there in a few."

Kate felt numb, like she'd spent hours on the frozen tundra without the comfort of clothes. She was cold to the bone. Shea had been in the same house, nearly the same room as Rich—as her and her baby. Shit was right. This whole situation was bad. But not just for her. Rich was in danger too. If Shea had slashed the painting, she had something sharp in her hand, something that could have just as easily killed him.

Shivers raced up and down her spine and her lungs gulped for air. Tears stung her eyes as she wrapped both hands around his hand. She cursed the console that separated her from Rich. Right now the only thing she wanted was to have him in her arms, to be in his, holding on to him, making sure that nothing would ever take him from her.

Rich's body was tense, his back so straight it looked like his spine had been replaced by a steel rod. His hand was tight on hers as though he were truly holding on for dear life. His eyes were focused with worried intensity out the windshield.

Kate closed her eyes and concentrated on the beating of her own heart, the air coming in and leaving her lungs, and the life line that had her tethered to the man she loved.

He squeezed her hand. "I won't let anything happen to you—or our son."

Kate let the reference to her son slide. This wasn't

the time to debate that again. There was more at stake than the paternity of her little boy. The situation had literally escalated to life and death. "I know," she breathed. "Rich, she could have..."

"Don't think about that," he cut her off. And by the intensity of his voice, of his body, it was obvious that he wasn't going to follow his own advice.

She'd made fun of him for sleeping in her driveway to protect her. Mocked him. But here they were. Kate could no longer live her life as though Shea wasn't a threat. A piece of paper wouldn't stop her if she was determined to cause more heartache.

"We have to go give a statement to Reggie. It shouldn't take very long then we'll get you home where you'll be safe."

Safe, Kate thought with a shudder, wondering if she'd ever feel safe again.

Twenty Nine

Rich pulled into the parking lot of the police department, and Reggie was standing on the front steps flanked by a couple more officers. He turned to Kate and flashed what he hoped was a reassuring smile. "Wait here, I'll be right back."

She nodded and mumbled, "Okay." Her face was pale, her eyes dim as she offered a pathetic smile of her own. He opened the door, but the death grip on his arm didn't loosen as he tried to exit the car. Rich wondered if she even realized she was shaking.

He leaned across the seat and kissed her on the mouth. "Then I'm going to need my arm."

"Oh." She blinked, looked down at where she still held his arm then slowly, reluctantly, released him. "Sorry."

Reggie was all business as Rich approached the group of men. "Was the place wrecked when you left it?"

Rich's stomach fell to his toes. "No. Everything was fine. Well, except for the painting. Why? What'd your guys find?"

"If you wouldn't mind following me over." Reggie motioned for the other officers to move toward their vehicles.

The only thing on Rich's mind was Kate—and her son. "I don't want Kate to know any more than she already does."

Reggie's eyes drifted over Rich's shoulder. "Agreed."

Then a thought occurred to Rich and he narrowed his eyes at Reggie. "If you were just going to drag me back over there, then why'd you make me come all the way down here?"

"If Shea was..." Rich cocked a brow and Reggie amended, "*Because* Shea was in the area, I didn't want either of you anywhere near there. The good news is that she stuck around long enough to take her frustrations out on the house which means she didn't follow you. That is a good thing." Reggie ran his hand through his hair and looked at Kate again. "Forensics is going over the scene now in hopes of finding some tip that will lead to where she's been hiding. I'd just like you to look at things and see if something stands out."

"Okay, I need to drop Kate off somewhere safe then I'll meet you."

"Thirty minutes, Rich, that's all I can give you." His dark eyes bored into Rich's. "Can you be there in thirty?"

"I'll make it work," Rich said before turning toward his still running vehicle. Kate's eyes were wide, scared. He jogged to the driver's side and she unlocked the doors. "I'm going to take you to Nate's, then I've got to meet Reggie back at the house."

Tears filled her eyes and rolled down her cheeks. "I can't, Rich. I can't. You can't leave me right now. I need you. I need to know that you're okay." She sniffed and wiped at the tears with the back of her hand. "Please."

He went back around to her side and opened the door. Sobs burst from Kate's throat as she threw herself into his arms, burying her face in his chest. His hands cupped her head then moved slowly down the auburn strands, palming the arch of her back and holding her tighter.

"I won't ever leave you, Kate. Never. Do you understand that?" Her head moved against his chest.

"Okay, let's go." He helped her back into the vehicle and went to climb behind the wheel.

The ride back was quiet, and when he eased the car over to the curb in front of the place he used to call home, he cut the engine. He waited for Reggie to approach the car then opened the door. Reggie smiled at the officer standing next to him. "This is Officer Terry. He's going to stand here and keep an eye on Kate while you're with me. Is that okay, Kate?"

Rich was reluctant to leave Kate with Officer Terry, but Kate nodded and said, "Okay. It's okay, Rich. Really."

He leaned across the seat and cradled her head in his hand, whispering low in her ear, "I love you. I'll be right back."

She nodded. "I love you, too. Please hurry."

"I promise." Rich pressed a chaste kiss to her lips. His heart couldn't decide whether to fly with the knowledge of her declaration or to give in to the anxiety that was flooding his bloodstream.

Reggie stood on the front porch, his hands stuffed in his pockets. "You sure you're ready for this? It's kind of ... disturbing."

"Shea does disturbing really well," Rich muttered sarcastically under his breath, brushing past Reggie as he stepped aside.

Inside, everything was a mess. Shattered glass, broken lamps, shredded couch cushions, and that was only what could be seen from his vantage point in the entry. Yes, the order had been disrupted, big time, but the thing that caught his eye and caused his blood to curdle in his veins was the sight at the top of the stairs.

Kate's picture, the beautiful one from his room, the one he'd dropped when he saw the vandalized painting, was there being held to the wall with a butcher knife. The point going right through her smile.

"Rich!" Reggie yelled as another detective rushed to grab Rich before he was able to reach the top step.

"What the hell?" Rich growled. He went toe to toe with Reggie, careful not to touch the man in charge, but close enough to get his point across. "You. Find. Her!"

Reggie didn't flinch. "We will, Rich. I promise. I don't want anything to happen to Kate anymore than you do."

"Do you love her?" Rich asked. Reggie just stared at him. "Because I do, Reggie. More than anything in this world. You find that bitch or I swear that I will. And if I find her, you'll end up putting me in a fancy set of bracelets. I will stop at nothing to protect Kate. Nothing. Are we clear?"

"Rich, I know you're upset—"

"Upset doesn't even begin to describe what I am. That's Kate ... with a knife... That's a clear threat, as if we needed another sign that she hated Kate and would like to see her dead." Rich raked his hand through his hair then slammed a fist into the wall. The drywall gave under the force. "Dammit!"

"Look, we'll post an officer outside her house and one at the station just to be safe." A chubby hand rested on his arm. "I don't want anything to happen to her either, Rich. Kate's a great girl, and I really think a lot of her. I'm glad she has you. But I'm also concerned for *your* safety."

"Don't worry about me," Rich grumbled, but he was worried. About Kate, the baby—and himself.

Reggie waved a hand at the remnants of Hurricane Shea and asked, "Do you see anything that might give us a clue as to where she might have gone?"

Rich's eyes scanned the room from one end to the other. Everything that was made of glass or crystal had been smashed to smitherines. The painting above the fireplace had been ripped from the wall, the canvas shredded. The couches were bare, their cushions fluff covered the floor like snow. He shook his head. "I don't know, Reggie. I really don't know. I wish I did. If I think of anything I'll let you know."

Reggie extended his hand. "Thanks, Rich. We will get her. You have my word."

Rich shook the older man's hand, then returned to the vehicle where Kate was sitting, chatting with the officer. She smiled, but there was tension in her face. "You ready, love?"

"Yeah, you done in there?" Her head jerked toward the house.

"Um hum, let's get you home." He climbed behind the wheel. "Thanks, Terry." The officer tilted his head and mumbled a 'you're welcome', then he walked off toward the house.

Kate grabbed his hand. "I'm tired. Let's go home."

Home. It had been a long time since Rich had truly felt at home anywhere. Hell, it'd been a near eternity since he'd felt at home in his own skin. Kate had changed all that. Not only was she his home, she was his everything.

He'd not told her what he'd seen in Shea's house, nor would he. She was already scared. There was no need to have her afraid to leave her home. With Reggie's help, Rich would do everything within his power to protect her.

✕✕✕

Rich connected the last of the wires, then stood back to admire his handy work. The room where he currently stood was empty except for the television on the wall. But tomorrow, between noon and 4:00, it would be nearly bursting at the seams.

Kate was in the shower, freshening up, and Rich

was doing everything he could think of to keep his mind off that fact. He walked down the hall, fully aware that her room was eerily silent. The door was ajar and he listened, holding his breath. Through the quiet, a soft crying caused Rich's blood pressure to spike.

He pushed through the door and followed the noise into the bathroom. Kate was crumbled on the floor, a towel resting around her hips.

"Kate?" She looked up from the floor, tears streaming down her face. Rich knelt at her side, lifting the towel to assist her with a bit of modesty. "What's wrong? Are you okay?" He was glad he didn't sound as panicked as he felt.

"I slipped and fell right on my..." She lifted the bottom edge of the towel to show him traces of blood on the fluffy white bathmat she was sitting on.

The panic that had been under control just a moment ago shot through the roof. He scooped her into his arms, his pulse pounding like a jackhammer behind his ears. "Come on, I'm taking you to the emergency room."

She didn't argue, just sat on the edge of the bed as Rich rooted through the drawers for some clothes. A set of pink pajamas finally made the cut. He tenderly helped her dress then picked her up again.

"I think I can walk," she protested.

"When the doctor says you can walk, love, then you can walk."

She rested her damp head against his shoulder. "I'm sure everything's fine." The words themselves weren't convincing due to the tears rolling down her cheeks, wetting his shirt.

He kissed her head. "I'm sure it is. And in a few hours we'll know for sure." It was important to keep Kate calm, even if it was impossible to convince his own central nervous system that he should also be calm.

After getting Kate settled in the passenger seat, Rich took a deep breath before he got into the car. His every instinct was shouting that he drive like a lunatic, break every land speed record to get them to the doctor, but he forced himself to follow the speed limits.

Rich watched Kate bite on her lip and rub circles on her belly while they made the short trip to the emergency room. Rich pulled up to the front doors and threw the car into gear. "Wait here. I'll be right back with someone to help you." Then he jerked the door opened and ran inside, hoping he would be able to keep it together.

✕ ✕ ✕

Kate smiled as Rich ran into the double doors of the emergency room. He was so concerned—so was she, if she were going to be honest—even though he tried to hide it. When he scooped her into his arms, she'd never felt so protected, so loved.

A few minutes later, Rich appeared with a guy dressed in scrubs who was pushing a wheelchair. The hospital worker opened the door and smiled. "Hello, Miss Callahan, I'm told you need some help tonight." He tossed Rich an annoyed glance, then reached up to aide Kate into the wheelchair. "You're going to need to move the car. This space is for ambulances only," he told Rich.

Rich bent down on his haunches and took Kate's hand. "I'll be right in."

"Let's go, Miss Callahan." Mr. Scrubs pushed the chair away from where Rich was still squatted on the ground.

Kate heard a door slam, and an engine protest as Rich moved the vehicle to a spot where it could wait for them to finish up with the doctors. A soft chuckling caused her to look up at the man who pushed her through the double doors. "I'm glad to see that you two finally hooked up."

"Excuse me?" Kate felt her brows pull together.

"Oh, come on, the way you came rushing in when he got hit in the head... Congratulations on the baby, by the way."

"You remember us? That was..." She tried to calculate how much time had elapsed since the time she'd overreacted at Rich's head wound.

"Don't hurt yourself," he said with a laugh. "I don't remember how long it was either, but it was pretty obvious that you two would end up together."

"You saw that ... then?"

"I guess I'm just a good reader of people." He patted her shoulder. "And he acted the same way you acted when you brought him in with his head wound." He laughed. "You should have seen the way he came running in like a crazed man, saying how you were pregnant and bleeding. I expected blood to be gushing everywhere."

Kate felt the corners of her mouth lift and her heart soared. "Yeah, he tends to get carried away."

He raised a brow. "And you don't?" When she scowled, he laughed. "I'll see about getting you looked at sooner than later. Who's your OB?"

"Dr. Tipton."

"Aaron Tipton?" He sounded ecstatic and quickened their pace, wheeling her behind a curtain. A metal on metal sound ripped through the air as he yanked the curtain around to give her some privacy.

"Yeah." The blood pressure cuff was cold, then increasingly tight on her arm.

His pen scratched against the paper on his clipboard. "Good." He stuffed the cuff back into its holder and wrote down more notes. "I actually saw Tipton in the hospital, I'll page him and see if he has a few minutes to come down and take a look at you himself. That will speed things along for you."

"Thanks."

"If I don't see you again, good luck, Miss Callahan." He flashed her a smile, then stepped through an opening in the flimsy wall.

"Where is she?" Rich's voice was frantic.

"Right through there," came the reply.

The curtain whipped back and Rich stepped through the opening. "You okay? What'd I miss?"

Kate wanted to laugh. Rich was so cute when he was panicked for no reason. At least she hoped he was overreacting. "I'm fine, Rich. I think the bleeding has stopped."

He was trying really hard to be cool, to not show her just how nervous he was about the situation, but Kate could see his fear reflected in his eyes, could feel it radiating off him in waves. He was truly frightened— even more so now than this afternoon with Shea.

Shea. A shudder ripped up her spine.

"Are you cold?" His head jerked from side to side, scanning their surroundings for something to offer her. When there was nothing around, he actually tugged at the hem of his t-shirt.

"Rich, stop. I'm fine." She wanted to ask him for the only comfort she could think of—him, his embrace—but didn't. Instead she crossed her arms tightly across her chest and closed her eyes.

The sound of someone entering their little space brought her eyes open. A nurse held the familiar clipboard. "Hi, I'm going to take you up to OB where Dr. Tipton will look at you."

A relieved sigh left Kate's lungs. "Thanks."

The nurse took control of the wheelchair and Rich walked along side. He was quiet, reflective, his whole body tense with the nervous energy she felt, too. As if sensing her need to touch him, Rich reached down and took her hand in his. They continued their journey down the long corridor, up the elevator, and over the glassed walkway that would lead to the wing where little miracles were born.

She finally stopped in a room with two beds, a curtain between them. "This is triage. We've been slow so you should have some privacy, but I can't promise it will last."

"Thank you."

"Here, put this on, opening in the back." The nurse handed Kate a pale pink gown with little white flowers on it. "I'll let the doctor know that you're here. It shouldn't be long."

Kate and Rich muttered a thank you in unison then when they were alone, Rich turned to her. "Do you need some help?" There was no suggestive nature in his question, and honestly, yeah, she did want his help. If she were being completely truthful in her desires, she just didn't want to be away from him. Ever.

"That would be very..."

"Helpful," he supplied with a smirk.

"Yes, helpful." She scowled at him and bit down on her lip to keep from smiling. Her feet moved from the platforms on the chair and Rich frowned.

"How about we get the gown on your upper half, then I'll support you to take your bottoms off."

"Deal." She didn't want to take the bottoms off with him standing in front of her. The body he knew and loved no longer existed. Now she was enormous, her skin stretched so tight it actually hurt. And she still had weeks—she hoped—before this adventure was over.

Rich's fingers were warm against her skin, his face all business, as he helped her ease the fabric up and over her head. The cool air swept over her and Kate was flooded with the urge to use her hands to cover her chest, but refrained, stuffing them into the sleeves of the gown Rich now held.

"Okay, hold on to me. Don't let go. I'll help you get the bottoms started and you should be able to just step out of them."

She nodded into his chest. Apprehension caused her stomach to roll. Her belly was big, and so was her ass. The thought of Rich seeing it...

"Kate, love, step out." One leg lifted, then the other, leaving her pajama bottoms in a pool on the floor. He reached down and scooped them up, and jammed them and the top into a white plastic bag labeled 'my belongings'. "Let me help you get into the bed." He lifted the covers and helped her slide beneath the sheet. "Are you warm enough? I'm sure I can get you another blanket if..."

"Thank you, Rich." Her heart filled her chest, overcome by the love she couldn't express for the man in front of her. "I couldn't have gotten through today without you."

His lips curved up at the corners into a smile his eyes didn't register. "You wouldn't have had to if not for me." His voice was hard, bitter. "I'm sorry...for everything."

"Rich, please, don't be sorry. If not for you, I wouldn't—"

"Kate Callahan," the deep voice of Dr. Tipton interrupted her words. "I hear we're having a little trouble. What happened?"

Rich began the rundown of how he found her lying on the bathroom floor, bleeding. Dr. Tipton listened, but his face had a look of surprise on it. Kate had told him that the baby's father was dead and that she would be doing this all on her own. Rich's composure, his intense expression left little doubt that he was more than just her roommate, or her co-worker. Rich loved her.

And her heart ached to let him, but...

"Dr. Tipton," Kate hedged when Rich took a breath, "this is Rich, my—"

"Boyfriend." The smile he flashed her was defiant, confident—loving.

Dr. Tipton didn't miss a beat. "Nice to meet you, Rich." He turned to look at Kate once again. "Okay, Kate, let's get an ultrasound before we start poking or prodding. We wouldn't want to make anything worse."

"Yeah, we wouldn't want that." She tried to force a smile.

He stepped outside the door and tugged an ultrasound machine through the door. With Rich's eyes safely on the doctor and his contraption, Kate lifted her gown and pulled the blanket down to expose her swollen midsection. Deep blue eyes met hers for a moment before focusing on the mountain where her flat stomach had once been. She didn't want to need to cover it, to hide from him, but her hands moved of their own free will.

Rich smiled, his eyes twinkled brightly as they slowly drifted up to hers. "You're beautiful, Kate. I love you."

She blinked back the stinging sensation in her eyes, not wanting to turn into a blubbering idiot.

Dr. Tipton sat down on the rolling chair next to the bed and took the transducer in his hand. "I'm sorry, this is going to be a little chilly." Goosebumps broke out on her skin as the cool gel hit her belly. "Let's see what we've got going on here." A few swipes later, he pointed to the monitor. "Right here is your placenta, it's completely attached, no problems there."

The sweet little man on the screen moved, and an audible gasp filled Kate's ears. It wasn't a surprise that Rich reacted to the baby—Jesse's baby. His eyes were the size of dinner plates with a deer-in-the-headlights expression that tied her intestines in knots. She may have fallen even harder for him in the last few minutes, but it looked like he was second-guessing his decision to be with her.

Tears filled her eyes and began to roll down her cheek. She sniffed and swiped at them which only caused them to come more quickly. She sent a prayer to the heavens, needing Rich to look at her, but his gaze was focused on only one thing—the baby.

"Is that..."

The doctor chuckled. "Yes, he's definitely a boy."

Rich laughed. "Yeah, *definitely* a boy," he said in a tone that sounded like awe.

The transducer moved slowly over Kate's belly, revealing more bits and pieces of the little person residing within her. Dr. Tipton pointed out bones and the internal organs. Rich gasped again at the tiny beating heart.

"And here's his face," Dr. Tipton said, not even needing to point at the little face that seemed to be smiling out of the monitor. "It looks like he might have a head full of hair." He turned to smile at Kate. "I guess we'll know soon enough." There was a soft scratching as he yanked a handful of tissues from the box, handing them to her. "I'd like to do an exam just to see if I can tell where the blood came from and to make sure that everything's okay on that end."

Kate wiped her belly, then scooched down on the bed and pulled her feet to her rear. She shot Rich what she could only imagine was a panicked expression and he smiled as he came to stand by her head, taking her hand and pressing it to his lips.

Dr. Tipton tugged at the blankets until Kate felt a rush of cool air hit her bottom. "Just a little pressure." He shook his head. "You're cervix has dilated to a two. A little more than I would like, but certainly not something to worry about. No thinning, which is good."

The doctor pulled back, and his eyes glanced down at her intimate area. A smile spread from his lips to his eyes. "Well, it looks like..." He met her eyes. "I'm going to touch you, okay."

She nodded.

"It looks like you have a cut on your labia. That's probably where the blood came from. The area gets engorged during pregnancy and a little cut can bleed quite a bit."

Well, that was a relief. She sighed, trying not to think of how painful a cut on her labia was.

The blanket was tugged into place, and Kate slid back up to the head of the bed. Dr. Tipton made a few more notes in her chart. "Here's our plan, Kate. I want you to cut back on your work load."

"But..." she protested.

Rich squeezed her hand. "No problem, doc."

"And since you've started to dilate, I'd like to place you on pelvic rest. If your cervix continues to dilate, or begins to soften, we may have to *dee*scalate your activities further." He shot Rich a pointed expression. "You okay with that?"

"Yes, no problem, I'll make sure she follows your orders to the letter." His warm, strong hand squeezed hers reassuringly, and she almost allowed herself to believe that he could still love her.

"Alright then, I want to see you this week. Call my office tomorrow morning and make an appointment." He put his pen back in the pocket of his white coat and said, "Take care," then left the room.

"I'm, uh, I've got to ... make a phone call." Rich's voice sounded weird, different, detached. "Why don't you start getting dressed and I'll be right back." And then he was gone.

Kate's eyes stung with emotions she didn't want to

recognize. His emotional detachment made her heart ache. And as hard as she tried to chalk it up to hormones, she couldn't. It was obvious that he couldn't get away from her fast enough.

It won't be long now, Katie, she told herself, *and he'll run like that right out of your life.*

✕ ✕ ✕

Never before had Rich felt so overwhelmed in his life. Seeing, actually seeing, the little boy whom he loved was nearly more than he could handle. He kept his eyes away from Kate, couldn't even think of looking at her, or the stoic façade he'd attempted to construct would have crumbled in an instant.

"Rich?"

"Hi, Dad." His voice cracked.

"Rich, what's wrong? Are you okay? Is Kate?" His dad's voice was full of the concern a father should have for his son.

"I saw him." Rich leaned against the wall and slid down until he rested on his haunches.

"Saw who, Rich? Who did you see?"

"The baby." He quickly relayed the story of the day, only giving the Reader's Digest version of the slashed portrait and near run in with Shea, then the fall and consequent visit to the emergency room. "It was incredible! The little guy was moving like crazy and has a ton of hair, the doctor thinks. I can't wait to meet him in person."

Richard started to laugh, and Rich could hear his mother's voice in the background. "It seems that our son is in love." Marilyn let out a squeal that nearly stole his hearing.

"Come on, you guys, that isn't a surprise to you."

There was a shuffling of the phone and then his

mother said, "We're just glad you're happy. It's been a long time coming, you know." Rich snorted unable to deny that to get to this point had taken forever. "When are you bringing her to meet us?"

The thought of Kate meeting his parents was one that both excited and scared the hell out of him. Marilyn could be hard on the girls he dated. She'd hated Shea from day one. And now he realized that she'd been completely right. Marilyn could also be overbearing and opinionated and—a mother.

"You know what?" she continued. "We'll meet her when we get a chance. Go back to your girl, Richie. Love her and don't let her get away from you."

"Will do, Mom." Rich closed his phone and went back into the small room to find Kate, her legs dangling over the edge of the bed, still in the hospital gown, and she was crying. "Kate, honey, what's wrong?"

"Nothing," she lied, rubbing at her cheeks. "I just want to get out of here."

"Okay, let me help you." He rushed to her side and took her elbow to ease her feet to the floor. His hands riffled through the plastic bag and pulled out her pajamas.

She snatched them from him and waddled toward the bathroom in what seemed to be a huff. "I can get dressed myself."

"I'll be right here when you're ready."

She muttered something under her breath that sounded very much like, "Sure you will," before closing the door with emphasis.

Rich leaned against the wall and smiled. His eyes closed and behind the lids he could see the picture that would forever be burned into his memory; the little boy smiling at him on the screen. A boy. A son. *My son.*

Thirty

"Yes, Mom, it really is fine." Kate had said the exact same words or a variation of them at least a thousand times in the last two minutes. "The doctor said that everything will be fine. I just have to cut back my hours at work, that's all." Kate saw no point in sharing that she also had to rest her pelvis—like there was any likelihood of it getting a workout.

Rich had been quiet, too quiet, all the way home. It was as if his mind was spinning and he had trouble keeping up with his thoughts. He was probably trying to come up with a way to leave, to bow out, without looking like a total ass to everybody that knew them. She would never blame him when he left. In fact, part of her wished he'd just get it over with. Better to have her heart broken now, rather than when she had a chance to fall even deeper in love with him.

"Okay. Are you sure I can't do anything for you? Because I—"

"Mom, I'm fine. *Really.* Besides Rich is here if I need anything." *For the moment anyway.*

Kate could hear her mother's smile in her next question. "How are things between you? Is he treating you well?"

"Rich is a good man. He's better than I deserve and—"

"Kate. Don't. You deserve all the happiness this life

has to offer, and if Rich makes you happy, then Daddy and I are happy for you." She paused and Kate could hear ruffling noises on the other side of the line.

"What are you doing?"

"Packing. I'll see you in tomorrow afternoon." And then the line went dead before Kate could tell her to stay home. She tried calling back, but after two rings the call went to voicemail.

A half-groan, half-scream ripped from Kate's throat, and within seconds, Rich stood in the doorway of her room, completely panicked. "What's wrong? Do you need something?" He was dressed in a white t-shirt and a pair of jeans so tight they should be illegal, and to complete his outfit was her pink and green striped apron.

Kate started to giggle, a real giggle, and it felt good to feel happy. She sat up against the pillows and asked, "What are you doing in there?"

"My girl's gotta eat—my boy, too." He held up a spaghetti spoon. "I hope you like Italian."

"Yes, I do." Her stomach growled as if to add its agreement.

Rich leaned against the door jamb and crossed his arms. "Would you like to tell me why you were screaming?"

"I didn't scream," she protested. He laughed and raised a brow. "Okay, so maybe it was a little *groan* of frustration."

"And what exactly has you frustrated?"

She huffed, and blew at a stray lock of hair that was tickling her forehead. "My mother. She's coming."

He stood there, smiling, looking handsome as ever, but said nothing.

"My mom tends to overreact. When I told her I'd fallen, she … well, she'll be here tomorrow afternoon. Dammit! I really don't need to deal with her right now." She slammed her fist into the mattress. "She's probably going to want to see the cut."

Rich's deep, warm laughter bubbled in the air around her, and Kate, despite her best efforts, joined him. The action felt good. She let the giggles continue and grabbed at her sides when they began to ache.

She was still laughing when Rich said, "I called Dale, you'll be working the afternoon shift until the doctor says otherwise."

Her laughter broke off abruptly. "I could have done that myself."

"I was only trying to help. You don't need to do everything yourself, Kate. I also talked to him about me working the evening shift so that I can drive you to work then bring you home on my dinner break."

Her eyes narrowed at him. "Dr. Tipton didn't say anything about not driving. I can drive myself." She crossed her arms over her chest, irritation coursing through her veins.

"I don't want to fight, Kate. Please just let me take care of you."

That sounded so good. She wanted to let him take care of her, to love her. But the voice in the back of her head kept screaming that she shouldn't give her heart to him. She would have to push him away eventually, after the baby was born, and then her heart would break in two.

✕ ✕ ✕

Rich woke up, in Kate's bed, alone. His arm stretched out across the mattress, but still came up empty. She was gone. He jolted into the sitting position. "Kate," he shouted into the silence.

She appeared in the doorway that led to the bathroom with just a towel on. Her auburn hair was damp, making it look like deep mahogany, and her skin was still red from her shower, glistening delectably in the light. "What?"

"I woke up. You were gone." His groggy brain tried to sort through the fear he'd awakened with and the relief of finding Kate safe and sound—and sexy as hell. "Are you okay?"

Her teeth bit lightly on her lower lip. "I'm fine. You?" Her dainty bare feet padded into the room, to the dresser where she opened a drawer and began pulling out lacy underwear. He bit back a groan. She was surely trying to kill him.

The doorbell rang and both of them jumped. Kate's face took on a panicked expression to match the one his face surely wore. He immediately thought of Shea.

Kate, however, thought of someone else. "My mom! Crap!"

There was no way that it could be Mrs. Callahan though. It was only 10:00 in the morning, and it would take Anna all day to make the drive from Flagstaff to Salt Lake. "You wait here, I'll get the door." His feet hit the floor just as the bell rang again. "Kate, please wait here."

"Like I could go out there like this."

He tore his eyes from the sight before him and slid his jeans into place before *carefully* tugging the zipper into place. Rich's skin was buzzing, his entire body preparing for whoever might be on the other side of the door. Never in his life had he wished he had a gun more than in this moment. He needed to protect what was his.

The incessant knocking was followed by a voice Rich recognized. "Rich? Richard Adam Spencer, are you in there?"

He jerked the door open. His eyes widened with the presence of the two people on the front porch. "Mom? Dad? What are you guys doing here?"

Marilyn   Spencer   practically   leapt   through   the doorway and threw her arms around him, kissing his cheek. "It's so good to see you." She kissed his other cheek. "You look so ... happy. Doesn't he look happy, Richard?"

"Yes, Marilyn, he does look happy." Richard Spencer stepped through the door and extricated his son from the death grip his mother had inflicted. "Let the boy breathe, Marilyn. It's good to see you, son. How are things?" He looked over Rich's shoulder. "Where's Kate?"

"Right here." Kate stepped out from around the corner. Her eyes accused Rich as she asked, "Your parents are here?"

"Yes. I didn't..."

"What a nice surprise." Kate came closer and Marilyn closed the gap, wrapping Kate in a hug. "Welcome to our home."

Our home. Rich liked the sound of that.

"We're glad to be here." Marilyn released her hold and stepped back. "I'm Marilyn and this is Richard. We just had to come and meet the woman who has captured our son's heart."

Rich felt an uncomfortable heat flood his cheeks, and he avoided Kate's gaze which he could feel burning a hole through him. "Captured his heart, huh?" Kate sounded amused.

"So, Mom, really, why are you here?"

"Well, you said that Kate couldn't travel—"

"You...?"

"I—"

Richard stepped in to save them all. "After speaking with you last night, we just thought we'd take a little vacation to come visit you and to ... meet Kate." He wrapped an arm around Marilyn's waist. "I hope we're not intruding."

"Not at all." Kate held out her hand to shake Richard's. "You are Rich's family which—"

"Makes you hers," Rich interrupted, stepping forward to mimic his parent's pose. Kate tensed, but whether it was the reference to her being their family or the contact he'd just imposed, he couldn't be sure. "You can take the bed that's being delivered today, and I'll take the couch."

"No," Richard said, shaking his head. "We're staying at the LaQuinta Inn. We wouldn't think of completely intruding." He chuckled softly and Rich realized for the first time ever that his father's laugh closely resembled his own. "Your mother might, but I never would."

She reacted just as the two men expected. She launched an elbow into his side, a blush rising to her cheeks. "I would not."

"It's okay, Mom, we're glad you're here."

The woman, whom he strongly resembled, smiled, her blue eyes flashing. "Kate, how are you? How is my grandson?" She reached out toward Kate's stomach.

Kate stiffened at the mention of the baby, and Rich realized that there was a storm brewing—the same storm that rumbled whenever he made reference to the child's paternity. "Good. We're both good," Kate said through a smile that didn't come close to appearing real. "If you'll excuse me, I've got to um..." She pulled away from Rich and started down the hall. "Excuse me."

Marilyn's eyes were wide. "I'm so sorry. I didn't mean..."

"It's okay, Mom. I'll just check on her." Rich followed Kate into her room where she stood in front of the window, her arms crossed over her chest. "Kate?"

She whirled around to face him, her eyes a blistering accusation. "How dare you?" she hissed through her teeth, careful to keep her voice low enough so that the people in the other room wouldn't hear her.

Rich stepped inside the doorway and closed the door. "Kate, I don't know what I've dared to do now."

Her teeth ground together as she continued to glare at him. "As if it wasn't bad enough that Nate knows what happened between us, you told your parents. Come on, Rich think of how that makes me look." The second the smile lifted his lips, he knew he'd made a mistake and her reaction verified his suspicions. "You're an ass, Rich."

"Maybe. But not because I've told anybody what happened between us ... well, except for Nate." He waited until the realization of what he'd just said sunk in, then continued, "They don't know that little boy could be mine biologically speaking, love."

"Then why did your mother—"

"I've been very open and honest with my parents, my father especially, about how I feel about you." Rich's fingers ran through his hair while blowing out a slow, controlled breath. "They know their son, Kate. That's all."

Rich watched as her whole demeanor softened, almost as if the anger melted away at his words. He wanted to continue, to tell her how much he loved the little boy growing in her belly, and that he'd also told his father that but knew better than to start that debate again. Not while his parents nervously waited in the other room.

"So they came here to meet me?" she asked as if totally shocked at the idea.

"Yes, love, just to meet you." He smiled when she did. "And I think you're kinda freaking my mom out. Can we go back out there?"

"Oh," she gasped, running past him. "Mrs. Spencer—"

"Call me Marilyn," Rich heard his mother say.

"Marilyn," Kate continued, "I'm so sorry. My hormones seem to be out of control these days, and I..."

"There's no need to apologize." Marilyn's blue eyes

met those of her son, and the two of them smiled in unison. "Hormones are just a way of tormenting womankind, I think." She leaned close to Kate and stage whispered, "You think pregnancy is bad, wait 'til menopause."

"Mom," Rich voiced his mortification. He was just about to apologize to Kate when a laugh caused him to smile instead. Kate had a hand over her mouth which did little to stifle the humor of Marilyn's statement.

"Come on, Kate, surely you've got some chocolate in this place." Marilyn threaded her arm through Kate's, and Kate led the way into the kitchen.

Rich watched the two most important women in his life as they laughed and disappeared into the kitchen. "What the hell just happened?"

Richard chuckled, clapping his son on the shoulder. "I think they just bonded." And as if to verify his father's statement, a ferocious bout of laughter boiled from the other room.

"Well, that's a good thing...I think." As the laughter continued, and continued, Rich wondered what he'd unleashed. A lump formed in his gut. It was good the two most important women in his life were getting along, but the only thing they had in common was him. And *that* was so not a good thing.

× × ×

Kate handed Marilyn a steaming cup of hot cocoa and a piece of Hershey's candy bar to use as a spoon. "I know it's the middle of summer, but this is my favorite when I need a chocolate fix."

Marilyn smiled, her blue eyes twinkled. "I knew I liked you, Kate." She looked over her shoulder, then leaned forward and dropped her voice. "Now that Rich is gone, how are you really? He called last night after you fell. He was so worried, but he tends to overreact." She laughed sardonically. "He probably got that from me. You're okay though? Is there anything I can do for you?"

This woman sitting across the table from Kate was nearly as prying as her own mother. Her mother, who—*Crap!* –would be here in only a few hours. Putting these two together would surely to cause more problems than it would solve.

"I'm fine, Marilyn, really." Her hands moved to the same spot they tended to go when she was nervous, her stomach. "Just a little sore, but I'm okay."

"Is he being good to you?" There was no doubt who the *he* was in her question.

"Marilyn, I have to say that you raised a good son. Rich is a good man, better than I deserve. He doesn't need to saddle himself with—" She waved a hand up and down herself. "—any of this."

"What if he wants to?" She leaned forward and took Kate's hand in hers. "Listen, honey, I have never seen Rich so in love. When he came to visit us after spending time with you in Phoenix, I saw it even then. He loves you, and nothing's going to change that." Her eyes started to glisten. "Please don't hurt him, Kate."

"Sometimes I think that's unavoidable." Kate's voice was barely a whisper.

"Do you love him?" the nosey woman asked. "You don't have to answer," she said when the silence dragged on between them. "Just promise me you'll be honest with yourself, that you'll listen to and follow your heart."

A throat was cleared from behind them, and both women looked up to see the men they loved standing in the doorway. They were posed the same, leaning against opposite sides of the jamb, arms crossed over their chests.

"How long are you two going to sit in here and

discuss me?" Rich was smiling but there was an anxious tone behind the nonchalant exterior.

Marilyn winked at Kate then looked at her son. "You know you're my favorite topic of conversation, Rich."

"Come on, lovely wife, we have to go check in at the hotel." Richard stretched out his hand. The chair scrapped across the tile as Marilyn pushed away from the table and stood. Richard wrapped her in a hug and smiled over her shoulder to Kate. "It was really nice to meet you, Kate. I can see why Rich is so taken by you."

"Thanks." Kate felt the blush rise in her cheeks. "I'm kinda taken by him too."

Rich's parents were beaming as they left her sitting at the table. Rich stuffed his hands in his pockets. "I'm just going to see them out."

Kate nodded and took a long pull on her hot chocolate. Meeting Rich's parents hadn't made any of this easier or helped her decipher her feelings. It only made her love Rich even more. His parents were so loving, so perfect. And they actually liked her.

Her heart broke at the knowledge that it would all end. The day was quickly approaching when the baby would come and then Rich would leave her. She didn't want to think of it, but couldn't force the thought from her mind. Rich was so sure that the baby was his. What would happen when it wasn't? Because it couldn't be. *It can't be.*

"Kate, why are you crying?" She hadn't even realized she was until Rich asked. He sat down in the chair his mom had left. "Did my mom say something that..."

"Your mom was wonderful, your dad too. I just..." Her voice broke. "I don't want them to hate me."

His thumbs rubbed lightly on her cheeks. "They aren't going to hate you, love." He kissed her softly on the lips. "They'd like to bring back some lunch. Is that okay or should I call and cancel?"

"No, lunch would be good." Her stomach growled and Rich laughed.

"I need to shower and change." He ran a hand over his still bare chest, and Kate allowed herself to study the cut of each muscle. He was lean, with hardly any fat on him, but he was strong and the muscular contours of his abdomen made Kate ache to reach out and touch them. She forced herself to behave by stuffing her hands in her pockets.

✗ ✗ ✗

Lunch was nice. His parents had managed to humiliate Rich with stories of how he was as a child. Pranks he pulled. Even relayed a potty-training story that caused soda to spew out of Kate's nose. Hearing Kate laugh was one the best thing in the world, but being the butt of the joke that caused that laughter was beyond painful.

Kate's phone rang, and she was still laughing as she answered, "Hi, Mom." She nodded, and smiled. "Oh, good, we'll see you in a few hours. I've got to go, we'll talk when you get here. Love you." She closed the phone and said, "Mom will be here about 4:00."

Then the doorbell rang, and they all looked at each other. Kate was the first to realize who it would be. She jumped to her feet and waddled to the front door. "Check the peephole first," Rich warned, hurrying to be there if she needed him.

"We have your delivery," the big guy announced, holding a clipboard out to Kate. "Can I see the room where it's going?"

"Sure, this way." Kate took off down the hallway with Bubba on her heels.

Twenty minutes later, the bed was set up, and the delivery guys were on their way out the door. "What a beautiful bedroom set," Marilyn commented from the doorway. "Do you need some help getting the sheets on it?"

"That would be great." Kate walked out of the room and came back with black silk sheets.

Marilyn raised a brow but, for once, didn't comment on the thought that raced across her mind. Rich couldn't hold his tongue. "Silk sheets, Kate?"

She blushed and bit down on her bottom lip. "I just thought..."

He held up his hands. "It's okay. I like silk." Actually he hated it, but couldn't stand the disappointment on Kate's face.

Marilyn pushed past him. "Let's get these on the bed." Kate handed her the sheets, and the two women walked down each side of the bed. "Rich, why don't you go grab the pillows."

Rich shot Kate a questioning glance to which she responded, "Hall closet, top shelf."

It took all of thirty seconds for Rich to head down the hall, grab two pillows, and come back with them tucked under his arm. But when he reentered the room, the bed was completely made with his mother just brushing the wrinkles out of the sheets. Marilyn tossed him a pillowcase which caused him to fumble the pillows, dropping them in the floor.

He bent over and picked up one of the pillows, shoved it into the case. Making quick work of shoving the fluffy rectangle into its cotton case, he threw it onto the bed to repeat the action with the other pillow.

Kate smiled at him, her hands resting on her stomach. "Are you happy with it?" She ran her hands over the headboard. He nodded and she said, "Good, because I am. I think it's perfect."

"So this is for you?" The question sounded accusatory to Rich, but he was sure his mother hadn't meant it that way.

"Yeah, this is my room." He could see the 'You're roommates?' question on the tip of his mother's tongue and held his breath in anticipation.

"Do you need some help in here?" Richard's voice eased Rich's tension.

Thank you, he thought. Rich waved an arm toward the wall. "Yeah, could you help me grab some boxes from the other room?"

"Absolutely."

Rich was glad his father had picked that exact moment to show up in the doorway. The situation had just become tense with his mother's realizations. And Marilyn Spencer was not the kind of woman to hold her tongue, especially when it concerned her son.

"So she's not comfortable having you in the same room, huh?" Richard asked as soon as they were alone in what would soon be the nursery.

Rich shook his head, unable to confirm the question verbally.

"That's okay. Which box?" Richard waited for direction then picked up one marked clothes. "You're in the same house, Rich. And it's obvious the girl loves you. Be patient, son, you'll soon be in her room, in her bed. It must be really confusing for her. She loves you, but must still feel a loyalty to the father of her baby."

Rich's teeth ground together, but he dropped his head to avoid his father's eyes. He scooped up a box. "At the end of the day, all I want is to be the man in her heart. As long as I have that...well, that's all I need."

Richard chuckled softly. "Since I'm a betting man, I would put everything I had on a bet that you're already there. In her heart, I mean."

"That's all I need." Rich brushed past his dad and went back into the guest room, his room.

Kate and Marilyn were each lying on the bed and, as Rich came around the corner, Marilyn put her finger to her lips. "Shh."

Kate's full lips pulled into a smile, her eyelids fluttered. "I'm not asleep, Marilyn, just resting my eyes."

Thirty One

As if having one mother in the house wasn't bad enough, the doorbell rang, announcing the arrival of a second. Rich felt his intestines wrap themselves into a knot as Kate once again carelessly rushed to the door. Whether it was the certainty—or the uncertainty—of who was on the other side that made him nauseous though, Rich couldn't be sure.

The last time Rich had seen Anna Callahan had been at Jesse's funeral. Kate had been an emotional basket case, and Rich wondered if Anna had any suspicions of the feelings he and Kate shared. If she doubted at that time, Rich had left little question with his weekly dose of flowers.

The door opened and Kate rushed into the arms of her mother and both of them burst into tears. Rich shook his head and bit back a chuckle. He would never understand that kind of reaction. He had missed Kate immensely, but didn't *cry* when he saw her after those excruciating six months.

Technically he did cry, he reminded himself with a pang of remorse, but not because of the reasons the two women in front of him shared.

Anna kissed Kate's cheek. "Your dad sends his love. He wanted to come, but couldn't get away."

"I understand."

Anna's hands moved over the belly of her daughter,

cooing as she felt the little person within kick. "I can't believe how much you've grown."

"That's just a nice way of saying I'm huge."

"You're not huge," Anna and Rich said in unison. Anna turned to him, her dark eyes sparkling, and she smiled, a genuine smile. "Rich, how are you? It's good to see you under happier circumstances." She stepped toward him and pulled him into a hug, kissing him on the cheek. "Thank you for taking care of my girl," she whispered in his ear.

Rich smiled. "Glad to do it, Mrs. Callahan."

Kate was practically beaming, the smile on her face spread clear across her face. "Mom, I'm so glad you're here. Come in. You must be so tired."

Anna threaded her arm through Kate's and they walked into the house. "Call me Anna," she said over her shoulder. "Oh, you have company. I'm sorry to just barge in on the party."

Richard and Marilyn were on their feet and smiled at the approaching woman. Rich stepped around Kate and Anna when Anna's feet stopped moving. "Anna, these are my parents. They popped in for a visit."

Rich had never seen anything so bizarre in all his life. The two mothers all but ran into one another's arms, embracing as if they were long lost sisters. Then Anna hugged Richard, placing a kiss on his cheek. It would have been easy to be creeped out by the *Twilight Zone*sque events unfolding in front of him if not for the soft touch of Kate wrapping her arm around his waist.

"Weird, huh?" she whispered.

"Yeah," he only breathed the word. His arm eased around Kate's waist, and he watched as the two older women began to plan a future he could only dream of. Kate stiffened next to him, her hand formed a ball at his side, as they began to delve into the nursery and how they were going to paint it yellow because...

"Yellow stimulates the brain and makes the child smarter," Marilyn informed them.

Kate stretched up on her toes and whispered, "I don't like yellow."

Rich nodded in agreement. He wasn't a big fan of the color either. "Um, Mom." Both women turned to look at him, each had a look of surprise on their face as though they were shocked to see him and Kate standing in the room with them. "How about a nice blue?"

Marilyn's laugh oozed sarcasm. "Oh, Rich, honey, *this* is what I get paid for." She looked at Kate. "Your nursery is in great hands."

"It's not the hands I'm worried about," Kate muttered under her breath, "it's the walls."

Rich chuckled softly. He gripped the back of her neck and whispered in her ear, "No matter what they do, we can *un*do it as soon as they go home. I promise."

Kate kissed his cheek and he could feel some of her tension fade. "Thanks ... for everything."

The moms were laughing as they walked past Kate and Rich, talking accent colors to the hideous yellow theme. "Black and white," Marilyn said.

"With a bit of red," Anna added.

"Yes! We'll have the smartest grandson on Earth."

"And the cutest," Anna insisted which caused another onslaught of high-pitched laughter.

Kate shook her head. "Unbelievable," she spat the word, "un*freaking*believable."

Richard cleared his throat and Kate held up a hand in apology. "No offense, Richard. I love her, and I'm sure she's really talented and would... It's just that I would really like to decorate my own nursery."

Rich knew his father's hard expression was only to tease Kate and make her squirm. Rich shot him a glare. Richard smiled. "As if I don't know she's overbearing. This is her thing. She gets a little excited and..."

"Goes a little crazy," Rich finished.

"We'll leave before she can do too much damage," Richard promised.

Kate breathed a sigh of obvious relief, and Rich could feel some of the tension leave her body in that breath. "But—" Then she sucked in another breath and stiffened. "—what about *my* mom?"

Rich and his father burst into laughter. Rich pulled her to his chest and kissed the top of her heard. Richard spoke through his chuckles. "Well, honey, there's not much I can do about her."

× × ×

Kate was grateful for the stabilizing influence of Rich and his dad. She adored her mother and she'd quickly learned to love Rich's mom, too. But together, the two moms were going to drive her insane. They had successfully bonded and were at this very moment decorating the nursery of *her* baby. If she wasn't careful, they'd try to name him too.

As if her thoughts called to them, the moms reappeared from down the hall, still chatting about little yellow duckies and fluffy white clouds. Kate was sure she didn't want to know the specifics of that particular topic.

"Marilyn," Richard interrupted the high-pitched planning, "I think we should head out for tonight."

"But..." Marilyn protested.

"We'll see you tomorrow, Mom." Rich didn't give her a chance to protest further. He gave her a hug. "I love you, Mom."

"Okay." By the fall of her beautiful face, it was obvious that she was disappointed and she smiled to hide it. "We'll see you tomorrow." She kissed Rich on the cheek. "Love you." Then hugged Kate. "Sleep well."

Kate's irritation melted into guilt. She considered asking them to stay, but refrained. "You too."

Marilyn hugged Anna then headed for the door. Kate couldn't let her leave without telling her one more thing. The door was open and Richard was already outside before Kate was able to pull her thoughts together.

"Marilyn," Kate yelled, rushing to the entryway, "in answer to your earlier question—" She paused for only a moment, feeling every eye in the house—and the yard—on her. "—Yes, I do. Very much."

As Marilyn's eyes filled with tears, Kate was certain she knew exactly which question had been answered. It was bizarre that she was hesitant to tell Rich that she loved him, but felt completely comfortable revealing it to his mother. She felt like she owed her that much.

And maybe she owed Rich that much too.

Richard escorted Marilyn to the car and they waved as they left the driveway. Kate watched from the doorway until the taillights disappeared around the corner, unable to go back inside and face Rich.

He stepped up behind her, wrapping his arms around her waist. "You do very much what?" he purred in her ear.

Kate's heart skipped a beat and she whispered, "Love you."

His breathing was steady, and Kate could feel the strong beat of his heart, but there was no other reaction. She wasn't sure what she expected, she'd hoped for elation, but this wasn't it.

Time seemed to stretch on forever. Kate knew he loved her—or she thought she did. But as each second ticked by, drops of doubt fueled the fear festering in her soul.

"I'm sorry," she finally whispered, cursing the

damned tears that burned her eyes.

His lips were warm and soft as they pressed a kiss to the tender spot just below her ear. "Kate, don't." Strong hands urged her to turn around.

She reluctantly faced him, but kept her eyes lowered, not wanting to see the rejection she deserved sparkling in his blue eyes.

"Kate." He lifted her chin with a gentle tilt of his fingertip. His breath was warm against her cheek. "Open your eyes and look at me." She considered leaving them closed, but ultimately, slowly, opened them. There, reflected in the deepest blue of his eyes, was so much love it opened the floodgates. "You do love me?" His voice was low and full of emotion.

She nodded and sniffed. "Very much."

"That's all that matters."

It wasn't all that mattered though. There was so much more at stake than just the two of them and their feelings for each other. She would have argued, debated the same old points, but suddenly a new thought had her mind racing. "Where's my mom?"

By the look on Rich's face, he'd forgotten that there was still a parent within earshot. "I'm uh, I'm not sure."

Rich's fingers wrapped around her hand and comforted her as they began their search. Kate's bedroom door was open, and there was a rush of water coming from the bathroom. "I'll wait here," he whispered.

"Good idea." She cradled his face in her hands and kissed him hard on the mouth. "Thank you, Rich. I really don't deserve you."

"You sell yourself short, my love." He kissed her softly, chastely. "Go find your mother."

Anna sat, fully dressed, on the side of the bathtub with the water running. She looked up as Kate asked, "Mom? Are you okay?"

Her eyes were soft, understanding. "Yes. Are you?"

With a flick of her wrist, the rush of water stopped. "It sounded like you and Rich needed a moment without an audience."

"Thanks. We did."

Anna's lips pulled into a disapproving line. Kate knew the look well. It was the same one she'd seen it hundreds of times over the years. "That man is crazy for you, Kate. Can't you see that?"

"Mom, please don't. I'm confused enough without you adding guilt to it."

"Kate," she said while she stood, brushing a lock of hair from Kate's shoulder, "I know you're an adult and that you're going to do as you please, but I just—"

"You love him," Kate interrupted.

Anna started to laugh, tossing her head back. "I do. And his mom is awesome."

"She is pretty great." Kate had no reason to argue. Rich's parents were just as wonderful as their son, and when the day came that Rich left her, loving his parents too would make it all the more painful.

✕ ✕ ✕

The rest of the evening progressed along comfortably. Rich was at complete ease as he watched the news with Anna. Kate was curled up next to him on the couch, her head on his lap, fast asleep.

"So this is your station?" Anna asked quietly, her eyes still focused on the television.

"Yes. That's Clayton. He's a jerk most of the time," Rich noted, shaking his head as the jerk in question delivered his tag. "Poor Nate's my best friend."

"He must have drawn the short straw today then?" There was clear amusement in Anna's question.

"Yep, either that or he pissed off Jordan again."

"Jordan? I met him at the...funeral." Sadness

flashed across her face at the mention of Jesse's services.

"Um hum. Him and his wife, Olivia."

Her eyes lit up with understanding. "Kate talks about Olivia a lot. She's never been one to have close girlfriends. It's nice to see she has one now."

Kate stirred and moaned something unintelligible. Rich shook her awake. "Kate, sweetheart, why don't I help you to bed?"

"No, I'm fine. I just drifted off."

"An hour ago," Anna laughed. "It's okay. I'll still be here in the morning. We can talk more then."

Kate sat up and rubbed at her eyes. "You're sure?"

Anna nodded and smiled the same reassuring smile her daughter had. "I'm sure. 'Night, baby girl."

Rich stood and offered Kate his hand. She slipped her small hand into his and used his strength to pull herself to her feet. She pressed a kiss to her palm and blew it to her mom. "Good night, Mom. I love you."

Rich wrapped an arm around Kate's waist. "I'll be right back," he told Anna.

"You'll... You're... What are you two going to do after I'm out of the room?" Her green eyes were wide with panic.

Rich ushered her down the hall. "The same thing we do with you *in* the room. Paranoia is not very becoming, love."

"I am *not* paranoid, just ... tired," she said through a yawn.

At her bedroom door, he paused. "Are you okay or do you need my help?" He raised a suggestive brow.

"I'll be okay. I'm pregnant, not an invalid." She rolled her eyes and snorted. "Good night, Rich."

"'Night." He pressed his lips to her forehead. "I love you."

A heavy sigh was audibly blown from her lungs. "I

love you, too."

He didn't want to feel the smug elation he did, nor did he want to grin like the damned Cheshire Cat, but there he stood, his heart pounding in his chest and his cheeks hurting because his smile was so wide.

She shook her head and slapped playfully at his chest. "Like you didn't already know it."

"I will *never* get tired of hearing you say it." He swatted her small bottom. "If you need me, just holler." The door closed and Rich couldn't help his laughter which he was sure she heard on the other side.

Anna was still sitting on the chair as Rich re-entered the living room. She smiled and used the remote control to turn off the television. The action made Rich's stomach roll.

"You really do love her." It wasn't a question.

"More than anything." Rich eased himself into the comfort of the opposing chair, feeling anything but comfortable.

Anna leaned forward to rest her arms on her knees. "I thought so." Her face hardened, every subtle line became serious. "What about the baby?"

Rich had been taught that answering a question with a question was rude, but... "What about the baby?"

"They're a package deal; Kate and the baby."

He had to bite back the big ol' *'duh!'* that was on the tip of his tongue, opting instead for... "Yes, they are."

"Can you love him?"

"Yes." This line of questioning was quickly frying his last nerve.

Her face softened and she leaned back in her chair, lifting her knees to tuck her feet under her. "It's important that you understand what kind of man his father was."

The grinding of teeth echoed through Rich's head. *I already know what kind of man I am!*

She continued talking as though she hadn't noticed his reaction. Maybe she just chalked his stiffened body up to her mention of Jesse. "Jesse was liked by everybody. He was so good to Kate, and was always honorable. Knowing that a little piece of him will live on is a wonderful thing." Her eyes filled with tears and she paused when her voice cracked, only to continue about how wonderful Jesse had been.

No wonder he died, Rich thought bitterly, *he was a freakin' saint!*

It was difficult not to let his eyes glass over when Anna's voice took on the Charlie Brown 'whah, whah, whah' tone. But he forced himself to listen to her drone on about Jesse's sainthood, determined to be able to teach the little boy who would be his son about the father who couldn't be there for him. *If* Jesse was the father.

"Anna," he interrupted, holding up a hand, "I don't care who the biological father of that little boy is, I love him. And I want nothing more than to be his dad."

Her smile grew with each word he spoke until every last tooth was exposed. "Ken and I want that very much. You're a good man, Rich." Her mouth opened and she used a hand to stifle a yawn.

"Why don't you take the bed?" Rich offered.

"Oh, no, I couldn't."

"Yes, you can. If my mom gets word that I made you sleep on the couch.... Do you have any idea how much hell I'd catch?" He motioned toward the bedroom. "Take the bed."

Rich had little doubt that Anna could out argue him. She *was* Kate's mother after all. He held her gaze, refusing to even blink—since she'd probably take that as a sign of weakness. They sat that way while the seconds ticked by. Finally she blinked and dropped her eyes for just a moment. Rich fought the urge to gloat at the victory. He bit the inside of his cheek and waited for her to concede.

She smiled and nodded. "I'd hate to get you in trouble with your mother." She stood and started toward the new bed that was meant to be his. "Thank you for everything you've done for our daughter, Rich. We appreciate it."

"My pleasure," he muttered. Rich waited until he heard the door close softly before laying down on the couch. He tugged the blanket off the back, covered as much of himself as the small throw could handle and prayed for sleep.

✕ ✕ ✕

Kate watched in horror as Shea broke the window and elegantly crawled into the room. Tucked under her arm was a tiny blue blanket. "I'm going to take everything from you Kate, everything you took from me—and more."

Kate clutched at her stomach. "You can't have him." She sounded surprisingly calm to her own frantic ears.

"And which *him* are you talking about?" Shea tossed her head back in an eerie laugh. She exposed a knife and unfolded the blanket with a snap. "It doesn't matter. I plan on only taking one with me—alive."

Kate's body jerked into the sitting position, sweat beaded on her forehead and a drop began its descent between her heavy breasts. Breath rushed from her lungs and refused to reenter her body. Her eyes did a quick inventory of the room, gratefully realizing that the window was still intact and that she was alone.

She concentrated on her heartbeat, nibbling on her lip. Her hands moved over her stomach, rubbing soothing circles, which did nothing to actually soothe her fears. There was only one thing that could do that, and he was sleeping in the other room. All it would take was a panicked shriek to bring him running, but there was someone else who would also arrive in the doorway.

The only choice she had was to go to Rich.

The door opened with a soft click and Kate held her breath, listening for any indication that someone else heard the sound. When there was only silence, she padded on bare feet into Rich's room.

Thanks to the moonlight seeping in through the blinds, Kate could easily make out Rich sleeping on his side. Which was weird, he usually slept on his back or his stomach. He looked a little small, but she climbed under the covers, snuggling up to the warm body.

"I really need you to hold me," she whispered.

"Sure thing," answered the feminine voice.

Kate screamed ... and so did her mother.

✕✕✕

Waking up to the horrified scream of Kate had Rich freaking out, but to have Anna's added to the choir sent his heart racing at supersonic speeds. His sluggish, still asleep feet painfully tingled as he stumbled down the hall.

He rushed into Anna's room and flipped the light on. *Shit! That wasn't the brightest idea.* He clamped a hand over his eyes. "Kate, Anna, are you okay?" Frantic blinks, through parted fingers, eased the bright light.

The two women were in the bed facing each other. Anna had a smug, knowledge-filled smirk, and Kate wore a bright crimson blush that made her all the more adorable.

"Kate?" Rich's brows pulled together. "What are you doing in here?"

"What am I...?" She huffed and plopped her hands

on her hips. Her ferocious glare moved from Anna to Rich. "Why aren't you in here?"

Anna giggled softly, but bit down on her lip to stop it when Kate glared at her again. "Rich is a true gentleman," Anna began, "and he all but forced me to sleep in his bed. Which brings us back to the question of why are *you* in here?"

Kate rolled her eyes and with an exaggerated annoyance she got out of the bed and stomped past Rich, who still stood dumbfounded in the doorway.

Anna cleared her throat. "Go to her. She needs you."

She needs me. She *had* actually come into his room, his bed, looking for him.

"Why are you still standing there, Romeo? Get out of here and turn the light off on your way out."

Rich did as Anna had ordered, closing the door as an added bonus. He walked through the open door of Kate's room, also closing that door. She was lying on her side in a heap on the bed, her knees pulled as closely to her body as her stomach would allow.

"Honey, are you okay?"

Her face stayed hidden, but her body expanded with a deep breath. "I have never been more humiliated in my life."

He smiled, amused by her overreaction. "Oh, it's not that bad."

"You weren't there!" she wailed as she flipped onto her back and yanked a pillow over her face.

"Well, what did you say to her?" He tried to hide the humor—and elation—he felt. "How suggestive were you?" His brows rose. "You didn't feel up your mom, did you?"

She rolled to face him, clearly unamused. "Can you *be* more smug?"

"Shut up and slide over."

For a split second he expected her to kick him out

on his sorry butt, especially when she got off the bed and crawled under the covers, lying down on the pillow. "Are you getting in?" she asked in a huff.

He looked at the beauty in front of him and was suddenly overcome with emotion. This woman was truly the only one who could complete him—make him whole.

She cracked a lid. "Please?" Rich crawled in next to her and she cuddled right into his arms. "Thank you."

Thirty Two

Having their parents visit had been nice—and excruciating. Kate loved having her house back. Just her and Rich—and the baby. Everything was falling into place. Her health was good, the baby's heart strong, as verified by Dr. Tipton only an hour ago.

Rich wanted to go to the appointment with her and looked really hurt when she'd refused. It was bad enough that she was second guessing her decision to keep him at a distance. Then to make it even harder, the wonderful man just kept being...wonderful. He was kind and patient—and loving.

She didn't deserve him.

Her thoughts drifted for a moment to Jesse. His reaction to the situation would have been so very different. There was no way he would have considered loving her with even the remote possibility that another man's baby grew in her womb. Hell, all it would have taken was to tell him she'd had sex with Rich for him to hit the road—after he raged and most likely put his fist through a wall.

Jesse was one man who wasn't capable of loving another man's child.

Rich though... Was he?

Kate pulled into the garage and let the door close before unlocking her door and opening it. Her swollen feet and ankles looked hideous. The ankle bone had all but been absorbed by the water-logged skin. Not to mention the ache that went along with it.

The house was quiet—and messy—as she entered the kitchen. By the look of things Rich had made dinner. She inhaled, sucking in the strong scent of lemon and other delicious aromas she couldn't name.

"Rich?" she called.

A loud crash and juicy curse answered from down the hall.

Her feet quickly carried her to where she knew Rich would be. The stench of paint fluttered up around her, assaulting her olfactory system. All of the doors were wide open, except one. Rich was in the nursery with the door closed. A lump clogged Kate's throat as she was once again reminded of his thoughtfulness.

Kate turned the handle and eased the door open slowly. Two things rushed at her, nearly knocking her over, paint fumes and heat. The window was wide open and sitting in the middle of the room was Rich. Blue paint smudges marred the perfection of his glistening bare chest. Both thighs of his light blue jeans had traces of a new hue, and even his brown hair was frosted with blue tints.

The walls now wore a coat of fresh paint, the most beautiful color that was nearly the same shade as Rich's eyes.

Scattered all over the floor were pieces of what would someday be a crib. Its box was leaned against the wall as if he were using it for assistance, like you would the lid of a jigsaw puzzle.

"Damn it," he muttered, a screw held between his teeth.

"Do you need some help?" she asked quietly.

He looked up to her, his frustration melting into surprise. Long fingers plucked the screw from his lips. "I didn't hear you come home. How did everything go? You okay? The baby?"

She nodded and leaned against the door jamb, her arms crossed over her stomach. "Everything's good. We're both healthy." Her eyes scanned the room with exaggeration. "Looks like you've been busy."

His eyes surveyed the disaster area then he smiled sheepishly and ran a hand through his hair. "Yeah...I was hoping to have it finished when you came home, but I'm...having a little trouble with the crib." He glared at the offensive pieces.

Kate laughed. "I can see that. Are you pulling the macho, I'm-a-guy-so-I-don't-need-instructions thing?" She waved a hand from the pieces to the box.

"I couldn't read them." He picked up a few more screws and tried to shove them into holes much too short. He shot a frustrated look over at the box and Kate couldn't contain her amusement. A laugh burst from her and she clamped a hand over her mouth when he glared at her. "You think you can do better?" he spat.

"I think you're making it harder than it needs to be. If you'd just use the directions...

"The directions, Kate—" He threw the unfolded, poster-sized directions at her which fluttered unoffensively at her feet. "—are in *Chinese!*" His exasperation only caused her to laugh harder. "Can you read Chinese, Kate? So much for your internet deal." A controlled throw deposited the screwdriver on the floor. "I need a shower then I'll finish dinner," he said, standing.

"You cooked?" Rich was full of surprises today.

"I can follow directions when they're in English!" Although her mood was light, his was still tense.

"Rich."

"What?" he snapped.

She walked over to him and wrapped her arms around him. He didn't return the embrace, just stood stone stiff against her. She pressed a kiss to his lips. "I love the paint. It's perfect. Thank you."

He sighed and his arms slowly slid around her. "I'm glad you like it." He turned her in a slow circle, keeping her tight against his chest, so she could admire each inch of the room. "I like this shade a lot."

"Me, too." She cradled his face between her hands and looked deeply into his eyes. "It's a very comforting shade."

His eyes twinkled as he smiled. She was suddenly overwhelmed by the need to feel his lips against hers. Their gaze was locked until at the last second when her eyes closed. His lips were soft, yet firm, and so deliciously warm, causing her blood to turn to lava.

He broke the contact after only a few brief seconds and gave her a quick chaste kiss, then rested his forehead against hers. Even that contact felt wonderfully familiar. Their eyes were again locked, and she felt him peering to her soul.

She loved this man with every ounce of who she was.

Her heart, her soul, screamed for her to throw caution to the wind and give into everything she'd been denying. *Don't think, just feel.*

But feeling led to heartache, and one day, when Rich walked away, if she let herself give in now, she would be devastated, irrevocably broken.

Her eyes closed and she concentrated on Rich; the scent of his natural cologne, his strong heartbeat, the steady pace of his breathing...the unmistakable growl of his stomach.

She started to giggle and a low, deep chuckle rumbled next to her ear. "Sounds to me like you're hungry," she noted, her hands rubbed the bare skin of his toned abdomen.

"For more than just food," he answered suggestively,

his hands rested on her bottom. "Damn pelvic rest." She didn't answer but had often had the same thought. "Give me ten minutes and I'll shower, then you can help me finish dinner." He kissed her quickly before escorting her out of the room. "Kate, I don't want you to go back in there for a few days because of the paint fumes."

Kate wanted to laugh, wanted to explain that lead paint hadn't been used since the 1970's, but placed his hands on her belly and smiled. "I won't set foot in there until you say it's okay. Okay?"

"Thank you." He closed the door and left her standing alone in the hallway.

When the shower water turned on, Kate tried not to think of Rich, completely naked, with water and soap suds caressing every inch of his glorious skin on the other side of the door. Knowing him the way she did, she would wager her last dime that the door wasn't locked— and that he wouldn't turn her away.

Her body heated with that knowledge—that *very* dangerous knowledge. She had to keep herself occupied until Rich was dressed. Television. Yes, that would be a great distraction.

Kate curled up on the couch, using the remote to flip from one uninteresting show to the next. Her eyes were on the flashing pictures on the screen, but her mind was concentrating on only one thing. One hot, delectable, make your toes curl with a kiss thing.

✕✕✕

Rich tried not to think of the sweet moments he'd just shared with Kate. He'd been frustrated and intoxicated by her all in the space of a few minutes. She'd loved what he'd done so far with the nursery, and that warmed his heart. Made him want to pound his fists on his chest like Tarzan. He was male, taking care of his female and their child.

A growl rumbled in his chest, and he had to laugh at the overwhelming surge of testosterone driven absurdity.

Rich loved how natural things were between Kate and him. When she let them. It had been good to get his parents approval, but getting the thumbs-up from Anna had been more satisfying.

He rinsed the soap out of his hair and stood under the luke warm spray for another few seconds before shutting the water off, ripping the shower curtain open. The towel was soft as it absorbed the water from his skin.

His legs stepped into a pair of boxers then a clean pair of jeans. With a quick swipe of the brush over his hair, he tried to calm the insanity before he tugged a t-shirt over his head and ruined the attempt.

He was both excited and nervous as he jerked open the bathroom door. Kate had a tendency for changing her mood so fast it put Shea to shame. Rich knew it had to do with her hormones, and hoped she would still be the sweet, teasing Kate he'd left a few minutes ago.

He rounded the corner to find her perched on the couch, remote in hand, concentrating a little too hard on the TV. Rich could hear the announcers and said, "I didn't know you were a fan of bull-riding."

Her eyes flashed to him and the TV flipped off. "Oh ... there's um ... nothing on," she stammered through a blush.

He smiled and eventually so did she. "Do you want to hang out here or..."

"I'll help with dinner. I really need something to get my mind off things."

"What kind of *things*?" he asked with a suggestive undertone.

She raised her brows and blushed a deeper red, and

Rich knew that it had to do with at least one of the things that had also been on his mind. His lips lifted as did his brows. She rolled her eyes. "Let's eat," she snorted and headed off in the direction of the kitchen.

He laughed as her hair swished along her back with the shaking of her head.

Once in the kitchen, Rich put Kate to work with a couple chicken breasts and the George Foreman grill while he followed the recipe he'd printed off the internet. Delicious scents wafted through the kitchen and his taste buds ached to sample just a morsel of what they would soon receive. But Rich abstained. He wanted Kate to taste it first. Watching her eyes close in bliss at the taste of the food he'd so lovingly prepared with his own hands would be reward enough.

"You almost done?" she asked as the chicken met the plate. "Should I slice these up or what do you want..."

"Slice them, please." He added a few more shakes of the seasoning he hadn't heard of before today.

The knife met the wood of the cutting board with a staccato rhythm then Kate came to stand next to him where he was whisking the bubbling mixture. She sucked in an exaggerated breath. "It smells awesome."

"I have your favorite ice cream for dessert, if you'd like to start there."

"No, I can wait." She smiled.

Rich turned off the heat and pulled the lid off the sticky rice. After grabbing two plates from the cupboard, he filled them with rice, chicken, and the special, homemade sauce.

They sat across from each other and Kate filled her fork. She smiled at him then opened her mouth and wrapped her lips around the fork. Just like he'd hoped, her eyes widened then fluttered closed. "Mmm," she moaned, lifting her napkin to her lips.

With a great sense of satisfaction, Rich filled his fork and popped it into his mouth. His taste buds revolted as his gag reflex kicked into gear. He leaned over his plate and spat the contents of his mouth back onto the plate then downed the contents of his glass.

Kate giggled softly and Rich stared at her. "Aargh!" he groaned, swallowing hard, "That's horrible! Please tell me you didn't swallow that crap."

She unfolded her napkin to expose the mouthful she couldn't consume. "Where'd you get the recipe for *that*?"

"The Iron Chef made it look so easy, and I printed it off the internet." Rich shrugged. "The only problem I had was finding the lemongrass. So I made it."

"You *made* lemongrass?" Her eyes narrowed with suspicion. "How did you do that?"

He suddenly felt like a fool and was sure his explanation wouldn't redeem him. "Well—" *How to explain this?* "—I went out back and carefully cut some *grass* then I brought it in and soaked it in lemon juice all morning."

Her green eyes twinkled as she smiled and tried not to laugh.

"Where else was I supposed to get it?"

She laughed and pointed to the windowsill where five little potted plants resided. "The one that looks like grass." A laugh exploded out of her. "Lemongrass."

"Well, hell!" Rich couldn't believe he'd been such an idiot.

Kate gathered her plate and carried it to the counter before she returned and took Rich by the hand. Her hands were strong, warm on his as she tugged him out of his chair. She wrapped her arms around him and sighed.

"Thank you, Rich, for everything. The fact that you tried to make a great dinner *does* count for something."

She leaned up on her toes and soft lips touched his. "Come on, pizza or Chinese?" She winked. "Maybe we can get the instructions for the crib from a fortune cookie."

Thirty Three

With a whistle on his lips, Rich strolled into the kitchen. Kate was sitting at the table, stirring the mug of hot chocolate that had replaced her morning coffee. He leaned down to kiss her on the cheek before going over to pour some coffee into his mug.

"What are we going to name our baby?" he asked as he sat down.

"*My* baby," she answered, just as he was afraid she would.

They'd lived under the same roof—sleeping in the same bed—for days and nothing had changed. He still loved her and she still pushed him away. His teeth ground together and he ran a rough hand through his hair. He was so tired of having this fight with her. She was full of excuses as to why they weren't a perfect fit, and he was beyond tired of hearing them. "I can't do this anymore." His voice was quiet—steady, confident.

Panic flashed in her eyes but quickly vanished under a composed face. "I expected this to come at some point."

Rich stood, the force knocked the chair to the floor with a crash. The grinding of his teeth and rushing of blood echoed behind his ears. "I can do *this*." He motioned between them. "What I can't do is deal with your insistence at pretending to be bipolar. I lived that life once. You once told me to love you or hate you. Well,

I'm making the same request. Love *me* or hate *me*, Kate. You have to choose."

She opened her mouth, but Rich held up a hand to stop her before she could utter a word. He hadn't said his peace yet. "I love you, Kate. I love you so much it hurts sometimes. Haven't you figured out that I don't care if your son is born with purple spots and orange hair? I love that little boy growing inside you, and if you truly believe me incapable of continuing that love once he's born, then you, my dear, don't know me at all."

He righted the chair and purposely avoided eye contact with Kate. His speech had gone from honest to over the top and, knowing Kate, it had brought her to tears. If he stayed long enough to process those tears, the dramatics would be for naught. Two strides took him to the counter, where he plucked his keys from the basket.

"When you figure out what the hell you want, call me." And with his back to her he growled, "Until then, leave me the hell alone."

She sniffed, and it took every ounce of control he had to not turn around and comfort her. *Damn fool!* But when she didn't mutter another sound, it made the departure slightly easier. He'd laid his ultimatum out on the table, made his intentions clear. The ball was now in her court.

Safely in the confines of his car, he turned the key and began to drive down the street, with the phone conspicuously on the passenger seat. At the stop sign, three houses down, it rang.

That didn't take long, he thought with smug arrogance. "Yeah," he snarled, not wanting her to rethink her apology.

"Is this Rich Spencer?" the male voice asked.

He sat up straight in the seat and checked the caller id for who the voice might belong to. A local number, not one he recognized. "Yeah, who's calling?"

"Rich, I'm calling about your wife, Shea."

"Ex-wife," he corrected. "What about her?"

"This is Reese Raskey. Shea used to ... work for me."

"Yeah, so?"

"Mr. Spencer, I regret the affair that Shea and I had, and I ended it as soon as I realized how much I truly had to lose. When my wife found out, I nearly lost it all and I... Never mind. I just wanted to let you know that I think I know where Shea is."

The validation of an affair should have been like a sucker punch to the gut, should have made him feel like a complete and utter fool, but all Rich could think about was Kate and keeping her safe. "Did you call the police?"

"No, I can't get involved with that crazy bitch again—in any way. Someone seems to be staying at my wife's family's cabin up Immigration Canyon. She's been there at least a month—with all the comforts of home." He then rattled off an address and Rich pulled over to the curb to draw himself a map as Reese described the twists and turns of where to find the cabin. "Do what you want, Mr. Spencer, call the police or don't, just leave me out of it."

The call disconnected without another word. Rich pounded some numbers into his phone.

"Chief Brown," Rich barked.

"And who's calling?" The woman on the other side of the line sounded a little miffed by his order.

"Rich Spencer. I have news on the whereabouts of Shea Spencer."

There was no response except for the hold music in his ear. He sucked in a deep breath, through his nose, blowing it slowly between his lips. If Shea really was at the cabin, this could all end today.

"Tell me you're not just shittin' me." Reggie sounded practically giddy.

"No shittin' here." Rich relayed the information he'd gotten in his brief phone call, and as he pulled into the Sheriff's Department parking lot, he said, "I'm right outside, let's go get her."

Reggie walked through the front doors and gave Rich an *'are you kidding me?'* glare. The Chief studied his face for a few minutes then shook his head and ordered one of his men to grab an extra bulletproof vest. Rich eagerly fastened the Velcro straps, making sure that it fit properly, then ducked into the passenger seat of the patrol car—his camera tucked safely in the backseat. There was no way he was going to miss catching the moment they shoved Shea's crazy, guilty-as-sin ass in the back of a patrol car—sporting a set of fancy, new bracelets.

With an entire Swat team in tow, they headed up the canyon without sirens. "No need to let her know we're coming," Reggie told him with a smile.

The radio traffic was a tactical operation in the making, strategizing and re-strategizing. There was actually a rookie behind the glass in the backseat with a topo map of the area, debating the best route to take.

"Time is of the essence," Reggie told Rich. "We have to strike while the iron's hot." And Rich couldn't agree more.

× × ×

The rattle of the mail truck putted down the street, and Kate lifted the blinds to watch as letters were slid into the box on the curb. She needed something to take her mind off the fight she'd had with Rich, and the mail would do it for a few minutes at least.

Her hips moved from side to side in a waddling motion. *This part of pregnancy sucks!* she thought with a soft groan. Truth be told, most parts of pregnancy sucked. The only promising part of the ordeal was the prize you got in the end. That made it worth the sickness, the uncomfortable months, and the fatness.

The box opened with a soft rasping of metal against metal and Kate peered in to see a stack of three letters. She plucked them up and closed the box again, starting back for the house as she sorted which ones needed immediate attention and which ones could wait. A bill from Directv, which wouldn't be a surprise since the same one had come in an email only two days ago. She tucked it under her arm and looked at an envelope from her doctor. Two rips later revealed a statement of charges that had been sent to the insurance company.

The third letter, however, had Kate's curiosity piqued. There was no return address and it was hand addressed to her by what looked to be a female. Kate tore at the envelope, carefully aggressive since she didn't want to harm the contents. It was probably just junk mail, but what if it was something important.

The white piece of paper was folded in thirds and, as Kate entered the house, she unfolded it. The curvy letters formed only a few words...

Kate,

I will take back what is mine.

One way...

Or another.

The contents of Kate's stomach rose up the back of her throat, and she rushed into the bathroom to give it a place to spew. The letter was still clutched in her fist when she bent over the toilet, and as she dropped it to the floor a picture fluttered from the envelope.

It was of Kate and Rich coming out the front door, smiling. There was a red circle with a slash over Rich's face. *...Take back what is mine,* Kate thought, the knot in her stomach growing, the lump in her throat holding the vomit from coming out.

Her mind raced with the ramifications of that letter—that picture. One, Shea knew where she lived. Two, she was determined to take Rich away from her by any means. Just like she had Jesse. Three, Rich was gone.

Rich!

Kate raced into the other room, locked the door, dead-bolted it, and ran to find her cell phone. Speed dial was a great thing when you were in a hurry, and a panic. His voice answered after only one ring, voicemail. She hung up and tried again—and again.

If she thought it'd been panic before, now she was drifting into the realm of complete and utter terror. *One way … or another. One way … or another,* Kate's thoughts chanted.

Shea was capable of anything—literally. She'd even proved to be comfortable with murder and she now had her sights on Rich.

Tears stung Kate's eyes as once again she dialed Rich's cell. "Dammit," she screamed, releasing some tension when her fist made contact with the wall. It actually felt good to feel a physical pain instead of the emotional one plaguing her.

Tender, swollen fingers dialed the police station. "Chief Brown, please." Her voice shook.

"I'm sorry, he's out."

Kate could hear that there was more to the story than just that he was getting a cup of coffee or was in the men's room. "This is Kate Callahan and I...I've received a letter from Shea Spencer."

"Okay, I'll let him know."

"Did you hear me?" Kate could hear the frantic tone in her voice and cringed. "I said Shea Spencer threatened me … in a letter … that came to *my house!*" She tried to tell herself to get a grip, not that it did any good.

"Okay, I'll let him know."

The line disconnected, and helplessness slithered up and around Kate to constrict the life out of her. Not only had a murderer figured out where she lived, but the police didn't care. She had to find Rich and warn him. He would care.

Her hands were shaking so badly that it took three times to finally punch the correct combination of numbers to get the station where Jordan answered, "KHB."

"Jordan," Kate whispered, panic clouded the word.

"Kate, you okay?"

She wasn't okay, couldn't be—wouldn't be—until she had Rich in her arms. "Have you seen Rich?" she asked with a quiver in her voice.

"No ... why?" There was no doubt she was making him nervous.

"Have you heard from him?"

"No ... why?" A scratching, then muffled speech reached Kate's ears, and she could hear Olivia in the background. "Kate, are you okay?" Jordan asked again.

"Yes. No. I hope so." She didn't know what she was. "I *really* need to talk to Rich," she said honestly. It was the only thing she knew.

✕ ✕ ✕

Rich didn't say much during the thirty minute ride up the canyon, just kept looking at his phone that only beeped with a message *searching for signal*. It wasn't as if Kate could get a hold of him anyway, he realized, and turned off the power. There was no need to waste the battery and the beep was grinding on his already raw nerves.

The windy dirt road was lined by pine trees Rich

couldn't name, the tall ones that seemed to touch heaven, and the trees with white bark that everybody in Utah called Quakies. Rich really liked them because of the snapping sound the leaves made when the wind blew. The scenery was beautiful, calm, the polar opposite of his mood.

Vengeance was forefront on his mind, and his temperament raged like a violent storm. He was so consumed by negative emotion he could actually taste the vile bitterness on the back of his tongue.

"You got any gum?" he asked Reggie, concentrating on the blur of scenery.

Chief Brown pointed to the glove box while responding on the radio to the latest question from the SWAT guys. "Yeah, looks like the road going into the place is about half a mile long, although not that far as the crow flies. Wait at the mouth and we'll go in on foot."

There was an affirmative response and then silence, the first bit since the whole adventure had begun only an hour and a half ago. It seemed like it'd been days since the fight—the ultimatum—he'd given Kate this morning. His stomach clenched as he realized that it had been *an hour and a half,* and he wondered if she'd even tried to call.

The car eased to a stop and Rich all but jumped from the vehicle. Reggie shook his head. "Nope, you're staying here."

"Forget that, Reggie." He tugged at the back door and yanked the camera from its padded case. "That woman has done nothing but make my life miserable for years, and she nearly killed the love of my life. I will not miss seeing you guys take her down."

"You'll stay out of the way."

Rich wasn't sure if the sentence was a statement or a question, but answered it anyway, "Absolutely. I won't even breathe if it will get me up there." He patted the camera with his free hand and smiled. "And it will all be preserved for future generations."

Reggie snorted. "Fine." He motioned to the SWAT team, who began to run in single file with their weapons tight to their bodies.

It didn't take long for Rich to realize he wasn't in nearly as good of shape as he'd thought. Reggie's feet thudded against the dirt at the same pace as Rich's, but the air still moved easily in and out of Reggie's lungs, whereas Rich fought the urge to huff and puff. He tried to blame it on the piece of equipment in his hand but knew it was only an excuse. The time in the gym had made his body rock hard, but he definitely needed to do more cardio. He tucked that little piece of knowledge into the back of his mind.

Reggie's hand flew up and the non-tactical guys all pulled to a halt. The camera was on Rich's shoulder in a blink and he surveyed the scene through the lens. The log cabin was set in the middle of a clearing, one car parked right in front—a bright red BMW.

"That's hers," Rich whispered.

Reggie nodded then put his finger to his lips.

As Rich zoomed in as much as he could on what was happening another thirty yards in the distance. The television could be seen through a window, and there was the horrible screeching that he recognized as Shea's singing. After all this time, all this worry and fear, she was here.

I'll be damned, he thought.

This was all really going to end today. Did he dare hope? With Shea out of the picture, one of the weights would be lifted from his shoulders—today. A smile spread to his lips as he thought of taking the news back to Kate.

Kate.

Damn, his thoughts always returned to her. Even

when he was supposed to be mad at her.

Two SWAT members approached the house and knocked, then stood on each side of the door and waited as if they were expecting the gunfire that came through it. Birds flew into the air with squawks of protest for the disturbance of their serenity. Rich had to admit he had a few protests of his own, like the fact that he'd just missed the first major event of this arrest. With a flip of his thumb, the red record light turned on.

✕ ✕ ✕

Shea wrapped her fingers tightly around the firearm that had just blown a hole through the door. She knocked the kitchen table over on its side and hunkered down behind the protection it provided. This was so not the way she'd planned for today to go.

"Shea Spencer, come out with your hands up. You're surrounded," said a deep voice, magnified by a megaphone.

Shea wasn't sure if she was more irritated or saddened that she'd been found before she was ready. She went with irritation, not wanting to sound weak. "I'll never come out, not until I have come up with a way to regain what is mine," she screamed back, unsure if they'd heard her.

"And what is that, Shea?" came the simple question.

"She took it all from me," she explained in a desperate yell. Her hand gripped the cool metal in her hand. "Don't you understand? I can't let her keep what is *mine.*"

"Who is *she*?" The voice trying to talk her outside was far too calm for her liking.

The *she* in question made Shea's blood boil. Her eyes looked at the wall where she'd put up a picture surrounded by a red lipstick bulls-eye, a constant reminder of who her target was. "That *bitch,* Kate Callahan. She ruined my life."

"And how is that?" the idiot asked.

Shea's finger was getting fidgety on the trigger, and she contemplated offering another warning. "Cut the shit! You and I both know she took Rich."

"She didn't take..."

That voice. That beautiful deep voice brought tears to her eyes. She ran to the window and looked out. "Rich?" she called, tears in her voice. "Rich, is that really you?"

Rich was there, standing next to the guy with the megaphone, a bulletproof vest strapped around his chest. "Yeah, I'm here, Shea."

Her heart soared. This was the moment she'd been waiting for for months. "Oh, Rich, I knew it was only a matter of time before you'd come looking for me." A movement drew her attention to the side where a slew of armed men surrounded the building. They drew their weapons closer. Her survival instinct flared, driving her back inside. "Why did you bring the National Guard, Rich, you know I'd never hurt you. I love you."

There was a long pause, then Rich called, "That's not why I'm here."

Bile rose up the back of her throat and her heart stopped beating for just a moment. This was not how she'd planned their reunion. She'd gone into hiding, been completely alone, miserable, waiting for this moment. Her sisters would've helped, even had the means to offer her the assistance she needed, but she hadn't seen them. Only that slimey brother-in-law of hers, Ray, had been around right after the stabbing. He'd proven to be an ally, one she would have never turned to. He gave her a KAHR 9mm, a shotgun, and an envelope with all the cash he'd had on hand. As a final farewell, he'd offered to foot the bill on a one-way ticket to Mexico.

She'd declined, walked out of the house, and out of her sisters' lives. Some days the loneliness was overwhelming. She didn't have anyone. Not her sisters—or Rich. Hot tears slid over the cold skin of her cheeks.

"Come on, Shea. Come out and we'll talk." Rich's voice brought her out of her misery.

"We'll talk? Does that mean you're done with that bitch and ready to come home?"

"Don't call her that," he snapped.

Blood bubbled behind her ears. "Why not? She wrecked our home, our marriage."

"Shea—" His voice was low, controlled. "—let's not do this by screaming through the forest. Come out and we'll talk."

"I hate her!" she yelled, not wanting to give in to the tears that threatened.

"It's time to come out now, Shea," the man said through his megaphone.

"Do you love me?" she asked through vocal cords that wouldn't work. Her throat was closing off with choked emotion. The question hung in the silence, and Shea wondered if Rich had even heard her.

"Please come out, and we'll talk."

"Do you love me?" she asked again, hating the desperation in her voice.

Rich's silence spoke louder than any words could have. She'd suspected, obsessed, known that he'd stopped loving her. But right here, right now, his lack of words was the final dagger in her heart.

Shea couldn't live in a world where Rich Spencer didn't love her.

✕ ✕ ✕

A gunshot rang out through the forest.

"Shea! Shea, are you okay?" For the first time since this all started there was a tone of panic in Reggie's voice. There was no need for the megaphone as he continued to yell, "Shea? Come on, girl, answer me. Talk to me."

But there was no answer.

"Shea," Rich called again. "Talk to *me*." The animosity he'd felt only moments before melted into pity. His brows pinched together. Did he actually feel sorrow to think Shea was dead? Yes, he did.

"Go!" Reggie ordered into the radio headset.

Men in black tactical uniforms flooded the house in a surreal motion that was exactly as Rich had seen it done on the cop shows on TV and in the movies. But this time he *knew* the dead body they'd find inside, and he had to bite back the bile that rose into the back of his throat. He wanted Shea behind bars where she couldn't hurt Kate—or anyone else—not six feet under. But Shea had decided otherwise.

It was over. The horrific ordeal Rich had been living had come to an abrupt end—a *dead* end. It was really over.

"She's ... dead," Reggie whispered from next to him. "I'm sorry."

Rich appreciated the sympathy, but straightened his shoulders, blinked back the tears that burned his eyes. Now that this chapter in his life was over, he needed to move on. He needed to get back to Kate. "It was her choice, not ours." He cleared his throat. "I just really need to get out of here."

Reggie nodded, the tender emotion was still in his eyes. "Go ahead and go back to the car. I have to get the investigation started. I'll get one of the deputies to take you back."

"That'd be great. I'd really like to get this video back to the station." He turned to look at Reggie. His entire body was numb, especially his brain. "That's okay, right? I mean, we can put this on the news, right?" *Always the news hound*, he thought, disgusted with himself.

"Yeah, if you can wait 'til the 6:00."

"Deal." Rich turned to jog back to the car.

"Rich." Rich stopped but didn't face the older man whom he considered a friend. "Give Kate a hug for me. I'm glad she's finally safe."

✕ ✕ ✕

It was the middle of the afternoon, and Rich was grateful for the lack of people in the newsroom. He walked right into Dale's office, regurgitated the events of his morning and watched as Dale's eyes bulged out of his head and he started to salivate.

"And you were the only camera there?"

"Yeah," he answered flatly. "I'll give you copy and the footage, and then I'm gonna need a couple days to ... recover."

"Fine. Yeah. Done." His head moved up and down with each new acceptance.

A computer would have been the fastest way to pound out the copy, but right now, Rich needed to feel close to Kate. Her desk was empty, her laptop at home with her. There were a dozen computers sitting unused but Rich parked his butt in her chair and began scribbling on a notepad.

Twenty minutes was all it took to have the story of what happened on the yellow, lined paper. He handed it to Dale. "You'll need to send someone for soundbites, but here's the copy for the voice-over. I'm outta here."

Grateful that he'd managed to miss Nate, Jordan, and Olivia, Rich slid behind the wheel and hurried out of the parking lot. Luck had been on his side thus far and he wasn't willing to press it.

He'd foolishly left Kate's with only the clothes on his back and, although he wouldn't have to work tomorrow, it would be nice to at least have a change of clothes and a toothbrush. He'd just stop by and grab a few things.... He knew he was lying to himself. All of those things could be purchased with one quick stop at Wal-Mart. What he wanted was to see Kate, to see if things had changed, to tell her she was safe now.

He used his key to open the front door and wondered if she'd request that he give it back when she kicked him to the curb. Kate was sitting on the couch, her arms wrapped around her legs, her forehead resting on her knees. She looked so beautiful, so fragile. He wanted to rush to her and hold her, to relay the events of the afternoon. Instead, he cleared his throat and waited for her reaction.

She looked up, her eyes puffy and red—and full of complete surprise. "Rich," she squealed. He'd never seen her move so fast in the months since she'd returned. She nearly flew across the room and threw her arms around his neck. Kisses covered his cheeks before lingering on his lips. "You're okay."

This was not the reception he expected, not that he was going to argue with it. "Yes, I'm okay."

"I've been calling all day."

Rich pulled his phone from his pocket and held the button to turn the power back on. "I was ah ... out of the service area and..."

She cut him off with another kiss. "Listen Rich, I've done a lot of thinking today. A lot," she added with a laugh. "I got a taste of what it would be like without you in my life. My mind can get pretty creative and I worried..." She shook her head. "All I know is that without you in my life, it's not really worth much."

A stab of panic pierced his heart. "Kate,

never...*never* say anything like that again. Your life is worth so much."

She shrugged. "I know, I'm just trying to say that I..."

Rich knew where this was going, and as much as he wanted to hear that she loved him and wanted them to have a future together, he wanted her to know that she didn't have to fear Shea. She didn't need to keep him around because she needed a live-in bodyguard. He placed his fingers on her lips and kissed the corners of her mouth. "Shea's dead."

"What?" she asked in a combination of shock and relief. "When?"

"Today. I got a tip and I...I was there when she stopped the police from taking her alive."

Kate was full of surprises and this moment was no exception. "Are you okay?" The question came with no hint of gloating.

Rich nodded. "I'm just glad the whole thing's over. So anyway, I'll just grab my things." He removed her arms from his neck and went down the hall to his room. Rich slid the drawer open and began to pull out a pair of jeans and boxers.

"Rich?" Kate asked from the doorway. "Did you listen to a word I said?" He chanced a glance at her face which was drawn into insecure lines. She walked to the bed and sat on the edge, then patted the spot next to her.

The bed dipped under his weight and Kate slid closer to him, only to move away. He worried that this was a bad idea until she lifted her leg and tucked it under the other while turning to face him. Her small hands grasped at his with gentle eagerness. "Rich, please look at me."

He'd never been able to deny her, and this moment was no different. She was so beautiful.

"I spent most of the day today thinking Shea had gotten to you, that she'd finally gotten her revenge on me by taking you out of my life." She explained about a letter she'd gotten in the mail, and Rich had to keep reminding himself that the threat was gone to keep from going ballistic. "In the hours that seemed to drag on forever, all I could think about was how things were left this morning and how I'd made the biggest mistake of my life by dragging this out for so long." She sighed and squeezed his hands when he looked away. "I love you, Rich."

"We both knew that already."

"Shh." She leaned forward and pressed her soft lips to his. "Please, let me finish." He offered her a small nod then shifted to face her a little more. "I do know that you love this baby." Her eyes made a subtle glance toward her stomach. "I also know that you're capable of still loving this baby even if he is Jesse's. I also know that it's not fair to make you raise another man's child." Tears glistened on the edge of her already puffy eyes. "I won't hate you if you decide it's too much when we know the paternity of the baby, but until we know for sure..." she paused. "Rich, I need you. I love you."

"I'm not going anywhere." He kissed her, his lips hard on hers. She sighed into his mouth, and the taste sent fire through his bloodstream. Needing to taste more of her, he traced the outside of her lip with his tongue. She opened to him and he plunged into her mouth, devouring her.

With the gentle pressure of his lips, she eased back onto the bed. He followed her, never breaking contact, careful to keep his weight off of her. Warm hands moved under his t-shirt, the cool air from the room blew across his back. He broke the kiss only long enough to tug the shirt from his body and toss it over his shoulder.

"Where were we?" he asked.

"Right here." Her hands gripped his face before a kiss he felt in his toes touched his lips. "And here," she whispered as her tongue tickled down his neck causing a serious case of goose bumps to be raised. Among other things.

He growled and took both of her hands in one of his to pin her to the bed. "Is torture on the itinerary?"

Her big green eyes flashed then darkened with desire. "I've been a very bad girl, quite naughty to you. I think you should... Oh!" Her hands pulled from his grip and flew to her belly, although Rich had felt the kick that had left her breathless.

He kissed her lightly on the lips then lifted her shirt to press another one to her exposed belly. "Thank you for reminding us, little one. Damn pelvic rest."

She groaned as her hands pounded the mattress. "Couldn't have said it better myself."

Thirty Four

Life was good.

Rich couldn't remember the last time he'd been so happy, so content with everything. Had he ever?

His clothes were still in the guest room, but each night he slid into bed next to Kate and held onto her with all his strength. She had become special to him the second their eyes met and had captured his heart in only a few sentences. The time it had taken to come to this point had been more misery than ecstasy, but here they were.

The baby was a few short weeks away, and then life would be perfect. Kate would see that the paternity didn't matter because Rich would be the baby's daddy. He pulled the ring out of his underwear drawer and examined it for the thousandth time. He ran his finger over the shiny diamond and smiled.

He wanted to rush into the other room and slide the tiny piece of gold on her finger while she showered. Not the most romantic of proposals, so he would wait. He had a plan for how it would happen and couldn't wait for the events that would lead to popping the big question.

"Rich?" Kate called from the bedroom.

He slid the ring back under the confines of the cotton underwear and called back, "In here, love."

She appeared in the doorway, fully dressed, trying desperately to get the strap of her sandal to stay on her heel. "Have you seen my other shoe?"

Life had taken on a very married feel, completely comfortable. Hell, he'd resorted to helping her look for her shoes.

Yes, he thought, *life* was *good.*

Walking back into their room, he bent to the edge of the bed where she'd undressed the night before and lifted the bedspread from the floor. He dropped to his knees and leaned over to look under. There it was. The lost shoe was about eighteen inches under the bed. No wonder Kate couldn't find it.

"Show off," she grumbled as he handed it to her. "There's no way I could have found that under there."

His hand gripped her by the shoulders as he kissed her quickly on the lips. He then leaned to whisper in her ear, "Admit it, Kate, you *need* me."

She reached around and filled her palm with one of his ass cheeks. "In more ways than one." Her brow arched while a smirk lifted the side of her mouth.

He kissed that smirk. "If you don't leave right now, two things are going to happen."

"Oh, yeah?" she baited him.

"One, you're going to be late." A trail of wet kisses moved up her neck toward the place he knew made her crazy just under her ear.

"Um hum." It sounded like a purr. Her dark lashes fell to cover her green eyes.

"And we're going to break the pelvic rest rule." His tongue traced her magic zone, and she melted against him.

"Damn pelvic rest," she muttered on a sigh and he laughed. "I really ... have to go." It was obvious he'd had an effect on her by the way she hurried away from him. Her hands tugged on the hem of her skirt, smoothing at it. "Do I need to fix my lipstick?"

He raised a brow. "Come here, I'll fix it for you."

"No," she said, holding up her hand, "I'll do it myself. Just go fix something else." Her feet moved as fast as they could in an attempt to get her away from him. When he followed her, she glanced over her shoulder. "Please Rich, I can't ... um ... you're too..."

Kate paused to gather her things, and Rich stepped up behind her, took her hips in his hands. "Too what?"

Her head fell loose on her neck as though she'd lost the battle. "Yummy," she whispered.

The deep male arrogance in him flew through the roof. Never before had he ever been described as yummy. "Really?" he growled in her ear.

"Rich," came the soft warning.

"Soon..."

A defeated groan blew through her lips. "You do know there's six weeks of ... no sex after the baby comes."

Two-by-four to the head. "No, I, uh, well..." The playful tone of the room was sucked out as if by a super-powered vacuum cleaner. "I'll wait. I love you," he told her with a chaste kiss to the lips, "and I can wait another six weeks."

He could wait. He'd wait an eternity for her to be his completely. Hell, it felt like he nearly had. Their road to happiness had been filled with potholes of every shape and size, some of them had taken up the whole damned road, but they would make it.

She stretched up on her toes, her belly rubbed lightly against his abdomen, and kissed him. "I love you, Rich."

Those words were ones he would never tire of hearing from her. Over the last few weeks since the scare, and death of Shea, Kate had been quite verbal with her feelings. Rich loved this new side of her. She'd stopped hiding from him—and herself.

"I'll call you when I'm on my way home." Keys

jingled in her hands. "Bye. I love you."

"You said that already," he reminded her with a smile.

"I feel like I have to say it now to make up for all the times I didn't say it since the day I met you." Green eyes twinkled. "You do know that I fell for you almost as fast as you fell for me."

"Good to know." He kissed her again. "If you don't get out of here right now, I'm not sure I'll be able to let you leave. I may just have to call in sick for you so I can hold you all day."

She laughed. "I'm leaving." He snorted in feigned offense, placed his hand on his heart as though she'd wounded him. Her head tipped to the side skeptically. "You know there's nothing I'd rather do, but I really need my sick time for after the baby comes."

"Maybe he'll come today," he said with a laugh. "Wouldn't that be great?"

"If he's coming today, you'd better get your butt in there and finish putting together the crib." She kissed him and slid past him to the door. "Call you later. Love you." And the door closed.

✕ ✕ ✕

"Hey, Kate," Jordan yelled when she walked through the door. "You're with Nate today. He's already got the address and you need to get going." He picked up the phone and his voice was now heard overhead, *"Nate Hughes to the newsdesk. Nate Hughes to the newsdesk."*

Kate skirted her desk with a glance to see if there was anything that looked pressing on the top of it. With nothing out of the ordinary, she walked over to where Jordan and Olivia had their heads together. "What's up?" Kate asked.

Olivia smiled. "Not much. How's Rich?" she asked

before Jordan shot a glare at her.

Everybody was still a little cautious of how to approach her relationship. Kate couldn't blame them. It had been an on-and-off kind of rollercoaster ride, she'd put more than just Rich through. She realized his friends—their friends—had been holding on for dear life too.

"Good." Kate turned to see if Nate was coming yet. If they were in a hurry, then he'd better...well, hurry. "Rich is putting the crib together. I think. At least he's got the English directions this time," she added with a giggle.

"Let's go, girlfriend," Nate bellowed from behind her. With his camera in one hand, he picked her bag from the floor, placed it over the opposing shoulder, and started to the door. "Be sure you buckle that seatbelt," he told her when she climbed into the passenger seat. "I don't need Rich's overprotective side coming at me."

Kate rolled her eyes, but forced the buckle together with a click. "Happy now?" He nodded and turned the engine over. "Where we headed?" she asked.

"Elementary school in Lehi. They're doing their own version of some Shakespeare play. I plan on being bored stupid."

I-15 at 75 miles an hour was not the perfect place to feel warm liquid running down your legs. Kate knew she hadn't just peed her pants. She was an adult for hell's sake. Adults did *not* pee their pants.

What possessed her to reach down and rub her hand on the fluid she wasn't sure, but what really shocked her was when her hand moved toward her nose. Then, to top it all off, she inhaled—deep.

At least it smelled like the ocean instead of ammonia. This was damned inconvenient, but it's not like she could control the when and where of her water breaking.

Her water breaking.

Her water *broke!*

She laughed out loud and slapped her hand on her thigh. Nate swerved, nearly into the other lane of traffic. "What the hell, Kate?"

"Um, Nate, I think you need to turn around."

His eyes were frantic as he searched for the reasoning of her bizarre request. "But the story..."

"Nate, my water just broke." Her voice was completely calm, which was a surprise to her.

Horns blared as Mario Andretti cut across three lanes of traffic to the shoulder where he decided to finally stop showing off his driving skills. His hands were clamped around the steering wheel, his face flashing from white to red which each puff of breath.

"Your water broke?" He sounded completely detached. "What do you mean your water broke?" The second question had the tinge of panic Kate expected.

"A baby is in a bag of water, and that bag breaks just before—"

"Wait!" His eyes flew to Kate's crotch and she jumped when he plucked at the hem of her skirt. "What the hell, Kate! You got baby-juice all over the seat!"

× × ×

Now that Rich had the English version of the directions Kate had printed off the internet, the crib went together quickly. He even took on the challenge of putting the sheet on the tiny mattress. That task was almost harder than putting the whole damned bed together.

When Kate asked his opinion, Rich had decided on a dinosaur theme for the little guy's room. Every little boy liked dinosaurs, right? After the blue paint had dried, wallpaper with pastel colored dinos finished the lower half of the room. Nate had helped nail the natural-stained chair rail to the wall. When it came time to hang the valance, Kate had held the ladder, just in case he fell—from the six inches off the ground. He loved that she worried about him.

Rich stood back and admired the room that had been transformed into a really great nursery. He leaned against the wall and slid down until he rested on his haunches. A little boy could be really happy in this room, he decided.

The phone in his pocket began to vibrate, and he reached around to pull it out. Nate's number flashed on the caller id which caused a slight increase in his heart rate. "Hey, man."

"It's okay Kate, I'm here and I can... Oh, Rich, the baby's coming." Nate had never sounded so hysterical in all the years Rich had known him. Rich felt a little hysterical in the seconds that followed, too.

He jumped to his feet and ran down the hall, grabbed his keys and headed for the car. "Where are you, man? Did you call an ambulance?"

There was a snapping of rubber gloves and Kate said, "Where the hell did you get those?"

"In my emergency kit." He sounded so pleased with himself. "Now just breathe, and I'm gonna..."

A slap resonated through the phone. "You're not gonna look up there."

Every muscle in Rich's body tensed and he had the sudden urge to slap Nate too. Slap him silly. "Nate!" he barked into the phone.

"It's okay, I've watched enough TV to be able to deliver a baby. I even recorded one for a crazy friend in college. I mean how hard can it be? Just put on the gloves and wait to catch it."

"Oh, that makes me feel so much better," Kate snorted. At least *she* still had her sense of humor. "Rich," Kate screamed, "I-15 just south of Thanksgiving Point."

Grateful to finally have a direction to go, Rich floored it. The engine roared in protest. He wanted to hang up, call 911 to make sure Kate had someone who wasn't an idiot to deliver their son, but didn't dare lose the connection.

The sound of movement reached Rich's ear. "I just need to find some towels. Hey, will a butt load of Taco Bell napkins work?"

"No!" Rich and Kate screamed at the same time, then Kate added, "You are not tying off the umbilical cord with a zip-tie, Nate. Just take me to the hospital."

"But—"

"Nate, step away from Kate."

"But—"

"Let me talk to her. Now!"

There was a shuffling of the phone and Nate's irritated voice said, "He wants to talk to *you.*"

"Rich, it's okay." She sounded too annoyed to be in too much pain—yet.

He thought back to everything he'd learned in their childbirth class. "How far apart are the contractions?"

"No contractions yet," she answered Rich, then said to Nate, "Dude, back off. I am not letting you see if he's crowning."

Rich was going to have to deck his best friend. Heaven help him, he was going to hit him—right in the nose. "I'm coming, love. Give me fifteen minutes. Have you called an ambulance?"

"Rich, there's no reason to. I'm fine. It could take hours before the contractions even start. My water broke."

"Baby-juice, man. Your woman got baby-juice all over my seat."

"Nate, shut up!" Kate snapped. "I'll pay for you to get it detailed, okay?"

"Okay," he muttered.

"No pain at all? You're sure?" Rich didn't want her to pull the I'm-fine-I-can-take-care-of-myself crap.

"None."

"Kate," he said skeptically, "you don't have to be brave."

"None," she answered again. "I just need you rescue me from this Neanderthal." Another slap. "Dammit, Nate, stop trying to lift my skirt!"

Rich couldn't stop the protective growl that rumbled in his throat. "Get off her, Nate." *Who's the Neanderthal now?*

"He's gonna have to kick your ass, you touch me again," Kate informed Nate.

Rich listened to Kate battle Nate, who kept insisting that he knew what he was doing, as he drove the last few miles to where he found the news vehicle with its hazard lights flashing.

The transmission protested as he threw it into park before the car was at a complete stop. He opened the door and ran up to where Kate was sitting in the passenger seat. She faced forward, her eyes trained out the windshield, her hands on her knees that were pressed tightly together. "No," she said, "get away from me, Nate."

"Nate," Rich roared, "enough!" He muscled his way through the brick wall that was his best friend and scooped Kate into his arms. "Thanks for everything you've done, but I'll take it from here."

✕✕✕

Hours passed and Rich wondered if the baby would ever come. By the time they'd reached the hospital at 12:14, the contractions had started. The clock said 1:33 when Kate said they were starting to *hurt a lot.* And at 2:55

she was screaming for an epidural.

Rich moved a lock of hair from her forehead and replaced it with a kiss. "You okay now?"

Her eyes were hooded, tired as she nodded. "Could you get me some more ice chips?"

He grabbed for the cup and offered her an ice covered spoon, watching as the monitor rose and fell with another contraction. "How's the pain?"

"Nonexistent. Epidurals are a gift from heaven." The ice crunched between her teeth. "Are you bored out of your mind yet?" she asked as her hand reached for more ice. "Have you eaten? You must be hungry. I'm hungry." Her stomach growled to punctuate her statement.

"I'm okay. Let's worry about you, okay?"

The door opened, and a short, heavy woman dressed in mauve scrubs waddled into the room. "Hello, Kate, I need to take your temperature and get an update on how you're doing down there."

It made Kate more comfortable to have Rich at her head anytime anyone looked 'down there', so he took his position. The nurse lifted the sheet, held Kate's knee and used her finger to...

"Oh," she said, her eyes shooting wide. "Don't laugh. Don't cough. Don't even sneeze or we're going to have this baby without a doctor."

"Wait. What?" Kate yelled as the nurse reached over her head to press the call button.

"Yes?" answered a voice.

The nurse started to pull the bottom portion of the bed away and lifted stirrups into position. "Get Dr. Tipton in here. Miss Callahan's ready to push."

"I am?" Kate asked, her eyes wide as she looked at Rich.

"You are," the nurse smiled. "In only a few minutes, that little one will be in your arms."

Kate wore the deer-in-the-headlight look, but Rich

couldn't find the energy to worry. He was consumed with an excitement that resembled Christmas morning before he knew Santa Claus didn't exist. He was minutes away from getting the greatest gift of his entire life. In mere minutes, he was going to be a father. A dad. The thought brought tears to his eyes.

Dr. Tipton came through the door and a flurry of activity burst to life. Three more nurses flooded into the room, each taking their battle stations. The doctor donned scrubs, little booties, and a pair of plastic gloves that nearly reached his elbows. He positioned himself at the foot of the bed, between her legs.

"You ready, Kate? I need a good hard push."

Rich mirrored the nurse, holding the back of Kate's thigh and put a palm on her lower back to successfully fold her in half. Her forehead crunched in concentration and she bore down.

"...Eight. Nine. Ten. Okay, take a breath and one..." Another round of pushing brought the head out, and one more brought a new life into the world.

Dr. Tipton tossed the baby from one hand to the other, not gentle at all. Rich wanted to tell him to be a little more careful with his son, but figured the older man knew what he was doing.

"It's a boy." He handed Rich a pair of scissors. "Dad, you wanna do the honors?"

Of course he did. He'd never wanted anything so much. By cutting that cord, Rich accepted responsibility for the boy, to be there for him, to teach him—to love him. He wrapped his fingers around the scissors and sliced through the rubbery cord in three awkward cuts. Tears burned his eyes and he blinked to keep them behind the lids.

A nurse snapped a thin white bracelet on his wrist. "This tells us that you're the daddy."

Two other nurses cuddled the baby in a blue

blanket, his head full of jet black hair the only thing remaining uncovered, and began to do their measurements against the far wall. It was obvious who the biological father of the little boy was. The baby had Jesse's blood running in his veins.

"I'll be right back," Rich told Kate, kissing her on the forehead. "I ... um ... there's something I have... I'll be back."

Then, with his heart and mind racing with what to do next, Rich walked away from Kate—and Jesse's son.

× × ×

Kate watched in horror as Rich removed himself from the room. The paternity was sure. One look at the sweet little boy left no doubt of which man had donated his half to the gene pool. The olive complexion and head *full* of straight dark hair that pointed in every wild direction verified that his father was Jesse.

And despite everything Rich had said, all the promises that he'd made, as soon as he saw that hair, the light in his eyes disappeared behind unshed tears. He cut the cord, but only because the doctor had practically shoved the scissors into his palm.

Tears welled in her eyes and poured down her cheeks as Dr. Tipton stitched the 'small rip' caused by the baby's exit. "It's completely natural to feel overwhelmed," he said softly. "It should pass as your hormones level out."

The nurse who had assisted her gave her a soft pat on the shoulder. "Go ahead and cry. None of us will mind."

They thought she was overwhelmed, that it was the delivery of her son that had her blubbering like a fool. But there was another piece to her puzzle that was missing. When Rich walked out that door, he took with him every hope, every dream she'd ever had. Her heart was breaking. That is what caused the tears to flow with such intensity.

Her body had just endured the greatest trauma to date, but it was the ache, the pain in her chest—the one she could still feel in her numb state—that had her reeling.

How was she going to raise her son alone? She'd convinced herself it would be easy, that she could do it, no problem—until Rich and his grand promises had convinced her otherwise. Now she was scared out of her mind and alone.

Completely alone.

The pillow soaked up the tears as they rolled from her cheeks to pool on the cotton. Kate wasn't sure how much time had passed since Rich had walked out of her room. It seemed like forever ago, and yet the recognition in his eyes as he stared at her son seemed to have happened only moments ago. And that moment replayed over and over in her mind.

The expression on his face wasn't recognizable, but the tears in his eyes were. He was hurt. She'd warned him, tried to protect him from himself. He'd been so damned determined to believe the baby was his. Hell, she'd hoped for it, prayed for it. But it seemed even a Higher Power couldn't change the paternity of a child.

She closed her eyes, but could still feel the tears as they trailed down her cheek. They'd taken the baby for his first bath, and Kate was glad that she had a few minutes to just sulk. The baby deserved a mother who wasn't a wreck and that is what she would give him from moment one.

"We're ba-... Kate?" asked a quiet female voice. "Do you want me to take the baby back to the nursery?"

"No, I ... I really want to hold him." She struggled to sit up with her lower half still feeling less than fully awake. When she was finally upright and propped against the back of the bed, her arms absorbed the tiny little boy. Another round of fresh tears started. These ones were the overwhelmed ones. "He's so ... perfect." Kate ran a finger over his plump cheek and the baby turned toward her touch, his mouth open wide. *He's rooting,* she thought, a smile on her lips.

The older woman smiled too. "Do you need any help breastfeeding?"

Kate hadn't thought to need help. Like Nate earlier, she wondered, *how hard could it be?* But now that the time had arrived, she wanted someone to at least show her the ropes. "Yes, please," she muttered, popping the buttons on her gown to expose her breast.

"Okay, cradle his head in your hand and guide him ... that's it."

A tiny mouth opened and accepted what Kate offered. The gentle tugging sensation sent shivers to her toes. It was weird and wonderful at the same time.

"Looks like he's going to be a good nurser." The nurse made some notes on the chart and turned to leave. "Let me know if you need anything."

"I'm a little hungry too, could I...?"

"Of course. I'll see what I can dig up."

"Thank you," Kate muttered. Her eyes were focused on the miracle in her arms, the little piece of Jesse that everyone back home had wished for. Dark lashes rested against tiny cheeks. Full lips were something else he'd gotten from Jesse. If she were honest with herself, this little boy looked nothing like her. He was all Jesse.

No wonder Rich left.

A war waged amongst her emotions. She loved this little boy exactly the way he was, but wished that his father would have been the man who could no longer love her.

The door to her room opened with a commotion; the

bouncing of rubber against wood and soft groans and grunts. When the blue and white balloons floated to the end of their strings, Rich stood there smiling with balloons in one hand, a vase full of roses in the other. Under his arm was the biggest stuffed dinosaur Kate had ever seen. And somehow, in the midst of everything else, he was holding a Sconecutter sack.

"Hi," he said quietly as he placed the roses on the table next to the phone. "I thought you might be hungry." A turkey sandwich and fries were pulled from the bag and laid out in front of her on the tray that he pushed over the bed.

She didn't know which emotion to give in to; the elation that he'd come back—with some of the best food Utah had to offer—or the anger that he'd walked out without a word. "Where did you go?" she asked quietly, unwilling to give into the emotions bubbling just under the surface.

He plopped down on the corner of the bed and gently ran a hand over the out of control hair of the baby. "I'm sorry I left the way I did. I just really needed to get some things."

"You don't have to do this. If you don't—"

"Kate." His voice was stern. "Don't. There is nothing I want more than to be with you and our son. I love you—both of you. I didn't run out on you."

"Then, what..."

The door opened again, another interruption. "Kate, I just wanted to give you the paperwork for the birth certificate." The nurse's eyes scanned the feast and she smiled. "Do you still want me to track down something for you to eat?"

"No, it looks like I'm taken care of in that department."

"Very good." She held up the stack of paperwork. "As I was saying, this is the stuff to fill out for his birth certificate. The sooner you can get to it the better." The stack was placed on the table by the roses and she turned to leave. "I'll let you get back to your meal."

Kate wanted to continue the conversation exactly where it'd been left off, but the moment was gone. She picked up a fry and popped it in her mouth. Rich rounded the bed and picked up the paperwork and a pen.

"You eat. I'll fill out this form." He waited until she pulled a one-handed manhandle on the sandwich and took a big bite. "Name? Well, I didn't get far before I don't know the answer." He looked at her expectantly.

She pointed to her mouth and chewed even slower as she tried to decide if the name she'd chosen would make him happy or send him running for the door again. When she didn't have any hope of pretending to be chewing, she opened her mouth to speak. "I was thinking of naming him Richard Jesse Callahan."

Rich's nose wrinkled and he tapped the pen on his lip. "Huh uh, I don't like it."

Her gut twisted and she nearly threw up the food she'd just swallowed. "Okay, well ... I guess, you should put Jesse Antonio Callahan then."

He frowned and shook his head. "That's not the part I didn't approve of." He clucked his tongue. "What do you think of Richard Jesse ... Spencer?"

Richard Jesse Spencer. Kate didn't miss the significance of Rich giving her son his last name. "Are you sure?"

He was already scribbling on the paperwork. "Yep, I'm already listed as his birth father."

"But..."

"As far as anyone will be concerned, Kate, he is mine. There will be no legal discrepancy. I called Claudia and had her look into it for me weeks ago." He stopped writing, looked up at her and smiled. "If you don't want to be listed as the mother, well, then I'm not really sure what I should put."

"Richard Jesse Spencer," she asked the little boy in her arms, "do you like that name, little one?"

He yawned and Rich laughed. "Good enough for me. Richard Jesse Spencer it is."

A few moments passed, and Rich placed the completed form on the table in front of her.

"All done. I just have one more thing to take care of." He again sat on the corner of her bed. "Kate Callahan, I love you so much it hurts sometimes. The days I spent without you in my life were miserable. I walked around as nothing more than an echo of myself. Let's build a life together; just me and you—and our son."

He stood and reached into his pocket and pulled out one of those big, bubble case things from a bubblegum machine at a grocery store. "It's not nearly as nice as the one back home in my underwear drawer, but I didn't want to leave you for that long. It's the only thing I could find between Smith's and the gift shop downstairs." A goofy smile lifted his lips as he popped the bubble and revealed a fuchsia plastic ring with a giant purple butterfly attached to it. "It took nearly ten bucks to get one this pretty." He held it up and took her left hand. "Kate Callahan, will you forever be the light of my life, the love of my life. Will you complete my family?" He tossed a glance at the baby. "'Cause Jesse needs a mommy, and his daddy needs a wife."

Tears flooded her eyes and her voice. The only answer she could offer was a passionate nod, which he accepted with an even more passionate kiss. The ring slid onto her pinky and Rich kissed the ring finger. "As soon as I can get home and back, I'll have the right one in place."

Kate held out her hand and admired her

engagement ring. "This one's perfect. Absolutely perfect. Just like you. I love you, Rich."

His large hands cupped her face, and she sighed into his mouth as a kiss that branded her as his was placed on her lips. Life was perfect. For the first time in a long time, life was perfect.

"I've got some calls to make," Rich announced when he broke the kiss. "Our parents are going to kill us that I've waited so long already." He took out his cell phone and flipped it open. "Are you okay if I tell people we're engaged or do you want..."

"I want you to shout it from the rooftops." Her heart was so full of emotion she was sure it might just burst. She was so loved and loved so much in return.

And while Rich made call after call, Kate was given time to reflect on just how much her life had changed over the last two years. She didn't regret what she'd had with Jesse. It'd given her a son and she would forever honor his memory by teaching little Jesse about the man who'd died before he was born.

But Kate couldn't deny the feelings she'd felt for Rich the moment they touched on that first day—and now she didn't have to.

She didn't think. She just felt.

And everything felt wonderfully perfect.

As a peaceful sleep overtook her, everything faded to black.

Epilogue

Five-year-old Jesse Spencer couldn't believe his dad was actually making him clean his room—by himself. Mommy always helped him because he was her little man. But Daddy had said she couldn't help today and that he was a big boy now.

If it meant he'd have to clean his room all by himself, Jesse would rather be little. His hand wrapped around the baseball that had been lying in the middle of the floor and he chucked it across the room. It bounced off one wall, knocked into another, before slamming into the picture of his Heaven Daddy, which landed on the floor with a crash.

Jesse's heart stopped, and he raced over to where the picture laid upside down, barely peeking out from behind the dresser.

"Please don't be broken," he muttered as his hand tugged the frame from where it was hiding. "Phew." Breath blew through his missing tooth, and he sat the picture back in its place.

"Hey, little man," Dad's voice said from the doorway. "You ready?"

Jesse tried to wipe the guilty look off his face before he turned to look at his dad. "Yeah, almost."

"Would you like me to help you finish?" Dad asked as he picked up the jeans and shirt Jesse'd been wearing a few minutes ago and stuffed them in the hamper. "We need to hurry if we're going to make Mommy's appointment."

Jesse was excited to go with Mommy and Daddy to the doctor's appointment. He was sure he was getting a sister and needed the doctor to tell everybody else. He'd decided they were going to name her JoJo like the clown on TV. She was going to be the best sister ever, not anything like Gracie, Nate and Roxy's little girl. Gracie liked to hit and bite and blame everything on Jesse.

No, JoJo was going to love him and be nice to him and let him do whatever *he* wanted.

Jesse couldn't believe how fast the room cleaned itself when Daddy helped. That always happened when Mommy helped too. When he had to do it by himself, it took forever for the toys to jump back in the toy box.

"All done," Jesse yelled as he ran to hug his dad. He loved the way his daddy's big arms wrapped around him. He always felt so safe.

"I love you, sport." Dad patted him on the bum and then took his hand to lead him down the hall to where Mommy was waiting in the kitchen.

"Are my men ready?" she asked with a smile.

"Yep, all ready and I cleaned my room all by myself 'cause I'm a big boy." He looked up with hopes that Dad would go along with the story.

Dad winked at Mom, which he did a lot, and said, "Jesse is definitely a big boy. His room looks great." He left Jesse standing by the door and walked to Mom where he kissed her.

Jesse cringed. "Ew! Dad, that's just gross!"

Dad—and Mom—laughed. "Someday, sport, you won't think so."

"Someday ... in a really long time," Mom added, kissing Dad on the cheek.

"My hope for you, son, is that you'll find someone you love as much as I love your mom, and that she will love you back." Dad's hand rubbed on Mommy's tummy. "And that she will give you two great kids to love."

"I want seventeen kids." 'Cause seventeen sounded so much better than just two.

"Seventeen?" Daddy laughed as Mommy's face looked funny. "Well, I hope you get a good wife who will give you seventeen kids to love."

Jesse watched as his dad helped his mom put the last of the dishes into the sink so that they could leave. He knew what he wanted when he grew up. "I want to love my kids, just like you love me, Dad. That's what I want."

He didn't understand why his mom started to cry and knew better than to ask because she couldn't ever tell him. And as Dad handed her a tissue, Jesse was really glad he had the dad he did. A kid couldn't ask for a better one.

Turn the page for an excerpt from:

In It To Win It
(Deadlines & Diamonds, #2)

Take one saucy sportscaster,
add baseball's notorious bad-boy,
throw in fifteen years of frenzied feelings
and an exclusive interview with strings attached…
and you get a reunion
that's sure to get knocked out of the park.

"If sweet and romance had a baby, this book would be the finished product." 5 stars from Romance Novel Junkies

"PIERCE IS HOT TONIGHT," THE COMMENTATOR said from overhead. "Swing and a miss."

Jane could clearly see Grayson from her vantage point just inside the tunnel that led to the locker room. He backed out of the batter's box and tapped the bat against his cleats. A quick roll of his head on thick shoulders and he stepped back into the box, hefting the bat into position. The tip circled for a moment before stilling. The navy batter's helmet with the large white *R* in the center was pulled down to his brows and his eyes were focused on the wind-up.

One more out—or one more run—and the team would be heading her way. Nate, her photographer and good friend, had the camera perched on his shoulder, waiting for the explosion of commotion that was only minutes away. He was all calm, cool and collected. Jane, however, had butterflies in her stomach.

Closing her eyes and sucking in a deep breath, she reminded herself that Grayson Pierce and his opinions no longer mattered. That hell called high school had been fifteen years ago. But she'd be damned if those scars didn't take eons to heal.

"...and a home run by Pierce brings in three! Rockets win by two."

Cheers and applause erupted, nearly shaking the walls of the stadium. *"Pierce. Pierce. Pierce!"*

The enthusiasm was enough to make Jane want to vomit. She swallowed hard and rolled her eyes.

In seconds large men flooded the space around her, making it suddenly seem like the walls were closing in around her. The smell of dirt, sweat and testosterone pushed her deeper into the tunnel until she was finally swept into the locker room. Nate was a big guy, easily as tall as any of the athletes with shoulders just as wide, and he captured b-roll to send back to the station.

Grayson, surrounded by his cheering teammates, entered and her heart nearly stopped. It had been years since she'd been so close to him and the effect he had on her was the same. Tears stung her eyes and she blinked. This was not the appropriate time to get emotional.

Come to think of it; *never* was the appropriate time to get emotional over Grayson Pierce. He didn't deserve her tears.

The one she recognized as Xavier stopped in front of her. His brows rose. "Hey, sweet thing. You lookin' for an interview?"

Instead of slapping him—which is what she really wanted to do—she stuck the mic in his face. "Great game."

"Thanks. Standing at the plate with men on the corners puts a lot of pressure on a guy, ya know?"

She bit down hard, grinding her molars to keep from rolling her eyes. "I can imagine," she said through gritted teeth, urging him to continue.

He did. "But doing it with a full count is enough to make you sweat." He chuckled and lifted his hat to wipe his forehead with the back of his hand. "It's a good thing I don't buckle under pressure. I thrive on it."

"You've had a decent rookie season—"

"Decent?" He laughed, looked over his shoulder and hollered, "Yo, Pierce, this chick says I've had a *decent* season."

In that moment Jane wanted to drop to the floor and dig herself a hole to hide in. The situation only got worse as Grayson lifted his chin and laughed. The sound was low and deep and—damn her straight to hell—sensual. He waded through the crowd straight toward them. Jane gulped and ignored the fact that he'd taken off his jersey. His navy uniform pants were so low on his hips she wondered if his cheeks would show if he turned around. His abs were damp with sweat and Jane felt the sudden urge to trace them with her tongue.

Which was absurd … because she hated him.

Grayson's eyes met hers and he lifted a brow. *Damn!* Surely, he didn't know what she was thinking.

"Thanks for the interview," she mumbled, trying to get away without having to talk with Grayson.

Surely there was another ballplayer that wouldn't thrive on trying to humiliate her. No doubt when Grayson showed up that's what would happen. And she didn't need those kinds of problems.

The news industry was highly competitive and challenging, but being a female sportscaster made it all the more grueling. Most athletes were respectful. A high percentage flirted relentlessly. She'd been given more than one hotel room key—all of which were placed where they belonged … in the trash.

Molly, her best friend since her college days at USC—Go Trojans!—insisted she wallpaper her bedroom with them. Or better yet, just hand 'em over to her. *She'd* be happy to *use* a pompous, egotistical man.

"Hey! Where you goin', darlin'?" A hand the size of a ham bit into her arm and roughly urged her to turn back around. She slapped Xavier's hand away.

"I am *not* darlin'. The name's Jane Alexander. If you'd like to stuff your testosterone where the sun don't shine, I'd be happy to put your ugly mug on TV. If not ... we're both just wasting our time."

Nate snorted, but didn't react further, professionally keeping the camera on the arrogant face that seemed momentarily stunned. But only momentarily.

"Listen, honey—" Xavier raised his hands in mock surrender. "—I didn't mean no disrespect."

"Listen, *honey*, if you can't call me Jane, then don't call me at all."

Xavier laughed and jerked his thumb in her direction—but the red tint to his cheeks revealed that he was embarrassed. "This one's a livewire. For real! Pierce, I think I'm in love."

Grayson finally made his way to stand before her. Those shoulders of his were even broader than she remembered—his body more toned with a wider chest, a narrower waist and more powerful thighs. The boy she'd known had become a delicious man. His dark hair was in a sweaty disarray, his cap having been removed, a dark curl rested against the tanned skin of his forehead.

He was sporting a goatee these days, trimmed close to his face, probably to hide the thin scar that she'd given him junior year. It was only fair; heaven knew that she wore enough scars from him. Hers were emotional—and still raw.

His heated gaze slowly roamed from her pink-painted toes, pausing at her hips and breasts, before coming to a stop on her face. Those perfect lips of his formed a smirk and her knees nearly gave out.

He stuck out his hand. "Hi. Grayson Pierce."

Wow!

Of all the reactions he could have had to seeing her

after so many years that was by far the last one Jane would have expected. It hurt—an honest to goodness dagger to the heart—that there was no recognition in his dark brown eyes.

She glanced down at his hand, but didn't take it. She forced herself to make eye contact as she said, "Jane Alexander, KHB, can I get a comment on the win?"

His grin widened and he shouted, jabbing his fists into the air, "Rockets—all the way to the Series!" He winked at her. "And you can quote me on that."

"Pierce!" a male voice yelled. "I need you over here."

"Duty calls. I'll catch you later, Jane Alexander." He held her gaze for a moment longer than necessary before turning to stride off through the crowd.

"Let's get out of here," she told Nate, refusing to accept that her heart had been bruised yet again. Would she never learn?

Turn the page for an excerpt from:

Out of Left Field

(Deadlines & Diamonds, #3)

Injuries and egos darken Dr. Frankie Holden's door every day, but nothing could have prepared her for Matthias Xavier, III.

Snap, crackle, pop.

Xavier enjoyed that particular combination of sound when it came from a cereal bowl, but coming from his shoulder ... not so much.

He ground his teeth. He closed his eyes, pushing the weight bar toward the sky. Focusing on the burn in his pecs, he relished the subtle pain that told him the exercise was accomplishing something. The pain in his shoulder accomplished nothing, except an assload of ache he'd sure as hell pay for tonight.

He knew he wouldn't be able to hide his weakness for much longer, but exposing himself meant ... well, exposing himself. He had learned a long time ago someone was always ready, willing, and able to use any vulnerability against him.

He blew a breath out through gritted teeth, making a half-whistle noise. He huffed and puffed, but not from exertion, as he set the bar in the cradle. He groaned and barely won the battle to keep from rubbing his shoulder. "I think that's enough for now."

From his position at Xavier's head, his coach and best friend, Grayson Pierce lifted a dark brow. "You didn't finish the rep. You okay?"

No. "Totally."

Skepticism shone in Grayson's eyes, but he didn't question further. Thank heaven. Xavier might be in denial. His shoulder, though, yelled with all the bells and whistles of a freakin' marching band.

"You just takin' a rest or you done for tonight?"

"I'm done."

"Good deal." Grayson grabbed a towel off one of the weight benches and scrubbed his face with it before folding it around his neck, holding an end in each fist. "I'm gonna hit the showers and take off."

There was no doubt where Grayson would go after his shower. Home. The photo adorning the definition of *family man* in the dictionary belonged to Pierce.

Xavier waited until he heard the door close before rubbing at the deep ache in his shoulder.

Yeah, this sucked.

He sat straddling the weight bench and considered his options. If he mentioned the injury to one of the trainers or the PT crew or, even worse, Doc, he'd be replaced until he healed. If he didn't say something, he'd face another sleepless night.

He stood. Decision made. Who needed sleep? He'd sleep when he was dead.

As long as he didn't move his arm he was fine. So he tucked it against his side and headed for the locker room. When only the echo of dripping water answered the call of his footsteps, he smiled. Alone. Alone with his thoughts. Alone with his shoulder. Alone with his pain.

He ducked into the shower, using the cold tiled wall as a support to keep his shoulder elevated. He scrubbed his hair and washed his face. Given his status as an athlete he really should have been more coordinated. But using his left hand to do things made him feel like an idiot. Like a child. Like a freakin' invalid!

"Xavier?"

"Shit!" He cupped himself and turned off the water. The quick motion of his arm brought back the rat-a-tat-tat of the drum cadence.

"I'm sorry to … um …" The blush on Doc's face made her almost adorable. Almost. She whirled around and he addressed her back.

"What the hell are you doing, bursting in here? Wasn't the shower a dead giveaway I'd be naked?"

The short blond ponytail at the base of her neck wagged back and forth. "Sorry, X."

He took the towel from the bar and rubbed at his hair and face. Left-handed. He was glad she couldn't see his struggle as he tried to secure it around his waist. After he'd tucked the edge against his hip, he stepped toward her.

"You can turn around, Doc, I'm decent."

Her cheeks were still pink as she faced him, but her expression was all business. "A little bird mentioned you might need to talk to me."

"Did this damn big stool pigeon look anything like Pierce?"

She rolled her eyes. "He only mentioned that your shoulder might be bothering you. Is it?"

"I'm fine."

Again with the eye roll. "I didn't ask about your overall wellbeing, X. I asked about your shoulder."

She reached out and stepped toward him. He stepped back. He felt his eyes narrow and his lips tighten into a scowl. "I said. I'm. Fine."

Instead of looking threatened or offended, the annoying woman had the audacity to smile. She actually smiled ... and laughed. He had the sudden urge to shake her. Didn't she know he was a force to be reckoned with when he was angry?

She slowly dropped her hand and slipped it into the pocket of her navy blue scrubs. She shook her head and murmured, "I can't fix stupid."

Bestselling Author, Morgan Kearns survived the intense and ever-changing insanity of television news before retiring to enter the jungle of raising four young children. Morgan believes Happily-Ever-After exists and is out to prove it one story at a time.

She lives in Northern Arizona with her wonderfully supportive husband, her four awesome kids, and her English Bulldog, Gus.

Morgan loves to hear from her readers and can be reached at www.MorganKearns.com.